Lucy Treloar was born in Malaysia, edu____ ___ Australia, England and Sweden, and worked for several _____ ___ _____ for her writing include the 2014 C_____ _____ Prize (Pacific Region). *Salt Creek* is _ ____ ___ ____ __ Melbourne with her husband, four ch_____

Praise for *Salt Creek*:

WINNER
Debut Fiction Indie Book Awards, the Dobbie Award
and ABIA New Writer of the Year

FINALIST
The Walter Scott Prize, the Miles Franklin Award and the
Readings Prize for New Australian Fiction

LONGLIST
International Dublin Literary Award

'*Salt Creek* is a raw and convincing addition to the canon. Treloar
writes with beauty and a winning compassion'
***Times*, Book of the Month**

'*Salt Creek* is a love song to a lost world… the precision of
Treloar's poetry stops the heart' ***Guardian***

'Empathetic and beautifully written, the story drives deep into the
pioneering experience with the confidence of a writer perfectly at
ease with her subject' ***Daily Mail***

'An impressive debut … a haunting story' ***Sunday Times***

'A historical novel in its grittiest, most real form'
Good Housekeeping

SALT CREEK

Lucy Treloar

Aardvark Bureau
London

An Aardvark Bureau Book
An imprint of Gallic Books

First published in Australia in 2015 by Picador, an imprint of
Pan Macmillan Australia Pty Ltd

Map by Laurie Whiddon
Illustrations by Robyn Molyneaux

First published in Great Britain in 2017 by
Aardvark Bureau, 59 Ebury Street, London SW1W 0NZ
This edition published in 2018 by Aardvark Bureau

A CIP record for this book is available from the British Library
ISBN: 9781910709450

Typeset in Garamond Pro and Didot by Aardvark Bureau
Printed in the UK by CPI
(CR0 4YY)
2 4 6 8 10 9 7 5 3 1

FOR DAVID, JACK, WILL, CATHERINE AND JAMES, AND FOR
DADDY (ALWAYS MISSED) AND AILEEN, WITH LOVE

SALT CREEK AND SURROUNDS, 1855

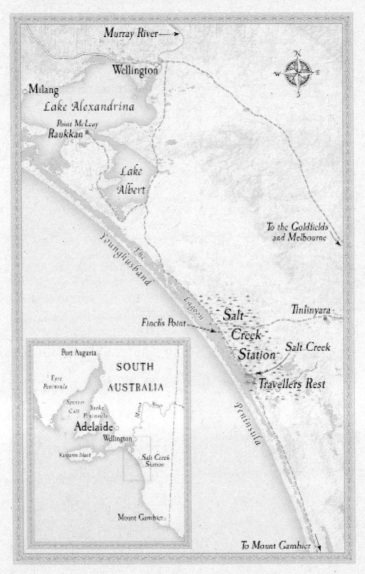

South Australia Act 1834
An Act to empower His Majesty to erect South Australia into a British Province or Provinces and to provide for the Colonisation and Government thereof

15th August 1834

Whereas that part of Australia which lies between the meridians of the one hundred and thirty-second and one hundred and forty-first degrees of east longitude and between the southern ocean and twenty-six degrees of south latitude together with the Islands adjacent thereto consists of waste and unoccupied lands which are supposed to be fit for the purposes of colonization And whereas divers of his majesty's subjects possessing amongst them considerable property are desirous ... that in the said intended colony an uniform system in the mode of disposing of waste lands should be permanently established Be it therefore enacted by the King's most excellent majesty ... and that all and every person who shall at any time hereafter inhabit or reside within his majesty's said province, Or provinces, shall be free and shall not be subject to or bound by any laws orders statutes or constitutions which have been heretofore made ... But shall be subject to and bound to obey such laws orders statutes and constitutions as shall from time to time in the manner hereinafter directed be made ordered enacted for the government of his majesty's province, or provinces, of South Australia.

From the Letters Patent under the Great Seal of the United Kingdom erecting and establishing the Province of South Australia and fixing the boundaries thereof

(19 February 1836)

On the North the twenty sixth Degree of South Latitude On the South the Southern Ocean—On the West the one hundred and thirty second Degree of East Longitude— And on the East the one hundred and forty first Degree of East Longitude including therein all and every the Bays and Gulfs thereof together with the Island called Kangaroo Island and all and every the Islands adjacent to the said last mentioned Island or to that part of the main Land of the said Province ... **Provided Always** that nothing in those our Letters Patent contained shall affect or be construed to affect the rights of any Aboriginal Natives of the said Province to the actual occupation or enjoyment in their own Persons or in the Persons of their Descendants of any Lands therein now actually occupied or enjoyed by such Natives.

1

CHICHESTER, ENGLAND
NOVEMBER 1874

Mama often talked of this house when I was a child, and of its squirrels with particular fondness. She missed them as she missed all about her life here. They were fastidious, she said, and always prepared for flight. Their plumy tails jerking, they would hold a nut in their tiny hands, turning it and turning it looking for the weak point, angling their heads and tilting the nuts, their tiny teeth flashing, yet could not always penetrate the shell. I watch one now through my drawing room window as it flickers beneath the oak, stopping to pounce, to sample, to bury, before flaming up the trunk. It is cold now; the breeze blows in and I shut the window. The squirrel glares at me from its branch. It has its habits and instincts that it must follow, as most of us do, I suppose. There was no point in my mother preparing for flight. Her sense of duty and her love were together too great.

I am a lady now and have a fine house and garden and a long walk to the gate. I even have a lake, with bulrushes and ducks and swans. I saw such birds constantly, many years ago now, on my family's property, which stretched as far as a person could ride across in a day, where birds filled the sky and the lagoon by our house; where the swans were black.

About that time I remember a great deal, some parts more clearly than others. There is a trick of the light here, late in the afternoon, late in summer, at the end of a spell of hot days, when looking from a window upstairs to the lake my mind slips and for a moment I am not here. The grasses are silvered and the waning sun lights them up and the damselflies hover and I expect to see Charles striding up the path with Skipper at his heels, to see a slender raft skimming around a corner, and Addie laughing and Mama for a wonder in good spirits. But it is not so.

It is strange to me that I never felt so alive as then, when we had so little and the possibility of death was our constant companion. Here where I want for nothing it is dull, but I have made my choice and must live with it. I imagine myself sometimes like a thwarted squirrel, holding my life, chewing and nibbling with no way to get inside.

I am respectable now, without taint as Grandmama advised, lest people become curious. What choice do I have? There is my boy to consider and no blemish must attach to his name. I have Grandmama to thank, for sending me here and leaving me this house, for saving me. Why she had always been fond of me, I am not sure; perhaps it was only that she liked my way with horses. And now I am a widow, with wealth enough to indulge my whims. I run a school for the town's orphans and poor. Finally all my learning, like this house, has a purpose. Mama taught me well.

Beecham is grander by far than anything Papa ever dreamed of building on the Coorong or of any that I saw in Adelaide; it is too big for me. Yet I would give it up for a week, a day, an hour in the valley of shells among the sand hills of the peninsula, or for the touch of the first north wind of spring against my face. A part of me will always live at Salt Creek though it is on the far side of the world.

It has been closer to me of late, its outlines growing clear again. Not two weeks ago letters and an old tin trunk crammed with items from the past arrived from South Australia. It was dented, dusty still, and a finger drawn across its skin left a smudge on my fingers. Could it be the grime of the Coorong after such a journey? On a whim I licked it from my fingers – salt – and swallowed to keep it safe. Superstition. I visited Fred in London only last week, and we talked of those years in Salt Creek. Now I can think of little else.

It is a Sunday today, and quiet. I miss the sounds of the young voices. I will ring for tea soon and Ruby will bring it up, then a walk perhaps. Our dear old hound Sal will be slow and Kitty will bound in loops around her. Leaves are falling outside the window. Autumn is here. And there is Joss coming up the drive, hat on and scarf about his neck against the cold. I would know his walk anywhere. Early home from his rambles today. He wishes to become an architect and has many fine ideas; drawing has always been a great love of his. He lifts his head to the windows, searching them, and I see that it is not Joss, but someone taller and older. It is my past come to meet me.

2

THE COORONG, SOUTH AUSTRALIA
MARCH 1855

The journey to that place was like moving knowingly, dutifully, towards death. I have seen beasts as resigned. People say it is not so, that they are ignorant to the end, but this is only what people hope. I knew our purpose in travelling there, how Papa had pinned his last tattered dreams to it, which I imagined visible as a flag slipping listless above the dray. Although Mama was as sad as I ever saw her, yet we knew or thought that our all, our very lives and futures, depended on Papa. It was unthinkable not to go with him.

Two days by horse and cart to Wellington, the river crossing, and three more days on a dray had brought us to the edge of our new property – our home, if such it could be called – the bullocks blowing and slobbering at each plodding step. It must be familiar to Papa and Hugh and Stanton. They had hardly finished taking the cows down the stock route to Salt Creek before they had to return to Adelaide to collect us. I did not believe any crop could grow on it or any livestock thrive. Everywhere were rolling grey shrubs and here and there a tree grown slantwise in the wind, I supposed, though it was still enough that day. If the land was an ill-patterned plate, the sky was a vast bowl that curved to meet the ground a very great distance from us in any direction we cared to look. There was no going beyond its rim.

Hugh and Stanton rode ahead and Papa drove the bullocks. The way was so worn down that its edges were a foot up the sides of the dray in places. Sandy soil spilled onto the dry old churnings of hooves and wheels. The route spread wide elsewhere, its centre as uncertain as an inland sea, and Papa had to stand in his seat to see where we should go: empty now. Prospectors and the gold escort had come this way once, but the inland track had stopped that, Papa said. A person might think, to hear him, that such scarcity of life was a virtue.

I was in the dray with Addie and Mama and Albert and Fred and the new babe, Mary, who was fretting. Her white fists waved about and battered at Mama's breast. Hungry again. Mama unbuttoned herself and obliged. I looked away, not that there was very much to see about us, but it was preferable to Mama's sad face. Grandmama and Grandpapa and dear friends left behind for Papa's newest venture.

When news came that the ship carrying the fine fat sheep that Papa had purchased had gone down off the coast of Van Diemen's Land, Papa had paced the drawing room, backwards and forwards across the window, tall and straight as he moved from shadow into light and back again.

Mama, hovering in the middle of the rug, said, 'You will come about. You will. You have us safe.'

Papa looked at her. His deep set eyes were rather empty. 'Yes,' he said absently, when she approached him, and patted her arm.

'It might be a blessing. Who would oversee the flock? Everyone has left for the goldfields. *You* could not do more.'

It was true. For the last several years Papa had often been away at the dairy farm in Willunga, taking Hugh and Stanton with him. The house was quiet in their absence, which we did not like, though Mama said it had been worse in the whaling station days when a month or more would pass before he could come back to us from Encounter Bay. Of course, we had two maids then, and a cook, so it would not have been very hard on Mama despite there being four of us already and her soon to have Addie. He had made a loss on the whaling station, whales not being as plentiful as they had been, which was a bitter pill. He had been obliged to sell most of his subdivisions in Adelaide to cover costs. At least the dairy had prospered. As Grandmama said one day: 'If only he had been

17

content with that.' He borrowed against it to buy sheep, and then it seemed that everything began to go wrong, and this time there was nothing to fall back on. The bank foreclosed on the farm and finally the house in Adelaide must be sold. At least Papa had kept the stock, and before collecting us from Adelaide had driven them through the hills and down the stock route to Salt Creek.

Now, Addie hung over the back of the wagon, holding a stick against the dust to make a trail. It was not safe and a girl of eleven was too old for such childish games, but if Mama did not bestir herself to say something, I saw no reason why I should. Albert and Fred began to squabble over a grasshopper that had jumped into the dray. Albert wished to tie thread about one of its legs and keep it as a pet and train it to do I know not what, while Fred wished to examine it.

'Give it back, Al. It set on me,' Fred said, and after a jostling wrested it back and held it in his cupped hands. A grasshopper claw protruded between his fingers, pushing at the air. It would be warm and sweaty in there, with a strong odour of boy, and not very comfortable.

'Hester,' Mama said to me wearily. Once she would have put the creature into a jar that we might observe it, the spring in its muscular legs, the joints, its bulging eyes. It would have been an opportunity for learning. 'See, it has its bones on the outside, while we have our bones on the inside,' I imagined her saying, and since she didn't, I did. Fred and Albert glanced from me to Mama, who remained silent. I wished Mama would take herself in hand. They were growing disobedient. Fred wouldn't be a boy for much longer; he was growing fast. It made poor Albert appear even younger. Fred was beginning to draw away from him in his interests. It took the quickness of a grasshopper to bring them together again.

I would have given anything to ride ahead with the boys. Stanton was only a little older than me, and Hugh was a clumsy rider. He had laughed and teased at his first sight of me on the bullock dray. 'Look at Miss Hester in her fine carriage.'

His self-satisfaction made me boil up inside. I sat straight, and held my hands in my lap and looked down my nose at him. 'Where you should be, Hugh. Away from those reins. Look at poor Birdie. You'll ruin her mouth.'

He jabbed the reins, sending Birdie shuffling and dancing. His moods travelled down the leather and he did not know the way of stopping it. He was missing an audience for his opinions and his amusements afresh, I daresay, having spent part of winter and most of spring on the Coorong with Papa and Stanton building the house, and was no happier than I at the turn our lives had taken.

'It will be five years and more before you go back to town, if it's as soon as that,' he said. 'What use will your fine gloves be until then?'

'I will, I tell you. I'll be back before you,' I said, though I knew it was not true, for how could I, a girl, hope to escape? I felt very wretched when people talked like that, but it wouldn't be my fault if I were not in town before then; I had made up my mind to that before we left.

Now I looked down at Fred, so like Addie, with his dark hair and pale skin. 'Show me,' I said.

He opened a well into his hands between thumb and forefinger. I looked, but it was so bright outside his hand, where we were, that I could not see in. At a lurch into a pothole we threw out our hands to brace – Fred too – and the grasshopper, a brown flecked bullet, made good its escape over the side. 'Oh,' we all said, for a moment united in loss. Any amusement, even one as slight as this, had been welcome.

Hearing the commotion, Addie pulled her stick in and scrambled down the dray, her knees and boots tangling in her petticoats. 'What? What is it?' in her little hoarse voice. She was our English rose, so Papa said. Grandmama said different. She said Addie was the apple of Papa's eye. I supposed that if she were an apple or a rose I was a bramble. It was ridiculous how fast I grew; on that there was general agreement. My dresses were always too short. The boys would tease, and nothing that Mama and Papa said stopped them.

In Adelaide Mama had tugged at my skirts as if she could make the fabric stretch. I was forever having fittings until the money ran short.

After that Mama would look at me, her eyes fixing on the expanding gap between hem and floor. 'It will have to do until you are finished growing.'

'Or the sheep stop drowning,' Stanton said, sitting on the edge of the kitchen table, his hands in his pockets, and swinging his legs.

Mama frowned. 'Stanton, I believe you are needed elsewhere.'

He lifted his brow, smoothly jumped from the table and sauntered out, his hands still in his pockets, as if it were his own choice rather than Mama's request that had made him leave. The girls went wild for Stanton, with his ruddy curls and hazel eyes and dandified clothes – flowered waistcoats and the like. He was like a hot cat blinking in the sun. They would all like to pet him.

Mama returned her gaze to the problem at hand, which was me. 'If you bend a little it will not appear so bad.' Since I must also stand straight it was quite confusing. Once I heard her say to Papa, 'She's fifteen. Where will it end? Surely soon, else no one will want her.'

Strange to say, I would have preferred she say such things again, though I did not like it then. Since the little ones died she had cared for nothing. First Louisa, not one year old, after Papa had lanced her gums to ease her teething. Then dear Georgie. The flux and a hot spell had been enough to take him away. He was the dearest little fellow.

We had all been sad since, and Addie fearful that she might fall ill again. For a few days it had seemed we might lose her too. She put her hand to her forehead often. 'Feel me, Hester,' she said. 'Am I hot?' I could not reassure her, only distract. In quiet moments when I found a place to be alone I sometimes touched my own forehead and cheeks and pressed against them a handkerchief sprinkled with a little of Mama's rose water to cool myself, and wondered. I did not wish to die.

Now, Addie shook my shoulder. 'Hester, tell me.'

'Just a grasshopper, Addie. Gone now.'

'Oh.' Her mouth was round with disappointment. She scraped her hair from her face.

'Where's your ribbon?' I asked.

She looked about at the parcels and trunks. Her eyes lifted to the broken way behind us. She shrugged.

'Never mind,' I said. 'There will be something in Mama's workbasket that will make you nice again.' Really she was old enough to manage on her own, but we had fallen into the way of babying her while she was ill.

She scrambled over our possessions to retrieve the basket and returned. I found a piece of cherry thread and combed my fingers through her hair and made a plait, binding its end with the red thread. Addie tried to pull it around so she could see it, but her hair had been cut short when she had the fever and had not grown again.

The dray continued its abominable lurching. We were on our run, but it made no difference to anything. We were here, not home. The journey was not flight; it was scarcely movement. I conceived of travel as sleek as water, not this dull connection with the ground and the wheels with a seeming will to plough deeper into it. I wanted to go and go and never stay still and have no one tell me what to do now or tomorrow or ever.

Midday. The sky was high and hard, and my face scorched by wind and sun despite my bonnet. A patch of skin showed between the end of my sleeve and the top of my glove. I tugged the glove up and eased the sleeve down. Now I could blush to think of the care I took of that inch strip of white skin, as if my future rested on it. We were filthy, Papa and the big boys worst of all, the sweat and grime making muddy rivers down their faces. The dust that dragged in the air about us was a cocoon we could not escape.

I rested my chin on my hands and my elbows upon my knees and Mama said not a thing. The track flattened into a river of sandy soil bordered by scrub and grass trees and lifted towards a rise. And then Skipper, our dear greyhound, lifted her head and gave a warning bark and I did see something – two women standing a way off above the rutted track. They carried baskets on their backs and wore a sort of grassy fringe at their waists. There was a boy with them of about Fred's age, I would say. He appeared so at ease, as if he'd merely paused at his front gate and looked over it to take in the passing traffic. Strange to think this desolation must be as familiar to him as town was to me. How fortunate we were to have clothes. Perhaps they would become civilized under our influence, as Papa hoped.

The face of one of the women was pockmarked. She stared at us, which I did not think polite, and looked fierce and haughty and wary together, and I remembered the stories about the wreck of *The Maria* somewhere along this coast and how its passengers were murdered, including nice Mr and Mrs Denham and all their children who used to live nearby in Adelaide. (I did not remember them, of course, because I was a baby when those shocking events occurred, but Mama spoke kindly of them.) Papa said there was no reason to be fearful now, that the blacks understood justice, and I tried to remember that.

Addie got to her feet and called out, 'Hello, hello.'

'Adelaide!' Mama said. 'Sit down.'

But Addie waved again, and I had just enough time to see the younger of the native women break out a grin – her teeth so white, like the whites of her eyes, that they startled me – before Mama reached across, squeezing Mary who set up a cry, and gave Addie a hearty slap. 'Sit down at once!'

'Huh,' Addie sobbed on a sharp indrawn breath, and threw herself off to the other end of the dray to sulk. She would not have been so forward in the past. Mama had her better in hand before Georgie died, but she had become disobedient of late.

'Mama,' I said.

Papa turned at the commotion from his high seat up front and showed us his narrow face of disapproval. We were all shocked – Mama too. She did not believe in striking children; she said that kindness and gentleness were better teachers. I had never before spoken so to her, yet she was the one to hang her head.

The natives appeared horrified: savages judging us. The boy plunged a hand into the bag slung across his chest and drew something out and loosed it at us with elegant power. The object could scarcely be seen. I ducked on an instinct and it thwacked harmlessly at the back of the seat next to Mama and Mary and bounced away. Mama flinched. It was a smooth round stone, about a quail's egg in size, which Fred picked up and threw gamely back. His face was twisted with rage and effort but it travelled only half the distance.

'Fred,' I said. I shook my head.

Mama's face was wet from crying. Fred and Albert fell to playing a quiet but fierce game of thumbs. We were as oblivious as any creature to the future. The people we passed were no more than curiosities; confirmation that we had exceeded a boundary and were now in wilderness. When I think of what they became to us and how long I have been thinking of them I would like to return to that day and stop the dray and shout at our ghostly memories and the natives: 'I am sorry. I am sorry for what is to come.'

'Listen,' I said. Everyone lifted their heads, suddenly alert at a distant thundering.

'It's the sea,' Mama said.

It sounded more like a storm than the waves we had seen once or twice before. From town to the coast had been a morning's drive across seven miles of cut up ground and mud. Mama and Papa had camped there years before while Colonel Light was determining the site for the town. I pictured Mama looking out to sea and dreaming of England, and Papa gazing inland through a shimmer of heat to where a civilization must be created, and Hugh paddling in the low curls of water. The waves there had sounded nothing like this roaring.

Mama took a handkerchief from her tucker and wiped her face and dabbed her nose. 'Look at the birds.' We followed her gaze to a flock of pelicans flying in – enormous white things in which flight seemed improbable.

The sun moved behind us and as we passed along our shadows rode beside us growing longer, taller, stranger in the falling sun, rearing up against trees and faltering across bushes and plummeting to the ground. Their lives were filled with interest.

Finally, late in the afternoon when the sun had turned to brass, the cart began its descent down a side track. We were so tired and benumbed with boredom we hardly saw the low structure built on a rise, the wide ribbon of water below, or the strip of land on the opposite shore, or heard the teeming birds along the water's edge. The boys dismounted and the weathered timber wall they stood against took shape. They opened a door and went inside. We pulled up and Papa got down, his expression hovering like one of the small birds we used to see all around the flowers in our garden in town, trying to decide where to pause and insert their slender beaks. He seemed caught between pride and shame, which was strange. It was something to have already built this stable where there was no timber and no stone. I supposed the house was somewhere beyond, obscured from view. He held out a hand to Mama. 'Come now, my dear,' he said. She stood and I saw then, finally, that this was our new home. Now there was reason to cry.

There was not the time with evening drawing near to look about the house, to step back and see if it improved from another prospect.

We boiled over the edge of the dray. Addie ran up and down the weedy path from dray to door. 'Is this our home? Are we living here now?' Albert and Fred found sticks as boys always seem to and ran in circles mad as young dogs about the house, wider and wider, whipping the tall grasses until the seed heads flew in the late sun. Mama's eyes flicked from them to Papa. His clothes hung looser these days, his cheeks were a trifle sunken and the corners of his eyes were whiskered with lines from his hours squinting in the sun. Papa lifted her down with care – she was a brittle thing those days, a dry twig – and led her to the door. There was no porch at the front, only dirt and crushed grass about the house, growing longer against the walls where feet had not trod, and a veranda at the back which stared down the long strip of water.

For a moment it was silent, with Mama and me in shock and Papa waiting for someone to speak and the bullocks dumbly standing. There was just the sea and the wind: a mournful conversation.

Papa bent his dark head to Mama, so slight at his side, and smoothed back a strand of her soft brown hair that had fallen loose. His voice, when he began to speak, was quick but without trajectory, a ramble of sounds filling a space. 'When there is more wood, Bridget, I will make you a porch. And when there is stone to be had, and the dairy is growing, we will build the finest house hereabouts. More people will move here when they see what this land can do. There will be company then, of that you may be sure.' His beard moved on his chest with his words. He stroked it and smoothed it. He was a handsome man, as Mama used to tell us in her tales of the time when they were courting. She spoke of his optimism and high spirits. Grandpapa was cautious and mistrusted enthusiasms; if ever a person were praised, or spoke in a way that he considered boastful, he would remark, 'Pride *goeth* before destruction, and an haughty spirit before a fall.' Papa must have seemed exciting.

It was hard to imagine him as light-hearted now. He had tended of late to grave reflection and would look at us and our squabbling as if we had failed him and, worse, our civilization. He wished for us to be exemplars of the best of the empire so that people, by which Papa meant the natives and lower born settlers, could have a model to aspire to. For, as he said, 'Their condition is so mean that it can only do them good to see how we live and prosper and make use of this land.'

'Do they not use the land, Papa?' Fred asked.

'No, not use it, merely live on it and eat what is there and hunt what lives on it or passes through. We wish to make something of it. They also can profit from that.'

Looking about me, those ideals seemed distant, the situation as hopeless as could be imagined.

Papa stroked Mama's arm, shoulder to elbow, as a person might a trembling horse. 'We will make it nice, Bridget. I know we can. You will see. You have such a way with things, and there are the girls to help.'

I moved away. Much help Addie would be.

My mother's limp skirts shifted in the wind, gusting salty now, shifting south, pressing them against her. Papa grasped the rim of his hat against a strong buffet and pushed it firmly down and then he thought better of it and doffed it, tucking it beneath one arm –

a movement I knew well from when we went visiting or when he arrived home from some business venture – and took Mama's hand awkwardly, since she was holding Mary, and rubbed it.

She said nothing, but blinked and obediently moved her eyes about when he released her hand and began gesturing towards the narrow strip of water – the lagoon, Papa called it – a sort of pink-grey now, and the spit of land beyond. He was a conductor of our future at that moment, summoning a vision from the landscape. Such a dreamer. Strange that it could be a gift and a curse.

Mary's hands waved pale as moths in the dwindling light, and her wailing started up, thin but insistent. Mama pulled the shawl from her face with two fingers, tucking it beneath Mary's chin, and her tiny goldfish mouth started its blind searching. Truly, babies sometimes disgusted me, though I must not say that. They were just little animals. I didn't notice so much with Georgie or even Louisa. More was expected of me now. At least Mama had stopped talking to me about becoming a grown woman and what I might expect. I must be thankful for that.

Mary's cry intensified and Mama looked at me. She held Mary so loose.

'Here. Give her to me.' I took Mary and put her to my shoulder and patted her back. 'There. There.' She was so soft, boneless almost. Georgie had been all muscle and spring. Mary's head banged at my neck and shoulder, working herself up to something. My arm was about her, lower, and a dampness began to spread across my arm through her shawl after the sharp smell of her reached my nose. More washing and who was to do that?

'Papa,' I said, and, 'Papa,' again when he took no notice. 'Mary needs seeing to.'

'Yes, let us go in,' he said, and lifted the latch on the door.

I would not willingly go through that night again, or that first week. I suppose that is true for much of life. To experience so many things once is ample. Not all. Some things you would live again and again. I knew that things had gone ill for Papa, but when we entered the house I felt it too. We were inside our new life then.

Mama stood in the dark hall – the only light appearing from its end – as if she were wedged there, and in squeezing past her, Mary still squalling in my arms, a splinter caught on my dress. There was the hiss of tearing fabric as I jerked free. Mama said nothing and did nothing until Papa went back and took her by the arm and led her down to the half-light of the parlour, as he called it, speaking low, though I would not say she was frightened precisely, rather, quiet and tentative in her movements. Mary's waving hand found her mouth and she started a furious sucking of her fist and growled like a small animal at a bone.

'We'll soon set it to rights.' Papa's voice rolled along. 'Come now and sit here.'

Mama blinked once or twice at the words and sank onto the sofa, not troubling to smooth her skirts, though they would crumple, as she would have said once.

Papa plumped the cushion behind her. 'There. I'll bring you Mary,' and then addressing me, 'the baby,' and he beckoned me over with fingers aflutter, trying to create some picture of her that might anchor us to this place.

I handed her over and there was snuffling, a whimper of frustration, silence. The dampness on my arm struck chill without Mary to keep it warm. I said nothing, only looked around the room.

Our house in Adelaide had two storeys and a cellar. The wainscots were fine cedar wood and the walls whitewashed within and stonework without. There were sixteen-paned windows all through the house, two of them in the drawing room. Here, the room had only a small four-paned window, and the thin light that came in revealed little of the inside, which perhaps was just as well, or of the outside, which was unvarying. Papa had brought a few household goods before he came to collect us: a wooden settee, a chaise longue that Mama liked to rest upon, the large bureau with barley twists, the piano. As pleasant as it was to see these old familiar objects, they were a poor fit in this parlour, like a crowd of slumberous oxen in a small stall – dark shapes seen more in my memory than in that moment.

The walls were grooved planks and the roof was wood too, and all of it brown. Without light how can there be colour? The room smelled stale and close after the days of travel.

Papa was watching Mama. 'That's better,' he said.

But it wasn't better – Mama staring numbly at the brocade chaise that she had last seen in town, looking at the window and at the uninterrupted view of the fading sky outside. Her head fell. I knew the picture that Papa had in mind: Mama in her chair in the drawing room, her skirts crisp and her hair smooth, always a babe in arms whose head she would stroke absently because her love and her calm were boundless and fathomless; a book about her and a child at her side, sometimes me, who she would be reading to, and Albert on his stomach on the fine red Turkey carpet, playing with a toy, Fred drawing at the table, his tongue working. There had been no end to the serenity of her.

I went into the hallway, and through the open door came the sounds of bags and baggage and trunks crumping to the ground. They would be covered in dust. Stanton and Hugh's voices were steady enough, getting the job done: now, lift, no, out of the way, Addie, go and ask Papa where he wants this, find Mama's things.

Then, 'Come now,' Papa said to me, 'lamps first, and then let's see about the fire.'

This was all of the house: a wood-lined room for the boys with narrow beds one above the other built hard up against the walls like shelves or a ship's cabin, two more – one for the girls, the other for Papa and Mama – and the parlour and a dining room with scarce space for the table beneath a low skillion roof of thatch and wood. The walls of this last room were of mud and wattle: rough but whitewashed so it seemed lighter than the rest of the house. There was a stove there for winter and a separate kitchen for summer below the veranda at the back. The sounds of Addie and the boys shouting flashed past the window. Beyond them, up the rise, was the stable I supposed. Another path led to the privy at the edge of a stand of twisted trees.

Stanton came bellowing around the corner. 'Come help. Come

on now. Bring everything inside. You're big enough.'

'I'm racing, I'm racing, you can't make me, Stant. Try if you can,' Addie shrilled. And she swooped on by and then Fred and Albert because they could not see what had befallen us, only that their limbs were free again to run as they pleased. My heart hammered to watch them and something of it caught me and I ran too, in pursuit or escape, I don't know which.

'I'm coming to get you, Addie. Albert, I'm coming.'

Oh and they screamed – 'Hester's coming to get us' – and Stanton bellowed a laugh and they ran as if a monster were descending upon them and would sniff them out in the gathering gloom. I felt fierce then and strong and fast.

'Hester.' It was Papa, quiet and terrible in his disappointment at the door, dark and tall and straight, the stove door behind him open and the flames licking up as the wood caught, and the lamplight misting from the parlour, and he had his town hat on as if this were a formal occasion and we must present well to the neighbours even if they were not here nor ever would be that I could see.

I ran past him again, one more great loose circle around the house, and put my arms out, shutting my eyes for those straight steps, feeling the breeze on my face.

'Hester, I say.' Papa again, close, and I opened my eyes and he stepped out so I must veer to avoid him or stop. It was just his voice and that was enough. I came to a halt, panting and stamping and quivering. A shaking laugh came from me and Papa put his hands to my shoulders and pressed them in so I felt I was being fitted to a smaller space than I needed, a little tight box. In you go.

I looked to the side, away from Papa's vest, which I noticed had a button that needed replacing, if there was one that could be found to match. The sun disappeared behind the peninsula and the wind began to groan through the grass and the trees. Addie and Albert and Fred were standing a little way off, watching. It was time to come in, but they had not been inside yet and even though it was darkening outside I could see them wondering if still it were better where they were, which they knew a little, than inside which they knew not at all and where Mama would be sitting so sad.

'Hester.' Papa shook me gently until I turned and lifted my gaze to him. 'You must put away childish things and help while your mother is poorly. Come now, let us find the tea things and you can put the kitchen to rights. It's supper time and you must do it until your mother is herself.'

'Yes,' I said.

3

THE COORONG
MARCH 1855

The first morning I woke in darkness and when the light turned ghostly I left the bed, tucked the quilts about Addie and a shawl about my shoulders, and gathered my boots and stepped quiet across the rough floor up the hall to the front door and outside. Skipper came to me, caracoling with excitement that the tedium of night had passed and standing on her hind legs to paw my front. 'Down, Skip,' I whispered, and stroked her soft head. She ran about sniffing, stopping to relieve herself – gazing away intently to show me that it was a private matter – while I sat on the doorstep and pulled on my boots. The earth still turned and we had almost reached the sun. Pink clouds were taking flight from the horizon and the bushes and scrubby trees moved about easily as if they also were stirring and preparing themselves; it was the temperature that Fred calls coolish-warmish, which is a perfect temperature for anything.

If this were to be my cage for the next few years I wished to find out the extent and margins and possibilities of it, and if Papa needed to succeed here to effect our escape I vowed I would do all I could to help him.

I went up the rutted track, retracing the route we had taken the night before, and when I reached the first bend I looked about and could persuade myself that our home wasn't so bad except that since it had no stone but that in the chimneys it appeared as temporary as an outhouse or a shed. It was a puzzle of the raw new timber and painted windows and doors that Papa had brought here when he was building the house, and materials scavenged from the Coorong:

silvered wood, mud and wattle and thatching – incoherent shelter when considered together. The track down the slope forked above the house: one arm leading to the veranda steps at the back of the house, and the other leading to the front door. There was a small sort of dam not far from the house where the land dipped. I saw now as I had not the day before that the house was on a spit of land projecting into the lagoon. Around its feet the water glinted blue and the vapour lifting above the peninsula gave its sand hills and vegetation the appearance of a watercolour, as if it represented something real but was not real itself.

The track's curve drew me uphill. The house was concealed and I could almost imagine myself to be escaping, and as one shallow bend replaced another with so little change in the surrounds a fair distance had passed before I stopped again, breathless with the pace I had set myself. There was little enough to see – dry grasses and low shrubs in sweeps down to the lagoon, an arm of contorted trees hugging the slope from the low ridge and modest folds of land – a bed risen from like my own and its covers pushed back to hold the warmth of night. The colours were not intrinsic. A dry grass stem in shadow could be as drab as sightless eyes or gold in sunlight or silver in moonlight, but I did not know that then.

Skipper snuffled at the grass to see what I had found that she had not, but detecting nothing bounded off, leaving only the occasional movement of the tops of bushes to show her whereabouts. Everything stilled and sound and sight and the warmth of early sun resting on me were faint. There was just the low drone of insects and the higher calls of birds; even the waves, so loud the day before, were muted. All that space around me.

Somewhere distant, Skipper set up her excitable bark, and thundered back into view desperate for an audience, dancing at a gap between the bushes, the entrance to a narrow track, which she disappeared into once more. It was well trodden and not more than twenty inches wide and pleasantly cool about my legs. The grey-green brush undulated in height about me, to my waist, even to my shoulders, so that I would have presented a strange sight from the track, my body rising and falling from the leafy sea as if riding the back of a half-tamed leviathan.

The path ran alongside the lagoon away from the house and after some distance forked, one arm descending towards the shore, the other rising to the ridge. But Skipper's baying came from below and I ran towards it, my nightgown held high, my shawl flying out behind and my plait bouncing and the bark came closer, also other sounds – growling and shouting and something high and shrill – and I burst into a clearing above the shore: a native encampment. I was part way across the grassed space before I was able to take in the enclosures of interwoven branches and a small fire, on the other side of which was a tall black man with a huge beard wearing a great cloak of fur. His spear was poised behind his head and three sandy coloured dogs, legs stiff and backs roached, were advancing and Skipper was as menacing as I had ever seen her, her shoulders up and head low and teeth bared and a growl gravelling out.

'No,' I screamed. 'Skipper, no.'

Skipper leapt before me, and the man stilled his spear and his eyes flickered from me to her, horrified by us both. A baby somewhere behind him began to cry and two women, their voices shrill with alarm, retreated at the sight of me. A child poked its head out of the shelter and hands appeared from within to drag him back.

The native shouted and waved his spear at me, brandishing it towards the track, and kicked one of his yelping dogs, which fell away with a scream. He could have killed Skipper in an instant yet he did not; he neither advanced nor retreated. His voice moved like close thunder, loud enough to frighten. Why hadn't I heeded Mama's advice to be less impulsive? How I wished I were properly dressed. I would feel better, even if they could not tell the difference. Ridiculous thought. I could die. No training had readied me for such a moment.

'I'm so sorry,' I said in the stupidest voice, as if I'd arrived at a tea party uninvited. Somehow, I grabbed Skipper's collar and she lunged and reared at the end of my arm – her yelps strangled now – so that I was yanked about until I clouted her haunches and suddenly she became obedient and I was able to heave her towards the path, though for a terrible moment when I searched about I wasn't sure I would be able to find the entrance to it in the wall of bushes. I did not like to turn from the man with the spear but in a few seconds when I looked back they were already hidden from view. Then I was afraid they might surprise me further along and that my legs would not obey me. Legs, hands, voice, all were trembling. Skipper seemed to catch something of my mood, moving at my side rather than charging ahead when I let her go. A clammy sweat broke out on my face and I felt so dizzy when I reached the fork again that I had to stop and bend over until my spinning head and shaking legs stilled. Now Skipper wanted to go back and tore ahead down the hill towards the house, my home as I supposed I must call it now, which was so far away.

If I expected uproar at my disappearance, I was mistaken. The veranda door was still shut, and inside the lacklustre heat from the stove and the kettle pushed back told me that no one was up. Skipper skittered along the hall, sniffing at one door, whining delicately at another, scratching at the boys' and, getting no response, returned and threw herself into her nest of blankets.

I did not like to wake people after the long journey, so I put the kettle on and stoked the fire and refilled the wood box and began to feel calmer despite my mind running through the events just past. It was the bearded native I was thinking of and his reluctance to strike. Fear had been on his face, but it surely would not have been of Skipper who he could have killed in a second, for everyone says the blacks are most skilful hunters, and he could not be afraid of me, a mere girl. Of what, then?

The kettle lid began to rumble and scuffing footsteps came down the hall: Papa tying his dressing gown, his hair and whiskers frowsty from the night. I could not help running at him. In a moment he was holding my arm – 'What is it, Hester?' – and my story spilled out.

He took me by the shoulders and shook me. 'On your own? What were you thinking?'

'Nothing. Just of exploring,' I said.

At the sound of our voices Hugh and Stanton appeared and then the rest of them, Mama last of all. But she was the worst, her face white, the whole of her aquiver, and clutching her shawl about her.

'It is not safe. I knew it would be so. We should not be here.'

'There is no danger. See, Hester is unharmed. Even Skipper. That shows how little there is to fear. We need only be sensible,' Papa said.

'Sensible? Sensible, you say? We will die here. I know it.'

'There were no natives about while we were building last year, but signs enough that they'd been here. It was to be expected. We must not antagonise them, but do what we may to befriend them.'

'When they killed that shepherd not a year since?' Mama said.

'Shh,' Papa said and sent her a frown. 'We don't know who that was. Not around here.' As if we had not heard that news and other news like it in town when Papa and the boys were here building this very house, and wondered about where exactly it had happened. The natives were becoming bold, people said, and must be taught a lesson.

'We should move them on,' Hugh said, addressing only Papa, who he stood close by. 'We can't have them living so close. We must persuade them to leave, not befriend them. Where would that lead? They'll eat the stock.' He stood with his legs apart – which made him appear ridiculous with his bare feet and his bare legs emerging from his nightshirt – and his arms folded as if he were twenty-three instead of eighteen. He pretended to be a man and I do not know why Papa encouraged him because he was not in the least bit sensible. With his great size he would jump a horse over a barbed fence and be surprised when it sliced its legs to ribbons, and then who would be given the task of tending to the poor thing? Not Hugh with his clumsy hands and manner. Still, I had to admit that I would feel easier if the natives were not there, even though they had done nothing when they might have.

Albert went to Skipper and wrapped his arms about her neck. 'Skip, poor Skip. You could have died. Did you scare them? Brave girl.'

'The man could have killed her,' I said. 'Easily. I don't understand why he did not.'

'They do not want trouble any more than do we,' Papa said. 'I see no reason why there cannot be peace between us. There is game aplenty, and fish and fowl enough for us all. They will see that we mean them no harm, and we must keep a close watch on Skip.'

That evening for grace Papa prayed: 'We thank you Lord for bringing us to this corner of your creation. May we fulfil all of your purposes, high and low, bringing civilization and reverence for God to the poor wretches that live on this land, and prosper to the glory of your name. Amen.'

'Amen,' we said.

After we had eaten and the dishes had been cleared away and washed we remained inside although it was pleasant outside. Stanton took his knife and fell to whittling a stout stick from the wood box. It was hard not to watch the slivers of wood flying about and bouncing across the floor.

'The broom's on the veranda,' I said. Stanton looked at me. 'When you have need of it, which I think you will.'

Mama said nothing and Papa had his nose in his journal and took no notice. Stanton sped up his work until the scales of wood fairly flew. His aim, it seemed – apart from creating work for someone else, most likely me – was to make a weapon of some sort, perhaps the head of a spear. He lacked the patience for the task, cutting too deep so the object became smaller but not more dangerous or intimidating.

I went to the door and reached for the broom, which was precisely where I had left it, and took it to Stanton and held it out to him. He continued his work, such as it was, and I rested the broom against the side of his chair. It began a slow slide that ended with a clatter on the floor.

'Hester, be careful now,' Papa said.

Stanton smirked. I left the broom where it lay.

Mama emerged from her reverie. 'Only think, they might still be there,' she said, her eyes on the back windows, which were ablaze with the dark orange sun, and her hands twisted her handkerchief. 'They might come for us in the night while we sleep. How would we know? Like poor Mr McGrath.'

'Shh.' Papa was stern and flicked a glance towards Addie and Fred and Albert, who were staring. 'As you know, my dear, I have heard that he might have been at fault.'

'How so?' Hugh said.

'For making the blacks take him beyond their own territory.'

'To kill him for so trifling a thing. And you wish to befriend them.'

'You should not speak to your father so,' Mama said, but as if from habit more than feeling.

Stanton inspected the point of his stick and, detecting some flaw, rotated it and held the knife to its side and sliced it away from him again down the point of wood. The end snapped off and now he had whittled away so much that there was nothing to hold. In disgust he opened the stove door and threw it into the flames.

Papa nodded. 'It was a long time ago. It is different now, but they should not have done it. I do not approve it. As to trifling, how could we know? What might be trifling for one can be grave to another. People do take slights where none is intended.'

I would not say that I was not worried, but if Papa was not I saw no reason for showing weakness to Hugh and Stanton.

'I'll stand guard,' Hugh said. 'I don't mind.' He stopped his lounging and sat straight and laid his hands on the table. 'If I keep a lamp burning by me they will see that we are ready for them.'

'You will make a perfect target, all lit up, while they will be hidden in the darkness,' I said. 'If they wish to surprise they need only approach from the opposite direction and then where will we be?'

'What would you have us do then, Hester?'

I did not know what to say without admitting that I was not easy about the night to come. Fortunately Papa intervened: 'There is no need. They know what will happen if they strike; they understand retribution very well. They will learn that they may remain here only by our grace and if they do not learn, why then we will have to teach them.'

In the end Papa determined that we should keep lamps burning in the windows, front and back, and from the bumps and prowlings that went on in the night and their bleariness the next morning I deduced that Papa and Hugh and Stanton had kept some sort of watch. After breakfast, Papa, with me to guide the way, took Hugh and Stanton to the camp I had discovered for some purpose that was not clear to me: to see if they were still there or to befriend them or to move them on; kill or comfort. As we carried the musket as well as blankets and a few foodstuffs the expedition was ambiguous. It did not matter in the end because there was nothing there but a strong feeling of fresh absence, as if we had walked into a room with two doors: one opened by us, the other swinging shut from someone just departed. So certain was I that I ran to the pathway on the other side of the clearing. There was nothing but a lizard sunning itself, and at the fall of my feet, it scuttled into the dry grass.

'Are you sure it was here, not further along, or somewhere else, or that you imagined it?' Stanton asked.

'You only have to look, Stanton, to see the signs that they were here.' There was a beaten down circle of grass and a few charcoals that had been blown free of their sandy grave by the wind.

'Hester,' Papa said. 'You should not speak so to your brother.'

'No, Hester,' Stanton said.

And so we returned to the house in perfect antipathy.

The news that the natives had departed did not reassure, rather, agitated Mama. 'Why, they might be anywhere by now and we would not know.'

'Now, now,' Papa said, tucking a wayward strand of hair across her ear. 'It was just one of their overnight camps, I should think. They have bigger ones. Almost villages, I gather. They've gone back or moved on is all. We will see them again by and by.'

4

CHICHESTER, 1863

England brought Mama back to me; in some way I came to know her here where she once lived as I had not in South Australia. Grandmama and Grandpapa had furnished me with sealed letters for a lawyer in Chichester and the housekeeper, Mrs Wickens, at Beecham, which was the name of their estate, to assure my welcome.

Mrs Wickens was between amazement and dismay at my arrival, as might be expected, but seeing my condition and learning my sad story turned motherly. 'To be widowed so young. Now, now, it will be lovely to have a babe about. Come sit, Mrs Crane, and I'll bring you tea and then we shall see what to do. I've made up a room – your dear Mama's it was – but you must choose as you see fit, and how long did you say you'd be staying? Some time, Mrs Back's letter said.'

'Yes,' I said. 'Tea would be lovely. You are kind.' And I remembered tea made on a clanking old stove in a house of drowned wood and the lagoon filling the window. I cried for that and other things, which Mrs Wickens believed was because of my poor widowed state. It was a fortunate disguise for the feelings I was then suffering from, including homesickness.

At first Beecham was overwhelming even though I knew of it from Mama's descriptions. The drawing room would have contained our whole house on the Coorong. In South Australia, after the sun had set and it was time for dinner, Mama would creep down the hall and, as if bracing for the effort, pause at the doorway to look in at us milling about the dining table. She came in and if she spoke, it was of England and her home and her childhood, and her voice being so soft made us unsure if she was reminiscing to herself or wished for an audience.

'The house was large and fine, with a circular drive for the ease of the carriages, you know. The breakfast parlour faced the east so it was pleasant at that time of day, and to the west was the parlour with a fine oak tree outside and parkland. There were three maids – imagine! – and a cook, housekeeper, footman and butler. My sisters and I had a governess but I'm afraid that we teased her more than we should and hid and did not pay attention. Oh, Papa – my papa, that is – used to lecture us.' And on she went. Her sisters had died, one of fever after having a baby, the other of convulsions before. I am the namesake of one – Mary the other – and although I do not resemble her, yet I feel her with me as if her hand is hovering at my back.

It had made us sad. With every word Mama told us she would rather she were not there in the Coorong with us, but in that lost green world where we had never been, not even in memory. It was strange to be wished out of existence. She had not often spoken of England when we were in Adelaide, but at Salt Creek she drew her childhood around her as if it were a cloak that might comfort and protect. The thought of Adelaide and our life there was not far enough from the Coorong to console. Perhaps it is inevitable to miss what is gone. If Papa had been less proud everything might have been different.

When riding the lanes in my trap I felt Mama's gentle presence by me and heard her voice in my ear: 'See the fields, how wide they are and how green? Just as I said.' And the interlacing of hedgerows and meanders through unblemished fields – all those bulrushes and reeds and no one making use of them – and castles and churches emerging like thrilling geographical formations and the blush of late winter woods and shadows as soft as blossom and sheep like clotted cream. The flint buildings, though, put me in mind of Papa's face towards the end, as if the skin of him barely stretched to cover bone and gaunt muscle and terrible feeling. If my mind drifted to the scrawny and nervous creatures and the salt bone bleached world of the Coorong I am sure that will not surprise.

These are the moments I wait for. Sometimes when half-asleep at night and lying in a particular way the past aligns with the present and I forget my plump pillow and the feathers beneath me and am in my old bed again, the ridge in the sheets where they have been turned to mend a tear, the salt smell of everything, my book shelf and lamp, the rough wooden walls, Addie tossing nearby, the heavy winter quilts holding me safe.

The Coorong, 1855

After that first foray we clung to the house, going about with each other for company if we had a mind to explore. I could not help glancing back. As insubstantial as the house was, and composed of so many of the elements that lay all about or grew from the ground or were of the ground itself, it seemed not unlikely that while my attention was elsewhere it could fly away in a strong gust of wind or subside into sticks and mud in the rain.

In one of the bursts of energy that overcame Mama she found our old school books and slates and brought them out. 'You must keep up with your lessons,' she said, 'else you will all become savages.' It gave her some purpose. Her enthusiasm often wavered and it fell to me to keep our school going between times. Hugh and Stanton were too big, and there was nothing I could teach Fred except mathematics, and Addie did not wish to learn and Albert would rather be out of doors. He was not interested in schoolwork, finishing it quickly to be done and then chafing at Fred to leave with him. But Fred stayed for as long as he could.

Mama was often seen looking from a window or holding to the rail of the veranda as if on a ship on a stormy sea. At first I waved, until I perceived that nothing would reassure. Still, for her sake, for weeks after we lost our fears we did not go beyond the limits that Papa had set for us: up to the stock route, a half-mile away at least, to the shores of the lagoon and around the curve of our point. There were paths all across the land leading to and from different places: an expanse of cockle shells below the house, a small hill from which we could see a long way up the lagoon, a good suck of water nearby, a stand of she-oaks. As we accustomed ourselves to the space and explored further we began to feel and not only think of it as our own.

In those days Papa was sure of our future success. He rode the run to check on the cattle, which were eating their way along the lagoon shore and into the scrub. Each day, Papa and the boys laboured to fence new areas, creating paddocks that they could be moved between. He wore his gaucho's hat, which he said all cow hands wear in Argentina, tilted down rather severe at the front, which a person could not help thinking of as foreign even if they had never left these shores. He had it from his travels before he married Mama and never wore another when he was out working and would not part with this one, old as it was. From a distance we could tell Papa from anyone by his hat, which had a wider brim than was usual and the dimple in its crown almost disappeared with age. I wondered whether Papa missed those carefree times and being here returned him to them.

At first we were in the expectation of seeing more blacks. I overheard a low conversation between Papa and Mama one evening on the subject.

Papa stretched his legs towards the fire, warming his feet. His chin was sunk against his chest. He watched the flames rather than Mama, and spoke as if he hardly expected an answer. 'They are wary, naturally. Who could ever know how many of the black women have been taken.'

'Have they?' Mama asked.

'I know it to be so. Those Kangaroo Island men are rough: whalers and sealers, and escaped convicts too. They row across and up the lagoon; take the women when the men are hunting, I suppose. With determination, it's not so far, and they are the most proficient rowers. They are accustomed to the pursuit of whales, my dear. If you saw them … I assure you they are most impressive. Even if the blacks here saw a boat coming, what chance would they have in their bark crafts? I daresay more than one has killed or been killed.'

'Dear me,' Mama said.

Days passed and were marked by nothing but the daily tasks of cleaning and washing and lessons and work, and by the flocks of birds, which shrilled upwards, their opposite selves, black shadows, swarming across the ground and water faster than anything could travel on those fissured surfaces. The weather was cooling and they were preparing to leave, and the weight I felt while watching them was as much of the body as the spirit. We saw no one. Yet wherever I went I could not rid myself of the uncanny sense of someone temporarily absent or recently departed, as if I were exploring a strange and empty house.

One day I took an old bone-handled knife from the kitchen – seldom used and not valuable – and placed it among the fallen seed cones beneath the she-oak trees. I hardly knew what I hoped for walking the lagoon path next morning – some sign, perhaps only of life other than ours, though who would bother coming out to our point I could not imagine. We were so far from the stock route that we would never see any white person unless they happened down our track. The moment I entered the shade of the she-oaks I knew it would be gone, and so it proved to be. I searched in the needle leaf fall. No creature would take it. I wondered whose hands were touching it now, and the thought made them feel close. At luncheon I examined everyone's expressions again for signs of concealment, but saw nothing unusual: only Addie pining for company, Hugh and Stanton wishing to go hunting for kangaroos, and so on. What need would they have of a blunt old knife? And how could I say what I had done without becoming an object of ridicule or censure? I repeated the experiment the next day leaving an old tablespoon and a battered enamel bowl with the same result. What could such things mean to a savage?

I had no way of knowing whether there was a connection between the knife and the spoon and the bowl and the appearance thereafter of one or two natives, seen by us all. Perhaps it was only that they had become accustomed to our presence and saw that we were no threat. They walked the tracks 'quite as if they owned it', Hugh said. 'It will not end well, Papa.' But Papa tipped his hat back and scratched his beard thoughtfully and said, 'I think not, Hugh. There is land enough. Consider how useful they might become to us. I have seen them working very willingly in the hills and at the lakes. Why not here too?' and he clapped Hugh on the shoulder and went on his way. Mama stayed indoors.

One morning we found a dead kangaroo, still warm, at the veranda steps, which, kangaroo meat having become so expensive in town, was very welcome. Another day there were three ducks.

Papa was delighted. 'See, Bridget,' he said to Mama. 'They wish to be friendly. When we see them, we must reciprocate.'

By degrees as autumn deepened the natives drew closer, as if our lives were aligning. Early one morning while I was letting the chickens out there were two canoes at the lagoon's centre and poised figures as lean and black as arithmetic spearing fish over the side, perfectly still until the darting strike, and then the impaled fish was flipped aboard. My impulse was to run for home, but they were at such a distance and had not even noticed me so I could not see the harm in watching. Another day, Fred and Albert were passed by some blacks out with hunting equipment: spears and clubs and curved sticks which the boys observed them throw great distances and which curled in the air most ingeniously, returning to the person who had released them. I had heard of them in Adelaide but never seen them demonstrated and envied the boys.

'They were so close, you would not believe it,' Albert said.

'Were you frightened? I would be,' Addie said.

'They didn't even look at us,' Fred said. 'It was as if we weren't there. And we saw that boy, the one who threw the stone. I'm sure it was him.'

'What were they wearing?' I said.

'Cloaks,' Fred said. 'They had sort of cloaks on, and string bags on their shoulders. There were ducks in the bags.'

'Do you suppose it was they who left us the ducks and kangaroo?'

'How would we know?' Fred asked.

'Don't tell Mama,' I said. 'It'll only worry her.'

But Mama overheard and was agitated and told Papa. His eyes

lit up. 'I wonder where their camp is.' He sawed his meat with enthusiasm. 'It can't be far. I must find out and we must learn some language, a few small tokens. We can invite them to one of our services. They might be of use about the run. Do you see how it happens, my dear? So, we begin to civilize them, from a small beginning such as this.'

'There is no beginning,' Hugh said. 'They did not communicate; they showed no interest. They are savages.'

'We will see, Hugh,' Papa said. 'I expect us all to be friendly if we see them. Greet them, smile. They must know that we mean them no harm or else we fail.'

Hugh and Stanton shot looks at each other across the table.

'At least they have decided that we mean them no harm and I count that as progress indeed, eh, Bridget?'

Mama did not reply.

Thinking to improve Mama's spirits, Papa put a slatted roof over the walkway between the kitchen and veranda, and at the base of the posts planted grape vines and geranium cuttings brought from Adelaide. He began looking about for timber to improve and enlarge the house. There were trees thereabouts, which grew thickly in parts, but they were twisted and knotty and hard, suitable only for fencing. There was just one large one at the turnoff to our track, which leaned across as if it were fleeing the sea – shaped by the wind as was so much else. Papa and Stanton felled a smaller tree growing nearby. It had a straight section of trunk and Papa wished to see what could be made of it. Hugh and Stanton tried to dig a sawpit but the sandy soil slipped from the sides no matter how they tried to shore it up. Papa went out to survey their progress, folding his arms and nudging at the soil with his toe. Then for a wonder he smiled for all it was such a pitiful mess.

'Well, boys, dig it a little longer and we can call it a grave,' he said.

They stood around considering the possibilities and poking at the pit's edge with their shovels. It had become an amusement. Stanton climbed in and lay there, tipping his hat so it covered his eyes as if to go to sleep and all that was visible from a distance was his hat's battered crown and the bobbing head of the grass stalk that he was chewing and his booted feet crossed casually at the lip of the other end where his legs were too long to fit. It made me shiver to see Stanton lying there beneath the ground's surface, and to see them mock it. Georgie's grave had been smaller than this and the mound over it a hump that a small child could have jumped with ease and all about it had been the dried grasses of summer that bent stiffly with the wind.

I picked up my skirts and ran at them, stamping my feet when I drew near. 'Stop. Stop it. Get out, stupid boy. If Mama should see.'

Papa looked at me mildly. 'Just a little fun, Hester. They meant no harm. But you are right about your mother. It would not do if she came out,' and he looked around to make sure she was not approaching – but of course she was not. 'Quickly now, Stanton.'

Hugh gave me that look with half-closed eyes and a faint smile of his ridiculous rosebud mouth, which made my blood boil, as if he were doing me a favour by conferring his attention. His self-regard was a mystery to me. Nothing could dent it. He kicked some dirt over Stanton who bellowed something low and rough and leapt up alive again and lunged at Hugh, tackling him to the ground and they rolled about, growling and laughing and slapping. I stepped around the grave and up the slope away from Papa's outstretched hand.

'Now, Hettie,' he said, but did no more to stop me.

I heard the boys laughing and did not turn and soon I was over the top of the rise and able to look around without my gaze falling on them.

They rigged up some larger sawhorses and tried to cut the length of the trunk, but the grain of the wood was fine and its torsion was against the direction of the branch so the saw blade stuck and then broke and they gave it up as a bad job.

Papa had brought one load of new timber down the stock route from the hills when building the house, but twice it had overturned in the ruts and he would not contemplate it again. Hard work would find us the materials. We fell to scavenging for wood on the peninsula.

After a storm the boys walked miles up and down the sea beach. Small lengths, broken pieces and driftwood were for the fire; longer lengths from the wrecked ships that had gone down hereabouts were prized – a terrible labour though. They had to be rowed back and if there was too much the boat wallowed and seemed likely to drown. Albert was sturdy for a boy of ten. He and Fred worked together, searching and dragging back pieces they could manage to the point opposite our house, and Hugh and Stanton loaded the boat and rowed back and forth with their shabby treasure.

Curved pieces from the ship's sides were weighted to dry flat; straight bits, which Papa said were from decking or walls, were best; they had been planed smooth – fairly smooth at any rate. He showed me other places in the house where shipwrecked timber that he and Hugh and Stanton had found last winter and spring had been used. It was curious to walk through the house and know that so much of it had once been afloat, and when the house sighed and shifted in the cold of the night, it was easy to imagine that we were at sea ourselves, that whales and shark fish were passing beneath us with a lazy roll of their backs along the belly of the house, and on a windy night that sails above were catching the driven air and we were slicking through water, and on a still night that we were anchored in the limitless sea to stop us foundering on the rocks.

All through the winter storms we were on top of each other and all about us was disorder and the big boys swearing they'd get more sleep out with the bullocks. The baby screamed until Hugh said, 'Cut her gums and save us all, Papa.'

'Don't,' I said. 'I'll mind her at night. Think of Louisa.'

Hugh was quiet at that, and I remembered that Louisa had been a favourite of his.

Papa said, 'It was a fever, the same as Georgie's.'

I said, 'I'll take her and keep her quiet. The tooth's nearly through.'

Papa agreed, so then it was Addie and Mary and me all in that one bed in our narrow room. Often during those colourless hours I rose to her cries and walked her from front door to back until she slept again.

As busy as we were with collecting wood and caulking the gaps in the walls and battening the roof to withstand the wind's sting we did not notice when the natives had gone, only that by June we had none of us noticed any for some time.

'They've seen that we mean to stay,' Hugh said.

Papa was hopeful. 'We have given them no reason to leave. They may yet return. We shall see.'

Mama's spirits shifted about, lifting at the thought of the blacks having gone, falling at her situation. The space unnerved her. She kept to the parlour and its reminders of her old life, only smiling obediently at Papa when he came to sit with her each day.

'We have extended the fence towards the stock route,' he might say.

And she would nod, 'Oh yes.'

'Which will prevent the cattle straying so far.'

'Yes. I suppose so.' She plucked at the fringes of the velvet cushions and shrugged deeper into her shawl. She took a turn about the room as if she'd decided on a purpose and went to the kitchen door and stared at the lagoon or stood at the parlour window, gazing onto the track up the grassy slope as if hopeful that someone might come visiting despite the hour being advanced and there being no company of any kind, suitable or not.

We rowed her across to the peninsula one day thinking to divert her and even persuaded her up a tall sand hill. At the summit she turned around and looked as far off as she could see along the waves of sand and water and sky and the light splintering across it all, and shuddered.

'Please, let us go back now,' she said.

'Just a little longer. Come see. I want to show you something,' Fred said.

But she became agitated and she would not thereafter be removed from the mainland side of the lagoon and its closeness to the stock route. It was the slender cord that connected her. I held onto the thought myself and had to believe that I would travel it one day with

Mama and we would return to our old life. Still, I liked the peninsula. No one knew what we did there: throwing ourselves down the sides of hills with our skirts held high and drawers showing, running after the gnawing waves and screaming away when they reached for us. I leapt across a snake once when running down a hill – there was no time to stop – across its unnatural diagonal movement, and at the bottom laughed that I had cheated death.

We persevered with school. Fred began to record the natural environment of the Coorong and he brought plants and flowers and insects to the table, which he would draw and describe in his note book after he had done with his lessons, a task he disappeared into so completely that he hardly heard his name.

Addie looked at the sentence I had set her to parse and stuttered her pencil on the table. 'Why must I do this, Hester? I'll never use it.'

'You might. Women are in as great a need of a well-furnished mind as men.'

'That is only what Mama and Grandmama say. Minnie says no man likes an educated woman.' Minnie was Addie's friend in Adelaide. We were all familiar with her many opinions.

'Papa does.'

'Look what's befallen Mama despite all her learning. I have other things on my mind.'

'Such as?'

'Living in town and marrying a kind, rich gentleman and never weeding or washing again.'

'You don't do those now. If we work together to help Papa we might return to town one day. How else will you meet such a man?'

'But parsing a sentence, Hester. How does that help?'

I began a new topic in Davison's *System of Practical Mathematics*. Inside that neat and predictable world my circumstances became illusory. There was a great deal in it that could have a practical application for Papa if he would but listen. Truly, I believe that mathematics saved me that first winter: that and the pianoforte, which I do not know how we came to bring. It had value and might have been sold. Perhaps Mama insisted, though she had so little of insistence left in her. It was sleek and large pushed up against the shipwreck wall, and was hardly to be believed.

Finally in spring there was sufficient wood to build an addition to the house, a bigger room for Addie and me and another for the boys, so they had two rooms, each with two beds. But the wood was not quite dry and as by day the house drew in dust and grass seeds and insects and heat, by night it released the sea: salty, briny, the breath of the deep, thin at first, then thickening and souring as it dried. I thought of the people who might have died inside the wood clawing for escape, or reaching for it to save them, or who were washed from it or dragged from it by fish and eaten. Was it any wonder that sometimes I shrank from its walls?

Papa built me a little shelf by my bed in the new bedroom where I might put a lamp and read. When I took the lamp into my room on the first night the light fell on a word, SAL, a name I supposed, scratched into the wood, and I wondered who it might be. Was it a girl, Sally, leaving her mark, or a sailor's or passenger's sweetheart, a whole name, a nickname, did the ship go down before the word was finished? I showed it to Addie and she made a game of hunting for other signs around the house. The thought of a person having been close by in another time was peculiar, as if days or years or deaths long past were no more than another room that we might walk into. Sometimes Sal was more real to me than anything. I wondered about her, wanting as I was for friendship. She was short and dark and lively, as I imagined her, kinder than Addie, less selfish, but with a quick tongue and fond of dancing. She thought me too bookish and looked out to sea, not at anything here. Her skin took the sun, turning dusky, and her eyes were pale as a calm sea close to shore, like the sea glass I found one day among the shells. Mama said it was rare. Who knew where it had come from or where it had been? I also kept a piece of driftwood, which was differently transformed. It had

50

turned to silk and weighed nothing at all. When I stroked it against my cheek it was like the touch of another.

It was my purpose to travel one day, as those objects had. Only I hoped I would have more will, more power, than a bottle thrown from a ship at sea or a twig washed from a distant shore.

5

THE COORONG
SEPTEMBER 1855

At first that spring Tully was merely one more native in the distance, differentiated from the others who appeared on the run once more only by his comparative pallor. It was the sight of him with two women walking the lagoon track a little closer to our house than usual that brought back our first day and the boy who had thrown the stone. Even then I might not have known – they were walking away from me – but for the turn of the taller woman's head at a duck lifting from the reeds so that her cheek caught the sun. I saw the marks of smallpox on her.

Tull was quite tall already and narrow. He was no one in particular to us and over some months it was as if he were resolving under Fred's microscope, until he was part of our lives and moving among us. A remarkable person: he altered our course, not only on the Coorong, but for always.

The cows were calving and Papa and the boys rode the paddocks each day to check them and move them to fresh pasture. Tull began to linger wherever they were, and gradually drew closer until finally they were able to converse. To hear Papa on the subject he might have been tickling for trout, so delicate was the task of waiting for the boy to approach so that they could communicate with or even befriend him. He put choice morsels of food as close to him as he could get – treacle-filled damper, a few slivers of dried apple, and drew back so that the boy might advance without fear. Why he might be frightened I didn't know, for no harm had come to them at our hands.

In the evening despite his fatigue Papa became animated on the subject, going so far as to enact the stealth of the boy's movements and his watchfulness. Mary, in my arms, was wide-eyed at the sight of Papa in his stockinged feet, lifting his legs high in a particular way and placing them with such care. Stanton and Hugh watched with a blank cast to their features; evidently they did not share his aims or fascination. I enjoyed hearing about it; I looked forward to it (any news was welcome) and I think Mama did too. Her spirits were improving somewhat with the warmer weather.

'He came close today and spoke, Bridget,' Papa said in excitement on his return home one afternoon. 'Only think, he has some English already. Where would he have that from? A great mystery. I was thinking of a small gift perhaps. Something to show that we mean well and wish to help, to begin our work. Jam. Yes, perhaps that. Do we have a pot to spare? Something sweet.' He was quite distracted.

'Some dried peas?' Mama said.

'That will do very well' – he kissed Mama's cheek – 'and a packet of flour. I'll get it from the storehouse,' and at Mama's sharp look added, 'A little only. I will be back in a minute.' He banged through the back door and could be heard whistling his way across to the storehouse in search of enticements. Mama looked after him for a moment and went to the inside larder and presently I heard the drawers opening.

Addie having disappeared exactly when her help might be needed, I began to set the table and then Fred and Albert came in hungry after their afternoon of work.

'Did you talk to the native?' I asked.

'Talk?' Fred said. He fossicked for oat biscuits in the biscuit barrel and slid it across the table to Albert. 'A bit. He made himself understood well enough. He speaks English, did you know? His name is Tully – an Irish name, is it not? He said he has another name, but he didn't tell us it, or speak a word of his own language. He wanted to know what we called things.'

'Is he nice? Did you like him? What did you think of him?'

'He's not very clean,' Albert said. He wrinkled his nose.

'No, he's not,' Fred said, and then seeing my disappointment at the lack of detail, 'I don't know. He's different.' He shook his head. 'He just watched us. We were notching the fence posts. He wanted to hold the axe. Papa wouldn't let him in case he ran off with it. He didn't mind.'

'Are you talking of the black boy?' Hugh asked, appearing at the door. 'If you'd like to know what I think, he might show us more respect, instead of behaving as if he were our equal and we were visiting him. Lordly, he is.'

But Papa said, 'There's time enough to teach respect. We must first make a good impression.'

All through spring the boy, Tully, approached them when they were out. He always knew where they were working. The transparency of that country was an illusion; its flatness beyond the stock route concealed dips and folds within which anything might be hidden.

'Slowly goeth the Lord's work,' Papa would say.

Hugh and Stanton held other views. 'Encouraging this familiarity,' I overheard Hugh muttering to Stanton one day as they removed their boots at the door. 'He will come to regret it. Do you know what the boy told me today? That we shouldn't have chopped that tree down and then showed me which ones we should use, can you believe it? Didn't have all the words but did very well making his thoughts known. I told him we would use the wood that we saw fit since it was ours, not his, and did not trouble to conceal my feelings. That gave him pause.'

'That's why he left?' Stanton said.

'Will he visit us here, Papa?' I said at dinner.

'Yes,' Addie said. 'We should know him too. I want to meet the black boy.'

Mama shook her head at Papa.

'He is not a toy or a pet, girls. And he has no clothes.'

'He does have a cloak,' Albert said.

'Which he removes when he is warm,' Hugh said.

'Some breeches?' Papa asked Mama. 'And a shirt? For the girls' sake. He would come closer, I think. We could persuade him. And the others might follow.'

'And the smell? What of that?' Stanton said.

'He is not coming inside, only visiting,' Papa said. 'That is, I hope he is.'

With a little more encouragement Mama found the clothes and Papa took them and in some way persuaded Tull to don them – tying them about his narrow waist with a cord for a belt – and he came closer to the house, and began to wait at the stable in the morning for Papa and the boys to begin their work, which just then was building a cheese-making shed from tree branches and wattle and mud. The boy became a willing helper. Addie and I watched sometimes, not too openly, from the vegetable patch or the poultry run. He was careful and precise in his weaving of branches and in applying the thick mud that coated them, and expected nothing in return, only, they said, that he talked a great deal and liked conversation and that his English improved quickly. I did not converse with him when he first made himself known to Papa, so I could not judge as to his improvement.

The first that I spoke to him was one morning when I went into the stable in search of Papa. It was shadowy in there and sweet with the smell of hay and Tull was looking about curiously. The horses did not mind him and he did not mind them – they were acquainted already, I suppose. He turned at my footstep and it was a shock to find myself so close to him; we might have collided had I been moving faster. He was almost as tall as I, but younger: slender and with a boy's frame and smooth cheeks. His hair was almost to his shoulders and curling and knotted and stuck with a few burrs. He smelled, as Stanton had said, his skin being rubbed with some animal fat. He was not someone whom Mama would welcome into her home, no matter the cause.

My own surprise was matched very well by his horror. I believe I was the first white female he had seen close to.

'Excuse me,' I said. 'Tull, isn't it? Is Papa about? Mr Finch, that is.'

He backed away and backed away and his eyes darted about and, feeling sorry for him, I withdrew until I was outside once more. When there was enough room to get past me he came out and moved towards the yard fence before he spoke to me, nothing more than a simple greeting and the information that he was waiting for Mr Finch and the boys. He spoke well, lacking only a few words, but the rhythms of his sentences were unusual to my ear and the ends of his sentences rolled away into nothing, like water disappearing into dry ground. It was not at all like the blacks that I had heard in Adelaide before they became so scarce.

'Would you like a drink while you wait?'

His eyes flickered across my hair and face and dress and at my shoes and ankles – which anyone could see but polite people would not stare at so because they should have been covered – and back to my hair and face very quick, which he had to look away from again.

'Of water?' I said.

He moved away again a half-step at a time until he ran into the yard fence, which he then climbed over, and to spare him I went back inside.

The cheese-making began, using the small moulds from the old dairy farm. I washed them and dried them to make them ready. The night before it was to begin, Papa chose a little bobby calf and led it and its mother down to the yard. At first the cow rolled her eyes and thrust her horns at anyone approaching the calf too close. She kept it safe between her and the wooden fence until the enticement of a few handfuls of oats was put in the trough, and the calf touching against her side became calm. It was curious and put its soft whiskered mouth against my hand and its mother stared at me as if making a judgement, and I lied in all my actions and the tone of my voice and she let me scratch the little calf on its head where the nubby horns were pressing against the skin. It butted its head into my touch.

Addie came up to the shed with me – to help, she said, but I think it was that she was curious. I was glad of her company. There was the condemned calf suckling and pausing to take us all in before returning to his pressing task, and his mother bewildered at being tethered to the fence. When the time came Papa led the bleating calf away from its mother out of the yard and around the corner of the stable where it was concealed from sight if not sound and Stanton or Hugh held it while Papa dispatched it. This part I surmised from the bloody knife in Papa's hand when he reappeared. The cow's lowing distress echoed about. Birds stopped singing.

Addie clapped her hands to her ears, 'Make it stop, Hettie.' And she ran away down the path.

It *was* a piteous sound. I wanted to row across to the peninsula and sit looking out to sea where there might be a ship that I could imagine was taking me away. Of course I did not do that. I had to be sensible. I went to help.

Fred and Stanton hauled the calf up and suspended it. Blood dripped from its neck into a large bowl beneath. The rope creaked with its weight and the calf swayed and its round brown eyes with their delicate lashes stared. There was a smell of metal. Hugh removed the bowl of blood and replaced it with a clean tub and Papa took his knife and made a long even cut into the calf's belly, his face twisting, and pulled out all the entrails. They landed heavy and wet in the tub and blood splashed onto my skirts. More washing. Hugh reached out his toe and pushed back a loop of intestine that had fallen over the edge of the tub. It slid very slow down the inside edge. Another smell rose which, combined with the sight of the grey pink loops of intestine, made me retch. I did not run, though I did look aside when Papa began to rummage. Only one of the stomachs contained rennet.

Papa and I went to the kitchen and he showed me how to prepare the stomach, first opening, then washing and drying it. It was hard to cut, being the texture of India rubber, but I managed to slice it into small pieces, which we set to soak in salt water with a little vinegar added. The rennet would be ready in one or two days.

'I don't know how you did it,' Addie said later, while we washed and dried the dishes.

'I don't either. It's not for the love of farm life, I can tell you that. There is nothing we can do. Nothing will change if you upset yourself. The calf will still die, the mother will moan, we will still need the money. We will be here. You cannot change anything by your tears, but you can change some things by your actions.'

Two days later Papa showed me how to make the cheese. It took only a little of the rennet mixture stirred through the heated milk to form it into curds. We scooped the curds out and pressed them into the muslin lined moulds until the cheeses had set sufficiently to be released. Lined up white and pure on the storehouse shelves they were a pleasing sight at the end of the day and gave me a feeling of hope. I looked at my hands grown strong from work, and my forearms speckled from working out of doors, and felt a curious mixture of pride and dismay. I had changed from the girl I had been in town, and I did not know if I could change back.

Papa was not to be thwarted in his wish to have Tull come inside, and by degrees he wore Mama down, first by inducing him to have a bath with soap in the washhouse. I did not witness that, but Fred told me of his refusal to have his hair washed or trimmed: most vociferous he was in his protestations. Albert came inside to tell us the news, also carrying a message from Papa that a jacket was now needed for Tull since he couldn't stop shivering.

'That will be the shock,' Mama said, rising from her chair where she had been sewing, curious despite herself.

'He's only cold I think,' Albert said. 'Not frightened any more. He's furious. It was quite funny, if you want to know what I think.' He grinned.

'Be kind, Albert,' Mama said, in gentle reproof. 'Come and help me find something,' and she put her arm about his shoulder in the way she had used to and Albert, surprised, leaned against her.

'You should have seen it, Mama. You would have laughed. You couldn't help it. He was worse than Skipper.'

It was such a little thing that Mama was doing, noticing Albert. Seeing the two of them so affectionate – Albert with Papa's long pale face and Mama's soft brown hair, but with a child's plump cheeks and small nose, and Mama tender – made me see how Albert missed this. There were just these moments when she seemed to remember how to be her old self, as if there were a trick to it. I could try to be like her for Albert's sake, but he looked to Fred for attention rather than me.

Each Sunday morning Papa held a worship service in the parlour, which we must all attend as neat and clean as could be managed and in the correct state of mind: reverential, humble, collected. Beforehand, I took Papa a cup of tea on the veranda and he sat and drank it by way of collecting his thoughts, and on one such occasion, seeing Tull coming down the fork of the track that came to the back of the house, Papa waved his arms in sweeping arcs and called out, 'Hello, Tull! Please come in, meet Mrs Finch and my daughters, Hester and Adelaide, that is. The boys of course you know. Come and worship with us.'

What Tull made of that I could not imagine. He approached the back of the house, and stepped up to the veranda, pausing there and moving his feet against the flat wood. Papa smiled in encouragement and went to the door and beckoned. The sight of Papa so close in the doorway made him stop. Fred edged around from behind him and said, 'Tull,' and smiled at him as if they were the oldest of friends. It was the nicest thing about Fred: he was quiet and his sombre colouring made him fade beside Stanton. Still, there was a gentleness and warmth about him that drew people in and made them wish to lighten his mood. It was in part a trick of his physiognomy, gone in a second when he laughed, but they didn't know that at first. Some of the tension went out of Tull and he came closer. Papa beamed and moved into the house and Tull at first peered and then stepped after him and by degrees, following Papa, made his way past Addie, sparing her barely a glance, up the hallway to the parlour. We followed.

'See who has arrived, Mrs Finch,' Papa said.

Mama came to the door and said, 'Good morning, Tully,' with a gentle smile. Mary, in her arms, stared and stared and sucked her fingers.

Naturally we were curious to have a native inside the house with us. Mama began to count the seats and I saw what she was thinking: that Tull could only fit in if he squeezed onto the sofa with the boys or if he sat on the floor, which would have displeased Papa as lacking in hospitality.

'I'll fetch a chair,' I whispered.

'You're a good girl, Hettie.'

When I returned with Papa's ladder-back, Tull, neat as a cat, was exploring the room and everyone there was watching him. He touched the chest of drawers with a single fingertip and ran his hands across the window and moved his head from side to side to take in the distortion in the glass and felt its smooth hard surface, very delicate in his touch. And we watched him in our own wonderment and curiosity, seeing our house through new eyes. It was very strange and fascinating. Papa went out to call the others (he liked to be punctual and we were already running late); Tull looked after him as if to follow but Papa said, 'Wait here if you like,' so he did; it was as if he must steel himself to stay in this small room with us.

'See this, Tull,' Addie said and went to the piano and lifted the lid. Mama frowned at her boldness, but Addie paid no heed, which was nothing out of the ordinary. I expected her to play a crashing chord for the fun of shocking him, but she touched her forefinger to middle C and depressed it once, just enough for the hammer to sound against the string, clear as a bell, and sweet. Tull blinked rapidly, but was otherwise calm, and watched Addie and the piano in expectation, waiting for what she might do next. She played the same note, and then another, higher, G, and played them together, and added an E to make a chord, luring him in by degrees. He came closer. Mama had become curious too and did not interrupt or reprove.

Addie nodded at Tull in encouragement. 'You can touch it, Tull. Go on. Play a note.' She struck a key, and took his arm (Mama drew in a sharp breath), startling Tull though he did not pull away, and led his hand to the keyboard that he might play a note on his own, which he did, loosing a smile that I think must have been part relief. There came the sound of the boys at the back door, of Papa shushing their weekday voices, and of them tramping through the house. Then they were in the parlour and the space shrank.

Tull watched intently as one after another we sat. Fred was the first to understand his confusion. 'Move, Albert.' He pushed Albert further along the sofa. 'Here, Tull.' He patted the space beside him and Tull looked at it. Fred turned him around and pulled him down. 'There.' They bounced together.

From what I saw from the vantage point of the piano – which was nothing at all while I was playing – Tull sat through the service with fair patience. He fidgeted a little through Papa's sermonette on the subject of gratitude for bountiful riches and blessings etcetera, which we had heard variations on many times before, but we were all guilty of that. My stratagem of giving the appearance of listening while setting myself mental calculations to while away the time having worked quite well, I could not attest to the details. Papa chose the old hymn 'Soldiers of Christ, Arise', which we had sometimes heard in Adelaide before we left, and sang with gusto, even for the line 'To keep your armour bright, attend with constant care', which advice I could not help feeling was unlikely to be followed. It put me in mind of housekeeping rather than war, and made me want to laugh. Hugh's voice rang out for the warrior lines: 'tread all the powers of darkness down' and 'take to arm you for the fight, the panoply of God'. (Looking back I have come to see that he was one of those people who seemed always to be presenting a picture of himself – noble warrior, determined pioneer, chief advisor – but seldom inhabiting his true self.) We made a poor army.

Papa invited Tull to stay to dinner. Tull watched the table being set and the other preparations of serving dishes being taken to the kitchen and Addie outside collecting a bouquet of whatever flowers she could find to make the dresser nice for Sunday. Without saying a word, Tull went past the table and out of the back door and flowed up the slope and away. He did not come to the house the next day and he didn't seek out Papa and the boys out on the run. He was gone again, we had no idea where, and in the week that followed Papa would not stop blaming himself that he had progressed too fast with him.

6

CHICHESTER
1874

I was fortunate in three things, none of which I deserved. My mother and father believed daughters to be worthy of education, Grandmama favoured me, and although we were ourselves poor, there was sufficient money in the family to save us from the very worst that poverty could inflict when we came to the time of severest trial. Together, they saved me. Now, all that I have from those early days, which were both terrible and wonderful, are some flints, a basket and a few stone tools.

Two books in my possession have been a comfort: one by a Mr Gould about the birds of Australia. A few of the birds in it are familiar – swans and pelicans and emus and gulls and so on – and are so lifelike in colour and in the cast of their eye that when I pass the book left open on a stand in the gallery they sometimes startle me, as if a breeze had lifted a wingtip or caught a tail or they are tracking my passage past.

The other book is by Mr Angas and contains many fine sketches and watercolours of natives, including on the Coorong, which he made while journeying in Australia. (It is not the copy we had in South Australia. Fred might have that one.) We used to look at Mr Angas's book when we were preparing to leave Adelaide and Papa would try to reassure Mama of the gentleness of the Coorong tribe.

'They have spears and clubs. See them there,' and Mama had poked the page, 'and there. Everywhere. Savages.'

'For hunting,' Papa said. 'For animals, not to fight people – not white people at least.'

'People *are* killed. What about *The Maria*?'

Everyone knew the story of *The Maria* – I couldn't remember a time when I had not known how the survivors of a shipwreck had been helped by natives on the Coorong and after a time had been turned on and murdered – all of them – and their possessions stolen. The governor had ordered a search party to be sent to discover who had done it and two natives were hanged and more than one shot. It was hard not to think of sometimes, when so few of us would be living in so remote an area.

'And people have also been helped. Other survivors would have died without the natives' help. I do not believe them barbarous, merely uncivilized, and that can be remedied. They have treated others with kindness as we will treat them and I believe that charity is rewarded, as I hope it will be for us when we are living among them.'

'Oh.' It was a drawn out despairing sound and Mama put her handkerchief to her mouth to stop it. 'And no one there but us?'

'There is an inn run by man and wife, the Robinsons.' At this Mama brightened. 'But ten miles further down the lagoon,' Papa added.

Mama's face became bleak again. 'Ten miles,' she repeated. 'Too far to walk. Too far for company.'

Papa gave his sweet patient smile. 'We must do this, Bridget,' and his voice was low and pleasant and his arm about her holding her to his side. Mama's forehead rested against his chest and he stroked her hair so gently I could almost feel its silkiness myself. 'It is our best chance; it is our only chance. We will become paupers else. I will not see our station so reduced.'

Mama's head moved against him, as if she were grinding her feelings and thoughts into him. 'If I ask Mama—' she began.

Papa stepped back and took her by the shoulders and held her away from him. 'No. We will not do that. We will not accept their charity.' And he shook her once, not with any violence, but in emphasis that was enough to shock. 'No more of that.'

'I am sure she did not mean, they did not mean—'

Papa released her and stepped back and the distance between them continued to increase as he spoke. 'Let us not discuss this further. It is not to be thought of. I will not give them further reason to question my duty to my family.' He stepped backwards again. 'It is *my* family. I will not be beholden again. I will not be lectured.' He was at the door by then. 'Let that be the end of the matter.' He opened the door and was gone, leaving Mama trembling behind.

She turned to me. 'It's not that they— They only wish to help. I am all they have left, you see, your Aunt Mary and Aunt Hetta being gone.'

'Mama.'

'They came here to be with us. To leave them here in town – I cannot feel it is right.'

'We will be back, Mama. I know we will.' Mama began to sob. 'Please, Mama. Don't feel it so,' I said.

'How can I do otherwise?'

I did not know what answer I could give Mama that would reassure, so I left the room too, which I should not have.

I did not altogether blame Papa. Grandmama was accustomed to managing people and set his back up. 'Surely not another lease,' she once said, and her eyebrows lifted and her thin cheeks flushed. Mama said that I took after her. She was tall and straight-backed, with an abundance of faded red hair and fine pale skin that was much admired. 'A bird in the hand,' she would say, and look at Papa. She and Grandpapa were much the same height – he perhaps a fraction shorter – and they seemed so much equals to me that it surprised me when he said, 'Now my girl,' and touched her arm in mild admonition. Then her eyes snapped and she sometimes left the room in such a rush that her skirts flew out behind.

I followed her once and found her further along the hall with her hands pressed to her cheeks and wearing a rather wild expression. When I asked what the matter was she said, 'To spare you all my terrible tongue, Hettie. It does no one any good. Mind what I say now.' She stroked my cheek – 'You're a good girl' – and then, collecting herself, gave it a smart pat and said, 'And if you will take my advice, never forget your bonnet. Dear me, what will become of you all?'

There was no more talk after that. Not even Georgie's untimely death the week after could delay departure. It was hard for Mama to leave his grave behind. All the sadness of that time became muddled.

I have Mama's old flint arrowheads that she discovered near this house when she was a girl. They were from the ancient Britons who lived here when the Romans invaded. They were something like talismans to her. I keep them in a case in the gallery with a spearhead and a stone axe and a carved wooden club that Tull left behind. I thought Papa might discard them and took them with me when I left. Of course, flints are not so remarkable to me now that I live in a country and among buildings that fairly bristle with them. In the Coorong, they brought to mind Mama and her stories of traipsing lanes and meadows and woods; more often now I recall Tull making use of them, how quickly he understood them and released their energy to make fire or implement or weapon, how they became more than stone in his hands.

And finally there is my Coorong basket, acquired through a trade I made with someone I knew at Salt Creek, which gives no indication of the purposes for which it was made or used. Addie said that the women who made them told stories while they were working; the stories were woven into every strand. For a while I had it on a shelf in the gallery, a mere artefact, but it began to lose meaning, almost to die before my eyes, so I put it to use thinking it better for it to wear out and break – to live and die – than to be shelved as if it were a fly drowned in amber. One summer morning I lifted it down and took it with me into town. 'Who would think savages could make anything so fine?' one lady of my acquaintance said. Several others touched it, which I did not like. Now I use it to pick flowers or fruits or vegetables about the garden and it has come alive again; it pleases me to see it returned to unremarkable utility.

*

Two weeks after the church service Tull returned. Papa was jubilant, and invited him to attend our small school. He had no idea of Tull's finer qualities at first, of the acuity and retentiveness of his mind. His invitation was nothing more than part of his goal to civilize. Perhaps he offered some inducement at first; I don't know what they talked of when they were out working on the run. What we saw was Tull being more often with us around the dining table for lessons than outside at work. Most days, Mama set a lesson for each of us, and tested us in turn and if she did not come to the dining room the job fell to me, but Tull worked with her; if she was not there he worked alone, on a slate. He valued reading above anything. He was so neat with his hands that it was no wonder that his writing was clean once he had the way of holding first chalk, later a pen. I could not tell if he derived pleasure from it, if curiosity drove him in the way that it drove Fred. It was as well that Papa had decided that Stanton need no longer trouble himself with school, else Tull would have had a harder time of it with him. He and Hugh had left earlier with a great jostling through the doorway and a nervous laughing energy that I could not fathom.

'Have a good day, Hester,' Stanton said at the door. 'Among your pots and pans.' He appeared so brown and free, his hair grown with no barber around, and he was filling out. He would be a big man one day, with broad shoulders. His jacket would not fit him much longer. He had the swagger of a person who lived in the expectation of admiration. There was none of that hereabouts; we must wait in the hope that neighbours would one day arrive. Until the district became more closely settled he would be thwarted. Love and other such matters were mysteries to me, but I do not think they were to Stanton. All I knew then was the teeming energy and frustration in him. Hugh had it too but contained it better. He contrived to be neat, to maintain some of the habits of town life. He hung his clothes at day's end while Stanton, from his dishevelled appearance, must have left them where they fell.

His mocking tone made me hot inside, but I would not show him that. As coolly as I could, I said, 'And you, Stant. Let us hope the cattle are able to elevate your mind.'

'Oh, I will have a good day. You need not worry on that score. And it won't be because of the cows.' He laughed.

'Stanton,' Hugh said, sharp now when he had been joking before, and Stanton turned to go.

I would not say that I hated my brother, but I did dislike him and could not stop myself saying, 'Yes, yes. Off you go. And if you later need assistance with matters that might require intelligence, I'm always happy to oblige.'

He turned back. 'You be careful, Hett. With your sharp tongue no one will have you even if they can bear your ridiculous height.' And he swung out of the door.

'You can't help it, Hester,' Hugh said. 'Stanton doesn't mean it. There will be someone.'

His pity and his kind, pompous face were worse than any jeering of Stanton's.

'Stanton does mean it and so do I. He *is* stupid. I would not trade my mind for anything.' But it was not true, as the tears that rushed into my eyes told Hugh most eloquently. 'Go. Go. I don't want to see either of you.'

There was the banging and stamping of them pulling on their boots and of them thundering down the steps and the clatter of the gate and soon after the diminishing crunch of hooves.

We became used to Tull's presence through that summer and into autumn – more than that: we were impatient for his arrival each day. He was the most alert, conscious person I had ever met, poised for anything: flight, danger, contests of strength or will, and to learn more – always that. We liked him for the games he knew and taught us, short as we were of entertainments. There was one in which we made two lines and kicked a ball from one line to the other and the people opposite jumped and wrestled for it; and another in which he set a disc of bark rolling and we tried to hit it with the fine blunt spears that Tull made for us. At first he laughed at our clumsiness and the way we stood and threw our weapons. Stanton improved and hit often enough, each time yelling a triumphant 'Hah!' Try as he might he could not leap as Tull did for a third game in which the boys took turns to throw things at him from a distance, and he evaded them. He was never struck. His litheness and agility were an amazement to us. From standing he could jump more than a yard in the air and twist and writhe to avoid being struck as if suspended and twisting in the wind. From a run he could leap even higher. But he brushed off any praise, the abilities of other boys of his acquaintance being greater, he said.

We knew only a little about him, and that what Papa had noted – that he seemed to some degree to be less favoured than other boys in his clan. His mother's husband was not his father, Papa said. They did not discourage his contact with us even if they did not wish for contact themselves.

From us, Tull learned how to play chess and draughts and marbles and he would play them with anyone who cared to late in the afternoon when the work had been done, or at other times if it was raining. It was a novelty for us all to pit our skills against someone new, one who saw with a mind that was innocent in a way – of this game and its traditions at least. He had never heard of a king or queen or knight or bishop and without a sense of hierarchy saw the game differently. He played as if the king were no more important than a bishop. 'He is weak,' he said. 'Why do the other pieces protect it?'

'He is important,' I said. 'The most important.' I had never thought of it, in fact, and wondered now. 'He must be wise, he and the queen.'

He picked up a knight – 'This one is good' – and he lifted it high and began shifting it from place to place, trying out its moves as it was permitted as if imagining the nimble leaps and turns of something real. 'You think you know what it will do, but you can't know.'

'Unpredictable,' I said. 'That's the word.'

I watched him absorb it. 'Unpredictable,' he repeated.

'We have a government too, men who make decisions about laws – rules, that is,' I said. I had in mind Papa and his desire for us to impart civilization. 'And bishops who know about God and the church and religion, the things we sing about on Sunday. Do you have people like that?'

'What are rules?' Tull asked.

'The things people may and may not do.'

'Oh yes. We have that too. A *tendi*.'

'I did not know.'

'We don't eat some birds.'

'Why not? Is the taste bad?'

'No. They make us sick. Boys, like me. Men can eat them. Other things too, some animals.'

'Which animals?'

'I don't remember.'

'We have so many rules I can't remember them all. About manners and clothes and respect. People may not kill other people, or take things from them. That is stealing. We may not steal. And other things too.'

'Take what?'

'Well, cattle – kill and eat them, that is. And we may not take your possessions.' I could not think what they had that we might wish for. One black had a shell necklace that I admired. I had heard people in Adelaide liked the carving on their weapons and collected them. 'Your spears and clubs, for instance. But you can sell them, if you like.'

'Fish? Kangaroos? You kill and eat them.'

'They are wild. They are on our land, but you may eat them, Papa says.'

'You can eat them too?'

'Us? May we eat them? Why ever not? Anyone may, I suppose, if they are passing along the track. It would be polite to ask, but I daresay people would not bother even if we made it a rule. How would they know that they could not do something here that they do freely elsewhere?'

Tull appeared troubled, but I could not explain it better. The king just was; our cattle and the land they grazed upon were ours; weapons and nets and canoes were theirs; game was anyone's. Tull said nothing more on the subject but reapplied himself to the chessboard.

I knew of Tull's progress, if not its scope, but it was Fred's work that I remember more clearly. There was a purposeful quality in what he did. In the afternoons he must help on the run; the work of building fences and other structures – the dairy, the storehouse, the washroom – never ended, and at other times there were the cows to be herded and milked, the cheese to be made. But he made the morning his, completing his schoolwork quickly – well enough not to be found wanting – and then sat behind the ramparts of his materials, among them Mr Angas's book about his visit to South Australia. I took it up to reacquaint myself with it. The pictures of the Coorong and the lakes were like and also not like the things I had seen. The people were not like any natives I ever saw on our land. They appeared as small and as meek as tamed animals, which could not have been further from the truth, as if they had nothing better to do than sit there, as if they spent their lives waiting for fate to have its way with them. Tull didn't like the book. He had looked at it once and glanced at us while he was doing it and put it aside with distaste. The camps were rendered with more realism. One was quite like the encampment that I stumbled upon with Skipper: spears rest against a wurly's roof, pressing into the grasses, and there is a big striped club on the other side, and clean picked whalebones piled neatly by the entrance. In the centre is the fire with its smoke rising straight. A still day, then: a rarity.

Fred said, 'See how his plants are not correct? The leaves are ridiculous, like wool or string. They are like nothing I've seen here. And the colours are wrong, the light is wrong, the ground is wrong.'

'But see the smoke in his fires. How does he do that?'

Fred took the book and held it close. 'It is quite well done,' he conceded. 'But the plants—'

'They're not as good as yours.'

'No, they're not.'

There was something similar in the pictures, though. Fred drew the plant, not the glass that held it or the kitchen or anything else that lay nearby. Mr Angas's drawings showed one or two natives or a detail of an encampment, but there was a smothering stillness in them. Even the smoke appeared more like a tuft of fleece than any other thing when I looked at it more closely. The natives were as fixed as pinned butterflies, for display only, when the space they lived in was vast and the sky without limit. They flowed through it as sure and inevitable as gravity, as if the space itself were a living thing and part of them and they part of it. I do not know how to explain it more.

Watching Fred, I began to wonder if it was something other than interest and curiosity alone that drove his actions. He was so purposeful in what he did. Self doubt did not occur to him; he was able to look only at the thing, the task before him. I wished that I could do the same. My own self was mysterious to me. Oh, I knew what I did, but other than that I was invisible to myself. Of course there was a mirror in the parlour and another hanging over the washbasin outside for Papa and the boys to tend their whiskers; I knew my appearance. It was not that, but that I did not see or know the difference that I made, the space I occupied in this world. I was no more than a phantasm flickering past people. I wished to know of what like and substance I was. I could see the work of translating from three dimensions to two, but could not understand how it was done. I could not feel it in my brain, though I could feel how to calculate the area of a leaf or the angle at which it branched from a stem or the regularity of its branching. There was so much else to do: churning the butter and cooking and cleaning and washing and planting and cultivating, and Addie and Albert to be helped with their lessons, and Mary to be managed if Mama could not.

But Tull: I did not think of him until I paused in my playing one evening to search through the music in the piano stool for something 'more melodious – no, more celebratory!', as Papa had requested. He was in good spirits. The cheeses made in spring had been sent to the market in Adelaide through an agent at Wellington and had fetched a good price, though the cost of transporting it had been higher than Papa liked. Since I had been practising exercises from Mama's old Clementi (*Introduction to the Art of Playing on the Piano Forte*), anything would fulfil his request.

'I don't know what to think,' Mama murmured to Papa. She clicked her knitting needles and jerked some wool free. 'He's a native.'

'It is your fine teaching and your gentle manner,' Papa said, with a look of tender regard. 'You have a civilizing influence, my dear. On us all.' He rested his hand on her cheek and Mama rubbed against it a little, as a cat might. The warm summer had improved her spirits, and we hoped it would last despite the evenings of late autumn drawing in.

Noticing me, Papa pulled his hand away and Mama became herself again. She shook her head. 'It's not that. The progress he's made. It's not winter yet. You would scarcely believe it. He is something quite out of the ordinary. What are we doing? He will be a misfit forever. What need does he have of knowledge?'

'He will be – he is – a bridge, as I hoped from the beginning.'

'There will be no one for him.'

'As to that we cannot judge. We must trust in the Lord to provide.'

Evidently Papa's curiosity was piqued. At breakfast next morning he announced that he would come home early that day, before we had packed away our books for lunch. 'And then you may all show me a little of your learning.'

I resolved to do something to make him proud. In the event I didn't know how. My hand in dictation and composition was as untidy as ever, and though my equations were orderly enough for anyone with understanding, Papa was not mathematically disposed and his eyes drifted unfocused across my work. 'Very good, Hester,' he said, already looking past me, and that was all. He tweaked Addie's curls. 'Now, Miss, I hope you are attending to your Mama.' His tone suggested that he thought it very likely she was not and he did not mind, which made Addie giggle. Fred's map of the run, the location of its sucks – the freshwater springs that formed natural pools – and its hills and tracks made him pause and stroke his beard and rest his fingertips on Fred's shoulder. But this was just by way of arriving at Tull's side.

Tull had been tense all morning. He held his pen too tight for neatness and seemed on the edge of running. It was months since he began to attend our school, and not once had Papa visited while our lessons were in progress.

Mild and quiet as could be Papa drew up a chair and sat alongside him. Tull darted a glance at him. 'You read well, Mrs Finch says. I wondered if you would read a little for me. Anything you care to.'

Tull gazed towards Mama.

'You may read from today's dictation, Tull,' she said.

He drew his slate close and cleared his throat, and began. His voice was not quite smooth; he halted at some words – 'void' and 'heaven' gave him some trouble – and lost his place once, before putting his finger beneath the line and continuing: 'And God saw the light and that it was good: and God divided the light from the darkness. And God called the light Day, and the darkness he called Night. And the evening and the morning were the first day.'

We all stopped to listen. We would have in any case, out of the strangeness of Papa's presence, but it was the surprise of watching Tull too, as if a new person had come among us. We knew that he could read, but we had not heard him read so much or so clearly. Mama was in the habit of drawing him off to one side. I had thought she was sparing his feelings at appearing ignorant among us. We continued to stare when he finished, which made him fidget and rub a hand on his breeches.

'Well, well, Mrs Finch is right. You read very well, very well indeed,' Papa said in a quiet sort of voice. His face was more eloquent – rapt, as if he had witnessed a miracle – and I had to look away.

'Well? He reads better than Stanton,' Fred said.

Addie snorted. '*Albert* reads better than Stanton.'

Mama pressed her lips together and frowned and shook her head, and said, 'You do read well, Tull.'

Tull looked about in confusion. He had no idea what he had done. He could not know that Papa had never before looked at me or at any one of us so.

Papa gave three small nods and swept his hair back from his brow in a curiously youthful gesture, as if had a hat been there he might have tossed it into the air. 'And God said, Let there be light: and there was light,' he said.

'What does it mean?' Tull asked.

'It's about the beginning of the world. Creation,' Papa said. 'About knowledge and sin. How we fell from God's grace. Not that bit – that's further along. The part you read is just night and day and how they came to be.'

'Oh,' Tull said, looking back at the words and running his eyes over them again, slowing more than once, and frowning, in no way enlightened. Papa couldn't see that.

We were spared further encomiums by Skipper's warning bark. Papa went outside and we followed, and it proved to be two troopers riding down to the house: a great novelty. We watched him walk towards them.

Seeing them, Tull slipped back behind us all. 'Why are they here?' he said.

'How would we know?' Addie said. 'Papa will find out and tell us.'

'Are they the same ones? Does Mr Finch know them?'

'The same as what?'

'As a long time ago.'

'Whatever do you mean?' I said. 'We've never seen troopers here.'

Papa had reached the gate and they began to speak. New people, who I had not seen for more than a year, appeared stranger by far than any native painted and carrying weapons and wearing fur and grass and seaweed and other things so connected by colour and substance to what was around us. The troopers' clothes were blue and their buttons bright.

'A long time ago. People, blackfellas, saw men like that with Mr Finch.'

'Troopers, do you mean, with Papa?'

'They know his hat.' His hand inscribed a curve above his head – Papa's gaucho's hat.

'Papa's? I suppose it's not the only one of its kind,' I said. 'The man with the hat, what did he do?'

'He was there with troopers when some blackfellas were killed.' He nodded towards the troopers. 'Two.' He circled a hand about his head and drew tight on an imaginary line and jerked it up and his head flopped to one side.

Addie shrieked – 'Don't, Tully' – and I drew a sharp breath. He was so lifelike in enacting death. Everything about it was clear, even the diameter of the rope. His eyes had rolled around, very white.

Tull let go the rope and loosened the noose and slipped his head out and dropped the ghost rope. We waited for the sound of it reaching the floor but it never came.

'Papa would never do that,' I said. 'What are you thinking of? If you are so worried about him, why are you here?'

'I waited for a long time, till I was sure. He never did me harm.'

'Of course he wouldn't harm you. He's a dear old thing,' Addie said. 'Anyway, he wasn't here before.'

'Not here,' Tull said. 'A long way that way,' and pointed down the lagoon.

'Hanged,' I said to Tull. 'Whoever did it and those who helped must have had a reason. People do not get hanged for nothing. Had the blacks attacked this man with the hat?' I said.

Tull said nothing, but stood in the doorway keeping an eye on Papa and the troopers while I resumed clattering about, clearing the books away, flinging the cold tea off the veranda, banging the kettle on to boil, wondering at him sitting there thinking Papa a murderer and accepting our charity. Then for no reason that I could see he left where he was and went in a quiet shadowy sort of way through the heart of the house and the front door and south along the lagoon path away from Papa and the troopers who were coming down the hill towards us. It was as if he were being propelled by them, their paces being so similar.

Papa invited the troopers inside. They had come about Mrs Robinson from the Travellers Rest, whose husband had gone missing, leaving her 'in high hysterics' Sergeant Wells said, tipping his tea neatly into his saucer to cool before drinking it, his magnificent whiskers resting upon its rim like a hearth-rug. They wondered if we'd seen him, which we had not. We had no news at all, but we could not bear to let these new faces and unfamiliar voices depart. We crowded about the dining table to hear, Fred and Albert leaning against the dresser.

'More tea?' Mama said more than once, and Addie bestirred herself to carry around a plate of biscuits. But eventually they had to leave. They had miles further to ride. And all we could do was wonder what might have befallen Mr Robinson for the next while.

Papa was curious to see what use could be made of the peninsula, as it was part of our land. Two weeks later he and the boys drove a small herd of cows down the lagoon and crossed them to the peninsula, taking them north again until they were opposite our house. They stopped at the Travellers Rest on their return and there learned that Mr Robinson, his throat slit, had been found in a swamp miles from the inn by Policeman Jack, a native. I hated to think of it.

'Poor Mrs Robinson,' Mama said. 'Would a native have done it?'

Papa just shook his head. 'A native would stab you or spear you. I would not think they would cut a man's throat. I heard talk of the coach driver who had been with him. He says they were out hunting. But why would he do it? He's gone, in any case.'

'Was it he then?'

'Why would he? And where's the proof? I would call it common sense to leave in the circumstances. The Celestials perhaps. But they keep to themselves.'

The Celestials came from China, and since they were taxed for landing in Melbourne, they docked in Adelaide and walked down the coast to the goldfields. Papa was the only one of us lucky enough to have seen them. They had built a few wells along the stock route, none on our run: 'a useful service to all passers-by,' Papa said.

We couldn't tell Tull that he had nothing to fear, or pass on the news that the troopers had brought. As it turned out, he was gone again for the winter. Word came that Mr Robinson's death had been ruled a suicide, but that didn't stop Mama fretting or the rest of us staying closer to home than usual. Any death must be a reminder of one's mortality. We felt safer bunched together, as animals do when pursued.

7

CHICHESTER
1867

The wonder in our first years in Chichester was the rebuilding of the cathedral spire, which had fallen a year or two before my arrival there. That something that had stood for more than seven hundred years could fall so quick was miraculous to me, in the sense that it could scarcely be comprehended.

No one was killed, the event having been expected and the area cleared, which many called a blessing and a sign from God that it was not punishment that was intended. I held my counsel on that point for I had seen enough of people to know that they can persuade themselves of anything at all regardless of the merits or justice of a thing. It was the predictability of the fall that saved people, not justice, and where there is no justice I do not find the hand or the presence of God.

I had never before seen a cathedral and this one appeared caught between two states of existence: construction and decay. All around it heaps of stone were piled up waiting to be restored to their proper place. People were accustomed to the sight, though Mrs Wickens said it had not always been so. 'It was like it had had its head cut off, Madam.' She put a hand to her stomach. 'If a cathedral can fall, anythin' might happen. And I saw it fall, mind, I felt it in my feet.'

I dreamt of the collapse once or twice: the air and ground thunderous and the cathedral spire subsiding as the mast of a sinking ship might be swallowed by heaving sea, and people swarming in and out of the black spaces of its blasted doorways, as frenzied as ants.

Some things collapse slow, and cannot always be rebuilt, and even if a thing can be remade it will never be as it was. I heard the rebuilding of the cathedral called an abomination, a view that was not generally held. People were glad of it; they loved it more tenderly, I think, seeing its fragility. They knew what might befall even something so vast and old.

Joss and I came to know those involved: the workers, the architect, the engineer and the benefactors, these last glossy with wealth and importance. The calculations, at least, I could discuss sensibly. I had not known that buildings were so mathematical. People are not, of course, which is a pity. The stress points are particular to an individual, and are not always visible to those around. A person might appear to be complete and be invisibly crumbling, or might appear to be falling apart and yet persist despite all expectation. Connections between people are not so different.

Observing the work on the cathedral was Joss's favourite entertainment. It put me in mind of the duck that Fred and Albert left to rot once as a scientific study after the visit from the troopers, the ants mining it for life, and of a story that Tull once told of ant people swarming across the land.

The Coorong, November 1855

Winter began in earnest, worse than the last. Thick rain and squall came from the ocean across the peninsula and the sand hills were no more than a ripple in their path. At first we were cosy within, the saturated sky and clouds and air and ground outside something to endure. Soon enough it began to find out the house's true deficiencies, the porosity that its roof of shabby thatch had developed since the spring, and we placed bowls about to catch the drips and squeezed into the dining room. It was as warm as it could be with its various draughts; better at any rate than the veranda which, deep as it was, was wet to the door. Drying clothes steamed on racks over the stove and over the backs of chairs, their vapours misting the windows and obscuring the view until someone went over and smeared the steam and water aside to peer out. But it was just water outside too, veils slipping in the air and flopping about in the lagoon. The peninsula was a smudge.

Once, maddened with confinement, I went walking in that weather and saw an old man throwing on his possum cloak, hands stretching it out to either side so it was a rich curtain he stood against and he swept his arms in, one and the other, the slow beats of huge wings. I tried it with my shawl but it was nothing that would hold me up and keep me warm. It was wet in an instant.

Fred and I took turns milking the house cows. They gave only a little milk at this time of year. The other cows were let loose. They became wary, staring at us with the eyes of scarce-remembered obedience if we chanced upon them, or sheering away into the bush on their way to becoming part of it. Sometimes they became stranded between soaks and the boys would splash towards them or circle from behind with windmill arms and the half-broke shouts of burgeoning manhood, and Skipper wild with the excitement of pursuit charged at them. Lacking any instinct for self-preservation, they enmired themselves at the edges of soaks and thrashed themselves deeper – rolling their eyes and bellowing until, exhausted, they slumped and settled and waited for death. Papa and the boys dug them loose and pulled them free by degrees and encouragement and they lumbered away in a state of bovine jubilance until hunger restored them to unthinking life. There were times when there was the sign of a great struggle: gouged and churned mud. We thought that they had broken free is all, that they had been fortunate or strong.

Papa was out each day, sometimes overnight with Hugh and Stanton. They found a gap burned in a fence, which they had to repair before travelling further afield to see if stock had strayed beyond our boundaries. After a night curled about a campfire they came across a native encampment that they hadn't seen before. They were quiet when they returned, even Stanton, and sat so close to the heat that the steam lifted from them.

Papa said: 'I have not seen them so ill this far south before. It was as if they had no fight in them. It wasn't only their bodies that had sickened, but their spirits also. Chills and fevers for the most part. And their stores run low. We gave them what we had.'

'All of it?' Mama said.

'All. We told him not to. They'll die anyway,' Stanton said.

'Yes, why slow what is inevitable?' Hugh said.

'They are people, Hugh. That is why,' Papa said.

Hugh would not meet his eyes. 'Where are those cattle, eh? They can't all be hiding in the scrub. The blacks will be stealing them. It's no wonder people take matters into their own hands, and I say it's time for us to be thinking of it.'

'If they are taking the cows, why would things be so bad that they needed provisions?' I said. The things Hugh said were like equations that could not balance.

'You could not possibly understand what it's like, Hester,' he said.

'Take me. I'd gladly come. I would like to understand.'

'Hugh, Hettie. Enough,' Papa said.

'Oh dear,' Mama said. 'Hettie, we must do more potatoes,' and she left the room pushing her sleeves up as she went. I believe she really thought they might be murdered each time they were gone from home, and their return was marked each time by her small surges of purpose.

'Papa,' I said, pausing at the door. 'Was it Tull's family there? Did you see him?'

'No, not his. I didn't know them. It was a long way from here, north of McGrath's. In spring he will be back I daresay and then we shall see.'

It seemed the cold would never end, but there came a day when the air turned soft and I took the dishes and the basin to the end of the veranda where the sun skimmed it in the morning, and filled it with hot water from the kettle and washed them. In the week that followed birds teemed in from the north and flung themselves at the lagoon and began a cacophonous calling. They were urgent in all that they did, action coming from impulse rather than consideration and duty. It would change when their eggs hatched.

Fred and Addie and Albert sat on the veranda to do their lessons, Albert kicking and fidgeting, their heads lifting to gaze at the lagoon. It was more molten metal than water. I could not help feeling my spirits rise and shut my eyes to feel the warmth on my face and when I opened them again Tull was there. He stood poised at the top of the steps waiting for a greeting, a welcome, whatever form that might take. I never met a more conscious person on the particulars of manners and customs.

'Tull. It's Tull,' Albert said. Everyone leapt up.

Tull was embarrassed at this effusion, and smiled in relief and came forward and was one of us again. His teeth, so white, startled me afresh. He had grown again and was pale, for him, after the short days. He wore a cloak and Stanton's old trousers. There was the stitching I had done at the thigh where they had caught, their worn knees, the frayed heels above Tull's ankles, which gave a curious sailor's look to his attire.

He began to stay with us more constantly, and after Papa found him asleep on the back step one morning wrapped in nothing but his sea-grass cloak for warmth he said he might stay with us if his family were agreeable, which they were. They knew we were no danger to him by then, I daresay. Papa built him a room of his own by closing off a narrow section of the veranda's return. Fred envied it. In it was a simple bed of wood that Papa had made, two hooks on the door to hang his clothes from at night, two carved clubs, a shield and several spears, which bristled in the corner behind the door.

The early morning was taken up with milking and lessons, and we took turns with the cheese in the afternoon, but there were occasions – Sunday afternoon, or before the evening milking – when Fred and Tull could slip away on explorations, either along the lagoon or across to the peninsula. Fred preferred Tull's company to Albert's, which I know Albert felt. His eyes followed them. Fred did not mean any harm or malice; he was oblivious. If Albert wished to go with them, Fred agreed – 'Only try to be quiet this time, or you'll scare everything off again' – but it is never pleasant to be merely tolerated and Albert began to go about with Papa and Stanton and Hugh even if his help were not needed.

If the weather was fine and Mama and Mary were napping and the chores were done I sometimes rowed to the peninsula with them. Papa and Mama saw no harm in it as a Sunday activity. We roamed the sand hills together, Fred with his note book and a satchel containing collection jars and the cloth bags that he used to keep his plant specimens safe and Tull with a spear and a net bag.

The ocean side of the peninsula must always be visited to experience the waves smashing the beach and the salt spray on our faces. The wind roared from the south, driving the fine white sand into clothes and hair and faces. Tull melted away high up between two sand hills. When I scrambled up to see where he had gone he was already at the far side of a sand-filled valley. Fred came up behind and we went into the deep hollow, and flopped in the lee of the hill. In an instant, the sounds of the sea beach became muffled.

All about us, erupting from the sand, were spiky single-stemmed plants about a foot tall: hundreds, thousands of them, irregularly spaced, neither sparse nor dense. I lay with my front against the warm sand, my chin separated from the sand only by my flattened hands.

'What are you doing?' Fred said.

'Everything is different from here. It's like being in a forest.' With my gaze at the height of some small creature I could imagine the plants about me to be strange trees towering around. 'They're like pine trees,' I said. 'Only miniature. Look, Freddie, how neat they are and all exactly the same.'

'They're not conifers,' Freddie said, shifting his gaze from his drawing to the plants.

'They might be.'

'They're not. They're euphorbias. At least I think they are.'

'Oh.' I thought of Papa's stories of visiting Japan during his voyaging days, how people there liked to transform tree seedlings into miniatures of their grown selves by pinching at their roots and leaves, and contorting their limbs into the shape that they saw fit, regardless of their natural inclination. I could not do such a thing to a living thing that had its own design and purpose, and so I said to Papa, who replied mildly enough that I saw nothing wrong with pruning a rose bush or a lilac, which was true, but the degree of interference made it different to me. It was more than enough, it was marvellous to see the ingenuity of pure nature on those windswept slopes, the plants responding to wind and moisture and light. Papa would say it was God's genius. Whether he was right or not I did not know.

'Do you remember those plants Papa told us of, when he was in Japan?' I said.

Fred gave one of his frowns of patience balanced with impatience. 'I suppose,' and was intent again on his work.

When he had finished his drawing and notes and there was still no sign of Tull, Fred arranged himself in imitation of my posture. 'I see what you mean. We are become Lilliputians, Hett. Imagine if a lizard came through: a monster, half the height of the trees, crashing them out of its path.'

It was an alarming thought, but I could see nothing when I raised my head. Instead, a millipede entered the canyon between us, its legs writhing and antennae feeling the air.

Fred scooped it up and observed the slow ribbon of it flowing across his skin. 'It doesn't know that I am dangerous, that on another day things might end differently.' He touched it and watched it coil, then uncoil, before releasing it.

'Is it a sort of diary that you're writing?' I asked when the millipede had gone. I had turned a few pages of Fred's book once. He drew the whole plant, and then details: the set of the leaves, the shape of the flowers, with notes to the side about the colours of both, the location where they grew, and the date. I thought his work showed some talent.

'No. A record of what's here, of life here. A book.' His voice was quiet. He put his hand to his satchel where the book lay. 'Biology, botany, geology. Not the natives. Mr Angas has already drawn them.' He seemed reluctant to speak of it.

Then Tull was next to us, when neither of us had seen or heard a thing. I wondered if there were a trick to his lightness that could be learned.

Another time on the peninsula we found charred sticks in the lee of a tall hill; evidently we were not the first to sit and watch the world from this lookout. A ship slid across the sea and we took turns with Fred's telescope to see tiny figures moving about the decks and the gossamer rigging. I vowed that one day I would be on a ship like that and sail the length of the world, and looking at Fred's face I did not think it was so different for him.

The stinging sand of the peninsula made our eyes sore and they crusted overnight so that in the morning we could barely open them. Tull showed us how the juice from the succulent plant that he called *ngunungies* rubbed gently across our shut eyelids would soothe them.

That is just one example of the useful knowledge that Tull possessed. He knew the correct reed to make string from and the sedges used for baskets or bags and the time of year when the mullet and the eels came into the lagoon, and many other things besides. He and Fred often sat in the kitchen while I cooked late in the afternoon, and I listened. It was quieter there than the dining room. I had made it as pleasant as I could: the jugs and pans and bowls were neat on the shelves, the table was scrubbed white and the small red flowers of Grandmama's geranium flowered in the window.

I had thought the blacks did as they pleased, roaming this country and never doing a day of school. But they had many rules: don't bathe until a particular flower has finished, pay attention to what birds tell you, leave the mullet for the men, don't walk about at night in case a bad spirit gets you, and many more besides. He saw things that we did not and told us which plants might be eaten and what other purposes they had. *Ngunungies* can also be eaten, for instance. I imagined the little fat leaves would have a slimy, snail-like texture (though I have never eaten a snail) but it was astringent and not unpleasant and could be eaten raw or cooked.

How To Catch A Duck

The natives were most ingenious and skilled. It was a delicate and patient task to catch a duck. I only saw it once when I was concealed within a stand of saltbush, from a distance. My dress would frighten anything wild away, Tull said.

You must first have string or twine to hand. Tull's was native-made (the women chew a particular reed and the men twist that into string) and was prized by all who use it. Attach a good length to a long stick and fashion a hangman's noose at its end. The hunter must be downwind of the prey and move with the utmost stealth, manoeuvring the noose slowly until it is close to the duck's head before dropping it about its neck and drawing it tight. The duck protests, as might be imagined, scaring every other bird about into flight. You must succeed at the first attempt, or else move to a place where the birds have not been disturbed. It is an easy matter then to dispatch the duck.

Tull spoke of another way of catching waterfowl with huge nets that the natives stretch above an expanse of water, which the birds fly into when frightened, but this is a job for many people when a large gathering is expected, such as for a *ringbalin*. Tull could catch a duck without a great deal of trouble and light a fire in a trice.

How To Cook A Duck

I only ate duck cooked in this way on a few occasions; Fred enjoyed it quite often. And now Joss wishes to try it.

Tull did not trouble to dress the bird but flung it into the flames until its feathers were burned away, then he dug a hole and heaped coals into it and lined it with grasses. The duck went in and was covered with more grass and coals and we waited. When he said it was ready we scraped the lid of coals back. It tasted a great deal better than stew. Sitting in the hollows of the sand hills while tending a fire was a delightful way to eat. There was no need to plan – in spring and summer at least – for food was at hand wherever we were. Besides the birds there were fish in the lagoon or crayfish in the reeds or cockles that we could dig from the sand, though Tull would only do that if all else had failed. There were plants, too, and small fruits we might eat if we were hungry.

When we had finished, Tull covered the fire with sand. The blacks were much given to setting fire to the land. Papa did not allow it on the run because of the danger to the stock. Fred once asked why they liked to do it and Tull looked at him in a pitying way.

'After the fire, it rains and the grass grows,' he said, as you might say two plus two.

'Yes?' Fred said, as uncomprehending as I.

'And the kangaroos come,' he said.

We waited.

He picked up a nearby stick and drew it back – 'and we kill them' – and it flew so straight and true that I could almost see the slain beast of his imagination.

'Like baiting a fish trap? You burn the land so the kangaroos will come?' Fred said.

'Yes.' Tull smiled then, as if he was pleased that we were not as stupid as he feared.

There were some things Tull would not eat, even if he were hungry.

Hugh and Stanton came home late one spring morning in great excitement over a duck that Skipper had flushed out of the reeds. The poor bedraggled thing, a female, was likely frightened from its nest, and now hung from Stanton's hand, its wide-billed head swinging and its eyes closed. The feathers on its tortoiseshell wings were broken.

'I had a devilish time getting it away from Skipper, I can tell you that,' Stanton said. 'Its wings flapping as if it were possessed, and the noise it made. I tell you I ran, and then Skipper dropped it and I managed to pounce. Look.' He thrust it towards me. 'A fine fat specimen.'

Tull was shocked. 'You can't eat it. You should have left it. You'll be sick. It will make your legs will grow weak.'

'Our legs go weak?' Stanton said. 'Why?'

And Hugh rounded on Tull. 'It will not. It's a duck, boy. It'll do you no harm. It's our land, and they are all our ducks and we may eat them as we please and when we please, but you needn't if you are frightened to, if you are frightened of a little bird.'

'Some people may eat them, but not you, or me. Not this one, a *Kalperi*.' Tull was very shocked, his eyes round and black, and he drew back from the duck and from Hugh and Stanton.

'Pluck it for us, will you, Hester?'

'Pluck it yourself,' I returned. 'I have other things to do and if you wish for a meal at this time of day *you* may get it.' I glared at him and he turned away, looking at Addie. She shook her head and he stormed outside, with Hugh following after. Presently, we saw downy feathers wafting past the window and Skipper came inside with a large wing feather drooping from her mouth. We attended to our lessons as best we could, or pretended to at any rate. It was a poor-looking specimen that Stanton brought back a little later. He had given up on the pin feathers and some of the down. Hugh got the big knife and hacked the bird into rough pieces.

With a clatter, Stanton pulled the black pan from the rack over the stove and drew back the stove lid and slammed it down on the hot plate and gathered the bowl of lard from the winter pantry and the flipper and when the pan was hot scooped out a hunk of lard with the corner of the flipper and set it in the pan. It ran about sizzling and hissing, releasing its meaty smell. Hugh, somewhat hesitant, carried a bowl with the pieces of duck to the stove and Stanton threw them in the pan and it hissed and smoked. Stanton snatched his hand away and sucked the back of his hand. The smell of feathers frying was sharp and hot. Stanton did not look about at any of us, but said, 'Anyone else want a piece? Fred? Addie?'

'I'm not hungry,' Fred said, which I doubted was true. He pretended to ignore what was happening, instead working in his sketch book and pulling a flowering branch in a jar of water before him a little closer. He resumed drawing, and from the way he did not so much as glance at Tull I knew that he was aware of him and was ashamed in some way. Stanton and Hugh were only acting in defiance of his words, and though I could not see what could be wrong with eating a duck when there were so many of them nesting all about, I had seen how certain Tull was about food, and what could be eaten safely and what should be avoided. I did not like to go against his words. From Fred's darting glances I thought it was the same for him. Also, I would not add to Tull's distress.

Stanton made a snorting sound of disbelief. He hunkered down over the stove, pulling against the resistance there was in the kitchen to cooking the duck, as a bullock will pull against a heavy load. But he was determined on this course of action.

'Get some bread,' he shot over his shoulder, and Hugh obediently found the bread and cut two rough slices of it, which he placed, one each, on Mama's small dark Staffordshire plates. Their dainty flowers presented a strange appearance with the sawn bread, but soon enough they were hidden by the pieces of duck with their blackened skin and frizzled down, which Stanton forked onto them. As the plates were too small, they overhung the rims. He poured the remaining lard over the meat and it began to slide from its dark surfaces and down its edges, finally falling to the floor, setting there in waxy drops. Stanton slammed the plates onto the table.

'Do you mind?' Fred said and drew his books further down the table.

Hugh got a knife and fork for each of them and they pulled chairs back from the table so their feet squealed against the floor, and sat and began to eat in great mouthfuls, sawing the duck to reveal the thick seam of fat and mopping the bread in the bloody juices and shovelling the food into their mouths, glaring about from time to time. Addie stared, aghast, as if she were waiting for them to die, or at least to sicken, and Tull as if he were watching drowning men but had no means to save them. I scraped the fat off the floor with a knife before anyone could slip on it.

Once, Hugh looked up and said to Tull, 'You. You can stop staring and get out. We don't want you in here. You should not be in here, and while my father is not you can stay outside where you belong. We've no need for your superstitions.'

Fred got to his feet, but seemed uncertain what to do next. Tull looked at him.

'You can't order Tull,' I said.

'And *you* will stop me?' Hugh said.

He was much taller and broader than I and I thought it wise to be quiet, even though I hated to hear him speak so and I did not think he would hit his sister. Tull moved to the door and put his hand to the doorjamb. Some compulsion held him there, mesmerized by the sight of their daring. Stanton picked up his remaining crust in his hand and wiped it all around the rim of the plate and circled the middle, gathering up all the last drops of the fat and blood, and stuffed that in his mouth, which was overfull, so the hunks of brown bread and the red meat could be seen as he chewed, and then he picked up the plate and threw it at Tull. It was a low, fast throw and if Tull had not jumped straight up in the air with utmost nimbleness and strength and celerity the plate would have struck its target in the moment before he fled. But it merely hit the door and shattered and fell to the ground in pieces, so that all Mama's china flowers were as scattered as a posy in the wind on the floor.

'Stanton! One of Mama's plates. Look at it. For shame,' I said. 'Have you gone mad? What will she say?'

'I am sure you will tell her when you see her so we can all find out,' Stanton said and leapt to his feet and stepped across the shards of china, shoving past me and flinging out of the door. Hugh finished his meat but with no pleasure or speed, only determination. He put his plate in the washbasin and with the broom swept the broken china into a heap, and scraped it into the dustpan.

'Here,' I said, taking it from him. 'I won't give Mama any more reason to be sad.'

Hugh stood dumb as an ox, while I swept and scolded. Then his throat began to work and he rushed past me through the door onto the veranda where he hung over its edge and was very ill. His shoulders heaved and his head sawed up and down. When he had finished he remained bowed, resting his forehead on his forearms as they lay upon the railing.

I went onto the veranda to see if there was anything I could do. Fred came out too. Tull was by the stable and a moment later Fred was climbing the short rise to see him.

Stanton stared at Hugh from the stairs. 'Too rich,' he said. 'That's all it is, Hugh. Don't go thinking there is any truth in those superstitions.'

'Hugh?' I said.

Hugh rolled his head to one side and his face was grey and sweating so it did appear as if he might have been poisoned. He staggered to the settee and lay down with his arm across his eyes and there he stayed. Stanton came and stood over him. 'You are all right, Hugh. As well as I be.'

I thought he did not look very well. Stanton then made a great show of his good health, drinking a cup of tea and playing a game of chess with Albert, which he did poorly. He lacked imagination and did not see the consequences of his actions, qualities that I suppose must be as advantageous in some situations as they are disadvantageous in others. I took Hugh a cup of tea and he sipped it tentatively and by lunch had recovered to the extent that he could contemplate some toast.

From having been so ill from the duck Hugh could not tolerate this particular duck or any duck at all again, but seeing that Stanton was unaffected, Albert and Papa and Stanton ate them, indeed Papa set about the task as his Christian duty, to prove that superstition held no sway with him. No harm came to any of them. But Tull told me later that it didn't matter if Papa ate them, so Papa hadn't proved anything except in his own mind. I do not care for ducks since they are so fatty and Addie refused to eat any thereafter, which I did not understand, and Fred would not out of a desire not to hurt Tull's feelings. I wondered how Tull explained this to himself but did not ask, merely observing that I never saw him eating one.

8

THE COORONG
JANUARY 1857

One day in the kitchen at the beginning of that year Tull told Fred a long story of an ancestor, Ngurunderi.

'He's like God,' Fred said to Tully when he had finished.

'Mr Finch says God is good,' Tull said.

'So people say.'

'Then Ngurunderi is not like God. He was a man. He made things, but because of what he *did*, not to *make* them, not like God. In what he did he created, but this was not what he meant to do, only what happened while he was chasing his wives. There are many other ancestors, Wyunggaree – another hunter. He made the lagoons with the skins of big kangaroos. He stretched them out. I don't know all the stories. There are many more, but you have only one?' He looked so pitying.

Tull grew fast through that summer and by autumn was taller than Hugh or Stanton or Fred and his wrists and ankles appeared from the shirt sleeves and breeches that had once been theirs. It gave him a gangling effect. Occasionally he was gone, for days or even weeks. We had grown used to his absences. I did not stop to wonder what might be happening in his life when he was not with us, or understand that he existed in two worlds.

Once we caught sight of him with some other natives when he was dressed as they were and we all paused to watch. He moved so easy along the track above the house but made no sign of recognition to us when they passed, and didn't look back as they walked away. In that moment he was something to us even if we were nothing to him. It made me feel small and temporary in that place and I saw on Papa's face how discomfited he was too.

'Girls, inside now,' he said, rather harsh.

'Why?' Addie said.

Papa looked about as if someone else might appear to explain the matter to her, but no one did and in the end he said, 'It's Tull.'

'We know that.'

Hugh slipped one hand inside his coat front as if he were Admiral Lord Nelson and pronouncing on matters of state. 'We should tell them to stay away from the house. The girls shouldn't see.'

'Yes, yes,' Papa said, a trifle impatient. 'As I said already.'

'I don't mind,' Addie said. 'I'm sure nothing could surprise me these days.'

'You should not see him so, Adelaide,' Papa said.

'Why not? He is black, isn't he? Well, blackish, and they hardly wear a stitch,' Addie said. 'We knew that before.'

Fred gave her a look to wither, and said, 'You know the difference. He's one of us too.'

From long practice this glanced off her. She raised an insolent shoulder and said, 'He's not one of me, Fred.'

'Addie, stop it. He is almost a brother to you,' I said.

She became serious. 'He's no brother of mine,' and although she came inside with me nothing I could say would induce her to leave the window until he had gone. It was as if she'd never seen him before.

Fred spent the most time with Tull, though I did see him for lessons and meals and around the run if they were not working at too great a distance. We conversed mainly about books and chess: more than I did to Stanton and Hugh, less than I did with Fred.

Tull liked to listen to Fred reading, though how it came about – Fred reading a passage before explaining it, Tull asking him to continue – I do not know. At such times I had a sense of Tull needing respite from the effort of learning so much and so fast. Of course, it might be that it was simpler to ask questions of Fred or anyone else around when words were spoken aloud.

That winter I began to notice how differently he saw almost everything compared to us. Mama might say that the colours of winter reminded her of the highlands of Scotland, and I might say that the sky was sapphire or that the washing lines were like cobwebs on a cold morning. Hearing these things perplexed him, as did so much else – the encumbrances of our clothing, our impractical hair, our heavy boots, the fences that we built – which he made apparent by his stillness or his incredulity and in other ways that I do not recall.

One day he asked why we had so few stories to tell and so few songs.

'We have bible stories,' I said. 'And novels. Of course we have stories and songs.'

'Books. You don't speak them. Or sing them. Our stories are different.'

'Tell me some of your stories then,' I said, but he would not. It was by chance that I heard him sing once or twice when he was about his work and I was tending the vegetable garden. It was not like our music and the words were not in English, yet he took pleasure in it I think.

He liked the Old Testament. I would have said it was his favourite part of the bible from the frequency with which he looked at it. I was not sure, though, whether pleasure and displeasure meant anything when words were before him. It was more as if there were a play on a chessboard that he could not read clearly. Fred's expression when drawing or thinking was something like it.

'You like this story, don't you?' I said. He was reading Genesis again, on the veranda. We had grown so used to him that it no longer seemed strange for him to sit on our chairs and to eat from our plates.

Seeing that I had some time he asked me again about heaven and hell, sin, the Fall, the vastness of the world and its shape. 'Is it about the white people?'

94

'All people – about the beginning of everything.'

'We have stories too, about the beginning of this land.'

'Like the one you told Fred? The man chasing his wives?' I asked. Tull nodded. 'Is your story true?'

'Most people think it is, that it happened this way,' I said. 'But Papa believes it is a story that shows us how we all, people, became what we are, sinners who do wrong, that is, that they were tempted and chose their fate.' Tull still appeared confused and I did not know how to make temptation and the Fall clearer to one who had never even heard of God. 'Is your story true?' I asked.

'What is true?' Tull gave me one of his steady looks and moved his face by infinitesimal degrees, and how could I know what that meant?

Towards morning's end Mary often became fretful and Mama took her for a walk, leaving us to finish our work. With no one there to focus our attentions we fell to talking. Later I wondered whether we should not have encouraged familiarity, that it would have been better to keep some distance between Tull and us. But we were young and curious about him, as he was about us.

'Tell us, what did you think of us when we first arrived?' Addie asked, leaning on the table towards Tull who sat opposite.

'We saw people like you before, a long time ago.'

'*You* did?'

'I am not old enough to see the first people. We stayed away from them.' He gestured towards the track. 'When my family saw white fellas the first time, the cattle frightened them. The sound was like thunder. Everyone screamed and ran away across the water.' He pointed towards the peninsula. 'They hid there and waited. They thought the horses were their women.' He laughed at the thought and at Addie's expression.

'Horses? That is ridiculous.' Her face flamed. 'Why would they think that?'

'They carried everything, like women.'

'But if they knew white men were men … We know your men are men – why would they think that?'

'They knew the men were men. They stole our women.'

'Kidnapped,' I said, remembering that overheard conver-sation between Mama and Papa. 'What did you think when you saw real women then?'

'We thought you had no legs,' he said.

'Legs? Of course we have legs.' And Addie leapt up, pulling her skirts to her knees.

'Addie, for shame,' I said. 'Have you lost your senses?'

'Tull doesn't mind, do you?'

He tore his eyes from Addie's legs and their fallen stockings.

'Tull, if you would go and see where Mama is – Mrs Finch, I mean – I should be grateful. Mr Finch too. Thank you.'

Tull didn't move. 'When we saw you we were afraid,' he said.

'Of us? We were children.'

'Of Mr Finch.'

'I tell you it was not Papa,' I said.

I daresay some would opine that Adelaide was not London, but the most provincial of outposts, and so I learned to see it years later. I had known nothing other than Adelaide and the Coorong and the road in between so that was no odds to me. When we were in Adelaide, ships had come through with news from home, and we might order any book or journal we cared for and after that it was a matter of waiting for the riches to arrive. And if the waiting took a very long time it whetted our anticipation and increased our enjoyment upon arrival. You might imagine the excitement that stirred, and for the next while all materials might be exchanged, since so many of us were known to each other. Naturalists' books might be had, or fashion almanacs, or novels or scientific journals or records of the voyages of discovery that were then circumnavigating the globe. It is a time without shape to me: a continuum of pleasurable incidents, at the end of which were the deaths of Louisa and Georgie and our departure.

In the Coorong we lost society, its benefits as well as its strictures, those things that we had not so much as thought of. They were the air we breathed. Even so, two great excitements broke the monotony of that winter. The telegraph line went through along the stock route. We rode up to watch the making of it and after the rough men had gone on their way all that was left were the poles, which were like so many stilts with their walkers departed, and their shadows, which lengthened and shortened as the earth turned, making patterns of shade and substance.

And in the winter Hugh and Stanton happened upon a group of travelling musicians on the road and invited them to stay for the night. We killed a calf and roasted it outside on a contraption the boys rigged up, and the sparks flew and the fat hissed beneath. They played their music on the veranda and we forgot ourselves in the shabby wonderment of their dandy striped waistcoats and bright trousers and the twang and thump of their instruments. Addie sang. ('Ye should come along with us, little lady,' one of the men said.) We whirled around, and Tull did a dance, stamping his heels, which he taught us as best he could. He laughed at us.

It was hard to settle after they went on their way. If there were time I went for a ride or a walk on my own or with Addie, which Mama did not like.

'Oh, Mama,' Addie said. 'The lagoon path is not King William Street.'

'Addie,' Mama said.

'Sorry, Mama.'

'Truly, Mama, there's no one about to think us fast,' I said. What point could there be to demureness and decorum and restraint when there was no one to witness them? She could not compel us, as she knew too. Still, we waited.

'What of the blacks?'

'They're not back from their winter camp that I've seen. In any case, if they've done nothing yet I think we're safe enough. Tull would tell us if not.'

'Well, I suppose.'

'Thank you, Mama,' we said. When she had gone, Addie rolled her eyes. 'Next thing she'll be telling us to put our gloves on before we go out.'

After that we took more care, slipping away without her noticing so we did not cause worry.

It was the talk of King William Street that gave me the idea of taking Mama on a day visit to see Mrs Robinson at the Travellers Rest. She was the only female settler within two days' ride, perhaps more, and I thought the company of another woman might be welcome, and that it might also be a kindness to Mrs Robinson in her widowed state. Papa saw no fault in the plan. He had always spoken well of her. 'She misses her husband,' he said. He fell to rumination before rousing himself again. 'I have never seen her anything but uncomplaining and industrious.' He sent Hugh to arrange a time for a visit – the second week in September – and Addie and Mama washed and ironed our clothes, and starched the ribbons on our bonnets smooth.

'There,' Mama said when she saw us, 'if we are not fashionable, we are at least respectable.' Addie had to be contented with that.

All the way up the path from the house I twisted in the saddle to see Mary, and behind her Tull and Fred holding her steady on the fence rail. She was kicking her heels and, I was sure, reminding them both what a big girl she was now. Well, and she was; she would be three by Christmas. Mama looked back too and Mary waved each time. She would be like Mama one day; their hair was similar: waved and brown, Mary's still wispy. I turned one last time before we rounded a curve to see her reaching for Tull and him taking her and swinging her in a circle. There was her distant shriek of delight and they were gone.

Poor Mama was not easy leaving her behind. Once she seemed on the point of turning back, then Addie drew her attention and she set herself again. Mary was too small for such a long ride, and so Mama knew, and the dray was out of the question despite the dry winter; we might spend the better part of the day getting there. When we had travelled a little further, Mama became talkative, riding ahead with Addie and Stanton, who had come as our escort. But I would not let the pleasure of riding away from the run, to keep on riding, be spoilt by him.

The path – wide in places, and narrow where it squeezed between rock formations and water – wound along the shore's edges, sometimes cutting past small headlands that jutted into the lagoon. The islands that I had only seen from the distance came closer. They were thick with pelicans. The sun, which had early shone into our eyes, drifted higher, as bright as a new penny. Later in the morning we rode over some shallow hills and when they began to fall away, the inn – a low wooden building crouching on a rise – came into view. The creek at its feet was thick with bulrushes moving in the slow breeze, and further down where it met the lagoon there was a short jetty and a tethered boat bobbing in the water. We rode down.

The inn yard was neat: within, Lady Banks' roses speckled in bud climbed the veranda posts and pots of lavender framed a doorway, and on the slope behind the stable was a well-tended vegetable garden. From the back of the building, the kitchen I supposed, came a dab of a woman. 'Mrs Robinson', Stanton called out. She was no more than thirty I would say, with fair hair drawn back in a bun and grey eyes and a cross-stitched apron atop her sprigged dress. She came forward in quick, light steps. Mama smiled at the sight of her, and she was so pretty and neat that I did the same.

Then, 'Hello there, Mrs Finch,' she said, and Mama's face fell. She, Mrs Robinson, was Irish, and quite confident for a small person; 'Come along now, leave your horses there, that's right. They'll be quite safe, I do assure you,' all the time drawing closer.

Mama turned and passed the reins to Stanton, who tied them to the railing at a water trough. I thought from her expression, which was trapped, that she wanted to leave already. There was nothing to be done. It was not that Mama disapproved of the Irish exactly – I had seen her speak to several people from that country very civilly in Adelaide – but she thought them feckless and could not think of them as our equals, so few of them being well born in Australia. I am afraid her manner, though polite, became stiff, and she spoke in her crispest voice. 'How do you do, Mrs Robinson,' and handed her the tin of biscuits she had brought.

Immediately, Mrs Robinson lifted the lid. 'Oh, shortbreads. They'll be grand. And I've made a cake too. We can have a nice cosy conversation.'

We followed her through the stout door into a vestibule with an entrance onto the public dining room – poorly lit and the walls above the fireplace blackened with smoke – and in the other direction a dark hallway. This took us to a good-sized room, with whitewashed walls and two big windows looking onto the veranda. A plain Welsh dresser filled with Delft stood against one wall, and at the centre was a flowered carpet around which were a settee and several chintz-covered arm chairs with small tables between.

'What a lovely room,' I said.

'Yes, indeed,' Mama said. 'Very pleasant.'

Mrs Robinson bade her sit. She flicked a handkerchief at the chair as Mama crossed the room towards it. Addie looked at me as if she might burst with laughing. I shook my head, but Addie looked so merry that it was all I could do not to. Mama sat on the chair's edge, her back extremely straight. 'Girls,' she said, and we sat too. Stanton's gaze moved between us. He began to talk, and for once I could see how he might appear to others: pleasant, even charming. But of course he and Mrs Robinson had met before, when he and Papa and Hugh were riding this way.

'Any travellers this week?' he asked, and Mrs Robinson was able to talk.

'Not a one, not for a while. It's very quiet. We were run off our feet a few years ago. Travellers, people off to the goldfields. Then the Chinamen. The inland route's killin' us, so it is. And Robe. The Chinamen are landing there now. Closer to the goldfields, see. I daresay you'll have noticed.'

'We're a half-mile from the track,' I said. 'We see no one but natives; we never have.'

'Natives – willin' workers, I'll say that.' She bustled out to arrange tea, and presently a gawky young maid with a number of teeth missing carried in a tray with a steaming teapot and cups – also Mama's biscuits, which had become crumbly at their edges, and a tall layer cake filled with jam and cream. 'Thank you, Jane,' Mrs Robinson said. 'A nice piece of cake for you, Mrs Finch?' She cut into it revealing its buttery yellow inside, and passed her some. Mama was mortified. She could not take her eyes from her shortbreads. She gathered herself and was gracious about the cake, pronouncing it delicious. Presently we were all eating it – and I must say that Mama never spoke more truly – and drinking tea, and in this way we were able to pass some of the time.

Mrs Robinson began to ask Mama questions, about how many children she had, and not to worry if she felt lonely from time to time – it would pass, she said – and where she had grown up. It could not have been worse. Mama took her friendliness as an impertinence. 'On our estate in West Sussex,' she said, very cool. 'And you, Mrs Robinson?'

She became flustered. 'Ireland. I suppose you can tell that from me accent.' She laughed nervously and her hands twisted in her apron. All but Mama smiled, which I know Mrs Robinson noticed from the way her gaze rested on Mama's face. 'In fact I came from a poorhouse, Ma'am. We would have starved if our parents had not left us there. I was lucky to leave, lucky to be here.' Her voice was steady enough, but had become respectful rather than friendly.

Mama said nothing in reply and dropped her gaze to her plate as if the cake had become very fascinating. I saw her face from the side. She appeared almost stricken, and if I did not perfectly understand it then, I think I did later. Mrs Robinson was no comfort to her and never would be; she was the measure for Mama of how far she had fallen.

Addie said, 'This is the loveliest cake I have ever had.'

Mrs Robinson came to life, and said confidingly, '"T"is, en't it? A nice lady I was maid for in Mount Barker taught it me, gave me the recipe when I married my poor Willie. Knack and practice is all it is. I'll show you one day, if you like.'

'I would like that,' Addie said. 'May we come again, Mama?'

'We will see what might be arranged, shall we girls?' Mama said, and then to Mrs Robinson, 'Mr Finch can't always spare the horses. It's a busy time of year at present and I'm afraid we must take our leave.'

'Oh, so soon?' Addie said.

Mama ran on. 'It was so kind of you to have us to tea.'

Poor Mrs Robinson. Her face fell so. It was as if Mama had struck her.

Within a very short space of time we were riding home, Mama very quiet and Addie chattering. 'I still don't see why we had to go in such a rush.'

Finally, in a small strained voice, Mama said, 'She is just not the sort of person I would wish you to be around, Adelaide.' And then began to sob.

I drew alongside and was able to lean from my saddle and pat her shoulder. 'Don't, Mama. Please don't,' I said.

She drew a handkerchief from her sleeve and wiped her nose. 'What have I become? I'll send her a note. Will you take a note to thank her, Stanton?'

'Of course,' Stanton said, rather short.

'I'll write it just as soon as we're back. But what was your father thinking?'

'That you were in need of company,' Stanton said.

'He should have told me.'

Mama and Papa were cool with each other for several days after that, and Mama became fussy about our manners. Addie would not stop talking of Mrs Robinson and her pretty dress and pleasant furnishings. When we lamented the things we had lost, company among them, Papa said that we had been spoiled and should take advantage of this opportunity.

'What opportunity?' Addie said cheekily.

I was glad I had not said it.

'To think of others and not yourself, to improve yourselves,' Papa said.

My efforts to improve things for Mama had come to nought, but I did not like to remind him of that.

'See how Fred takes Tull with him?' Papa said.

'Actually, I think Tull takes him,' Addie said.

Papa ignored that. 'You might undertake something of your own when you've finished your work.'

The advice gave me no hint about details and specifics. I thought I would try to befriend a native of my own since it pleased Papa.

In the morning after all the breakfast tasks were done there was some time before our lessons started. The next day I walked up the lagoon path, as I often did for the quiet of it, to the place where native women sometimes worked. They had returned to the lagoon's shores from their winter camp now the weather was warming a little. They caught things at the water's edge or pulled reeds or collected small crayfish or dug for things along the slope. I never went close to them, but sat on a rock a little way off and they glanced in my direction, wondering about me, perhaps, as I wondered about them. Sometimes they laughed. The little ones, fingers in their mouths and eyes huge and round, didn't trouble to conceal their curiosity and would creep closer and scream in delighted terror and run back to their mothers if I smiled at them. Their talk and laughter made me lonely.

I took a little packet of sugar; Tull had a sweet tooth and I thought that they might too.

No one was there, but since there was nothing to go back for save more work and lessons, I set the sugar down on a dry rock and stood at the water's edge trying to see what they saw there to collect. It was just reeds and grasses and a few bubbles rising from the lagoon bed. Thinking they might be from crayfish I found a stout stick and twisted my skirts up out of the way onto my lap and began to dig, pulling and twisting at the reeds and their roots. Determination set in and I tugged and dug, scooping the silty sand to shore. A clump gave way with unexpected ease and I fell back and there was a shout of laughter from behind: natives – women, girls and small children, seven or eight of them. I recognized one of them as the one with the scarred face we'd seen on arrival. She was tall, about my height I would say, and wore a fringe at her waist and a grassy looking cloak and at her side had a bag that carried her tools: sticks of different sizes, some with pointed ends, and other things that made the bag bulge. Like all the women she had one long fingernail that had been sharpened to a wicked point, the purpose of which I could not imagine.

She gave me a steady look – not amused or annoyed or disturbed – resigned, rather, to something unpleasant. I scrambled to my feet and brushed the gritty mud from my hands onto my apron. The laughter stopped. The children slid behind the women.

'Hello,' I said.

And then, 'Whatever are you doing?' the woman said, the words running along in the way that Tully's had when I first spoke with him.

'You speak English?'

She didn't reply and her eyes moved across the mess I had made, the scattered reeds all different lengths and the roots mixed with the grassy tops and the muck I had splattered on the shore.

'I thought there was something there I could catch,' I said. 'You can have them if you like. The reeds, I mean.'

She regarded them and then me. 'Good for nothing now.' She looked away. I would sooner endure the worst of Papa's lectures than that disdain.

'I'm sorry,' I said, which was true, but I did not know what for, just that my being there was a sorrow.

She made a contemptuous noise and if anyone thinks natives dull witted one look into this woman's face would teach them otherwise. The other women hung back still, but the tall woman took my hand in both of hers and thrust it at the other natives and rubbed her fingers and thumbs across it, hard, lifting the skin on its back and releasing it, showing the other natives as she did it and she said something too, and they edged in until they were all around, and there were the faint nibbling touches and tweaks of their hands at my skirts and sleeves. I couldn't understand what they were saying, of course, but one word or phrase was repeated enough that I remembered it. One girl, bolder than the rest, lifted the bottom of my dress and looked at my stockinged leg and the cracked boots on my feet. It gave the others courage and soon both my hands were being held and squeezed and pinched and inspected – a strange feeling, as if my body were no longer my own.

'Your hair,' the tall woman said. 'Blood hair.'

'Red.'

She shook her head. 'Blood.'

I touched it. 'They think it has blood in it?'

'Yes.'

'Oh.' I wanted to sit then or hold something to steady myself, remembering Tull when we first spoke. It was not a pleasant feeling to be thought a horror. I reached up and untwisted my hair and it fell in dark red coils. They were aghast. I stroked my head and held my hand out palm upwards to show them how white it still was and lifted a curl in the air and teased it apart and bent over that they might touch it. One of the children caught the end of a curl and the children shrieked at her daring. I could have cried but I shut my eyes tight and the moment passed. I put my hair back in a plait as best I could without a mirror and seeing it some of the girls wanted plaits too so I showed them how, using a few of the torn reeds to bind their ends so they were not all wasted.

The women began digging some daisies growing above the shoreline and put their roots in the baskets they had brought. Having lost their fear of me they talked again, a sound that was as incomprehensible as birdsong or waves hitting a shore. I thought it the foreignest thing I ever heard, which much later made me blush to recall, and fascinating. I wondered what English might sound like to them, its words being so distinct. The tall woman paid me no more attention until I had to go, when I took her the packet of sugar, opening it to show her what lay inside. She took it from me with reverence almost and reached into the packet and drew out a pinch and tipping her head back released the sugar. She shut her eyes and her face was suffused with pleasure. Seeing her, seeing this, everyone gathered around and she showed them how sugar might be enjoyed, licking her finger and plunging it into the sugar and into her mouth, and each in turn copied her and was delighted.

Lessons would be starting and I wasn't there, but I wanted to take a proper leave, and for something to have changed. I approached the tall woman and the others made space for me. I said, 'I am Hester.'

She looked at me in a different way – not with warmth or as a friend. As if I were there and the fact of me could not be ignored.

'I am Rimmilli,' she said.

I went back home and wrote down a word, as best as I could remember the sound, which the women had said more than once, separate enough from the other sounds I had heard. I would ask Tull when he came back with Papa and the boys. They were clearing some land to let more sun in and improve the pasture, and that was after milking at first light. They were exhausted when they rode in and I waited until after dinner before I spoke to Tull about meeting the native women. 'What does "grinkry" mean?' I asked.

'Grinkry?'

'They looked at me and they used this word. Something like that. I wrote it down.'

There was a flash of comprehension. 'I see.' His eyes moved across my face, and then, reluctantly, he said, '*Grinkari.*'

'That's it. What does it mean?'

'It's just a name they call white people. Not only you.' But he did not meet my eyes.

'But what does it mean exactly?'

'It is a word for dead people. They are pink after their skin comes off.'

I made a face. 'We look like dead people?'

'It is just a name,' he said.

9

THE COORONG
OCTOBER 1857

It was morning and the sky was gathered up like smocking when I followed Mama to the shore of the lagoon. I took it as a good sign. At least she had left the parlour, which, so dark and shrouded and closed to air, put me in mind of the kennel of an old dog waiting out its time. Her spirits had fallen again in the month since the visit to the Travellers Rest and nothing we could do would lift them. The running of lessons and the household had fallen to me, which was not as bad as when we first arrived. I was older and had grown stronger from doing chores and hard riding and from walking so far, much farther than in Adelaide where we would go visiting in the buggy and need do no work in the garden save picking flowers for the house if we were of a mind to, and never mind if we were not because Violet would do it otherwise.

The sandy soil spilled from the path's edges over my boots and insects rushed away into the scrubby bushes that edged it. I lifted my skirts; I was not frightened of them precisely, but I preferred not to touch them or for them to touch me. The wind had shifted to the north, from inland, and now everywhere was the smell of warmth and grass and things that I could not see instead of the salt sea blowing over the sand hills and the lagoon from the south that I was used to, and my spirits could not help lifting despite Mama. I was thinking to speak to her, to see if I could divert her mind to our clothes, with all of us growing. We might talk about which clothes were ready for alteration or could be reworked into something respectable. The warm weather was coming; every day the sun was stronger and higher and the grasses and reeds sprang green and tall and we were not so different.

I reached Mama's side on the shallow slope, my skirts brushed against hers, and I put an arm about her thin shoulders and pulled her close and we watched the birds teeming in from their long winter flights. They were thick as storm clouds and plummeted to water where they made a living carpet and began to call, cacophonous as a group of musicians tuning their instruments, but conversational, social.

She was like another bird, fine boned against me. She gave me a faint smile and looked back again at the birds: gulls and gannets, terns, ducks and I knew not what else.

'Look,' she said.

'Aren't they funny?'

'They have so much company they can scarcely move,' she said. 'And I have none and can scarcely move.' And she shrugged and drew her shawl close about her shoulders though it was a balmy morning and not likely to get cooler until evening. I had already pushed back my sleeves.

My hair blew across my face and I brushed it away and tucked my arm through hers and stroked the back of her limp hand.

'They do not even see us.' Her voice became querulous and she pulled free of me, moving towards them, but they did not alter their behaviour in any way that I could see. She was nothing to them, not even something to be cautious of. She hardly existed.

'Come, Mama.'

And then from around the headland further up the lagoon came a small boat with a brown sail, the like of which I had never before seen on the lagoon. From the peninsula we saw ships passing far out to sea and would track their progress across the pale horizon, thinking of what they carried – sheep or passengers or other goods – and wondered whether they would arrive safely at their destination, wherever that might be, because sometimes they would not. Nothing was more certain than that. Once, while watching a ship with Papa while he was checking the cows, he had removed his hat and held it tight by the brim with both hands and bowed his head and murmured a prayer. 'The Lord bless them and keep them safe. Let the waves and the deep not claim them.' I do not remember the rest. He had a horror of shipwrecks and what might befall their survivors. It was a dangerous coast. 'There is help at hand now,' Papa said once. 'No need for the blacks. All will be well.'

The boat came closer – there were two men aboard moving about and adjusting sails, coiling ropes, their arms brown against their white sleeves – and we walked down to the landing place below the bluff, where our own boat was moored. Mama's hands fluttered about her hair, tucking in the wisps and looking at me as if I were a mirror that might reassure. She had not troubled to fix it yet. Later I might persuade her to sit out in the sun, her eyes shut, and I would brush it smooth and neat and coil it into a bun. We all felt better when Mama resembled her old self.

Then they were there, the sails were furled and they laid anchor a little way off shore and the men lowered a small boat and jumped into it – the younger steadying the older – and rowed to our beach in thick even strokes, heaving it clear of the water. They were father and son to look at them – lean and brown, the father with large side whiskers, the younger one a scarce-bearded youth, as Mama would say – but not workers though they worked well together, understanding the movements they made separately and together. They had done this often. They had put jackets on, which had the cut of gentlemen, being longer than practicality demanded and cut away at the front. Their trousers were town clothes too, but the boots – stout, dusty, thick soled – were country. They removed their hats and bowed so gentleman-like it made me smile and the younger one gave a grin, and they introduced themselves. Bagshott was their name.

For a wonder Mama became cheerful, smiling at things that were not the slightest bit amusing – the noise the birds were making out on the water, the difficulty of sailing on a flat day. 'We would be pleased if you would stay for a meal, if you have the time,' she said. 'If you have any news – any at all, from anywhere—'

My mind began to fly about, wondering how a meal fit for guests could be contrived. Some carrots and a few elderly turnips remained from winter. But they and a few sprigs of spring parsley would not conceal the fact that it was last night's stew warmed again.

'We'll tell you what we know, which is not a great deal,' Mr Bagshott said.

'Mr Finch will have returned by then – my husband, that is,' Mama said. And she forged the way up the path, chattering about the weather and what the men were doing here. I could not have found a space in the conversation even if I had thought of something to say. It was strange to hear so many words spilling from her. Could I create an equation to calculate Mama's words? How then to factor in a variable such as a visitor when no one knew when another might arrive? The younger man did not trouble to talk to me so I was able to pay attention to the conversation in front of us and to ponder my conundrum.

'I'm on a commission from the province.' Mr Bagshott's voice boomed out as if he were addressing a considerable crowd. Even viewed from behind, his gait was that of a person who had a station in life that had never diminished. His clothes might be as dusty as Papa's, but that was because he had been parted from civilization. 'Yes, we are undertaking a survey, principally of properties along the coast and rivers and so forth, and Charles, my son, is making a pictorial record of them and of other places of interest,' Mr Bagshott told Mama.

It seemed a peculiar profession, if it was such a thing, but people must use the skills they have here, or so Papa says. I could do nothing but mathematics, play the pianoforte, and read. My cooking was atrocious; I could make butter these days, a description of which I did not think would interest our visitors greatly. They had travelled by cart and horse along the Murray River and inland and had sailed across the lakes, Alexandrina and Albert, to the sea, and here they were. They had seen things that must be of interest to anyone.

'It is a strange life you have, then, Mr Bagshott,' Mama said, somewhat breathless at the quick pace she had set. She tilted her head to look up at him with bright curious eyes.

'We are become used to it. Each day is different so we are never bored. The company we meet is most various.'

The younger Mr Bagshott ambled by my side, looking about curiously, one hand in his pocket, the other tapping his hat against his leg. He was more than a boy but not yet a man, not quite, but tall and well made; anyone would have said that, with his dark hair swept back, dented where his hat had pressed it against his head and he had sweated, his ready white smile and his startling blue eyes and a manner that seemed easy. He did not have much to say; perhaps, like me, he had no conversation. He did not appear nervous or proud or uncomfortable.

We paused at the top of the rise when the house came into view again.

'Well now,' Mr Bagshott said, sizing it up with a thoughtful eye.

I feared what they might think. It seemed to me sometimes that we were as much like driftwood as the timber our house was made of, washed up here after the foundering of Papa's businesses, and now we must make a life out of what remained and hope that we could find shelter there. I wondered if our visitors thought the same.

'Your husband has been busy,' Mr Bagshott said.

'And our older sons, Hugh and Stanton.'

'Would you permit Charles to sketch your house? Perhaps your husband—' Mr Bagshott dragged his eyes from the house in the distance to Mama, so small at his side.

'We will ask him when he returns. I think he will be pleased.' And then, her face dropping and her voice less certain: 'He might be, that is. Yes, he has done a great deal.' It reassured her to say this, I believe. It gave a frame for the way to look at all that was about us, and I supposed she and Mr Bagshott were right. Even if the house was not comfortable it was at least better than a native shelter made of bark and grass and reeds.

With a clattering of boots we went up to the back veranda. We could not ask strangers and visitors to remove their boots, so it was a mercy that the ground had dried and they were not muddy. And we pushed the door and stepped into the dining room. As I expected, Addie had not cleared the dishes or the table but had just disappeared. Mama would never have permitted her laziness in town. Socks were hanging on the stove railings. A bee was caught at the window. I flushed with the shame of it and then had to turn from the light of the window until my complexion had calmed. But the two men did not judge or did not appear to at any rate, or even to notice, but stood taking up a great deal of room until Mama remembered herself and asked if they would like to sit, which they did, scraping the chairs back from the table. Charles gazed at the rough ceiling: just a small lizard and a spider as big as my palm on this fine day. I took the opportunity to remove the socks and put the kettle on and clear the dishes; there was nothing I could do about the rest. Mr Bagshott rested a hand on the table, his fingers idly gathering a small mound of crumbs. I was ready to sink through the floor.

He talked on, and it was fascinating to hear. The first parliament in South Australia had been elected earlier in the year, he said, since which time he and his son had been far into the interior of the country. They had named places and Mr Bagshott was drafting maps. He promised to show them to us later. It was dry inland – with expanses of desert where very little grew and there were no trees at all.

We drank tea and ate oat biscuits, which were all we had. 'We entertain so seldom out here,' Mama said by way of explanation, which was a huge exaggeration. 'Practically never' would have been closer to the truth.

'They are quite delicious, I assure you, Ma'am,' Mr Bagshott said.

I went and lit the stove in the outside kitchen, banging the door in vexation. As if they would not have known visitors were never expected the instant they passed the tubs of washing soaking in the sun and the house not swept nor cushions plumped, nor flowers anywhere and all of us shabby. I had seen it on our return from Mrs Robinson's, but with so much to do, and Mama not herself, it was hard to keep up. We had become ramshackle. And oh, my dress, my blue dimity, growing daily more faded. Why was I wearing it this day? I fetched the old veal stew from the pantry and took it to the kitchen, and scraped and cut up carrots and turnips and threw them in with the meat and into the oven.

Papa and the boys, Tull too, returned late in the morning and Papa took the Bagshotts on a small tour (how could it be otherwise when there was so little to see?). I followed along, not wishing to miss any news. From the rise looking back the house was homey enough, with the smoke rising and the horses stamping and twitching their tails in the fenced-off paddock. The bullocks were sober creatures and moved as imperceptibly as becalmed ships across the grassy land as if their slobbery noses were attached to the ground. Bullocks are a necessity, but they are not a pleasure. Looking at our visitors' expressions I saw how the house appeared to have run adrift into a dip in the slope and was set at an awkward angle – also the patchwork effect of the wood, the modest size of the buildings, the plain veranda posts and small windows.

Papa's face settled into moroseness. He put his hands in his pockets. 'Why do you wish to draw it?'

'For a record of these times to show how we are developing the land. That is all.' Mr Bagshott spoke very plain and dignified and I think this reassured Papa, who I knew felt the fall in his station. He spoke often of the civilizing influence of our presence and religion. 'Tull is the proof of it, my dear,' I had heard him say to Mama more than once. I found it hard to discern God in what lay about us but no one was interested in my opinion.

'If you had seen our house in Adelaide, and our old dairy farm. They were worth making a record of, I can assure you of that. Very fine.' Papa became hearty at the memory, rocking on his heels.

'I like this house. It's picturesque.'

'Picturesque,' Papa said slowly, as if he was testing the word. 'Well, I don't know. We will build a stone house when we are able, and then we shall have something worth drawing. No, we shall have something worth painting. Perhaps you will come by in another year or two and see what we have become.'

113

'Perhaps we will,' said Charles. 'I will venture to say, sir, if you agree, that the property appears to best advantage from the water. I would like to draw it from there if I may.'

Papa bowed his head in assent and we walked back down the hill. He insisted on taking Mr Bagshott through the front door, which stuck so that he had to put his shoulder to it, it not having been opened for so long and having grown damp in the winter storms. Poor Papa. It did not add to his consequence. When it could not be shut again he turned it into a virtue.

'A good airing for the spring, what say you, Hester?'

'Yes, Papa. I think Mama might like that,' and I followed after the Mr Bagshotts and Papa, who rubbed his shoulder where he had used it to gain the house.

I could not remember when I had last been through the doorway. The day of our arrival, when the hall had been a tunnel and the parlour a cave after our travels? For a moment I saw how like we had been to small animals creeping to the far closed end of our burrow. It made me hurry past the men when they paused at the parlour and into the dining room where I flung open the back door and put some wood against it to stop it blowing closed again and threw up the window sash, setting the curtains flapping. My heart slowed again.

'Feel better now, Miss Finch?' young Mr Bagshott said.

I spun around to see him leaning up against the entrance to the hallway. I had thought him still with his father and my father. Truly he had the bluest eyes in the world. 'Better? I feel very well thank you, Mr Bagshott, as I did before. No need to feel better than that. Hester is my name.' And I smiled to show how little his words meant.

'Charles,' he said. 'Anything I can do?'

I shook my head.

'Not that I'm much of a cook, more used to campfires, damper and billies, not the luxuries you have. An oven. A kettle.'

'Yes indeed. We have so much to be thankful for.'

'Oh. I did not mean to— We have been to finer houses than this – only because they are more established – but few so welcoming. It reminds me of home, because of your brothers and sisters, I suppose. And you've invited us in.'

'What else would we do?'

'The same as other people. Direct us to where we may set up our tent, show us the water and leave us to build a fire.'

I tried to gather my thoughts, to see something that might remind me what I should do next. 'The kitchen. I must see to lunch,' and I went outside.

He followed me, pulling up a chair and sitting in the sun beneath the blue sky and the grape vine's new shoots. It was hard not to look at him – his open sunburnt face and the leaf shadows moving on it. I fetched the flour and eggs and milk from the pantry and came back and mixed a dumpling batter and spooned them as neat as I could into the stew, Charles paying some attention to a task that seemed not very fascinating and made me wonder about each dumpling, whether it was too large or too small. What made a good dumpling? I didn't think my thoughts would interest Charles. I put the stew on the stove top.

'Don't people want to know what news you have and to hear about your travels?'

'You saw how much news we have. When they discover that our ignorance about home is as great as theirs and that we have not discovered new pastures or prospects or gold, they are finished with us, more or less. They don't wish to hear how poor the country is further inland, about deserts and thin sheep and uncertain water supplies. People prefer to believe in a lie or a dream and do not like the people who wake them. But that's as they wish and choose.' He shrugged and set his shoulders square again. 'They want to know the price of sheep and wheat and how others are faring. No better than they and if possible a little worse, they hope. When they know this we are free to set up camp and the next day to be on our way.'

'How long have you been travelling?'

'Months now. Five? I think it would be five. We return to Adelaide soon, where my family lives.'

'They will miss you.'

He shrugged again, but also smiled so I didn't feel I had been too curious.

Through the doorway I watched Papa and Mr Bagshott amble onto the veranda talking of I know not what, just that they nodded their heads in amity and their mouths moved in cordial conversation, the tour of the house and estate now complete. Mr Bagshott accepted the offer of a pinch or two of Papa's tobacco and they sat, beards wagging. Charles called out to them and they included him in their conversation, which came in through door and open window.

'And the natives?' Mr Bagshott said. 'Do you have much trouble with them? Any unrest?'

'Not to speak of,' Papa said. 'They were wont to steal cattle, or so I believe.'

'But you have one working for you?'

'Eh?' Papa said.

'The black you rode in with. A fine specimen of the local inhabitants I would say.'

'Oh, Tully.' Papa stopped there as well he might. (I wouldn't know how to describe him myself. I seldom thought of him as a native these days. He was just Tull, not a foster son or adopted or servant or companion. He was all of these things and yet something beyond, the embodiment of Papa's hopes, an instrument of civilization. The backward looking eye sees with less distraction.) 'He is—'

'Our friend,' Fred said, coming outside.

'Yes, that's it Fred. Thank you,' Papa said. 'We are proud of his progress.'

'Really,' Mr Bagshott said, surprised. Tull came out then and he spoke to him direct: 'You are fortunate in knowing this family, and in being on such friendly terms with them.'

Tull looked around rapidly to see what might be required of him. 'Good day, sir,' he said. 'Thank you, yes. I have learned a great deal.' Behind Mr Bagshott Fred and Albert grinned at Tull's predicament and at Mr Bagshott taking in his speech.

116

'He has lived with us for more than a year, Mr Bagshott,' Fred explained. 'On and off. He has his own family too.'

'Really?' Mr Bagshott said, stretching the word. 'Well.' And then to Papa, 'Very charitable of you.'

Tull gave a longing glance towards the lagoon and would have left then had Papa not noticed: 'Come, come now, Tull. No need to be shy.' He went to stand by Fred.

The dumplings were ready then and I took the stew inside.

Mr Bagshott sat next to me at the table. He was very weathered closer to, like paper that has been rained on and has dried again and yellowed in the sun, and seemed to fill more space than was available. His gestures were large and his voice and laugh loud and his tales long. Well-being and satisfaction radiated from him like heat from a stove. Papa's clothes were shabby.

Papa took the opportunity to deliver himself of one of his longer graces, finishing with, 'Let us remember the bountiful riches provided to us by our benevolent Father in heaven. Give us the strength to fulfil your purposes, to offer instruction and hope, provision the natives with food and employment, and teach them that their souls might be saved and eternal salvation will one day be theirs, as it is ours, and that they know you in their hearts as we do. In Lord God our Father's name we pray. Amen.'

'Amen,' we all intoned.

Part way through I stole a glance at Charles, who rolled his eyes so that I couldn't help smiling, and then, feeling disloyal, frowned, which made him smile again. (Papa's voice flowed on.) He seemed much amused by life.

Mr Bagshott spoke of England, which he did not miss. 'Yorkshire,' he said. 'I have not been there for twenty years, but I will never shake its cold and damp from my bones. No, this country is the future, of that I am sure. Riches for all who will work for it.'

Papa looked downcast at this – if there's one thing we had an abundance of it was a lack of riches – but his mood did not last and lunch was almost merry for all it was so plain. Addie, who had appeared the moment she was no longer needed, as usual was bumptious and in need of direction – not that Papa was going to supply it; he looked doting at the mere sight of her. And all Mama murmured at distant intervals was 'Addie, shh,' which just made Addie laugh the more.

She was a great show-off and made much of tossing her head so her black curls danced, and asking Charles questions that could only make her appear foolish: 'What do you like to draw best, Mr Bagshott? Do you miss your friends at school? I should like to go to school too, though I did not used to like it. In fact I used to think it the dullest thing imaginable. It is just that I miss the company – and dancing. I like to dance. Book learning is dull, don't you agree, Mr Bagshott?'

He raised an eyebrow. 'I didn't find it so. I would like more, in fact.'

'Oh,' Addie said, looking down at her plate.

Charles winked at me so fast I thought I was mistaken and grinned so I knew I was not and I couldn't help smiling and I blushed again. He did not invite her to call him by his name but treated her much as you would a kitten: a funny thing to tease and laugh at.

'You are a notable cook, Mrs Finch,' Mr Bagshott said, and he did seem to be eating with enthusiasm.

Papa looked at me so I knew I must not say anything. Mama was startled and glanced from me to Papa and mumbled a thank you and tucked a strand of hair across her ear again and again. She did not think it decent for a woman to show more than the lobe of an ear. I did not see what was so marvellous about an ear that it could inflame passion, but I am not a man.

Papa cleared his throat and offered Mr Bagshott more wine, what remained of the bottling from our vineyard in Adelaide. It might be that his tongue was loosened by the drink, or unfamiliar company (strange how a confidence is sometimes more forthcoming to a stranger than to a friend), but Papa began to speak more freely then than I had heard from him before.

'My parents thought it foolhardy to come here,' he said. 'They were not persuaded and would not support me, which is a matter of regret to me. I hope to show them wrong.'

His tone made me pity him rather, a feeling I did not recall experiencing towards him before. My thoughts ran over it, as a finger will travel to a scabbed wound, lifting its edges and exploring it.

'Do you see many changes on your travels?' Papa asked.

Mr Bagshott mopped his whiskers with his napkin. 'Oh yes, certainly. Farmland up and down the river. Clearing for crops and sheep of course and some excellent buildings. Places we hardly recognised on the return journey though we had visited them on the way up the river. A little trouble with the natives, as you'd expect, but their cooperation can be bought, and there is less trouble all the time.' Seeing Tull taking this in he shifted in his seat and busied himself with his food. As for Papa, he had become bleak. His moods swooped like a wagtail in flight.

We all knew of Papa's family and the work they had done towards the abolition of slavery; indeed the great William Wilberforce – a saint, Papa said – had been a friend. Quakers – the Finches among them – and Anglicans had worked together for decades to defeat the iniquitous trade. It was something of which we must be proud. When Papa was a boy there were slaves still, who could be purchased and sold as if they were nothing more than a loaf of bread or a packet of sugar – though I imagine that they were more expensive – and who lived in people's homes and worked without receiving as much as a penny in pay. All men are created equal, we have been told for as long as I can remember, and deserve the same rights and freedoms, and that is why we must treat the natives with respect despite their poor condition. Papa did not hold with people who believed that natives should first prove themselves worthy of such treatment. 'How can they know the right way to go about things unless they are entrusted with those tasks?' Papa would ask. But observing how the natives continued to live, choosing to live as they always had despite seeing a more comfortable manner of living, I was not sure what Papa now thought. He was given to instructing Tull on the art of fence making and animal husbandry and other such things. 'Remember this now, so you can tell others,' he would say.

Mr Bagshott could not know this and it was too late to tell him but he had seen Papa's fallen spirits. He said, 'I've seen no house finer than that you have planned for this vantage point and all of them of some years' establishment. Why, I am sure we shall see great developments here on our return to these parts, eh, Charles?'

Charles lifted his head from the plate and glanced at my father's face, hopeful and expectant just then. 'Indeed yes. A fine place for a fine family.'

I feared sometimes that Papa was rather vain, not of himself, but of his family. Perhaps proud was a truer word. He had an eye to how we appeared to those outside and liked his family to reflect well on him and his means as well as on all the things that he believed. Levity was not always something that he cared for, or only in moderation. He liked us to appear to advantage that we might set an example. He sat up straighter, he swelled a little at Charles's words as if he were sitting upon a carved oak throne in a stately home (which were in short supply in this country) and his supplicant tenants had come to pay a visit. Looking at Charles and his slow gaze at Papa and its sweep about the room I wondered if this had been his intention. I looked too at the clutter of things, seeing it through his eyes, at the layering of outer garments festooned from the door hooks, and the kettle steaming at the back of the stove, the overflowing wood box, the dresser in need of putting to rights – nails and twine and shears and a hammer and I know not what else piled up with the Spode. Our home was not much more than a shack in a desolate part of the world forsaken by all but a few blacks and people who did not have money to pay for proved land, but must gamble all on the possibility of a return. Whatever would Grandmama have said? Charles noticed and gave a look of what I suppose he meant as sympathy but I loosed a ferocious stare before I could stop it, at which his face lit up. It was plain that his family had never fallen on hard times.

'Are you too warm, Hester?' he asked.

'I am warm enough,' I said, and got up to remove the plates. 'Addie?'

She flounced about, using clearing the table as an excuse to swish her skirts, which had grown quite full.

'Did you put on every petticoat you possess?' I hissed at her, crossing the walkway to the kitchen. 'You look completely ridiculous.'

'You're only cross because you didn't think of it first.'

'I am not.'

'You are. *Charles*,' she said breathlessly.

'I do not say that.'

'You do a bit.' She darted ahead and clattered the dishes on the kitchen table and came skipping back past me. She was growing too and what was to be done about that? Her bodice was too tight. Perhaps a gusset could be inserted under the arm or one of Mama's dresses could be cut down.

Mr Bagshott was holding forth when I came back. 'I have found it to be a healthy environment here in general,' Mr Bagshott said, and he went on to speak of a visit he had made for the General Board of Health to a small town called Haworth in North Yorkshire, where almost half of all the children died before the age of six. 'Typhoid, consumption, smallpox, scarlet fever. Terrible. It was my unhappy task to determine the sources of the infection and to give advice. I tell you that it did not cease to rain or snow or mizzle or mist from one week to the next. And the wind: I thought I would be blown off those moors. All was damp, houses, animals, people alike. There was a family there who offered me lodging, but I declined when I heard of the recent loss of one of the daughters of the household. But she had died elsewhere, I discovered. The Brontës – perhaps you've heard of them. Writers they were. They wrote under other names.'

'Bell? Currer Bell, do you mean? And Ellis Bell?' I said.

'That's it. They both died, I heard. The last of them not so long ago – Currer, I think. Another sister was dead already. Quiet little things. They became quite gay after tasting from the cup. Their brother now, was another matter. Oh, a hard life. They were gently bred and reared and spent all their hours writing, or so I heard. But

I did not meet them often. You know of them?'

'Of course! I should think everyone must know of them. I had their books in Adelaide. Grandmama gave me them.' I almost leapt up; I could not help my excitement. Of all the strange things, that this man in the wilds of the Coorong had met the author of *Jane Eyre: An Autobiography*.

'You have read them? A girl your age?' he said.

Papa cleared his throat.

'You did not think them rather intense, rather exciting for a young girl?' Mr Bagshott said. 'I do not myself hold with fiction.'

'I will not say I was easy,' Papa said. 'But my mother in law thought them full of common sense—'

'And true feeling,' Mama said and they both laughed as if this were a favourite joke between them. It was the old Mama and we all turned to see her smiling so free, as if she might keep smiling for a while after, and the Bagshotts looked about the table in confusion.

'Well,' Mr Bagshott said.

'We believe that educating females is proper,' Papa said.

'As do I and my wife.'

'Including mathematics and the other branches of higher learning,' Papa said.

'Indeed?' Mr Bagshott said.

I said, 'Grandmama says, "Men know fools make the best slaves." Her mother was fond of saying it.'

Mr Bagshott turned his head very slow. 'Really.'

Papa cleared his throat, 'But those books – we were glad to leave them behind.'

'I was not,' I said. 'Tell us, Mr Bagshott, what were they like – the ladies, that is?'

All I got in response was a look of reproof so that I saw that I had appeared forward or outspoken or something of the sort. I could no more get information or knowledge out of Mr Bagshott than I could lift a limpet with my bare hands and I was so disgusted with him that I hardly knew what to say. Charles caught my eye as if he understood my feelings though I do not see how he could.

'Nothing could have saved them,' Mr Bagshott said. 'I decided then that I would not willingly pass further time in such inclement climes and resolved to find a new world, a real one, not of the imagination such as they wove in their fictions. I would not have children as pale and frail and stunted. The Americas beckoned but as luck would have it I attended a lecture given by the South Australia Company in London and was persuaded that Australia represented the best prospects. Soon enough my good wife and I had set our course for the Antipodes. Your children are as fine looking as ever I saw.' From this I deduced that he believed his own children to be finer looking as I have observed that people praise where they are conscious of being in a state of comfortable superiority.

'All but Hugh born here. And your son is an excellent young fellow. You must be proud,' Papa said, from which I deduced that he felt us to be superior. It is true that Stanton was larger and more muscular, doubtless from the physical work that he was obliged to do, yet his consciousness of his looks and stature made him less attractive, not only to me, but I felt absolutely.

Tull had been quiet at first but became at ease while talking to Fred, and after lunch they found the chessboard and sat playing on the veranda with Addie for company. She had given up hope of captivating Charles.

Mr Bagshott came out with his pipe and lit and drew in and blew out several quick, thick clouds of smoke across them, making a sucking crackling sound at each breath. Fred and Tull played on.

'Chess – an excellent game, which may be played with enjoyment regardless of the level of skill,' Mr Bagshott said to no one. 'Impressive that you have taught him the moves, Frederick.'

'Thank you,' Fred said. 'Do you play, sir?'

'I do, I do. I might be able to teach you a trick or two, young man.' He rocked onto his toes and back. 'Young men,' he amended, nodding at Tull.

'Why not play Tull, since he hasn't been playing as long? Some suggestions for a new player perhaps?'

Tull glared at Fred.

'Of course. I'd be delighted.'

'Very well,' Tull said. He sounded calm enough but I thought he was uneasy at the prospect.

Fred swept the board, which was a pity. The game had been poised with interesting traps about to be sprung. Perhaps Mr Bagshott hadn't noticed that. I would not say we were skilled players, rather that it was a diversion in the evenings and on Sunday afternoons. They reset the board and Fred moved aside and they settled themselves.

Poor Mr Bagshott. Stanton and Albert had long since given up playing against Tull. Hugh pretended he wasn't trying, but humouring Tull. It was the opposite; Tull did not play his best game with Hugh, leaving open enticing routes that might have helped him had he perceived them. He had bested me more than once of late. He played the game most originally – to us, that is. It was mathematical to me, a weighing up of lines of power and the opponent's strengths and weaknesses. Sometimes it was as if Tull was exploring the limits of a single piece's strength, or the ways it might react to threat. Then he would appear to forget about it, luring his opponent on another front before circling back. I was not so aware of this then, but have thought of it often in the intervening years and come to this conclusion, replaying moves while lying awake in darkness. (I sleep rather poorly.) Then, all I knew was that the game became new once more. Fred felt it too, I think. We seldom played each other. The paths our minds moved along were too similar to be of interest.

Tull did not spare Mr Bagshott, but Mr Bagshott persisted and the only agitation he showed was the increasing speed of his smoking, the clouds from it encircling his head in a thick mist. Once, to put Tull off his game, I think, he said, 'Quite an unusual home then – educating females and natives. I'm not sure—' He stopped speaking then; Tull had captured his queen. At the end he looked at the devastation and lifted his head, staring from Tull to Fred and back again. 'I see what you've done, the lesson you have taught me, and I thank you for it.'

'Thank you for the game, Mr Bagshott,' Tull said, polite but still uneasy. He would be wondering whether he should have let Mr Bagshott win, I suppose.

Mr Bagshott nodded and stood – 'I do wonder though what will lie at the end of it.' He put some more tobacco in his pipe and strolled away.

Charles rowed out to fetch his sketch book and when he returned put it before Mama on the cleared table – the rest of us gathered behind her to see – and sat at her side as she turned the pages, explaining the sketches to us and telling what lay beyond the edges of the pictures he had drawn. Some of the sketches were very fine, I thought, as were the houses in them. They appeared so light to me and must have been spacious. I would like to have opened some of those doors and walked through the rooms of those houses. What would they hold? Who would live in them?

'Where are the people?' Addie said. 'I want to see them and the clothes they wear. Are they young or old?'

'Charles is recording the houses, not their owners,' Mr Bagshott said from the other side of the table.

'No people?' Addie burst out.

Mr Bagshott lifted a finger in admonition as I wished Papa and Mama would. Addie subsided, which was a rare enough thing, and he sipped his tea and wiped his whiskers before he spoke again. 'The commission is for the homesteads, not the owners.'

Fred came forward to stand at Charles's shoulder. His eyes were alight and moved swiftly across the turning pages. 'That's a good sized book,' he said.

'It is,' Charles said. 'And the paper – see?' Fred felt the corner of the page Charles held with finger and thumb.

'It's heavy,' he said, surprised.

'Gives more depth.'

'Ah, I see,' Fred said. The longing in him for one of these books was plain. There was paper for writing and book keeping, but nothing like this hereabouts. Mama might be persuaded to write to

Grandmama to see if she could send a book or two. I would talk to her later. Fred asked for so little.

When Mama tired of it and rose and Albert and Addie and Tull had left, Fred remained and when Charles asked if he would like to continue looking he nodded his head but would not speak. Charles said, 'Be careful, now, you hear?'

Fred was almost overcome, but managed, 'Yes – sir.'

'Sir, am I now?' Charles asked no one in particular. 'I think Charles will do well enough.'

Later, towards evening but not yet supper, he found me on the shore looking at the changing light. It was one of our few entertainments in these parts and I had developed a taste for it. I could not help knowing that he had been anchored away from shore sketching our house for a good part of the afternoon while his father dozed on the veranda in the afternoon sun. I had moved further around from our small beach lest he imagine that I was watching him because I was not but was sitting on a tussock of grass that suited me very well. They made fine seats, some of them sat on so oft that they had parted and become bald in the middle like the parson's head in Adelaide. It amused me to think of sitting on him. He was a dull man, and quite *quite* determined to impart his views and thereby to improve us all.

Seeing me, Charles veered from the path through the saltbush, which came up to his waist. The bushes resisted, gave way and sprang back into place as he moved through them. Evidently he did not feel constrained by pathways. I smoothed the skirt of my dress, which was so faded these days that I had to look to remind myself of the old pattern of pink flowers against the blue. Charles tugged free of the bushes and approached and sat on the next tussock over – Fred's and Tull's, but he was not to know that.

He appeared uncertain and removed his hat and turned it in his hands. He had fine fingers, and long. 'Have I offended you?'

'Offended? No. It is just that I have become unused to company.'

'Yet Addie is friendly. Your father is friendly, and your mother too.'

I turned from the sky to face him. 'Addie is nothing but a flirt, Papa hopes to impress you and your father both and Mama is glad of company.'

'I *have* offended you.' He gave another of his boyish smiles.

'Do not think you can please me. I know quite well how we appear.'

'I wish I knew what I could say. I wish I knew what I could do to change your opinion of us, of me. I do not pity you if that is what you think. Do you miss town life?'

'I have no fear of my own company, if that is what you mean. It is the tedium. The sun rises and sets; the wind blows strong or a little; the rain falls or does not; and the clouds – their formations change, it is true. There may be reasons for these things, as Papa says, but I have little interest in them.'

'If there is something I could do, I wish you would say.'

'There is nothing. I do not know you well enough to ask anything of you or what wishes of mine you could fulfil.'

'No, you are very capable. You need for no one and nothing. I see that.' He put his hat back on and stood.

'Not nothing – books. I need to be thinking else my mind is a wheel and I wonder what is to become of us. It is a bad feeling.' I spoke hastily. I did not really want him to leave.

'No books, but perhaps you draw?'

'No, nor even write a great deal. I like mathematics.'

'Mathematics.'

'Yes.'

'For Fred then. I have another sketch book. He could have it if you think he'd like it.'

'Oh he would. He'd love it. I know he would.'

'And we have a little plain paper too – for yourself, I mean. Do you have a neat hand?'

'Small at any rate.'

'Better than neatness. You can come out to the boat and I'll find it.'

We walked the long way around, up to the junction in the paths

127

and back down to the shore, which was a relief. My dress would have been torn to ribbons if we had followed Charles's earlier route.

'Are there many blacks hereabouts?' Charles asked, but not as if he were interested. He was just making conversation.

'Quite a few.'

'Are you afraid to walk about here on your own?'

'I need never fear the blacks. No. They stay away from me. I know a few native women but they don't care for me. They stay away from us all if they can. They used to think I was dead. Not only me.'

'Dead? Why would they think that?'

'Our skin. They were frightened. They thought I was one of the bodies come alive or I reminded them of the bodies. I am not sure on that point. Pleasant is it not to remind people of a corpse? They know I'm alive. But I make them uneasy all the same.'

His eyes moved across my hair, which as usual was breaking loose. 'You don't look like a corpse to me.'

'I am so glad to hear it. It's compliments such as that that young girls dream of.'

Charles laughed and that made me laugh too. I was pleased to have amused him. I meant to. He plucked a tall stalk of grass and stuck its end in his mouth and began to chew it. He had very white teeth, and even but for one that broke the line. It was like a gate that had not been closed. 'I could tell you other things that would please you better,' he said.

'But I wouldn't believe you.'

'I could draw a picture of you if you would let me.'

'And why would you do that?' I asked. 'To mock me for my fine clothes? Do you wish to show how far a young lady can fall?'

'No, not for that. You could show Addie or Albert or Fred and they would tell you if it was a true likeness.'

'They would only tease.'

'Why?'

'Because of my height.'

'Ah. I suppose you are quite tall for a girl.'

We had arrived at the shore. Charles handed me into the rowing boat and pushed off, stepping in as the boat slid from shore.

Suddenly there was nothing to say. The wind had dropped and it was quiet and still in the middle of the watery space. I had forgotten how being in a boat with someone feels much like being in a small room with them. Not a single topic of conversation came to mind. Whatever would Mama think of me? Grandmama believed that girls benefit from instruction and that education was important even in the colonies – more important. We were to set a tone and an example for the future of this province. Grandmama said a woman of learning was always welcome everywhere, and should never be short of something sensible to say. I had not found this to be the case. There were few people interested in my command of algebraic equations, the major rivers of the continent of South America or the anatomy of vertebrates.

As if our minds had been travelling the same path, Charles said, 'I'm sorry about my father.'

'For what?'

'Girls. And education.'

'He doesn't approve?'

'Only watercolours and languages and the pianoforte. "Let a woman learn quietly with all submissiveness. I do not permit a woman to teach or to exercise authority over a man; rather, she is to remain quiet." That's First Timothy.'

'Do you disapprove?'

'I don't know. Really, I don't care. If I were a girl perhaps. But why it should matter … It is in the bible, I suppose.'

'There are a lot of things in the bible. If I don't teach them, I'm sure I don't know who will. Hugh and Stanton would never do it.'

'*You* teach them?'

'If Mama is not quite well.'

'Also: "If there is anything they desire to learn, let them ask their husbands at home." First Corinthians.' He couldn't meet my eyes and his voice in the recitation was flat. 'Not what I believe. I wish he had kept his opinions to himself, but he will not.'

'I would never learn a thing in that case. I have no great wish for marriage.'

'Why not?' He seemed startled, and stared at me as if he had not quite noticed me before.

'Why would I? I never met a man I would care to obey.'

'Are you a bluestocking then?'

'You make it sound very shocking. My Grandmama's mother was one, in the Blue Stockings Society. But how can I be here? There is no society, no school; I have only my books.'

'You think yourself superior to all men?'

'It does not follow that because I do not think myself inferior that I regard myself as superior. My acquaintances are so few here. My family, two police came visiting once, some musicians, and you and your father. That is all. I must obey my father, but I won't always.'

'Will you stay here forever then?'

'I hope not.'

'How will you leave?'

'I don't know. When the farm makes enough money, when the children are grown, when there's nothing here to keep me. My grandparents would have me, I could find a position, but I couldn't leave Mama. Papa would not allow it.' I looked overboard and beneath the water's surface could see forests of weed and clearings of sand, but no fish, scared into hiding by our boat, I supposed.

'What would you do?'

'I could become a teacher or governess.'

'Like Jane Eyre?'

'You've read it?'

'I borrowed it from a friend. My father doesn't know.'

'In any case, I do not see the problem. Adelaide is growing; there must be more schools, and they must need teachers. I will live on my own and never make another cheese. It is common sense not fiction that gives me hope.'

After several more strokes of the oars Charles looked around to check his course and made a slight adjustment with a delicate feathering of one oar. It was a relief when he spoke. 'I would like to draw you, Hester, if you would let me. I need the practice. That's the truth. A house and a farm is not the same as a person, and the owners of farms sometimes wish me to draw them and their families. If you would let me I would be grateful. Think of it as payment for the paper, if it makes you feel better.'

'Why not Addie? She would love it.'

'I would have to listen to her.'

I wouldn't say anything that was disloyal. In fact it seemed a cheek for him to say such a thing, but it was true too, and part of me couldn't help being pleased. 'Very well.'

We drew alongside the sailing boat, which loomed above us. The rowing boat bumped against it with dull thuds, moving away and back in, and the water slopped about. I didn't know how I would climb aboard, not with my skirts in the way. But Charles threw a loop of a rope over a bollard to steady us and leapt up and reached over the edge to heave me up and I was there, the smooth wood deck moving pleasantly beneath me, and I was able to explore. It was tidy without and within, the ropes neat, and the sails furled, and inside the cabin the narrow beds, one on each side up against the curved walls of the boat, were made up with red striped blankets and quilts, reminding me of the little houses we used to make under the big table in our town dining room, with cushions for beds and a space for our books and blankets all about the sides for curtains.

It was strange to be in the private quarters of men who were not family. It smelled different. I felt I had been caught spying. The roof was low over my head. I couldn't stand straight and when Charles poked his head through the doorway – 'I'll just fetch that paper,' he said – and came down the stairs and had to move past me I didn't know where to stand. There was so little space between the beds or at their ends and Charles was making for shallow cupboards above one bed. I thought we might brush against each other. I did not see how it could be avoided. I felt his warmth when the fabric of our clothes touched. And then he was past me. I did not look at him, but moved back to the stairs where there was the smallest wood stove I had ever seen, with room beneath for the wood that fuelled it, and a kettle on top and a billy and a saucepan hanging on hooks above that.

'You are good housekeepers for men,' I said, to fill the quiet.

'There's no room for mess, as you can see.' He was back at my side, both our heads bent as if we were whispering secrets, and holding two books towards me. They had brown covers and were about an inch thick and six inches tall and perhaps ten inches wide. There was nothing inside those pages but they seemed full of such possibility to me that for a moment I was fearful. I didn't want to spoil them with things of no importance.

'There are two here,' I said.

'One for Fred, to draw in. One for you for your mathematics.'

'It's too much. We can't pay.'

'There's no need.'

'I can't take them both.'

'But you can take one? There's no difference.'

I handed them both back. 'Keep them.'

He put his hands in his pockets. 'You are so quick to take offence. Come, Hester, it's not comfortable in here standing and I think you will not sit.' He went up the steps before I could reply but when I came into the light, taking the hand he offered me, he said, 'I have the answer. I'll make two pictures of you. You can earn those books with your boredom.'

I did not know what to say to that, so I agreed.

The next morning when the light in the parlour was good – Charles had walked about the house looking for the best position – he placed a chair near the window and bade me sit on it, adjusting my posture, and commenced to draw. He had little to say, so I fell into silence and was able to watch him or to look about as long as I didn't move my head.

'What does it matter?' I asked when he remonstrated once.

'It matters because every part of the light on your face changes when you move it. It's hard enough with the clouds.'

'There's not a cloud in the sky.'

'The sun shifting then.'

'I can't stop that, I'm afraid.'

'Oh,' then silence.

'May I move my mouth to talk?'

He bit his lip and his hand moved on the paper.

'Charles?'

His head reared up. 'What?'

'May I talk?'

'I suppose. But I must concentrate, so don't expect me to talk back.'

'Charming, gentlemanly.' I spoke in a voice that was so low and temperate Grandmama would have been proud. She would have offered up prayers of gratitude that it seemed I was coming to something after all, despite all her worst fears. It was strange, pleasant almost, to be obliged to sit still when there was so much to be done. Fred and Tull and Albert would be gone and Addie running wild and no one to make them attend to their lessons. Albert was only twelve and all he could think of was mending things or exploring or farm work. He liked to be doing things not thinking of them. It was not always easy to see the point of book learning here. But we all had to do it if we were to be fit to return to town. And even if they were to stay, they still needed to know how to keep accounts and write letters and to calculate quantities. It was as Grandmama said: education was important in any station of life. I don't know what she would have thought of the blacks. Would they need an education? News had come of a mission being started at Point McLeay to educate the blacks and to bring them to a knowledge of God. If Grandmama were here she would be involved. In Adelaide she took food to the natives in the parklands. It was the duty of those with much to give to those with little, she said.

'There.' Charles shut his sketch book and stood. 'That will do now.'

I rose and stretched. 'Are you not going to show me?'

He tucked the book under his arm. 'Just a few things I'd like to finish first, but I don't need you for them. After lunch we can do the other picture, I hope.'

'I can't give you a whole day, Charles. There's too much to do.'

'What do you have to do?'

'Everything.'

'Your mother? Doesn't your mother attend to things?'

'Not so much of late. She is tired now, she has not been well.'

He looked with sudden comprehension. 'I beg your pardon. I shouldn't have—' He busied himself rearranging his things.

'Oh no. She's not, that is, I don't think she is.' Now I had said something I shouldn't. What if he was right? Her appetite was poor; she was preoccupied. I had attributed these things to her spirits. If she were, out here so far from help—

Charles saw that he had almost made me say something that I should not, that a young lady would not. 'Of course. Of course.' He sounded like one of those gusting winds. 'Tomorrow? Could I draw you again tomorrow?'

'I'll see. Perhaps Addie could cook dinner tomorrow. Yes, perhaps she could.'

For a wonder, while passing through the dining room to the kitchen to see about lunch, Charles behind me, Mama was sitting with the boys and they were all bent over their books and slates, and Mama was explaining something to them. Albert looked up when I came in and his eyes were very round. We had a conversation with just our faces.

Me: eyebrows up.

Albert: shrugged shoulders.

Me: mimes writing on the slate.

Albert: nods.

Me: nods in comprehension.

Mama looked up when I closed the hall door. 'I thought I would do a little schoolwork with the boys and Addie this morning since you were busy.'

'Yes, Mama. We've finished. For this morning at least, but Charles has more to do.'

'This afternoon and tomorrow morning if I might,' Charles said.

'Of what?' Addie said. 'Do a picture of me.'

'Another picture of Hester, Mrs Finch, if you could spare her.'

'Why? Why do you need another picture of Hester? You have one already.'

'I have a portrait and now I would like to do a figure drawing. The same face as well as the figure, at a different distance, in another setting. You do not look alike.'

Addie scowled.

'Could you cook tonight, Addie?' I said.

'Cook? Me cook? What do I know of cooking?' she said, as if it were the most ridiculous idea in the world. 'I'm not cooking.'

'I'll show you then.'

'If you can show me, then you have time to do it and I need not. There.' She turned on her heel at the kitchen table and made for the door.

'Addie!' It was Mama. 'Come here now.'

Addie was shocked, as well she might be. We all were, unblinking, except Charles, but then he didn't know what she had been like of late, especially since Mama refused to allow her to visit Mrs Robinson again.

Addie stood before her. She was quiet, even meek. 'What, Mama?'

'I beg your pardon, Mama,' Mama corrected.

'I beg your pardon, Mama,' Addie said.

Mama put a gentle arm about Addie's shoulders. 'Come. We can cook dinner together while Hettie is busy.'

The oddness of the next two days was so varied: Mama cheerful, Addie cooking, the company of the Bagshotts at every meal, and I sitting idle with a stranger.

The Bagshotts left two days later after a hearty breakfast of toasted bread and eggs and a slice or two of salt pork. Mama came into the dining room – 'Fried eggs,' she said – and fled. We were quiet despite Mr Bagshott's hearty observations about life and Addie's attempts to entertain.

'Oh, it will be dull again once you are gone. There will be nothing but work and lessons and scolding,' she said.

'Scolding? Who scolds you?' I said. 'Or makes you work?'

'Why you, you, you, Hester. And you will be cross with me no matter what I do.'

'It is that you do nothing but what pleases you that makes me cross.'

She bent her head. 'See, it's started already.' Her tone was mournful, and then she lifted her head and laughed so that everyone else laughed too. Even I could not help it.

But our good spirits did not last. When the two men had drained the last of their tea and wiped their mouths and scraped their chairs back and risen it was to leave. Mr Bagshott smoothed his hands down his waistcoat over the swell of his stomach, and sighed with satisfaction. 'Well,' he said, as if that summed up all: life, the world and the few days they had spent with us.

'Well,' Papa said, standing, and a tide of movement began to flow outside into the morning light.

Charles held back at the door to let Mama and Addie through. I made to follow, but Charles took my arm and stopped me. 'Write to me,' he said and pressed a scrap of paper into my hand.

I looked at it and took in the scrawl of pencil. It was his direction in town. 'Write?' The words seemed indecipherable for a moment and his meaning opaque. What could his intention be? And a piece of paper – why, anything could happen to a piece of paper. It might as well be dust in the wind.

'If you would like to. If you have need of ought.' He appeared so strange and intent, bending so his face was close to mine.

'Need of ought? Do you mean note books?'

'Oh.' Now he seemed confused. 'Anything at all. Or just write – to let me know how you go on.'

'Charles!' It was Mr Bagshott shouting.

'Coming,' Charles called back. 'I forgot something.' And then turning to me again, 'I like you, Hester. That is all I mean to say. You are sweet.'

I took a step back. 'I am not sweet, Charles.'

'I think you *are*.'

136

'Oh.' And I could not help smiling.

Charles stepped forward and bent his head and kissed my cheek. He was closer than on the boat even, and he retreated and looked into my face. I could not speak but I believe that I was smiling and that this pleased him. On this point I am still not sure, but I persuaded myself of it later whenever I thought of that morning. 'Write,' he said again and I nodded and he was gone, plunging his hat on as he went through the door. He leapt the balcony's edge and turned, chivalrous of a sudden, and held his hand to me, though I could leap it as well as he, and I jumped and for a moment he took my weight. I could feel how he arrested gravity and wondered about Sir Isaac Newton, whether such a moment might have discovered gravity to him as readily as an apple falling, and about the forces that could arrest a fall. It was the moment when I felt for the first time, and knew it to be true and not an illusion, that life and self were not only matters of personal weight and burden and endurance, that they might be shared.

10

THE COORONG
NOVEMBER 1857

I stood on the tallest sand hill on the peninsula and turned slowly, looking all the while through Fred's telescope. To the west was the vast blue plain, the sea – empty today – and to the east across the lagoon was the long stretch of the landward shore, which Tull called *tengi*. Addie and Mary were feeding the chickens, a favourite task of Mary's. From this distance, it was as if they were scuffing through blossom. Mama had taken Addie in hand a little lately. She was in charge of the poultry now, and was learning to cook. Undulating to north and south was the peninsula's unending line of sand hills and saltbush and grass.

I had seen other things from there, on Sunday afternoons when no work could be done: the native women pulling rushes and sedges and laying them aside in bundles, the men poling along on rafts, or gliding in their canoes, fishing spears at the ready, or walking one of the tracks. The natives always carried spears and weapons, several each, which bristled above their heads. They were good fast walkers. Kangaroos had been a common sight once, but none of us had observed any of late – a pity for Skipper, it had been her favourite sport to chase them. This country, which we had once thought empty, was busy enough in its own way. A person had to watch and wait to see that it was not. We had to learn to see.

Not a week after the Bagshotts' departure we saw the most unexpected thing. The fish had been running in the lagoon, which not even Stanton failed to notice. He made himself a rod and for more than a week, late in the afternoon, had stood on our point, arcing back and forth like a pendulum weighted beneath, casting and dandling the line on the water. From atop the tallest sand hill, we watched two men, natives, wading waist deep and slow along the water's edge on the opposite shore, perhaps a mile from our house where the stock route pulled away from the coast to cut a curve in the land. Each of them held a stout pole, the two of which were connected by something, netting I supposed – a long stretch of it by the distance between the men. They moved so patient and particular. Fred and I took turns to observe, but Tull having once seen it did not look again. The sight seemed to annoy him. Slowly, one of the men changed direction, drawing his pole so that the open side of the loop faced the beach and the men came closer to each other and even though I did not understand what I was seeing I held my breath at the preciseness of the task. And the poles touched. Several other men entered the water, one of them with a rock which he used to hammer the poles into the lagoon bed. More poles were inserted at other points of the loop. The encircled water rippled at its surface and there was a splash: fish. They were the most ingenious people.

'Why not catch them?' Fred asked.

'They can't eat so many. We can keep them or smoke them when we are ready.'

'Like the chicken run,' I said and he nodded.

'So clever,' Fred said.

Tull's smile fell away. 'Oh yes, blackfella very clever,' he said. 'Blackfella catch fish, go hunting, dance.' His voice had changed. He performed a half-hearted staccato caper, staring at Fred.

I had never seen one of the natives' celebrations, though Papa had described them: they painted themselves and the women drummed on their possum skins and their singing thrummed into the dark. Seeing Tull dance in such a way while dressed in trousers and shirt was very strange.

'I didn't mean anything by it. I don't think of you as one of them,' Fred said.

'I am one of them,' he said.

'You don't think it clever?' I asked.

'We always do this. Clever?' Tull shrugged. 'You tell me what is clever. You think you know, that you are cleverer. That's what you mean, that you are the one to decide. Now I should say, "Thank you".' He gave a jaunty little bow to go with his mocking face. 'Look at that.' He pointed along the shore and towards the low bluff above it where the ground had been trampled and the grasses and rushes torn at by the clumsy cows. 'Are you clever? You are like children. You take and take.'

'We're making use of the land,' Fred said. 'We're farming it. Some spoilage cannot be helped.'

'Do we not use the land?' he said, as if it were a question, when the answer was obvious.

I did not like to argue with him or offend; what they did was not the same, as everyone knew. 'Why don't you farm the land?' I said. 'You could have and did not.'

He had no answer to that.

Like children: the thought of it. Were there others who thought the same?

At dinner Fred mentioned the fish pen to Papa, glancing at Tull at the same time, hoping to please Tull that he had thought it worth mentioning, I would say. It was the sort of thing that Papa found interesting, and he promised to go and see it. But Tull was not pleased. In fact he was nowhere to be seen that afternoon and in the evening hardly responded to one or two inconsequential remarks that Fred made to show that he bore him no ill will, and declined my offer of a game of draughts or whatever else he might feel like. He spoke only to Addie and Albert, quite friendly.

The next day after his week of disappointment Stanton returned with a fine catch of large fish, which floured and fried provided a welcome change at dinner. It was the same the next day and the one after until we wearied of it. Three days later two native men arrived at the house to speak to Tull. I was in the outside kitchen and watched from there. Tull must have seen them from the stable and come out to meet them. The men were tall – well made, Papa would have said – and heavy bearded. One of them was older; his beard was grizzled. Their chests were patterned with scars, lines and dots. Slung on their shoulders were baskets bristling with weapons and tools, and each held a cluster of their slender spears. It was hard to imagine things so fine causing any great damage, but they did. I had seen it. Flocks of emus sometimes waded the shallows of the lagoon and once while out riding I saw two of them struck by spears from a distance of one hundred yards at least. The speed and accuracy were very remarkable.

Papa appeared at the back door and Tull and the men came down, approaching quite close. The natives spoke, touching their hands to their chests, twice, the fingers relaxed, their wrists loose. I copied the gesture against my own chest, feeling the strangeness of it. It was as if their hands were suspended above a piano, the fingers descending with no more weight than was needed to sound a note, *piano*. They were light. Papa clapped his hand heartily to his chest and his voice grew louder. Their heads reared back. It seemed to mean one thing to Papa and another to the natives. Was it a warning to them? I went to the doorway to hear more clearly. They stood their ground and spoke some more. All I could hear with them turned obliquely from me was the roll and flexibility of the sounds and I felt my own tongue moving to try to make them myself. It was strange to my ear and not unpleasant. They raised hands and fingers and gestured towards the distance, as if pushing something away. Then Tull translated, and I stepped closer still and watched with the keenest attention. Someone had stolen fish from the natives' enclosure, Tull said, and he, they, wanted it to stop.

Papa didn't blink, and his voice was deep and unchanging calm. 'Indeed?' he said. 'Another tribe, I would suppose. Or Celestials. They are partial to fish, so Nellie Robinson says.' He cleared his throat.

Tull spoke to the natives, telling them what Papa had said, I presumed. By the time he finished speaking they had changed. I could see all the muscle of them tense. The older one spoke again.

'You will do nothing?' Tull said to Papa.

He did not reply. The natives stared at Papa, and the lids of their eyes drew a little closer and that was all, as if there was something that he was not saying that made things clearer. It was as plain to me as it was to them, I would say: Papa would do nothing.

Fred came to Papa's side and watched with him while Tull and the natives moved away across the grass, stopping to converse once more. Perhaps he wished to be noticed by Papa, as I did. I climbed the stairs and joined them and took in the older native shouting at Tull and gesturing furiously towards Papa or the house or all of us.

'George and Billy,' Papa said, his voice and face heavy. 'I would not have things become rancorous between us.'

'You know them?' I said.

'We have met once or twice,' Papa said.

Finally the two men strode away leaving Tull on the path. Tull began to walk back, slower than usual. I did not like to leave Papa just then. We knew that Papa had spoken an untruth and I think he realized that we were aware – the natives too. He was diminished to us all, himself most of all, and how could he recover from that?

'You go on now, Fred, Hester. Don't you mind me. I will come around presently,' he said. 'I always seem to.' He turned and went inside.

Stanton came banging through the door and down the stairs towards Tull, buffeting his shoulder – '*Excuse* me' – as he passed him, and grinning as if it were all a great joke. There might have been shame in him somewhere. I would not know; I never saw it unless it was there, in that bravado. Tull was close then. There was nothing I could say that would make a difference to him. My brother a thief, my father unprincipled. Fred raised his shoulder a fraction and forced a small smile. And then came a faint lifting of Tull's features, an easing of everything on it, which with the slow shift of his gaze, as if he were not with us, told me that we did not perfectly understand the fish in the pen and Tull's connection to them. But I didn't ask him and he didn't tell me.

The day after that the fish pen was gone. It might never have been.

*

142

I thought of Charles. I could not help myself. What is there to say of him though? I had liked the look of him, his long blue eyes, the horizontals of mouth and brows, the way his hair was cut old fashioned as if he did it himself by campfire with shears, straight at the bottom and tucked behind his ears to fall loose again. I thought of these things and remembered his mouth. Sometimes in the dark I put two fingers to my cheek where his lips had touched.

By November I was sure of Mama's condition: her belly was swelling again and I was filled with dismay. She was too old for another baby. As for Papa, I preferred not to think of his part in it. It was not for me to judge or disapprove, but I could not help thinking, only in passing, that he might not have indulged himself and thus spared her. Mama's spirits were changeable, but not as bad as they had been before the Bagshotts came. Papa was serious and sombre and given to prayer and advice and long graces before our meals. The food at least had improved with spring vegetables: young potatoes and peas, baby carrots and beetroot, salad leaves. There were bunches of grapes on the vines. I looked forward to the sweetness of them at summer's end.

Papa had other things on his mind than Mama. The small cheeses we had made in the past had sold quite well and grocers would buy whatever we had to sell. This was our third spring – the busiest time for cheese-making with the cows producing so much milk. Papa let them go dry in winter when they were in calf and we kept only a few in the home paddock for our own milk and butter. And now the cows had calved again and we all had to rise early to help with milking. Cheese-making would go on all summer and all autumn, but it was never as busy as spring. There wasn't enough feed close to home so some of the cattle must be left on distant pasture with their calves and Hugh and Stanton and sometimes Albert travelled the run to check them, camping out overnight.

Addie was the best of us at milking. She sat on a stool and leaned her head against each cow's flank and sang under her breath. The cows waved their ears towards her and flared their nostrils and let down their milk. I did not find it unpleasant for short amounts of time. The cow's rough coat against my cheek, the vibration of life all through it, and its sweet smell felt almost motherly.

The profits from the dairy had been modest, sufficient to live on but not to improve the condition of our lives to any great degree. Stores must always be more important than clothes. Papa brooded over his journal, reckoning up columns of figures in ways that never came out satisfactorily if repetition were any indication. It was the simplest of calculations. I had been through the figures twice, upside down, from the other side of the table and thought if I had to listen to any more of his scratching quill I would reach across and snatch it from him.

'What's the matter, Papa?'

'Nothing, my dear.' He stared at his book. 'It's no way to make money, like this, at a crawl. It'll take twenty years, more, to get back to what we were.'

Apart from his frown it could almost be said to be pleasant, all of us spread about the dining room and across the veranda enjoying the evening, reading and sewing and looking at catalogues and drawing. Hugh and Stanton played cards, and Albert joined them. He had grown. He would be a big man one day, like Stanton. He was only thirteen, almost as tall as Fred already despite being three years younger, and stronger when they had been much the same for so long. He had moved apart from him in other ways too.

'Come on, Fred, nose out of your books,' he said. 'Come play a game with us.'

Fred lifted his gaze absently from his reading. 'Later maybe,' and his eyes fell again.

'Leave the little bookworm,' Stanton said.

'Stanton,' Papa said. 'If you had spent more of your time so—'

'He could spend a hundred times as many hours and still be in no danger of being called a bookworm,' Hugh said, and though I do not generally agree with him I had to on this occasion.

Stanton said, 'Oh, Fred doesn't mind, do you, Fred?'

'Pardon?' Fred asked, which made us laugh.

Papa announced at breakfast the next morning that he would be away for ten days at least visiting Milang, on the other side of Lake Alexandrina from Point McLeay. He had some business matters to attend to and would also collect the new stores of dried beans and seeds and sugar and tea and so on. We had been keeping a list, which he took without comment and went out with the boys to hitch up the dray.

We passed a week that didn't vary greatly from any other, apart from our speculations about the day of his return. We could not help thinking of different foods: me of mustard (something with some bite), Addie of jam and cake ingredients, Albert of the cake itself and so on. It would be years until our fruit trees bore enough for jam, if we kept them alive in this place of salt air and salt water and salt earth. When a week had passed we rode along the track, galloping the few straight sections, slowing through curves and scrub and marsh and around the rocky points towards the north. We saw nothing but a broken-down dray which we made note of to collect for its timber, the blacks having stripped it already of any metal that could be pried loose: hinges and brackets and nails.

The following day we went out again and found Papa a few miles from home. A canvas cloth covered the contents of the creeping dray, tied down around the sides to shelter the load, which there seemed to be more of than usual. Fred and Tull took over the driving, sitting up straight and serious with the responsibility. I was glad to see them friendly again when they had been cool with each other since the incident with the fish. Papa came with us leading the spare horse behind, grateful to be spared half a day on that hard driver's bench. Addie's horse skittered around Papa's and barged into mine.

'Sorry.'

'Addie,' I said.

'Yes?'

'Collect your reins; ride your horse, for pity's sake. Tell it what to do.'

'We're going forward, aren't we? That *is* what I want it to do.'

'Girls,' Papa said, with no great feeling, just a small secret smile and a serene countenance.

145

I wish it were not so, but he filled me with misgiving. Something had made him buoyant. It could not be his accounts, which meant that it might be one of his ideas. He hurled himself at new ventures (sheep, a whaling station) as if he were a drowning man and they would sail him back to shore. He did not say what he was thinking and I didn't ask; I preferred not to know.

When Tull and Fred arrived hours later, we went out to see, Mary bouncing in my arms, and with a great flourish, Papa threw off the canvas to reveal the cause of his hope: thirty large metal cheese moulds. All but Mary were silent. 'Show me, Hett.' She patted my cheek and leaned towards them.

'More cheese moulds?' Hugh asked. It was hard to see our future prosperity in these still shapes.

'So we can make more cheese. We could sell twice as much as we make now.'

'Twice,' I said. 'That would take a great deal of milk. Will you bring all the cows closer? Do we have enough feed?'

He fluttered a hand in dismissal. 'It will pay, Hester. You will see. Think of the time we'll save making large cheeses, the ease of stacking, the quantity. Why did I not think of it before?' He clapped his hands together. His tone, though, was becoming querulous. I was not the only one looking dismayed.

Mama said, 'Where are they from?'

'A gentleman farmer of my acquaintance at Lake Albert.'

'I see. And did they cost a great deal?'

'It's an investment, my dear. We must spend money to make money.'

Such a summer. The house became a taut drum until it seemed a careless match or a spark would explode it into flames. At night it let out its heat in slow groans. I threw off the covers and slept in a shift and the air was like a hot touch on me. The sky was of the deepest blue and hard overhead and white hot on the horizon and the air above trees and water trembled and hurt our eyes to look at. Addie and I abandoned our petticoats and rolled our sleeves as high as they would go and undid our bodice buttons too if no one else was about. 'Girls,' Mama said sharply when she saw us and we waited until she had gone to rest again and undid ourselves.

What grass there was at Salt Creek was sparse and dried quickly and the cows produced not half the milk of the previous summer. Papa would not admit any concern. He was determined to prove the usefulness of the large moulds and we must all take our turn stirring the cauldron of hot milk and waiting for the curds to form, even if it was more than one hundred degrees in the shade. Through the open doorway of the dairy Addie and I watched the blacks disporting themselves in the lagoon, all shiny in the blue, the children leaping from the sides of their rafts and plunging about.

'I wish I could do that,' Addie said. 'What would be the harm?'

The curds formed and we called Papa, who came up the path, rolling his limp sleeves and wiping the sweat from his face with an old kerchief. He said not a word, just filled the moulds and left them to drain before departing on some other pressing task.

We watched until he had gone and then, 'Come on,' I said, and took Addie's arm and dragged her along the path – the heat from the hard packed earth pouring from it and filling our skirts – until the house was out of sight. 'This can't harm anyone. I shall go mad otherwise.' We were damp with sweat and our sleeves would only roll a little above our elbows; the material prickled against our skin and sweat trickled down our faces and necks and legs. We were choking in clothes.

We took off our boots and stockings and left them on the shore and lifted our skirts high above our knees and waded into the cool water – oh, the feel of it sliding up our legs: a silken density. I shut my eyes. Addie slipped on a rock and sat in the water and her skirts were like an anemone and she laughed. I sat too and suddenly we didn't care and were in up to our shoulders with our dresses wafting around us, dragging against us when we moved too quickly, holding us back.

'Hester, Addie!'

We turned to see Fred and Tull and Albert and even though I was shocked that we had been discovered I could not make myself leave the water. Addie scooped glittering handfuls of water across them. 'Come in, come in,' she screamed and soon we were all plunging about.

A wet dress is not easy to walk in. The folds of material clung to our legs on the way home. If I could see the outlines of Addie so clear, the same must have been true of me. I sent the boys ahead of us. Addie would not stop laughing and gave up on modesty, swinging her boots by their laces and holding her skirts high, and the boys looked back and laughed at the sight. Before we reached home the skirts were dried stiff as paper and we crept past Mama's darkened room where she lay panting on her bed, and into ours and when we removed them the salted dresses half-stood on the floor as if dwindled figures remained within.

We waited for the moments when a cold wind would drive in from south or west and the world would turn upside down, the heat coming from the baked ground beneath and the cool from above. They did not last and arrived without rain. Towards the end of summer Tull brought three black men to the back door one Sunday afternoon. I recognized two of them – Billy and George from their visit about the fish. One now wore a feathered ornament attached to his hair at the back; the other wore a sort of cloak, the same colour as a basket but of a thinner and more flexible material. There was a boy too, older than Tull – he had the beginnings of a beard – but his hair was longer and fell about his face. Tull kept his tied back when he was at home.

The native women of my acquaintance had become used to me, more or less. Once they showed me how to suck the sweetness from the flowers of a grass tree and laughed at my surprise and the children brought me more flowers and wanted me to keep enacting my surprise for their amusement. I did my best to oblige. On other occasions I had bartered sugar and flour for one or two of their useful baskets.

Now, the native men stared at me and their gaze left me and darted back again. They were curious (or horrified) to see a white woman at close quarters – if it was the first time. I did not like to stare back; would it be impolite to ignore them though? Grandmama's lessons in etiquette and setting visitors at their ease had not touched on entertaining blacks beyond the edges of civilization. The men stayed behind Tull as if he were a buffer of some sort. They watched him very closely; Tull, I would say, was nervous.

He said to me, 'Is Mr Finch about? They wish to speak with him.'

'About what?'

'Water,' he said.

'They can have water. There's the sucks. Papa doesn't mind.'

Tull shook his head. 'It's not that.'

'He's in the parlour.'

It being the day of rest, Papa was doing nothing but cradling his unlit pipe and feeling his tobacco pouch and reading the bible or Quakerish texts, as he did each Sunday. When the religiosity of the day was fading into evening he would smoke his pipe and watch the sun falling, and he might pick up one of the papers that he managed to get from a staging post on the track. But that time was some hours away yet. He seemed glad of the interruption. Mama said, 'Send them away,' but he said he would not discourage them for anything. 'For how will they learn about us if we reject them? No, I am sure the Lord will understand, my dear.' He had brooded after their last visit and had been short with Stanton.

From the parlour, I watched Papa walk towards them. Their fingers cupped the air and drew Papa on. It was a gesture that was hard to resist; Papa could not. A string might have attached the natives' hands to Papa's feet.

Mama peeped around the corner of the parlour after they had gone and squeaked in horror.

'You saw them?' she said.

'Yes, Mama.'

'You should not have.'

'How could I prevent it?'

'I don't know, I am sure, but I wish you had not. Addie?'

I shook my head.

'At least they weren't completely bare.'

There came the sound of the door banging and we went through the dark house to the veranda where Addie, holding Mary, stood watching after Papa and all the boys and Tull and the blacks fading up the hill path. Well, what could we do but wait?

It was an hour or more and close to dark when we heard their voices, cheerful enough, rolling down the hill.

'Quickly now, girls, get dinner ready. Dear me,' Mama said.

'Quickly, girls,' Mary said. 'Help, help,' she said. 'Mary help.'

I gave her two spoons and she began circling the table banging them together and then went outside where I could hear her voice: 'Boys, boys, Papa,' and banged the spoons again, and there came a laughing call back: 'Coming to find you, Miss Mary.' Fred's voice. Mary shrieked with delight and ran back inside and hid under the table. Yes, there were some good times.

Then they were back – except Tull, who had gone with the blacks – and all was explained. It was the cattle and two favourite sucks of the natives, which they were spoiling, trampling the edge of the deep sweet water. I had seen myself how the water turned cloudy and fouled as the cattle dumbly chewed any fresh shoots before lumbering to an unspoiled patch. It was worse this summer than in the past, the heat having dried the shallower sucks. The blacks wanted Papa to stop the cattle.

'How?' Mama asked.

'Fencing. They showed us which ones.'

'Our water,' Hugh said. 'They could go elsewhere, but no, it falls on us to provide.'

'Just two. That's all we agreed to. It's not much,' Papa said. 'An annoyance. It will rain again and won't matter so much.'

11

THE COORONG
MAY 1858

Mama stared out of the window at the sky, unblinking. 'I'd never noticed before how like clouds are to lily pads against the sky. See them, Hester, floating on its surface?'

'Be still now, Mama, and save yourself. Please.' I wet the cloth and squeezed it and held it to her brow, and pressed it to each cheek and she shut her eyes and for a moment her face was peaceful.

Her eyes flew open again and darted to the window. 'What lies beneath, do you suppose?' And her face began to gather up, different from the gathering of an infant's features on the point of crying. It was as if she saw something coming from a distance and it could not be stopped but only faced as best she was able, fearful as she was. Her concentration on it was fierce. She held my hand between hers and squeezed, then harder until I felt the bones of my hand, my knuckles, grind and shift against each other. A sound came from her – a soft groan. The sight of her face, the frown and the pallor and the set of her jaw and the tremor that ran all through her were too much and I shifted my gaze to the window and beyond, as she had. And the pain in my hand receded, Mama receded, until there were just the clouds: rafts drifting, ships sailing, waves scudding, birds hurtling. All of these things. The pressure on my hand fell away and I looked down. Mama turned her head and then her body until she was all curled up, her knees drawn up as far as she was able against her great belly and her face against her two cupped hands. Just so have I seen Skipper lie when she wishes for warmth and quiet and rest, her nose tucked into her paws. In this way the labour continued through the evening and on past midnight. I went out once to tell Fred and Addie to put Mary to bed and to go to bed themselves, and left them before they could ask any question.

Once or twice Mama panted. She took my hand and pulled me down until my face was close to hers. 'I'm sorry for this,' she said.

'Why, sorry for what, Mama? There's no need—'

She broke into my words, her head a trembling shake against the pillow, 'No. No. Leave here, Hester. Do not stay.'

'All will be well, Mama. Do not say it.' And I sobbed once because if she was frightened then I was right to be too.

She panted as the hens do in the heat: small hot breaths, as if someone were pressing them out of her. 'I will be here,' she said. 'It will be well. We will come to rights. Only if ever you get the chance, take it. Leave. Never come back.'

'Mama. The boys. Addie.'

'Promise.' This was a groan.

'I promise,' I said. I did not meet her eyes then, but stared at the ceiling lamp which seemed to hang at an angle, as if the world had tilted, and when I looked again her eyes were clenched, her fists were clenched, her legs were clenched tight together and neither of us said what we were thinking and by night time there was no more to be said. It began to rain. The time for words was over.

When the waves of pain had abated for that time I left Mama's side and went to find Papa. He was at the front door, and spoke to me pleasant and calm as if his manner would make the occasion come right. It is in this way that we proceed in life, by convincing ourselves in each moment that events are running smoothly or are about to because the truth is not to be contemplated.

'Papa,' I said. 'It is going ill with Mama, at least I think it is.'

'It is hard, always hard, but she has done it many times before and will come through again.'

'Please.' I took his hand and his arm and tugged. 'Papa.'

'Yes. Of course,' he said, and gave one last look up the path away from the house and turned to accompany me.

We heard her from outside the bedroom, the sound more animal than human: growling almost. At the end of the hallway Hugh peered around the door. I shook my head and he disappeared. We pushed the door open. Mama was in a desperate condition, rocking her head from side to side, her mouth open. I would have known that even without Papa's stricken face.

'Where's Stanton?' I asked.

'He should be back,' Papa said. He hesitated and then went to Mama, holding her hands to his mouth. But she was beyond comprehension and plucked her hands from his, fretful, and he turned back to me. 'Hester, we must do something.' He stood and moved away, as far from Mama as could be while still being in the room. His mouth worked and he put three fingers against it, and still his lips moved beneath them. He shut his eyes and swayed and took his hand away from his mouth and clutched the door and began to swing it.

'Papa,' I said, rather sharp.

'Eh?' he said, startled. 'Oh, the Lord bless us and keep us all.'

'Please.'

There was the sound of the back door slamming and heavy boots coming up the hall and I leapt up and pulled the door from Papa and flung it open. It was Stanton, his coat still on, his hat in his hands, wet from the rain, and the cold and life pouring from him. It would be winter soon. Water dripped from the bottom of his coat onto the floor.

'We can't get the dray through,' he said. 'A tree's down across the track. Even if it weren't it's not safe. To take her in this is madness. She's better here.'

'It's very bad, Stanton. Could someone come here?' I said.

'Who? How long would it take for them to come?'

'Stanton, we must,' I said. 'Else she'll—'

'Down the lagoon then, to the Travellers Rest. Nellie Robinson will know what to do.'

'What, row her? It's too far.'

'There is nothing else. Make haste now, Hett, do.'

When I think badly of Stanton and Hugh, as I often did then, I remember that night and all they did. They were calm when Papa was not, and held Mama firm when we had to move her despite the pain it caused. I had seen Stanton be as calm with cows struggling to calve, and how they appeared to trust him. Papa stood aside with his face buried in his hands while Hugh and Stanton carried her out – an awkward thing since she was crying out and struggling to break free of them – and I gathered up quilts to line the bottom of the boat to make her as comfortable as might be possible. Papa stumbled behind us to the boat and sat away from Mama. I crouched next to her in the bottom of the boat to do what I could to ease the pain, which was very little. I would have stayed behind to be with Fred and Addie and Albert, but Mama had hold of my hand as if it were the only thing keeping her from plunging into darkness, and she wouldn't let go, so Hugh stayed behind, watching on as we pulled away. The rain had cleared by then.

Rowing away from the jetty across the slap of black water I could make out the shadowed back of the peninsula vast against the sky and then we were lost in the dark with the chirrup and groan of the oars in their locks as they gouged the water and flung it back, the wind fingering the reeds, the soft croon and rustle of a million life forms and inside the boat Mama rigid at our feet, crying out at my attempts to bring comfort. She was an animal in a trap and we could not set her free.

Stanton rowed uncomplaining, but strong as he was he had to stop to rest. Papa spelled him twice and I did once. It was slow though and when Mama's moans died down I think we all lost heart, but kept going because to stop would be to admit that hope was quite gone.

Darkness began to thin on the horizon and pale gauze light drifted up the lagoon and flowed over and around its islands and in the distance we saw the place where the creek enters the lagoon and the short jetty a little way further in. We crept towards it and it began to loom. Finally, Stanton flung the boat rope over a stanchion and we drew alongside. He and Papa got out and went running along the jetty and up the slope towards the inn. Mama was quite still by then, her face clammy to the touch and cooler than I liked. Her hands when I held them and rubbed them were cool too, and unmoving.

I heard their voices before I saw them and then they were coming down the slope through the ghostly light, as if they were appearing from another world than the one I was sharing with Mama, their breath huffing out, hanging in the cold air before disappearing. Mrs Robinson was in her nightgown still, and with a coat on top of that, and her thin plait snaked from beneath her bed cap. Her boots were unlaced and she stumbled once or twice in her haste before righting herself.

They clattered up the jetty. 'Oh, Mrs Robinson,' I said when they reached me. 'I'm afraid.'

'What? What now, my duck?' she said. 'Let Nellie have a look and we'll see what we might do.' She stepped out of her boots and let herself down nimble and swift as a spider and held her weight with her arms at the jetty's edge to keep the boat steady while I shifted to give her room. She moved then, crouching by Mama's head, and stroked her hair from her face where it had stuck with the water flicking from the oars. She put the backs of her fingers and then her palm against Mama's cheek, and frowned. 'Come now, Mrs Finch,' she said. 'We'll have you out and see if we can ease your suffering.' And she put an arm behind Mama's head, at her neck, and tried to raise her. Mama's head fell back. 'Wake up now, Mrs Finch, if you please,' she said, and when she still didn't move Mrs Robinson picked up her hand again and rubbed it hard and pinched and twisted the small fold of skin she'd raised on its back, concealing it from us as best she could in the curve of her lap, but Mama still did nothing and, looking over her shoulder past Papa who stared dumb and listless to my brother, Mrs Robinson said, 'Stanton Finch, come help me now, my sweet, and we'll lift your mammie out and then we might see what's to be done.' Her voice, become a trifle hearty, set me shaking.

I clambered upright and the boat rocked again and Stanton took hold of my hand and heaved me onto the jetty and took my place in the boat. With the greatest delicacy they raised Mama until she was sitting, and looking down – suddenly as if from a great distance – I was able to see what they had not yet: Mama's white nightgown all dark with blood behind. I could not help crying out.

Mrs Robinson put her hand to Mama's neck and I knew what she had discovered from the way she took her hand away and touched her fingers to Mama's eyes, and told Stanton to let her lie back.

She was quiet before she spoke again: 'She's gone now and I am sorry for it, my dears. That's the way of it sometimes. The Lord taketh away, that he does, and there's no knowing when that time may be, as I know too well with my poor dear Willie.' She wiped a quick hand over her cheeks and pulled the quilts over Mama again, tucking her in – for all our sakes, if not Mama's any longer – and almost as an afterthought, with the utmost gracefulness (for which I will always remember her fondly, no matter what people said of her later) drew a loose fold across her face, hiding us from its uncanny stillness. 'Come now, my dears, and have a bite and a nice cup of good sweet tea. I'm so sorry for it. There's nothing to be done here, and a long journey back.'

It was the strangest thing that we did stop at the inn. At first I thought I could not leave Mama alone like that and sat on the jetty with my legs curled up inside my skirts and my skirts doubled and wrapped around me like a shroud and the rest of me hunched deep within my coat. But watching Stanton and Mrs Robinson walking away rather close (Mrs Robinson tripping on her bootlaces again, still untied, and Stanton's hand at her elbow) and Papa drifting after them childlike, and looking at Mama below – a thing now – I didn't like to stay and leapt up and ran after them. I never loved my body as well as I did that morning: all the life of me coursing through me, which I felt almost as an animal pleasure, and for the first time sensed an affinity with Stanton, what it might be like to live in his skin, but all these things were only flickers on the edge of my thinking. A small despicable corner of me was glad that it was Mama who had died and not I, even though she was the greater loss and I missed her already. I was alive, alive, alive, and did not want to stay with someone who was dead.

I was fast and with my skirts held high I caught Papa and Stanton and Mrs Robinson easily and didn't stop but went running along the rutted track leaving them and their shouts of surprise behind until finally, finally I could run no more and stopped, panting and sobbing, and I swore to myself right there that I would not allow myself to become like Mama, that I would never die in such circumstances because someone had decided my life for me. No one would make me live where I did not wish to. Becoming anything was so far into the future though, and there was this time to be lived through, and no seeing where it might end. Just, now, that there was the long walk back to the inn. I was hot even after taking my coat off.

Perhaps I went into the inn in a rush. Everyone looked up startled when I opened the door onto the crowded kitchen, where the maid, Jane, moved about tending the fire and pouring tea and bringing toasted bread and eggs to the table, which smelled more delicious than anything else I had ever smelled in my life. Stanton was eating with the greatest efficiency. Papa's eggs had been punctured and the yolks had spread. He poked at them and took a bite of toast.

'Come now,' Mrs Robinson said. 'Sit down here' – she patted the rough bench at her side – 'Jane will bring you what you would like.' She sipped her tea and regarded me. Her eyes were sharp without being hard. She was used to making judgements about people, I think. I hadn't noticed that about her when we last visited. Perhaps she had concealed it. 'Hard for girls like you.' Her voice was quite soft, too low for Papa and Stanton to hear – and they were sunk deep in their own thoughts.

'Why?' I said.

'You're not the eldest are you?' And then, 'No, there's your brothers, isn't that so?'

'The eldest girl.'

'The same thing. I know, my dear, I know. It's the expectations that hold you back. They'll kill you in the end, if you're not careful, suck the life right out of you. Run, I say. Run whenever you should have the chance, don't spare a glance back or you'll turn to salt or stone. When the agent came to the workhouse looking for girls to travel to Australia I put myself forward, made the most of that chance. I had no idea what might become of me; it was only that it might be something better but I took it and so should you when the time comes. There's more than one way to die, with all respect to your dear mama.'

'My mother said something like it to me just before she died.'

'A sensible woman then. Wise. Don't forget.'

'I must stay. There are my younger brothers and sisters.'

'Even so,' Mrs Robinson said. 'When the time comes, and it will, don't miss it.'

It was a long row back despite the current being with us this time. Papa sat away from Mama's little body and drank from a bottle that Mrs Robinson had thrust into his hand. I took the oars twice and the boat was heavy with all the bodies it carried.

There was nothing but sadness to meet us at the other end. Hugh and Fred dug a grave halfway up a slope a short distance from the house. Addie and Tull drifted around after Mary who kept looking for Mama, like a lost calf. The dismal sound of Papa hammering as he made the coffin in the shed rang out for the rest of the afternoon. That night he sat on his own in the parlour and when I went in to light the fire he watched while I arranged sticks over cones of she-oak. I took some coals from the stove in the dining room and the heat of them spread through the metal pan and up its handle and made me shiver. I felt I would never be warm again. When I returned with it to the parlour, Papa's glass was full again.

'Have you ever considered this room, Hester?' he said. 'What would you say it resembles?'

'I don't know, nothing but what it is.' I couldn't say that it had once reminded me of a byre.

'A ship's cabin, I would say,' he said. 'A weighted line will hang true, and yet see this lamp?'

'Yes, Papa.' It swayed a very little in some draught.

'It reveals to me that the house is not true, was not built true, that I am no builder nor ever will be. It is I and not the line that has failed. The walls and the floor and the roof conform in their wrongness – see? – while the lamp, which is true, appears the liar.'

He was right in what he said. The lines of walls and door and windows were not parallel with the lamp line, the same as in Mama's room. 'Papa,' I said.

He watched while I put the coals around the kindling and bent and blew, sending sparks and then flames crackling. A pleasant smoke pulsed into the room and sucked back up the chimney. It was a smell of life to me. We needed to be warm because we lived still.

The light of the flames that Papa now stared into threw shifting gleams and shadows across the lines of his brow and cheeks. It was getting dark. I picked a long twig from the wood basket and lit its end and went to light the lamp.

'Please don't, Hester. Leave me here like this. I prefer not to see the lamp line. On a night like this it makes me feel at sea. At any moment I expect a wave to roll beneath the house and rush the gap at the door and smash a window.' His voice moved like the sea itself, slow and regular and inevitable. He lifted his head. 'Smell the salt?'

We buried Mama the next morning. Papa spoke the words of the service. I could not help noticing the horror on Tull's face when we lowered her rough coffin into the ground and threw handfuls and then spadesful of earth over it and tamped it down.

12

THE COORONG
JUNE 1858

Papa said, 'We could have cleared the path if we'd discovered the branch sooner.' The smoke from his pipe was thick around him and he stared into it as if answers might be found somewhere within. 'It wasn't there two days before she— I should have thought. I should have looked.'

'Why would you? It's never happened before. That part at least is not your fault.' Oh, I should not have said that.

He swung around. 'I beg your pardon?'

'I meant only that it was night, Papa. It would not have changed anything.'

His gaze was fixed on me. 'It would have given us a chance.'

'No, Papa,' I said. 'I think it would not, a branch that size.' I was almost out of patience with him. His brooding could not restore Mama to us.

Tull had been gone for some days already. He had been mystified by us – not by our sadness, rather by our actions. He had watched us carefully after we buried Mama, as if expecting something more to happen or to discern more in our quiet. It was such a settled muffling thing. We were finished so quickly with disposing of her.

Papa wrote to Grandmama and Grandpapa to let them know the terrible news. That winter we dwelled in quiet, even Addie. It was a study to watch us all, as I sometimes did, but not an amusement. We never mentioned Mama except by mistake, and did not use favourite things of hers: a spoon, a tea-cup, a serving dish. Perhaps the others did as I did – found somewhere private when sadness struck. Except for Mary. She was like a small boat adrift and there was nothing we could do to settle her. Sometimes Addie had red eyes. She collected posies of winter flowers and laid them on Mama's grave – a solitary task.

Papa sat at the table or on the veranda if the weather was not too cold after the day's work was done, staring at nothing at all. When Mary put her hand to his knee and commanded, 'Up, up,' he looked at her, sometimes hauling her up absently. She clambered about his lap, patting his cheeks and teasing his whiskers and exploring his pockets until finally she had his attention. But she couldn't hold it. She wandered about looking behind doors. I found her part way up the track once on my way out to the washing lines, and she just a pale shape, a spent rose with its petals lolling in a breeze. When I called to her she ran faster and I had to chase her. And when I caught her and was holding her hot little body to me and smoothing her wispy hair from her face and asked what she was about, she said, 'Looking for Mama.'

'But she is gone, Mary. Quite gone. She won't come back, not ever.'

'I want her.'

'She can't be here, sweetheart. She's in heaven.'

'I want to go.'

'You can't. You're not dead.'

Meals were solemn occasions. Skipper was plush with the good fortune of our misery. Papa began to drink a little in the evening. He rode to the Travellers Rest for supplies and on his return reported that Mrs Robinson had married a Mr Martin, who was helping to run the inn now. We clung to Papa's presence; he was the only parent we had left. We avoided the parlour. It reminded us too much of Mama, with her sewing put by on a side table where she might pick it up when she had a moment to spare and her shawl tossed over the arm of her chair where she had dropped it during her first pains of birth. No one had moved them. The dining room was warm, and if it was overfull with people and furniture, the light within and the company let us forget the darkness closing outside.

A letter arrived from Grandpapa. We watched as Papa read it.

'What does it say?' Addie asked.

'He asked if we would care to live with them in Adelaide.'

'May we?' I said. My mind moved so swiftly. In less than a second I was in town.

'Naturally not. We cannot live on their charity.'

'Oh.'

'They wondered if they could visit us here. But I think not.' He nodded his head. 'I think not. The journey is too rough and we have nowhere to accommodate them. So, I will write to let them know.' He threw the letter in the fire.

Papa placed his knife and fork down one evening and drew himself up and cleared his throat. He had our attention. 'We will fell the tree. We should have done it before. We will do it now so it cannot happen again.'

There was a moment of silence. I wondered if there were more, but from his expectant look around the table it seemed that was all.

Papa said, 'We cannot have the path blocked. In another emergency we could not get through.'

'But you cleared that branch.'

'It might happen again.'

'We could move the path around the tree,' Stanton said. 'Easier by far.'

'We do not do things for the ease of them. We do not avoid every obstacle, every impediment in our lives. Imagine if we went around every tree when making a road. The expense of the extra distance; slowing for a winding track.'

'It's winding already,' I said.

Stanton leaned towards Papa. 'I just meant this one tree, because it's on our track not the main route, and because of its size.'

Papa put his hand to the table and I could not help studying his slender fingers, and how our life here had coloured them and scarred them and chipped their nails. 'No,' he said, quiet still. 'We deal with them, not retreat. We overcome them. I would hope that you could see the importance of that.' And he gave one of his looks of sorrow and disappointment, which we all hated so.

There was no point in further talk. He had set his mind to it as he had when he said we must move to the Coorong or face ruin. He reminded me of a picture of an Old Testament prophet I saw in Adelaide. Elijah perhaps. I do not remember. It was the cast of his features and the fixedness of his gaze, his outflung hand of command. It could not be opposed.

The work of felling the tree began. It was the largest thereabouts, with a dense canopy that the cattle liked to stand in the shade of on hot days. Each morning we made our way up the track in expectation. We were captivated by the excitement of the task, also by a wish to forget about Mama even for a short while. Despite our anticipation, melancholy grew. It was a noble tree. Its tips of wet winter growth were green gold and bright as stained glass. And it was so various in its structure; its branches were formed by wind so it seemed they were trying to drag the tree free and flee towards the inland desert that Charles and his father had told of. There was a great scar all down one side where the surface of the trunk had been cut away, and a thick rind of new growth, muscular, bulged about its edges.

'One of their canoe trees,' Fred said.

'How do you know?' I asked.

'I've seen them. You must have too – on the lagoon.'

'I didn't know. How would I?'

'They have no saws. They are very clever with what they have. Don't tell Tull I said that.'

'No, I won't,' I said, remembering the offence that Fred had caused over the fish pen.

It was a perilous task. There was the long two-handed saw, which Stanton and Hugh sweated with the effort of using, and Papa directing the angles of the cuts, chopping in at the corners with his axe, and Skipper running between the two groups of us, the cutters and the watchers, as if reporting important news. Sometimes the boys wiggled the saw free and began worrying away at a different place. It reminded me of a picture I saw once of a bear being baited by bulldogs. The tree appeared to tremble sometimes, but perhaps that was my imagination. In the evening Papa sat at the supper table and announced with great purpose and a rubbing of his hands that he thought, he really thought, that tomorrow would be the day when it would finally fall. 'Isn't that right, boys?' Hugh and Stanton would nod.

It was only after a few days that I began to see Stanton's fear. He shied away at creaks and groans or in gusts of strong wind. Papa's voice would carry, louder, all the way to us, 'Come, Stanton. The saw won't go with only one of you,' and he would be dragged back in. As the week drew on and Papa made his nightly prediction of success for the morrow, Stanton needed to be coaxed to agree.

'We should leave it to the winter storms. They'll bring it down soon enough.'

'We can't. It could fall on someone,' Papa said.

'He's right,' Hugh said.

'It could fall on us,' Stanton said.

Papa set his knife and fork down. 'We will finish the job we have started, and I'm afraid, Stanton, that you must help. Let that be an end of it.'

We wanted it to be done by then. We were tired of keeping an eye on Mary and running to rescue her and save her from all the consequences of her curiosity. She was so fast now and could disappear in a moment.

The next day Stanton set his course towards the ruin of the trunk, its wedges and gouges and the long wounds ringing it. He and Hugh commenced sawing downward to meet another cut.

Finally after all those days there was a deep creaking groan and something higher, screeching, and Papa bellowing, 'Away, away. Leave the saw.' It was as if the tree paused and gathered up its final energy, and there was in Hugh's face a mixture of excitement and terror, and in Stanton's just terror and his mouth open in a yell, and all of them fleeing as the tree fell with a great cracking, its branches and leaves rising and subsiding and rising again like waves in a storm, and Stanton submerged beneath. It stilled. It had been large while standing; it was vast now, bigger than our house, bigger than our house in North Adelaide even.

Addie clung to my arm and screamed, 'Stanton.'

Papa and Hugh ran back and began burrowing into the leaves, calling and calling, and we ran to help, darting around like so many terriers after a rat. Closer to I could see the torn red heart of the trunk. There was a voice from somewhere inside.

Stanton.

Albert found him. 'Blood. He's all over blood. He's bleeding, Hettie.'

Papa and Hugh were in a frenzy cutting him free, the branches flying away behind them, Fred and Albert pulling them out of the way, and they came to Stanton and heaved him beneath his arms out and upright. Thick red blood welled over one eye and eased down his face in slow ribbons, which he wiped at. Papa gripped him by both shoulders and peered into his eyes.

'You can see? Your eye? Close the other eye now. Here, let me,' and he put a hand over Stanton's undamaged eye.

Stanton jerked free and away and was on the point of shouting something, and his arms rose as if he might shove Papa but he didn't. He was still and then he swayed – as the tree had done on pleasant days – and Papa forced his head down. He put his hands to his knees.

'Water,' Papa said.

Albert ran in with a beaker from the pail. Papa took it and pushed it into Stanton's hands and he gripped it and staggered upright, Papa holding his elbow, and drank. Papa said something I couldn't hear and Stanton blinked and wiped his eye again and stared ahead and nodded. He was as bloodless white as Mama had been in death.

Papa shut his eyes and murmured something, a prayer of thanks or some such. Fred and Albert stood back. It is strange the respect with which an encounter with mortality is greeted. Stanton had always before gone about in a cloak of invincibility.

'You are going to have a terrible scar, Stanton,' Addie said.

'Be quiet,' Stanton said.

'Quickly now,' Papa said. 'We must get you back home and Hester can stitch it. It's too big to leave.'

'Please no,' Stanton said.

'It's Hester or Adelaide.'

Stanton looked with horror at Addie.

'A tree has just fallen on you and you're scared of a few stitches. Brave Stanton,' Addie said.

Stanton blazed now. 'Shut up, Addie. No one will want a tease and a shrew like you.'

Addie flinched. 'And who will want you now your pretty face is ruined?'

'Stop,' Papa said. 'Quickly now, Stanton.' He pressed a grubby handkerchief against Stanton's brow.

We blundered down the slope. I shoved Mary at Addie to mind so then Mary cried.

'Take her for a walk or something. Think, Addie,' I said.

'The chickens, Mary. Shall we see the chickens?' Addie said, and Mary was diverted.

We went into the house. Papa fetched Mama's workbasket and left the house again.

Hugh stood at Stanton's side. 'You said it wasn't safe. I'm sorry for it,' he said.

'There was no stopping him,' Stanton said.

I washed his face clean with water from the kettle and a little soap and dabbed it dry as best I could with one of the cloths prepared for the baby we never knew. The cut was to the bone and more than an inch long through the brow and the bleeding would not stop. Stanton gripped the table edge then crossed his arms, folding them in front and holding them tight, caught between bravado and fear.

I lifted the needle. 'You must stay still now, Stanton.'

Flesh is not like cloth: it is slippery and thick and resistant and fits snug there on the brow. The sewing of it is a finicky task. I didn't know how to approach it. Should I do a running stitch or cross-stitch, and how tight and how to keep the sides matched? Separate

166

knots so the stitches wouldn't pull against each other, I decided, and I would start in the middle to keep the edges matched up. I pinched the skin together and pushed the needle in and through one flap, then the other and pulled the thread through and tied a knot and cut it. The blood kept seeping, more at each new puncture I made. I gave a bundle of the baby cloths to Hugh and a bowl of warm water. 'Here,' I said. 'Give me the cloths when I say, wet then dry between stitches, else I can't hold the skin.'

Once, I remarked, 'When Mama taught me to sew, I don't believe she had this in mind,' which made Hugh snort. I will say this for Stanton though: he did not flinch or jerk away when I was working on him despite the effort it took to force the needle through his swollen flesh. There was just a trembling of him as of a frightened animal. I did not judge him for that. I would not be so calm. Addie would be in hysterics. Stanton's eye was half-closed in the end, and all about it was puffy and bruising up and there were the stitches creeping across it like beetle legs across a seam of meat.

'Perhaps I should have used another colour. Pink, something that showed less,' I said, standing back to consider, as if he were a sampler I had been working on.

Stanton leapt up and made for the parlour. His shirt was torn at the back and the skin showed through paler than his arms and face which had become so brown. He had a gash on his arm too and scratches everywhere. I followed and found him looking at himself in the looking glass on the barley twist chest, as best he could in the room's poor light, angling his head and the mirror.

'It will mend,' I said. It was not the moment for teasing. He looked at me with narrowed eyes as if he suspected I was mocking him. But the horror when he disappeared beneath the tree and the silence and his courage in the kitchen were with me still. 'It is only now that it looks bad. I truly think so. The swelling will go down.'

'People will laugh.'

'The stitches will come out and the black eye will go. The scar will fade. It will, Stanton.'

Stanton looked back at the mirror. 'It wasn't safe. He knew it wasn't and yet he would not stop. He is mad, Hett. If you had heard him out there. It was like the tree was, was possessed. I don't know what. What was he thinking?'

'Of course he isn't mad.'

'What would you say then? What would you call it?'

'He is determined. He will not be opposed. In such a mood he cannot admit defeat. He *will* not.'

'He is not safe to be around. He would let us die on a point of principle if he had to.' I had the feeling that he was speaking from a distance, even though we were but a foot or two apart.

I put my hand on his arm. 'What do you mean?'

'I tell you I will not be put through such a thing again. I will leave before. I had time while the tree was falling to know that he had killed me, I was sure of it. Not again. Not for me, not ever.'

I went back to the table and began setting Mama's sewing basket to rights, which in my haste to find a fine needle and thread had become a tangle. At the bottom of the basket, among bobbins and spare buttons, I came across a flint arrowhead – one of Mama's childhood collection from England – and went in search of the rest of them, finally going out to the stable to ask Papa, where he was sitting on a stool cleaning a harness.

'In the dresser drawer,' he said. 'In our— Wait.' And he dropped his work and went into the house, not speaking, with me following behind, and into his room for several minutes – enough so that I began to wonder whether I should knock – and returned with the small black velvet bag that I did not remember until that moment. 'Here.' He handed it to me expressionless and went outside, not even pausing to look at Stanton, who had come out of the parlour and now stood at the table pressing the swelling on his brow.

'Leave it be,' I said.

'There was no need,' Stanton said. He had said it already, but it still made no sense.

'No.' We all knew what Papa was like when he had the bit between his teeth, how we could not resist from habit and from fear of something within him. Not one of us would cross him lest he revealed something at his core that we could not help dreading and did not like to be reminded of, even though we could not have agreed that it existed much less said what it was. It was relentless. It would yield to nothing.

I did not know what more could be said about it. I spread a cloth on the table and emptied the bag onto it. Oh, I remembered the little flints so well, all their shapes: some smooth and flat and oval, with a ridge down the centre on one side so that they fitted cunningly into one's fingers and hand, or that had one smooth edge and one fine and serrated and seemed ready for something that I could not tell. Others had clear purpose: two arrowheads and a small spearhead with murderous points and raised veins and serrations down their edges. All of these intention-filled things inside a velvet pouch.

They had belonged to the people who lived around Chichester. Mama used to tell us how the Romans subdued them with their superior numbers and skills and weapons. I played them about in my palms. They made a dry sound, musical almost, as they rubbed against each other in my hand and again when I dropped them into a china bowl, and were translucent when held to the light.

The tree was too big to clear or saw through. Without saying anything more about it or involving Papa the boys cleared a new path around it and the tree began its long decay. Tull came back not long after, towards the end of winter. He asked Fred about the tree. But what could Fred say? That our father had gone mad? It didn't make sense to us either.

'We told him not to,' Fred said.

'It's been there a long time,' Tull said.

'I don't doubt it,' Fred said. 'I'm sorry for it. We tried to stop him. Tell your family that.'

Tull stared at him as if he was trying to decide what to say next, and when he couldn't he turned around and strode back up the path. I wonder now if he had gone to tell his people.

Papa stopped sitting on the settee that he and Mama had shared on mild evenings. He began something new in the shed on his quiet own. It was made from driftwood, that much we knew. As winter turned to spring and the sky was again filled with birds he took an interest in wood pieces we brought back from our roaming, tossing almost all in the wood basket, placing a very few other pieces neatly – as neatly as could be for twisted branches and twigs that had turned to bonewood in seawater or salt air. We began to see without speaking of it or knowing their purpose what he would save. The sound he made in his throat like a dog's low growl was the only sign of him taking pleasure in anything in those days.

Finally one day, it – a chair made for one – was done and he and Fred carried it down from the stable. The thing had a wild Viking air, as did he sitting on it. The top of its back curved, its ends twisting away like antlers, and its arms were attenuated at the ends and fingered the air. In the half-light they could have been part of him. He sat so still, as if he had been transfixed by the seat and the waterish kingdom before him. Once or twice I stood at his side and aligned my sight to his and stared down the lagoon and felt as close to him as I ever would again, for a fleeting moment understanding how his reluctance to leave might be as much to do with pride as bitterness. I could not hold the thought.

Things happened in the midst of monotonous sadness. The great wonder was the mail boat, which began regular trips down the lagoon. 'I call it providential,' Papa said. 'Imagine how much cheese it will be able to carry.' The sight of it chugging forward and its steam and smoke trailing back was a spectacle. A whistle alerted us to mail and one of us would row out to collect it. It was a cord that tied us to the world in a way that the track did not. Letters and papers arrived from town occasionally. If Mama had lived to see it, I think she might have felt better. Grandmama and Grandpapa invited us to visit them if we wished, which Papa would not allow, and they had a little news about town life. And I had a letter from Charles, which I took away to read in private. It began: *Dear Hester, I hope you are well*, and continued in a similar vein. That is, it said nothing, except that he had been on another expedition inland with his father, who was doing quite well with his business ventures, and how he, Charles, wished to become an artist, *which aim*, he said, *Father does not approve*. He finished: *Yours, Charles*, which could have been taken any number of ways. I carried it around in my dress pocket to keep it from Addie's curious eyes. I did not wish for anything from him, yet I could not help thinking of him and sometimes touching the letter in my pocket. It made me feel less lonely.

There were letters in a strange hand and with no direction other than Papa's. I handed them to him and he took them.

'What are they about, Papa?' I asked one day when he opened an envelope and, seeing its contents, shoved the whole into his inside jacket pocket.

'Business. I borrowed a little to purchase the cheese moulds, from a gentleman farmer on the lakes, Mr Baker, who sold them to me.'

'You mean you bought them on credit.'

'Well, yes. But there will be no problem in the repaying. He has a guarantee in any case. He is just reminding me that the payment will soon be due.'

'What could you guarantee?'

He looked away. 'Never worry about that. I have it in hand, my dear.'

Of course I worried after that, but he would tell me nothing more.

Once Albert came galloping down the track: 'The Celestials. Come see, quickly.'

He was in such a lather that Addie and Fred and Tull and I rode bareback up the track after him, Fred fortunately shutting Skipper inside or I don't know what might have happened. It was a long line of men with jet black plaited tails of hair, identically robed in sailor-like pants and light, loose collarless jackets, each carrying a pail suspended at either end of a yoke of wood. This flexed with their movement: all those rhythms and their appearance presenting a curious sight among the sheets of sky and sea and land. The ground thrummed with their movement. They spared us hardly a glance and what they would have thought of a band of ragged children with their legs hanging down the sides of their bare horses I could not imagine.

'Something must have gone amiss. Too stormy to dock at Robe perhaps,' Papa said at supper. We had given up hope of ever seeing them.

'There might have been a new strike,' Hugh said.

'I think we would have heard before they did in China,' Papa said.

'But think.' There was strain in Hugh's voice and he leaned forward in his chair. 'It could be the answer, Papa.'

'Hugh' – Papa's voice, normally reedy, was low now – 'I think not. Gold is for fools and speculators.'

'What are we doing here if not speculating? I could go.'

'Not on your own. It's not safe. Remember the Ballarat uprising.'

'With Stanton then.' He was ablaze now.

Stanton leapt to his feet. 'Yes.'

'No.'

But two days later when we woke in the morning they were gone, leaving a letter for Papa.

'What does it say?' Albert asked.

Papa looked at us sitting about the breakfast table, with dislike I would say, as if it was just a matter of time before we too betrayed him. 'They have gone to try their luck in the goldfields,' he said with frightening quiet. 'At the worst possible time.' Cheese-making was upon us. For more than a week he gave up directing any of us. He stayed away, leaving the house early and returning late, if at all, so I had the running of things. It wasn't so bad. Tull took charge of the yard work and the stock, working with Fred and Albert, and I managed the cheese. Without Stanton and Hugh we could not do all the milking. We divided the herd, milking one half, and leaving the calves with the cows in the other half. It was the best we could do until Papa was himself again.

I wondered what it would be like to be a man, to be Papa. I thought lonely; they are solitary creatures for all they work in each other's company. 'Hole in the fence there, wire's out back, rain later', they say, like the smoke signals that are used by the natives in some parts of the country. For all I knew it would not be so different for the blacks: 'Cold today, cockles for dinner, fix the fish traps, rain later'. They are all of them, as much as I can make out, free as gulls wheeling across water and earth and space alike around the belly of the world.

In some way it was the sight of Tull so busy and so able that seemed to settle Papa again. He looked up from his newspaper to watch him reading one evening.

'See, Hester, what we have created? But for his skin he is as white as any one of you. Others will follow.'

It seemed to me that Tull had made himself as much as anything, but Papa would not want to hear that. 'He is a remarkable person,' I said. 'But what will happen to him? Will he stay here working for you or get his own run? Who will he marry do you think?'

Papa rustled his paper and turned a page. 'He has connections with his own kind. Something will be arranged for him. He can teach them what he has learned. See?' The plan was so neat, so certain to him. Perhaps it would come right, but watching the game of draughts that Tull and Addie struck up, and the two of them talking and laughing, I was not sure.

A letter arrived from Hugh to let us know that they were at Ballarat having walked to the inland route and hitched rides on passing drays. Papa said, 'Well, happen they will strike it rich after all. We shall see.'

I imagined lighting out to seek my own fortune, leaving without a thought as if family had nothing to do with me, as if they had no corner in my mind or any part of me. My life occupied a small space; it was time that moved: days and weeks and months and seasons and years rolling across me as inevitable as night. Moving any great distance would be like a cut against the grain of time. How had Hugh and Stanton done it with such ease? Any one of the things that held me at Salt Creek – Mary or Albert or Addie or Fred – was enough to stop me running. I hated Hugh and Stanton for their selfishness; I envied it too. Sometimes I took Birdie and galloped her up and down the track until we both were panting. It gave me the illusion of flight.

In November, when Papa judged that the cheeses were ripe enough, he sent them up the lagoon to Goolwa and from there by paddle steamer around the coast to Port Adelaide. But the large cheeses, when cut into in the grocers' shops, were found to be spoiled. Even the small ones were poor quality. It was as if our misery had poured into them. A number of grocers demanded refunds but Papa could not repay them, having spent the money already. The grocers were not pleased and declined further risk, which I could not blame them for since they had been left out of pocket. We were left with the cheese moulds and our mouldering cheese and Papa's hopes, dashed again.

After we had the news of the cancelled orders I found Papa resting his arms against the paddock fence, looking at the cows. 'We'll have to let them go, Hester,' he said. 'I'm finished with them.'

'Could we go back to the small cheeses?' I said.

'There's no money in it, my dear, or not enough and never will be. If we don't know that by now, we have learned nothing.'

He kept only a few cows in the home pasture for our own use. The rest he and the boys drove out onto the run's expanses, planning to sell them when the calves were old enough to be moved.

When I look back at that year I see that we were all right until Mama died. I think we were. Every wrong and every setback that ever befell us began to concentrate then, like seawater drying until just a salt patch remained on which nothing would grow. Even when her spirits were low she'd had a softening effect on Papa.

And for me there was something else, beyond the loss of her and her gentleness, which it shamed me to think on, and that was that with her gone so also was my hope of escape. I had had no clear idea of when the future might arrive or what it might hold, but that I would leave Salt Creek had been certain. There would come a time when the children were old enough to be left to Mama and I was of an age when Papa could no longer make me stay. Now the failure of the dairy meant there was no prospect of a return to town. All that, a life of my own choosing, must be forgotten now and if I fell into despair sometimes when I was alone, on the sand hills or over a wash trough, I'm sure that would be no wonder to anyone.

Tull came into the kitchen one day when my face was wet. A magpie that I fed meat scraps approached the door and tipped its head and made a sound in its throat. Tull watched it with the same grave interest that he watched me. I wiped my face on my sleeve and threw some meat at the magpie and it plucked it from the ground and flew onto the veranda railing.

Tull said, 'What is it telling you?'

'That it's hungry.'

He shook his head. 'No, something else.'

'I don't think so,' I said.

'You need to pay attention,' Tull said. 'Listen. Watch.'

But I did not hear or see anything.

Life is so much absence and emptiness and vivid stretches and disconnected fragments when everything happens; things that light up in memory while all around is darkness. Some of the people I have known are no more than fragments themselves, because I knew only a part of them or because their lives were short. Mary is one. There are so few now who knew her, but for the time that we had her she was someone and I mention her even though she had no part to play really, except that she was sweet and loving and missed in her absence, and that the loss of her made us all grow harder. It would have been difficult for us to grow sadder.

She glances into my mind best when I am not thinking of her or of anything: at a movement of Joss's shoulder, the sight of a basket of eggs, a fistful of daisies. We took her out with us onto the sea beach sometimes. She clutched our clothes – a collar, a gathering of lace – and faced the wind, her eyes squeezed all but shut, sand in her lashes and her clothes billowing. The sound of them: a high snap like a small sail. She ground her fists into her eyes. I sank down in the shelter of a sand hill and pulled her onto my lap and bade her shut her eyes, holding her head against my shoulder and putting a hand over her eyes to hold them closed.

'Can't see.' She shook her head.

'Move your eyes, Mary, pretend you can see. It will feel better soon.'

Her lidded eyes rolled beneath my hand.

'Good girl,' I said, and presently, 'better?'

She nodded and I released her and her eyes flew open and she blinked at the sudden brightness and her pupils shrank.

She was curious about everything, leaning out of our arms to gaze at the ground and pointing imperiously – 'This way, there' – to set our direction. She liked shells and at first she put them to her mouth as if she were a puppy at a bone. When we put her upon the sand she ambled about until a slope or softness or a gust of wind or her petticoats caught beneath her feet made her collapse. She was old enough for pick-a-backs, and would ride us, droning in our ears, her fingers laced at our throats. Afterwards I felt her fingers still, a phantom touch upon my neck.

'Don't watch the sun, Mary. Don't look at it now.'

She screwed up her eyes and held her fingers above them in a veranda, looking up at Fred and Tull to make sure she had the stance correct and they stood, Fred holding her hand, all of them shielding their eyes and staring across the sea at the skeins of light. I wish I had let her look and look until she would look no more.

'Fast, Hettie,' she shrieked, bouncing up and down on my back. 'More fast!' and she set me galloping along the pathway from the sea beach through the valleys. She lived fast, like one of the summer insects that Fred liked to draw. And when she died of a snake bite it was the worst of that year, worse than Mama. I could not get past the length of her life and the place of it and hated Papa for it, more than for all else combined. Mama might have died even in Adelaide but the snake was in the Coorong. She suffered a great deal before she fell asleep in my arms and later died. I try not to think of her hot body and panting breath and how her death was a labour.

I missed her sticky hand in mine. I would have done anything to have her back, even though part of me knew that the loss of her brought freedom and escape closer. I was not the worst person yet, then. I took some comfort in that.

Afterwards, it was uncomfortable to be near Papa. In the evenings, Fred and Tull and Addie and Albert went walking along the lagoon and sat close to the moored boat, not so far away. If it was cool they lit a fire and the crack and smell of burning driftwood and the sparks from it and the sound of their talk and laughter came up the rise to the house. I went with them once or twice and felt what it was to be part of them – family again, but a different family than our own, nothing to do with Papa or the memories of people who had died or the things we had lost. I could not like him then. The shame of my disloyalty and inconstancy stopped me going with them more often.

Papa gave no sign of noticing. All through that summer the house felt empty and I wondered what difference there was between our current state and being orphans. I wrote to Charles about our year, only the facts, but they spoke well for themselves, I think. A little later I heard from him, a letter of sorrow, and a book, *Jane Eyre*. I took it down, away, to my own seat by the lagoon, and read a little, and cried for the people lost to me, and at the thought that the only person who knew me at all was so far from this shore.

Tull saw me one day in the vegetable garden, doing what I could to encourage the peas to climb their house of sticks. 'Who has cursed you?' he asked.

'Cursed? No one.' That word – the weight of it, as if the word itself carried the darkness of its meaning. I could feel it almost, as close as the salt air touching my skin. 'No one,' I said again, louder. 'Do not say so again, Tull.' I knew he was wrong. I wished I knew I was right.

13

THE COORONG
FEBRUARY 1859

I thought to try to reason with Papa, or at least to find out whether his intentions for us had changed with so much having gone wrong, and sat outside with him in the warm evenings – he on his driftwood chair above his watery kingdom, I on the wooden settee. The wind was coming in hot breaths from the north, slower than during the day and not less dry, wind that was thick and had travelled a long way and was heading away from the land. It was not dark yet, and I watched it ruffling and stroking its way across the water, and the plumes of Papa's pipe smoke travelled with it. It reminded me of our old drawing room, of Papa in his smoking jacket of silk and velvet and his tasselled pumps, enthroned in his brocade chair, tsking at *The Register* and passing on such information as he felt a woman of Mama's standing and breeding and education might be interested in hearing: another school being opened, a new shipment of goods having arrived and the like. Now his sleeves were rolled up roughly and his shirt had no collar. He had not troubled to polish his boots since Mama died, just stamped the dirt off if it got too bad.

He waved his pipe about at distant islands in the lagoon. 'It always puts me in mind of whales breaching. See them about to leap from the water? Fascinating creatures. A gift from God. The bounty of them.' His excitement fell. The bountiful times were over when he bought the whaling station. An old gamble.

Darkness became a shroud. I set a lamp on the table between us and its light bloomed a little way out. I pulled my chair closer and began to weave a darn into a sock, tilting it to the light. I said, because I had wondered, and because his presence appeared so neutral that such a question might not be remarkable, 'Why are we here, Papa?'

He looked at me and drew sharp on his pipe once or twice before allowing the smoke to escape in quick clouds. 'Why, to make our living; to recover what we lost; to do justice to our family; to bring glory to God; to bring God and sow civilization among the natives.' He measured his phrases out in thoughtful puffs and small nods of his head. 'You know that.'

'I mean now, still. Now that the cattle have—' I steadied the darning mushroom within the sock and smoothed the sock over its curve. 'Not done as well as expected,' I finished, weaving the wool in and out of the warp I had made, in and out. 'I wondered perhaps—'

'I have thought a great deal,' Papa said.

'Yes?' I finished a thread and cut a new length, pinching it over the eye of the needle and threading it. He watched as I doubled it back in the sock so it would not pull loose.

'You are like your mother sometimes,' he said. 'It is hard to see, but it is a comfort too.'

'I've been thinking too, Papa, that we could make a life in town. Addie needs society, and Fred needs school. Albert too. There must be something there, people who would help, who would find you a position.' I did not dare mention Grandmama and Grandpapa who would lend us funds at a moment's notice and likely not call in the debt, but Papa's stern stare told me he knew what was in my mind. 'Perhaps I could teach,' I said.

'You should not speak of things you do not understand, my dear. I have borrowed before on good terms and am sure I can do so again, if needed.' He rocked back on his chair legs, kicking off with his toes until he was up against the house. He puffed again and came down with the thud of an axe into wood.

'From whom?' I said.

He ignored the sharpness in my voice and took his pipe from his mouth and poked about in the bowl. It had gone out. He tapped it empty and drew his leather pouch from his pocket. 'Why, from one or two gentlemen farmers of my acquaintance,' he said, his attention to his pipe unwavering. With finnicking movements he pinched some tobacco and filled the pipe's bowl, pressing it down carefully and nipping off any tendrils that were too long and putting them back in the pouch. (He had a thrifty streak that came out in little ways.) He struck a match against the sole of his boot and lit the pipe, pulling in with his mouth until the filaments of tobacco burned red and the smoke rose sweet as any other old comfort. He closed his eyes; he felt it too, I think, how habits made things timeless and thereby restored for a moment things that had passed absolutely. His fingers moved and stroked the curved bowl of the pipe. Albert had a tortoiseshell button from Mama's town coat that he kept about him and liked to hold. It was a secret of his. Papa was as tender with his pipe as he had been with Mama.

He leaned forward in his chair and his pipe hung down in his slack hands and the smoke drifted up in the lamplight. 'I intend to do what is right for you all. You were not aware. The folly of town life, its vapid pleasures.'

'Just people being sociable.'

'But when our fortunes changed, people did also.'

'I don't remember.'

'You wouldn't have known. I cannot forget some of the things people said. Which I would not trouble you with.'

'It's just I think, I wonder, if this is the land for our purposes. Could land turn on us? I have heard that said.'

'Who would say such a thing?' And when I didn't answer, he said, 'That's superstitious talk, Hester, which I will not have in a Christian home. You should know better. I would hope that you had been taught better.'

I did not say that of course I had not been taught better since Mama was dead and I was the one who was teaching and the people we lived among believed us to be cursed and I couldn't help wondering if that was the only thing that explained our circumstances. It seemed common sense rather than superstition. My darning needle began to jerk in the wool. I couldn't stop it.

'No, we will bide a while longer. We are not finished yet. We are not what we were and I have sworn that we will be.'

'But the children,' I said.

'They appear quite well to me.'

'Addie is running wild. I haven't time to stop her.'

His face got that soft doting look. 'She is just lively, as she has always been. No, Hester. We will come to rights, my dear, nothing more certain. We are in God's hands.'

I jerked the thread then and it puckered the darn tight and was ruined. I could have screamed with vexation. I rolled the sock about the needle and put it in the workbasket and took it inside, into my empty room. The window was open. I leaned on the sill. It was all sound: insects and lizards in the thatching, the screaming of crickets and cicadas beyond, and the waves repeating against the sea coast. I was not more than any other thing.

Papa sold the cattle to a Mr Stubbs, who had a profitable run at Lake Albert acquired during the first land release, all of it rich pasture. I do not know what price he got, but there was enough money to purchase three thousand sheep from a gentleman farmer further inland, and he was well pleased for several days together, even going so far as to hum a few jaunty hymns as he went about his tasks. He took Albert and Tull to muster them and left Fred behind with Addie and me. His spirits on their return two weeks later were changed. The sheep were not in quite such good condition as the small flock he had been shown.

'However, a great deal less work than the cows,' he said, meeting no one's eyes. 'The flock will expand soon enough.' He did not provide further explanation, but we were familiar with his abbreviated sentences and the things he wanted us to believe. There was no need for him to tell us all the words. Signs of doubt or worry were taken as disloyalty. He drove some of the sheep onto the peninsula by the crossing south of the Travellers Rest. 'Think of the saving,' Papa said. 'No need for fencing out there.' Fred came back from his expeditions complaining about the mess they made. The remainder grazed our side.

Papa wished for contentment but could not persuade himself of it. There was the unease over the sheep. Occasionally if he were home at midday he looked about at his remaining family, but without pleasure or satisfaction. He began to chafe at Fred, watching him work on his book in the evening. He had filled the first sketch book, and was now using the one Charles had given me. 'Dost think, Hester, that this is the best use of Fred's time?'

'What should he be doing, Papa? He finishes his lessons quickly so he can do this. He will work on the run all afternoon. It's only a little time that he takes.'

Papa stood on the other side of the table, regarding Fred as he might a sheep or a cow, pondering its value.

'He is not much more than a boy,' I said.

'When I was his age—' But he did not continue.

'Were you not at school when you were fifteen?' I asked.

He took my point. 'Yes.'

'Fred would like that.'

He fiddled with his fob chain, following it across his front to the pocket containing his watch. 'He will have to content himself with the books we have and your teaching.'

Fred looked up from his work. His air was distracted and he blinked and rubbed his hair. He was just then drawing one of the spike-stemmed plants that grew about the sand hills, and now its stem rested in a little water in the base of a glass and the light from the window sent its toothed shadow across the table. 'Pardon, Papa?'

'I was speaking to Hester about what you are doing.'

'A drawing for my book.'

'Still? You are grown too old for such things, surely.'

He looked at his page and the intricate work of shading the leaves. 'I think, I hope, it might find a publisher one day. See what I have done?' He turned the pages carefully, one after another, so that we could see his drawings. So many of them. He had made notes too, in his small hand.

'Who would publish such a work?' Papa said.

Fred blinked, a nervous habit of his that betrayed him in ways that his voice did not. 'Grandpapa and Grandmama have connections in London.'

'We will not apply to them for help, Frederick.'

Fred's face fell and he shot a glance at me and when I shook my head said, 'Oh, may I not?'

'And you are too young and without credentials. No one will want a work from someone untrained in drawing and uneducated in botany.'

'These are not so bad, though. I have improved and if no one will want to publish it, they might offer advice.'

'Yes. There is no harm in trying at any rate, Papa, surely,' I said.

Addie came in with a basket of eggs, which she set on the table. She poured a cup of water and leaned against the dresser while she drank.

Fred stroked his fingers across the paper, as if he were trying to calm a frightened creature. The steady touch appeared to soothe him. 'Mr Bagshott might help.'

'Mr Bagshott? Why would he help? How would he?'

'His father is a friend of Mr Darwin and he might forward it to him. You know that Mr Darwin visited Australia?'

'I have heard you mention it once or twice,' he said in his old dry way. 'He did not care for it, as I recollect.'

'No, but think, Papa, if he had come here? I think he might have been interested. Mr Bagshott could send a letter recommending it to his publisher or something of the sort. I do not know exactly.'

'Do you know his direction?'

'Hester does,' Addie said. 'She knows Charles. She likes Charles.' She sounded triumphant almost. I shot her a look of fury before Papa's attention shifted to me.

'Indeed?' he said.

Next to him, unobserved, Addie was smiling. What softness she had, had gone since Mary died.

'As a friend only. And I know where he lives,' I said. 'We write to each other occasionally is all. There is nothing untoward.'

'And yet I did not know.' Papa was not angry precisely, wounded, rather, and shook his head so that I felt I had betrayed him. There had been so few letters, and their contents would be dull to any but me: weather and books, Charles's family, a visit into the hills; and from me to him only news of Salt Creek, which did not vary a great deal. The letters had not been a secret; if asked, I would not have denied them, yet it was true that I preferred that he did not know. Perhaps we all had things we would rather keep to ourselves.

I made Addie hang out the washing later and when she let the sheets drag in the dirt I said she would have to wash them again.

'You are a mean cat sometimes, Hettie,' she said, yanking them off the line.

'*I* am the mean cat? After what you said?'

'Well, you do like him.'

'I do not, and if I did how would you know?'

'You carry his letter about with you. I saw you touching your pocket and looked.'

'Because of you – that's why it's there. You can't be trusted. We're only friends.' I was glad I had hidden the other ones away.

'I know.'

'You read it?'

'Wouldn't you?'

'I was going to help you, but I won't now.'

'See,' she said. 'You are a mean cat, Hester Finch.'

Addie became even more wild and wilful, and galloped along the track on whichever horse was free, and if there was not one she melted away anyway. There was no point in asking Papa to remonstrate, not with Addie. I stopped her at the door one afternoon, holding it to prevent her escape. 'It's not fair, leaving me to do everything.'

'Don't do it then. I'm sure I don't mind,' she said, shoving at the door, against me. 'The boys are busy with the sheep, stupid creatures, and you will only clean and stitch and cook. Where is the fun in that? There is nothing here for me.'

I held the door and would not let her past. 'It is not my preference. I have no time for fun. If I don't do it there will be no food and holes in our clothes and we will be like the blacks grubbing around for cockles.'

'They don't really care for cockles.'

'I don't wonder at it, though I do wonder how you know such a thing.' I looked at her hard but she just folded her arms. I could slap her sometimes – do something to shock her. 'If you would starve otherwise, I suppose the taste is not so bad.'

'I've seen them scraping for them in the sand. I helped one day.'

'Addie.'

'Oh what, Hettie? Don't pick. I've tried them. They are not so bad cooked in a fire. Set them on a stone until they pop in the heat.'

'You will become a savage. Your skin. People will know. Your dresses will be ruined.'

'My frocks are not so fine and pretty these days. I would rather go about naked.'

'Addie.'

'Addie, Addie, Addie. Think, you could do anything. You could run fast as a boy. You could ride like a boy.'

'I do ride like a boy. I ride better than a boy. Bareback. But you mustn't tell Papa, else he will stop me. We are all of us ruined if something happens to me. Papa cannot manage you all, and you can't even manage yourself. What would Mama say if she saw you?'

'What would she say if she saw *you*? Anyway, she's not here.' She spun away from me.

'No.'

'And even when she was, she was not.'

'Not always.'

'At the end. What good did all her work for us do? What life did she have of her own? Where is the fun in that? And you wish me to follow her example. I will not.' The words just ran out of her.

'You'll leave it for me? Addie?'

She turned back to me. 'You know how it was. Do not pretend otherwise.'

I said, 'What is to become of us? I cannot do everything. You need to mind your lessons or you will be here forever. You will never be fit for town life.'

'I don't care.'

'A minute ago you were dull here. Remember what Mama said. A woman of learning can make a sensible contribution in any room she enters.'

'Oh yes, in the fine rooms of the Coorong.'

'In any situation in which she finds herself.'

'A sensible person would look at this and advise us to leave.'

'A sensible person wouldn't have come, or would have left years ago, gone to Grandmama and Grandpapa.' I let the door go. I shoved it for her. Let her leave if she wanted to.

Addie felt the door and pushed it in and out, twice. 'I wish he had let us.'

'Yes.'

'I'll do the dining room. Show me what I must do.' Her voice had lost its quick girlishness, and her face became serious. 'I am not as silly as I seem, Hester. Truly, I am not. But Papa likes me to be lively. It lifts his spirits. I do it for him. It's hard to stop, and it's dull when everyone is sad.'

'Poor Addie.'

'You are a little like Mama sometimes, how she used to be. Calm. You know the right thing to do and say, how to go about things. And you are clever.'

'I am calm because Mama liked me so and Papa needs me so. Inside I boil. This place.'

'Tull says the land doesn't like us. Is that possible?'

'We have moved beyond the age of witches, I hope. It was God's will, everything that happened.'

'It was not. Stupid God.'

'Addie! Do not say so.'

'I will. Why would he will such a thing? Why would he wish that on us? On Mary. What harm did Mary ever do? You are not Mama to tell me what I may say.'

'I am not. Yet you must mind me. And the boys. Or all is lost.'

She did more about the house after that conversation, while continuing her solitary explorations. She would not obey me as she had Mama – I was only her sister, after all – but understanding her better, I was kinder.

In the autumn Grandmama sent us a parcel containing a new sketch book and watercolours for Fred, a telescope for Albert, and cloth for dresses and shirts, which Papa with the greatest reluctance and only after Addie's pleading allowed us to keep. They were presents such as grandparents like to give rather than charity, she said. She was kept busy for the next while making them up. She was a better seamstress than I, and the occupation suited her. It was a comfortable feeling to be presentable again, which lesson I have always remembered. (All the girls in my school are well and warmly dressed and it makes a great difference to their spirits and demeanour and habits of learning.) When Addie called from the balcony early in the winter to let me know that we had visitors I didn't feel as bad as I might have, knowing that we were respectable.

She was leaning on the veranda rails, at the end by the steps, when I went outside, Skipper aquiver at her feet, watching two troopers coming down the track through glittering morning. What would they think of her, resting on her elbows?

'Addie,' I said to her back. 'Adelaide.'

She gave a lazy turn of her head over one shoulder with a look that was not impatience or boredom or amusement, but all of these things. I had learned to see the parts of her that she concealed. I might raise an eyebrow at her teasing and she would give a fleeting smile and suddenly she was a little like the imaginary Sal of those years ago: a friend. I poked her in the back, half in teasing, and would have again but for her quiet look, as if she saw right through me and pitied me for my tired habits, bones picked clean of meaning, when once they had been a way of keeping Mama close. A year now since she had died. They were nothing that would hold up life out here. Addie patted the railing at her side. It did not seem so terrible to join her, our shoulders touching warm on a cold day. Who would ever know that once we rested our chins on our hands and our elbows on a wooden rail and regarded two strange men with such frank interest?

They slowed at the sight of us – females being a rarity thereabouts – and in lifting their faces into the sun we saw that they were not strangers but the two police who had come by searching for Mr Robinson. Sergeant Wells's mutton chop whiskers had continued to flourish, becoming fascinating topiary work. He wiped his sunburnt face with a grey rag and tucked it away in a pocket.

'Heavens,' Addie drawled low. 'Those whiskers can't be real. Whatever are they made of? Possum tail?'

'Shh,' I said.

The troopers tethered their horses at the yard gate and fastened their jacket buttons, slicking their hair back before settling their hats again and coming to stand beneath us. Their dark uniforms were mud spattered and beneath that faded wherever the sun had struck most directly, on shoulders and forearms. The younger one, Trooper O'Grady, was not much older than Hugh I would have said and regarded Addie with the liveliest interest, setting his thumbs in his belt and his feet apart to look more impressive. He need not have troubled himself; Addie would flirt with any man regardless of dirty clothing and untidy whiskers.

'Well, the Finch girls. You have grown up,' Sergeant Wells said.

I didn't think that I had changed very much since last we saw them; and if Addie had in her appearance, she had not in her demeanour. 'You ought really to call us Miss Finch and Miss Adelaide,' she said. 'That would be the polite thing to do.'

'Addie,' I said, but she just tossed her head.

'Is that right?' he said with a slow smile. 'Miss Adelaide, I presume.'

'Papa and the boys are out with the stock,' I said.

'So you are on your own?'

'Yes. I mean no, not exactly. We have Skipper here to mind us'

– it was unfortunate that Skipper chose that moment to look her least intimidating, scratching at one side and falling over when coordination failed her – 'and Fred and Tull and Albert will be back soon. It is only for a little while and we are quite used to it,' I said.

'And the blacks?'

'They are no trouble if that is what you mean.'

They went on to tell us their business, which was a search for some missing travellers who had last been seen passing down the Coorong.

'I would not know them if I saw them. No one comes down here,' I said and then, 'Hardly anyone. Musicians, and an explorer and an artist.'

'And the police,' Addie said.

'Yes.'

'What a dangerous place we live in,' Addie said languidly.

'I'm not saying it's dangerous now, leastways not as dangerous as some say. I'm just saying keep your wits about you, don't be rash,' Sergeant Wells said.

'Was Mr Robinson rash?' I asked. 'Did you find out what befell him? Did he really take his own life?'

'That was the finding and who am I to say otherwise? But if you're asking me was it likely, well I think you know the answer to that. Who's to know what really happened, eh, girls?' He leaned in towards us and spoke in a confiding way, as if his hints were a sort of enticement.

We had to ask them to stop for tea after their days of travel from Wellington and their nights camping out, which offer they accepted with alacrity. I must have been poor company. Addie made up for it. Fred and Tull returned before they departed with news of their own. Something was ailing the sheep: their feet were rotting and cracked and bleeding.

'I've heard the same further up,' Trooper O'Grady said. 'I'm sorry for it, for your sakes. Not easy testing new land. I expect Mr Finch was aware.' They left not long after.

'And watch out for strangers, lassies,' Sergeant Wells said.

'As if we would not otherwise,' Addie said watching them depart.

We dreaded telling Papa about the sheep, but in the end we were merely confirming what Papa had discovered himself. Something in the land here was harming them, and there was nothing for it but to lease another run, inland, and to employ a native shepherd. Since the inland run, Tinlinyara, was not large enough for all the sheep, Papa's life thenceforth was punctuated by the tides of moving the sheep inland and then back to our shore. They all had to take their turn in suffering.

Poor Papa. He pitted himself against the land, yet it was impervious to all his learning and effort and incantatory prayers. The land had its own drives and they ran against Papa's, blunting all his purposes.

When the time for lambing came, there were fewer lambs than expected. Papa rode the run each day in diminishing hope. Finally he and the boys rounded the sheep up and penned them so he could inspect them properly. He was grim at the end of their several days of hard work. He sat on the veranda in his sock feet, his hand about the glass of barley water I had brought him.

'I should have looked at their teeth before I paid; half of them broken-mouthed. Took me for a fool. Took him for a gentleman,' Papa said.

'What does that mean?' I said.

'Too old to lamb.'

It was the same at Tinlinyara. And the fleeces were poor too, from their time at Salt Creek. The sand had blown into them, as they did into our hair, and blunted the shears. And they were full of burrs too. It could hardly have been worse.

For several evenings together Papa was restless and could not settle to anything, but looked around as if about to call us to attention, to make one of his announcements. Finally, one evening he spoke; it would have been November by then. He told Fred he would have to leave and work for Mr Baker, who he had bought the cheese moulds from. 'I'm sorry for it,' he said, 'but there is no choice.'

'To work at the lakes.' Fred's cutlery clattered to his plate. 'You go and work for him.'

'Frederick, look at me.' And Fred did look at him, which I did too. Papa's face did not move and its lines were not greatly changed from when Mama died – perhaps a trifle deeper – and his eyes were very dark and without expression. I could see the parts on his clothes that I had mended: an odd button, a binding of blue serge on his frayed cuffs and collar, the concealed patching on his trousers that had taken so long. There was nothing really that had changed about him, but that he had changed completely in a way that could not be seen was certain from the stillness that we stood within. Papa spoke again. 'You are too young to run Salt Creek. I cannot leave the girls alone. I am not talking of being away for a few days.'

'It's quite all right, Papa,' I said. 'Not that I would want you to go, but I don't need looking after. I can do very well, and mind Addie as well. There is nothing that I cannot do, that I do not do anyway.' Really, I learned then that I would miss Fred more than Papa. The thought of it was uncomfortable.

'They would not be alone; they'd be with Tull and me,' Fred said. 'We've done it often enough.'

'And me,' Albert said. 'I'm as good as Fred. Better.'

Tull watched with interest but said nothing.

'Three boys. I can't leave three boys to run Salt Creek.'

'A boy,' Fred said. 'That is all I am, is it? If you had been less strict with Hugh and Stanton it would not have come to this.'

'And why not you?' Papa asked. 'Why not? Are you afraid?'

'Not to leave the run, or to leave our family. But if I go only as far as Lake Albert there will be no way out. I must stay here else I shall never leave.'

'You must.'

'I work here. *Here*.'

'When you have the time, when you have finished one of your sketches.'

'That is not true, Papa,' I said.

Fred leapt to his feet. 'Please. A little longer.'

'You can work on your book at the lakes.'

'I can't. Everything is different there.'

'You must.'

'Send me and Addie to town,' I said. 'I could work there – in service, or teaching – and send the money back.'

'No. You are *my* daughters,' Papa said. He smoothed his moustaches with his tapered fingertips, and palmed the length of his beard. 'It is an arrangement we have,' he said to Fred. He took care not to meet his eyes.

'What arrangement?' Fred asked.

'I bought the cheese moulds from him.'

'On credit,' I said.

Papa stared at me. 'Yes, on generous terms. However the cheese failed and now the sheep have not produced as expected, so we agreed on an alternative payment.'

'Which is?'

'He will accept repayment in kind, or will commence proceedings against Salt Creek.'

'In kind? What does that mean? We have nothing he would need.'

Papa looked away.

'He means you, Fred,' I said.

A hand to his chest. '*Me*? I am "in kind"? Why stop there, Papa? Put a collar about my neck and a chain to lead me by and you may drag me there, for I tell you I will not go willingly. I am not something to be traded, and you are not my master that I must obey your bidding. I am myself.'

'Not until you are of age you will find. That's the way of it. A lesson to learn.' Papa spoke with an edge of ghastly amusement – at having outwitted Fred? I was not sure.

'Hugh and Stanton did as they wished.'

'Against *my* wishes.'

'How proud your father would be,' Fred said. 'William Wilberforce himself could not be prouder. Why stop there, Papa? I am a fine physical specimen, am I not? I would fetch a good price, enough surely to pay off your debts and allow you to be the gentleman.'

'Stop this. Stop. Both of you,' I said, clutching Papa's forearm, all its muscle tensed, and with my other hand taking Fred's, which was clammy and trembling. 'Only think, Grandpapa would help if we asked.'

Papa wrenched his arm away and his face worked. He half-lifted his hand. That was the first time I began to see of what like he was, of what purpose he was forged. I have seen it since, the ways that people are differently revealed: for a sliver of time I am outside myself and all that I feel – and curious. Even Fred's distress I regarded as if from a distance. Papa's will was not a part of him that could be altered, only revealed and tempered by circumstance. He was a person who would do what was necessary, but for his purposes alone, whatever he might believe them to be.

Albert stood then. 'I'll go, Papa. If you can do without me here, I'll do it.'

Papa was distracted. He lowered his hand.

'You're too young,' I said.

'I'm big enough, as big as Fred,' he said, which was true. 'And strong. I can work there as well as I do here, and Fred will be here still. He can do my work and his book.'

'Fred,' Papa said, turning to him again, considering him and finding him wanting. (Poor Fred: so transparent in that moment. He could not help hoping and his face could not help pleading, and he could not help hating himself for sacrificing his brother, but he would do it anyway.) 'Will you do Albert's work? I see that you will not, you couldn't. Your mind: it's no use to us here. If only you would put it to good use.'

'I do,' Fred said. 'It will be a good book, I know it.'

'It's not the country for you,' Papa said. 'It has no use for you.' He spoke with such dispassion, as if looking at an injured beast that would never come right.

And then Tull said: 'Fred and I can share Albert's work. And get another shepherd to work past the Travellers Rest. It won't cost too much.'

Papa paused. 'Yes,' he said, measuring him and his idea. 'We could do that. Very well. Let us try that.' And that seemed to settle the matter.

Later, Fred stayed in the kitchen while I cooked dinner, staring into the pot of boiling potatoes, poking at them with his pocketknife, eating a carrot. 'Papa thinks me useless,' he said. 'Imagine that. I'm worth less than a black to him, his own son.'

'He doesn't think that, you know he doesn't,' I said. 'It's because of the money is all, and his plans.'

'I will show him one day. He will take his words back. He will know what I am. I will make him see me.'

'He sees you now.'

'What could he see now? A son who thinks too much and will allow his younger brother to leave home in his stead? He is right. I should do it, but I cannot make myself. What can I do?'

'Make it a good book,' I said. 'And restore the family fortune.'

Fred laughed. 'Is that all?'

'All that matters to Papa,' I said. I went to the door and rang the bell and moved Fred aside. I drained the potato water into a bowl and put a good lump of butter into the potatoes and began mashing. 'Here.' I handed the masher to Fred. 'You do it, then some milk, not too much, salt, butter.'

'Me?' he said. 'Cook?'

'Yes. And think, Fred, it could be worse. At least you have a plan.'

14

THE COORONG
DECEMBER 1859

Albert had lived always in the shadow of Fred's intelligence and Addie's liveliness. It took his departure that summer for me to perceive what he had been: willing, not given to volatility, affectionate. I wished I had given him more attention when I might have. If Fred felt ashamed that he had allowed his younger brother to leave home in his stead, I did not think it unreasonable. He moped for weeks until the arrival of Charles Darwin's new book *On the Origin of Species*, and a new sketch book, restored his spirits. Grandpapa had heard of and ordered it even before it was published. 'I don't suppose there are many copies of it in this country,' Fred said, more than once.

'I tell you Hett, it has given me a great deal to think about, even its subtitle: "Preservation of favoured races in the struggle for life". It makes you think.'

After that, he wandered around the house at any opportunity reading aloud passages that were of particular interest – to him, if to no one else. He came into the parlour one night while I was playing the piano. Papa was reading, a glass of rum at hand.

'What do you think about this?' Fred said. 'This is on the subject of varieties reverting in some of their characters to ancestral forms. Darwin says: "they would to a large extent, or even wholly, revert to the wild aboriginal stock". He uses cabbages as an example. Cabbages. And asks what would happen if they were left to their own devices in poor soil.'

'Really,' I said.

'Papa,' Fred said.

'Yes,' Papa said.

'What do you think would happen if you removed all the accoutrements of our civilization so that we had at our disposal nothing but the resources that the natives possess? Do you think it would be we rather than the blacks whose population would decline?'

Papa said, 'People are not cabbages and our civilization possesses greater knowledge, which would enable us to make greater use of the available resources than the blacks. Pastures, for instance, or gold.'

Fred said, 'But we couldn't eat the gold and the sheep do poorly on the pasture.'

Papa gave one of his narrow stares and I knew that he had seen the direction of Fred's thoughts. 'We have resolved that problem. And see how the natives sicken in general?'

'Mr Darwin says it is the fault of Europeans who bring disease with them. Wherever he travelled he saw the same thing. It's in his voyages. He found the same thing all over the world.'

'Nonsense. They were sick long before we came. Smallpox. I have talked to the Reverend Taplin on the subject, a most sensible man. He believes that people who choose to live barbarously will always diminish towards extinction. As he says, "If ye live after the flesh ye shall die." If we have done anything, it is to slow their decline with the things we give them.'

'He thinks they were civilized once then?'

'So I would suppose.' Papa hated to be questioned in such a way. It made him become haughty. He sat very straight and stared Fred down.

'Well,' Fred said. He knew as I did that there would be no arguing a point that Reverend Taplin had made. Since he established a mission at Point McLeay and Papa chanced to visit him there they had maintained some contact. Reverend Taplin believed that native practices and traditions must be eradicated if the blacks were to become Christian and Papa agreed. I did not know what to think. Sunday morning was the dullest time of the week, though I was not to say so. But there was no denying that there were several natives about with the scars of smallpox, which they must have suffered before the arrival of white men in this area.

Fred opened the door and a burst of laughter came up from the dining room. Papa had settled to brooding once more. I left the room with Fred, who began to talk the moment the door had closed. 'Obviously interbreeding doesn't do any harm. Look at Tull. He is vigorous and healthy and intelligent – more intelligent than anyone I know, I would say.'

In the dining room Tull and Addie were playing draughts.

'Was he all right?' Addie asked.

Fred said, 'He said that people are not cabbages.' They burst into laughter. 'I thought you'd be pleased to know of his high opinion. Tell me, Tull. How long would I live if you left me on the peninsula, on my own?'

Tull looked at him thoughtfully. 'In winter you would die of cold – maybe two nights. In summer you would die of thirst, although you need not.'

'It wouldn't be food?'

'Cockles. And one day you might catch a duck.'

'Do you think so?' Fred's face lit up at this praise.

Then Tull said, 'No. But you could try,' and we laughed again.

'How long could you live there, Tull?' I asked.

He looked at me in a wondering way. Fred did too, as if I had asked the strangest thing.

'For ever,' he said. 'But I would need some company.'

'I could keep you company,' Addie said.

He turned to her and gave a shy sort of smile. 'Thank you.'

They had become quite friendly of late.

Papa came to the doorway. 'Well, well,' he said dolefully, 'you do sound merry tonight.'

It was as if we'd been shipwrecked on the Coorong that winter. The natives had left for their winter camp and weeks went by in which we saw no one but Mr Kruse on his mail boat. It was wet that year.

The soaks expanded and new ones formed, covering great stretches of the stock route – spreads of water that on a still day reflected the sky. When my boots got wet while walking I lifted my skirts high and strode those shallow lakes and with the clouds at my feet it was as if I were stilt-walking the sky.

Papa brought us titbits of news from the Travellers Rest: a report that some natives near the lakes had been given poisoned damper, which killed them. What purpose would that serve but to save a few cows? There was also a rumour of a black killed near the Travellers Rest, found in sacking weighted with stone in a deep waterhole. Papa gave it no credence since no one had seen a body. 'People are not animals,' he was wont to say, despite the evidence to the contrary.

Hearing the reports Fred said, 'Would you say our civilization is reverting to a barbarous state?'

'It's happened already,' Tull said, and grinned as if he had meant it for a joke, but I think he had not. I thought of the things that Papa had done for them, bringing provisions from the mission and fencing off sucks, but didn't say anything.

We were in the kitchen, where it was cosy at the end of a winter afternoon, the boys in from milking and feeding the house cows and a day driving the hay-loaded dray to sheep two miles away. Twice, the dray had bogged and had to be dug out. Now Tull whittled a spear and talked to Fred. It was blowing hard and grey outside, but inside the lamps glowed and the stove sent out its heat. Addie was making a sponge pudding, moving about to collect ingredients and mix them in their proper order. She had flour smudged on her cheek and Tull called her over and brushed it off; she held her face still for this and watched him and smiled a little. Everything seemed both ordinary and lovely at such times to me. A bowl of eggs in lamplight: if I could draw, I would draw this, or paint it.

'This isn't barbarous,' Addie said.

Tull said, 'No. But the men who took my mother were.'

'Where did they take her?' Addie asked.

'They came from Karta. The island of the dead people, where I came to life.'

'Kangaroo Island,' Fred said. 'Tull, Papa would not want the girls—'

Tull ignored him. 'And they took her there. They rowed across and down the lagoon and stole women from along here.'

'Tull,' Fred said, louder this time.

'How did you leave?' Addie asked.

'She took a boat, when I was a boy, and we escaped.'

Fred sighed at this, but did not bother to interrupt.

'I wonder who your father was,' Addie said.

Tull pulled his shirt-sleeve up and held out his arm, paler than his hands. 'A spirit,' he said. He was light skinned for a native, though still dark, like polished wood, and his eyes were lighter too, a golden brown, flecked. He looked what he was. 'My people don't like my skin. They say it's ugly.'

'Everyone teases me about my freckles. It is the way of things in families,' I said.

'If I had been younger, a baby, my Narinyeri father might have killed me.'

'Killed you?'

Tull grinned. 'I was too fast; he couldn't catch me.' Then, seeing our horror, said, 'I was too old. My mother wouldn't let him. But I am not as ugly as white people.'

'Ugly!' Addie said.

'I am used to you now. I don't see it any more. You are not too ugly.' He laughed at Addie's reaction. 'No, not ugly at all.'

I could not help thinking of Stanton: his skin blistered and peeled and dried into lizard scale before it flaked again, leaving it raw pink underneath. As vigilant as we were with hats and bonnets, we could not help the burning when we were outside so much. The blacks walked about with hardly a stitch on all summer with no ill effect. It was a labour for us to live here. What would Papa think if he knew what the blacks thought?

I went into the larder to fetch some potatoes and an onion. When I came back Addie was sewing by the warmth of the stove. Tull and Fred were still talking.

'Do all of you hate us?' Fred asked.

'Hate you? I know you. How can I?' Tull held the spearhead up to the light, inspected it and, finding it wanting, returned his knife to the task, scraping carefully now. 'But I don't understand you. All my family— They, we, were waiting for you.'

'Why not try and stop us?'

'How would we? We knew that you, *grinkari* would come with muskets. The ancestors knew about you.' He made a gesture with his hand next to his shoulder that I had seen before, his fingers feathering what lay behind. It meant a long time ago, generations. 'Everywhere you go, you stay and don't leave. And then you arrived, at first only a few and then more, always more. Like ants – ant people, we call you. We knew it would happen. Some people say we will be cursed if we don't help you and that's why people get sick and die, as they did before in other places. It makes no difference if we hate you or don't hate you. We must live with you; you must live with us.'

'We don't believe in curses.'

'But in the bible there are curses. The locusts, the floods.'

'They are stories,' Fred said. 'They're not real.'

'You don't think you are cursed? Your mother and sister are dead, your brothers have gone, your sheep are sick. A story does not have to be real to be true.'

'Why would we be cursed? We are a good family. We treat you well. No one is killing you here,' Fred said.

'But in other places?' Tull asked.

'Who knows if those stories are true?'

'They are true,' Tull said quietly. 'My mother has seen it. She speaks English. She learned from the men on Karta. When she escaped she was married to someone from this *lakalinyeri*. But she is not from here. She spoke English to me. She said I should speak it so I could talk to the white men when they came. The *tendi* agreed.'

'That's why you came to talk to us?'

He nodded.

'Do you tell them about us?' Fred said.

Tull hesitated then. 'I try to. They don't understand you.'

'And you?'

He shook his head. 'They share water and food. You take until there is nothing. They would like some land.'

'But you may live on our land. Papa told you that. He fenced off the sucks.'

'It's spoiled here. The water, the grass. The kangaroos are gone. We can't burn the grass and the bush. The land is going bad. It's not good for us here. They want land where white men don't come, to keep their women safe.'

'Safe from whom?'

'White men, of course.'

'Which white men? From the island? Those days are done. Or do you mean from travellers? Do you want land away from the stock route? Don't you need the sea?'

'From all white men.' He busied himself with his carving then, pulling back from the conversation in the delicate way he had when he didn't wish to offend.

Fred looked at Tull, rather stricken at first, and then angry. 'My brothers?' Fred flung himself at Tull and tried to land a blow, and grappled him, but Tull writhed away quick as an eel, not trying to defend himself, merely moving out of reach.

Addie and I shrieked.

Fred did not do anything more, just stood, panting. His anger burned out as fast as dry grass. Tull was quiet. He had only said what was true. He was not a liar, as Fred knew.

I stood at a little distance, waiting for the knowledge to sink into and become part of me.

'So much for Papa's dreams of enlightenment and reason,' Fred said.

'Do you want this – to live away from us?' I asked.

He would not say yes or no, but busied himself finishing his spear.

In the morning I opened the damper and the flue on the stove and fetched some kindling and some bigger bits of wood. The coals

201

were glowing orange by then and soft ash flitted from them and I placed the kindling carefully and, when it caught, bigger pieces of wood and shut the door to the fire and put the kettle on. It was early in August, cold, and I wrapped a shawl around my shoulders and put Papa's old town coat on top and stepped up the path to the rise. My breath came out in clouds and as far as I could see the light and the grasses were as waterish as the sea, and the succulents in the cold still water might have been a Turkey carpet, and the sea and the grasses and the sky and the air, even my breath, were like nothing I could find words for. I was as dumb as a beast of the field taking what pleasure I could in the touch of sun.

It had rained so much of late, the water flowing down the track and gouging down slopes – worst of all in the yards where the grass had been eaten low and trampled; rivulets of soil bled into the lagoon. Its current was swift now. Birds alight on its surface sailed past at a clip, turning their heads at their disappearing audience as if caught between glee and surprise.

Papa and Tull departed to Tinlinyara after breakfast. Papa could not wait any longer for the water to subside; the sheep might need moving to higher ground. The days stretched out. Everything, the house and our point, seemed empty. Addie moved from window to window and to the front door which she wrenched open, sending a flood of wind through the house to slam the hall door, and back to the veranda where she stared the length of the lagoon. The rain began again, lighter now. It was too wet to work outside. Fred sat at the table, contented with his paints and book, making a humming droning sound in the back of his throat, stopping sometimes to put wood on the fire. I played the pianoforte, one of the Goldberg variations (trying to make the notes sound the way they felt to me) until Addie burst through the door. 'For pity's sake, Hester, play something different or I shall begin to scream.'

I broke off.

'Do you suppose Tull is all right?' she said. 'It's two weeks they've been gone.'

'How would I know?'

'But do you think he is?'

'Of course. He always is. What would happen to him? It's Papa you should be worried for.'

'Do you think he's lonely?'

'Tull? Why would he be? He's not alone.'

'I don't know. He just might— No one but Papa to talk to. Imagine.' She left the room.

The house couldn't contain her restlessness and in the afternoon when the rain had stopped again I made her come for a walk in the blustery weather. We wrapped ourselves up and tramped above the lagoon path's edge, tussocky grass being preferable to mud. Despite our best efforts to hold our dresses high they were muddy at the bottom and spattered up the skirts and the next morning, when the sun by some miracle had appeared again, I began a washing, even though it was a Thursday and Grandmama's sampler said that Monday was washday. But it might be raining again by then.

Late in the morning Fred came around to the line where I was wrestling a sheet, the wind heaving its clammy folds against me, slapping my clothes and clinging to my face.

'You'll never guess who's here. Charles.'

I pulled free of the sheet. 'Charles? Whatever do you mean?'

'Charles. On his own.' He was panting from running. 'I saw him at the point and ran to tell you.'

'Damn.'

'I thought you'd be pleased.'

'Where is he?'

'Coming down the track. I ran, cut the corner – faster than him. His horse doesn't like the water.'

'The mud will be sliding under his hooves on the slope. They don't like it. Oh.' The wind had whipped up so my hair was flying and I fumbled about my head for it, Medusa-like by the feel, and twisted the snakes together and tucked them back and under the tethered parts – and smoothed down my mist-coloured skirts to no effect at all other than to fill me with dismay. There was no time to make myself nice, and no purpose in doing so. My dress was an old one of Mama's with a flounce added to the bottom and taken in wherever it could be. I straightened my sleeves, unrolling them and then pushing them up again when I saw how creased they were, and removed my apron. There was nothing to be done but to go and let Charles see how things were with us these days.

I walked towards the house. Charles was further across the boggy slope, coming down the main path. His hand was loose on his thigh, giving to his lanky chestnut's long easy stride; his face was concealed in the shadow of his hat brim. Fred opened the top gate to let him through and dragged it closed after him, and Charles continued on the narrow foot-path, his horse's ears twitching and its nostrils fluttering. They stopped at my side and I put my hand to the horse's neck and stroked down its length beneath its mane, glad of it to hide the trembling of my hand. Charles dismounted and took off his hat and stood before me, travel worn and mud-caked about his boots.

'Charles.' I held out my hand to him – to shake his hand as if I were a boy, and drew back into a bob and stopped that too. I had never before curtseyed to him, not even on the day we met three years before.

'Hester.' He reached out and took my hand. I clasped his in return. It seemed to be all I could do: to gaze at his hand surrounding mine and to feel its warmth and size and when I loosed my grip he continued to hold it until it became awkward for him too. I had forgotten the strangeness of another's flesh, its unpredictability.

'You are here,' Charles said. 'I thought you might be gone.'

'I would have mentioned it in a letter. Where would I go? I am— we are unchanged, as you can see.'

'You are not. And Fred must be six inches taller.'

Fred grinned. Charles's horse fell to cropping the scant grass, tugging Charles along. He heaved it back and stroked its shoulder and chest and the horse swung its head and bumped him.

'Loose him, if you like,' I said. 'What are you doing here?'

'I'm on my way to Melbourne. I finally persuaded Papa of the merits of the art school there.'

'Will you stay tonight or do you go on to the Travellers Rest?'

'I'll stay, if I may, if Mr Finch agrees. I wondered if I might stay longer – a week or two. I have the time.'

'He's away just now, but it won't be any trouble.'

I directed him to the stable and watched from the kitchen as he removed the saddle and wiped the horse down with a handful of hay and loosed him in the yard. I set myself to familiar tasks: stoking the fire and putting the kettle on to boil and making tea. When Charles was finished he came towards the house straightening his clothes, buttoning his collar, tucking his hair back – that old familiar gesture.

'Where is everyone?' he said at the door.

'Papa and Tull are at the new run – Papa's worried about floods. Stanton and Hugh are on the goldfields and Albert is working at the lakes.'

'Then there is no man here?'

'Not here.'

'Thank you very much,' Fred said coming past with an armload of wood.

'Except for Fred, but you knew that. We can look after ourselves quite well. It's only for a few days. Addie's gone for a walk to avoid the washing.'

Charles laughed. 'That sounds like Addie.'

'She's better than she was.'

He took off his hat and once inside the dining room looked around it as if he were reminding himself. 'You've made it so pleasant. Flowers. Where are they from?'

'Mama had them from Grandmama. They do well here.'

He gave a quick smile. He was a man now, his boyishness gone. The bones of his face were more visible and his shoulders broad, as if the light here had learned how to reveal him. His eyebrows were thicker. There was a scar at the end of one eyebrow that had not been there before. What do you say about someone you cannot help liking? I liked the way he moved and the way his hair fell and his smile and the graveness of him when he was not smiling. I liked *him*.

He looked around. 'It's so quiet these days.'

'Yes.'

'I was sorry to hear of your mother and sister.'

Suddenly, I could not speak. I held myself still and tense and contained the sob in my throat until I felt faint.

'Hester.' Charles put a hand on my arm, near the shoulder.

I could not help swaying towards him – just a reflex – but stopped myself. What was the point in weakening? It was not worth the moment of relief, especially when the comfort would be gone so soon. I shrugged from his grasp and his hand fell and returned to his hat, pinching at its rim. I drew in a shallow breath. 'It was hard, but we are coming about, all of us quite well,' I said.

He said, 'My father was sad to hear about your mother. He admired her. He thought her brave to live here.'

'I think she was in the end. Her spirits were better before— But she didn't like it. She never did. Papa was wrong to bring her to Salt Creek. I shouldn't say that. It would have been better to leave us all with Grandmama and Grandpapa in Adelaide. They came to Australia to be close to us.'

'But I would not have met you.'

'I'm sure you wouldn't mind that. You wouldn't know.'

'I would mind.'

'Thank you again for the book,' I said.

'I hope your father wasn't annoyed.'

'I didn't tell him.'

He had brought a sketch book for Fred and a note book for me, and was planning to do some drawings along the way.

'Why not go by the inland route?' I asked.

'To see what has changed, to see you all.' He took off his coat.

'Here.' I took it and his hat and hung them on the door and he sat and began to be more at home, telling me of his plans for the next year.

'Melbourne,' I said. 'A long way.'

'I suppose. This place, I've been thinking of it ever since I left.'

'Whatever could you care for here?'

He looked at me and then out of the window. 'The light,' he said eventually.

'The light?'

'Don't you see it?'

What would I say? That sometimes it seemed that every grass head, every insect claw, every tree root, every fleck of slobber about the bullocks' mouths had been carved by miraculous chisel. Or that sometimes the sea was a gaseous haze, or that a sea mist held its own glow and could be cut right through with an out-swept arm. 'Of course I see it,' I said. It was seeing him that was the problem. The conversations I had imagined between us were not like this conversation.

'I can breathe here. Don't you feel it?'

To distract myself I fetched the biscuit jar.

'Hester?' he said again.

'I feel as if I will choke,' I said. 'But then I cannot choose when I come and go.'

The tips of his fingers moved on the table as if they were seeking purchase. 'You *have* changed.'

'Yes. I told you. All of us. How could we not? As have you. This is what happens. You could at least stay until Papa returns and see what he says. He might need some help. But as to money to pay for it?' I shrugged. He stilled his face at that, and no wonder. I could not stop myself.

'No need for money,' he said, very quiet. 'Just offering as an old friend.'

'How nice for you.'

'You don't want me here.' He stood. 'I'll thank you for the tea and go.'

'No.' I shut my eyes and covered them with my hands, pressing them. 'Only give me a few minutes. I didn't know you were coming.' I opened my eyes. He was sitting again, waiting. 'You knew you might see me, all of us.'

'And you didn't.'

'No.'

Fred came in then, oblivious, and struck up conversation, bringing out his books, and Addie returned and began to flirt, but in the way of habit rather than conviction. Soon she had us all laughing.

Fred proposed a walk in the afternoon, to show Charles the things that had changed. Skipper brought down a kangaroo while we stood watching. A small mob was passing through (they'd become a rarity and we'd stopped to wonder at the sight) and when Skipper struck one lagging behind they became a ball of rolling fur. A second later she was panting and grinning over the kangaroo. She was useless as a working dog – only put her near a flock of sheep and she scattered them for miles – but a wonderful hunter. Try as we might to keep her and the natives' dogs apart, we could not. They would find each other. Papa had taken more than one of her puppies – tall, fast, variegated hounds – to the natives by way of making connections, and they prized them for their speed and strength.

One thing that was sad: it was a female kangaroo and in its pouch we found a baby still living. It was a sweet thing, its head part deer, part puppy, and with the longest back feet: a ridiculous creature. I found a soft old cloth – one of the baby blankets – and made it a nest by the stove where it sat trembling while on the other side of the oven door its mother roasted. Fred carried it about after that, tucked in his shirt, feeding it cow's milk mixed with warm water, and the next day it began lolloping behind him like a dog. Skipper stalked it with her eyes and whined until Fred shouted at her, which hurt her feelings and made her sulk. The creature became the sun to us; we orbited around the strangeness of it and in this way she drew us together.

In the week that followed Charles busied himself: chopping wood and attending to the house cows and riding out with Fred to feed the sheep or move them. He sometimes found time to work on his drawings in the kitchen while I was cooking. I stopped to make us both a cup of tea and while we were together I had a strange sensation inside watching his brown hands and arms and face and neck where the collar buttons were left undone and wondered how different his skin might be where it had been hidden from light, as mine was. Sometimes we talked and sometimes we didn't and it was fine either way.

We rowed to the peninsula one day, not talking of anything profound while crossing, just of the things of town life that I remembered and missed: school and company and dancing and nice clothes, books, and buildings made of stone, my grandparents, a place and a time where nature did not seem constantly to be conspiring against us. It was as if I were pretending to be someone else, the words I was saying and the things they represented no part of my life and not likely to be. Perhaps this was how Addie felt: a great separation between words and actions and thoughts and feelings. Charles was quiet for the most part, just letting me pretend. We arrived on the opposite shore. I rowed hard at it and leapt onto the sand before the boat could slide back and held it steady until Charles was clear too.

The weather changed while we were on the sea beach. The wind blew from the south and the waves thrashed the shore and I thought of Papa's dead sheep in the deep, draggled and grey, plunging in the water and taken down by the weight of their wool or eaten by sharks. But I suppose the ship was their coffin. The air was sickly yellow, as if the clouds overhead were the water's surface seen from below. I was beneath water once and opened my eyes and looked towards the skin that separated water from air and it had appeared so. I couldn't help shivering.

'Are you cold?' Charles said.

'Cold? It's not so bad. I've grown used to it.'

He took my hand – 'You're near frozen' – and rubbed it and took off his jacket and made me put it on, standing before me to do up the buttons. He was slow and his fingers were not as neat as I had seen them at other times. It smelled like him, of wood smoke and a little of sweat. It was warm. It was what I imagine being held by him might feel like. It was soft at the collar against my cheek, a worn velvet, rougher elsewhere, the colour of tobacco.

He pulled the collar up at the back. 'There.' He put his hands to my arms and rubbed up and down. I couldn't help liking the sensation.

'Thank you.'

'I'll need it when I go. I have no other.'

'It's as well I have one then.' Charles stepped back. I spoke so hatefully sometimes that it startled me as it did him. But I knew where all my feelings could lead. I could not stop myself inclining towards Charles but I couldn't help hating myself for it, and him for that too, and for having thought so much of him when he wasn't there and for imagining – knowing – what it would be like after he left. I dreaded it. What was to become of me, what was to become of me, what was to become of me? This was the pulse of me. What did Charles's pulse tell him? Draw, paint, travel? I didn't know.

Tull and Papa returned the next day. It was Fred who spent most time with Tull, and I thought missed him most when he was gone until I saw him greeted by Addie that afternoon.

She flew at him. 'You're back. It's been so dull without you.'

Tull held up his hands to fend her off and stepped back, but he was grinning. 'Addie,' he said.

She smacked his arm – lightly. That she touched him at all seemed strange, but there was the smile they held too and something about the space that smile created that was theirs alone. Fred frowned at the sight and went stamping out into the rain to help Papa. Charles looked from them to me.

'Addie,' I said. 'Could you fetch another packet of tea from the storehouse?'

'Why?' she said.

'Because I asked.'

'Tull can help then.'

So they went together when I had meant to separate them.

It took some minutes for Addie to crash back through the door, in better spirits now. 'That's the last of it,' she said. She tipped it into the canister.

Papa came to the door, grim as he always was after he'd been at

210

Tinlinyara. He scraped the mud from his boots and kicked them off and came inside and his clothes began to steam before the fire, sending out a strong smell of damp wool and mud.

'Papa,' I said.

'Yes?'

'Charles Bagshott is here – for a week or two.'

'Charles Bagshott? Whatever for? Where is he then?'

'Here, sir,' Charles said, coming through the hall door with a bundle of papers. 'My father thought you might like these. News. Some from England.'

Papa took them. 'I thank you for them.'

'I hope I may stay. Hester said—'

'Yes, yes, of course.' But it was evident from the way he dropped the papers to the table that his mind was elsewhere.

Fred chose that moment to come into the room, the baby kangaroo behind him.

Papa frowned. 'Where did you come by that?'

'Skip killed its mother.'

'You should have let her kill it too. It won't end well.' The kangaroo chose that moment to rub its nose with a paw – it was the sweetest thing – and Fred scooped it up. Papa couldn't resist any more than we could. 'Well, you have been busy taking in strays. I suppose you may try, if you have the time.'

'Hear that?' Fred said to the kangaroo. 'It's life for you,' and sat it on his lap and began tipping sips of milk from a tea-spoon into its mouth.

'Papa,' I said, since he seemed to be taking things quite well. 'Stores are running low. The tea's nearly finished, and the sugar, and—'

Papa shut his eyes and kept them shut. 'Some more tea if you please, Hester.'

I drained the teapot and began making a fresh pot.

'But never mind. I'm sure we can do without for a while, until it's convenient.' I refilled his tea-cup. 'Here, Papa, and some letters that came while you were gone.'

He opened his eyes again and gathered himself, opening the letters: one he threw into the fire, another he put aside, a third he read, his eye slowing more than once and returning to read a particular section. 'Well, I hope I know my duty,' he said when he'd finished it.

'What, Papa?'

'Reverend Taplin asking something of me. I'll need to go to Milang for stores in any case. Tull can come with me, I think.'

'He's just come home,' Addie burst out. 'Fred should go.'

'I'm sure he won't mind,' Papa said. 'A few days' rest first. And now to wash, I think. I'm feeling rather—' and he fluttered his hands at his side in some gesture of discomfort.

Charles was taken aback that evening by the sight of Tull reading by the fire and Addie nearby playing a soft tune on the pianoforte and singing a song of her own invention. 'He is quite at home then,' he murmured to me.

'He's lived here for years. He was when you visited.'

'I thought it was temporary.'

'You know Papa. "All men are created equal."'

'He was quieter then I suppose. I didn't notice him so much when there were so many of you.'

'He's almost family to us. We don't think of it.'

'If you saw the way they were treated elsewhere … What's he reading?'

'Darwin's new book, I think.'

'Good God. I'm glad Father's not here to see it.'

'Yes.'

Addie's manner and Charles's words made me see Tull afresh. He was very tall now, and wider only at shoulder and deeper only through his chest. His trousers were held up with an old belt and they and his shirts, although clean, were patched – and when outside he carried over his shoulder a reed bag. Despite this, or perhaps because of it, the way his self stood in relief against his shabby clothing, I saw how he moved, every step like the beginning of a dance, slow but with contained power and above that, above all, with a grace that was particular to him. Now it seemed obvious and made me uncomfortable to think so. If I could see this in dispassion what might it be like for Addie? If she felt towards Tull as I tried not to towards Charles – and now this did not seem ridiculous, but inevitable and unstoppable – things could only go ill for her. Tull made me fearful on Addie's account and I resolved to speak to her about keeping a proper distance.

Papa and Tull were home for only three days and after they left we had the joy of Addie short-tempered once more. Charles wished to do some sketches of the peninsula and since it was a calm day, and with the lure of escaping Addie, we rowed across once more, pelicans bobbing away on either side. I tied the boat to a scrubby bush.

'You must see this, Charles. You'll be amazed and then if you still want to you can do your drawing I suppose.'

I followed the path along the edge of the lagoon. We came to an opening between high sandy bluffs and I scrambled up, ahead of Charles, clutching snaking roots in one hand and my skirt in the other. 'Come on, town boy. Keep up. You are grown soft.'

'And you are grown outspoken.'

'Am I?' I stopped and looked back at Charles who was still below me.

'Not really. Or only a little more than you already were.'

'Oh no. It's what I say to Addie and now I have become it too. We won't be fit for town.'

'You'll be fine. I like it. You are—'

'Please, do not say unusual. There is nothing worse than to be unusual. Whatever would Grandmama say?'

'She is not here, so what does it matter?'

'But I plan to go back, to take Addie or she'll never be fit for town life. I should do it now, but I don't know how.' We had reached the top of the hill and the wind and the roar of the ocean were around us.

'Does Mr Finch approve?'

'He doesn't know, and you mustn't say it to him. You mustn't.'

'No. I won't, if that's what you want.'

'There's no money to get us there, but I will find a way.'

'Don't think of it now. There will come a time, I'm sure.'

'That's what Mrs Robinson, Mrs Martin now, from the Travellers Rest, said to me once. And Mama. People say these things but don't tell me how.'

The path sloped down and widened and the wind dropped and the sun fell on us. It was sheltered and warmer in here and white flowers were opening on the bushes around us as they did at the end of winter. Small bees dithered and the sound sent me after all this time to our garden in Adelaide, to its daisies and roses and the jacaranda that had been coming on so well when we left, that Papa had said would one day be a climbing tree, if not for his own children then for his grandchildren. People would look over the fence and gaze in for the pleasure of the colours and the scents. Once I saw someone with their face buried in the white lilac and when I commented on the sweetness of the scent the woman lifted her head and I saw that she had been weeping. 'Sorry, Miss,' she said. 'It reminds me so much of home that I couldn't help meself.' Well, I knew what she meant now, except it was the sound of the bees for me, and the thought of all we had lost, Mama included, but I would not cry. I looked back. Charles was ambling along, looking about with curiosity, as if everything, all of life and not just this moment, was the most wonderful adventure and had been put in his way for his pleasure alone. How comfortable the world was for him; how well he fitted inside it.

'Only a little further now,' I said. 'Here.' I left the path and scrambled up a hill. The sand fell away from my feet. At the top it was as if a doorway had been scooped into a lip of sand. 'There,' I said, when Charles arrived at my side.

Before us was an expanse like a shallow fluted bowl, but vast, more a valley, rimmed by more sand hills and covered at its base and curling up its sides with millions and billions of broken shards, a white desert, mysterious and glittering in the sunlight so that we were obliged to narrow our eyes against its brightness.

'Ah,' Charles sighed. 'What is it? What's it made of?'

'It's just cockles. That's all. Shells. All broken and worn.' I bent and scooped up a silky handful and tipped it from one palm to another. 'See how smooth all their edges are? And listen.'

Charles stroked his fingers across the shells in my hand – a tingling sensation – and I poured them out. He picked up a handful of his own and poured them from one hand to another and back again. 'But where are they from? How did they get here?'

I shrugged. 'The blacks eating them here?'

'Surely not so many. How long would that take?'

'I think hundreds of years. Thousands. I don't know. The blacks won't last for much longer. Papa says they're doomed, but they're not ill here yet.'

'It's beautiful. Strange though.' He dug his hand in and scooped up some more. 'How deep do they go?'

'Deep. I don't know.'

He squatted and swirled his hands about the surface of it. 'Do you come often?'

'Sometimes on a calm day. If I shut my eyes I imagine I am in our garden in Adelaide. A shock when I open my eyes.'

'Do you have it still?'

'Sold to cover the losses. Papa is quite entrepreneurial and I believe such people can be hard on their families. He is hoping now that Hugh and Stanton will make their fortune and restore what we have lost. He has spent most of his life hoping, I think.' I began to swing my leg about, toe pointed to touch the shells and the other leg a pivot, as if I were a compass and could inscribe a perfect circle about me. I drew my skirts up a little to see better. 'He is too much the gambler. He makes it, then loses it. It is like these shells. He picks up a handful and then they fall through his fingers and he is always surprised and then a little later he is hopeful again.'

'Is it really so bad?'

I stopped my turning and stood there in the middle of my circle with its border of gleaming shell. 'It's bad just now because of the sheep. Sometimes I feel like my life is galloping away, bolting, and because it's fast and the direction straight, I can hold on despite my panic. But when it slows— then, I have the time to wonder whether if I ran in an untried direction, where I pleased, the way would be better even if it were hard at first. Only there are Addie and Fred.'

'I had to fight my father to go to Melbourne.'

'But you're a man; it's different. He can't really compel you; you can travel alone.'

'I suppose. I wish I could do something for you.'

We walked on, our boots slipping on the shells.

Charles said, 'Does Mr Finch know this place?'

'We had more sheep out here for a while so he had to visit, but it ruined their fleeces. And their feet were bad. Papa doesn't care for it out here. He finds it desolate. He says it slithers beneath his feet and he cannot feel the ground. He says: "It is mine but I do not feel welcome here." And he tells me not to be superstitious. He used to go all the way around instead of across the middle to get the sheep on the other side. It's so slow. The sheep didn't like it either. They stood there dumbfounded, like this' – I gave Charles my sheep impression which made him laugh – 'and then they went back. They didn't believe it was real. Well, I don't know what they believed, but they wouldn't put one of their dainty rotting feet on it for anything.'

'You don't look like a sheep.'

'Or like a corpse. Wonderful. I will begin to save your compliments. It is comfortable too – as comfortable as any bed I ever slept on.'

'Show me.'

'Why, you just lie down. It's quite simple. Like this.' I lay down and wriggled to shape it to me. It was warm beneath and it moved so that it seemed almost a living thing. Charles loomed against the blue of the sky and with the sun behind him I couldn't see his face. I closed my eyes to better feel the warmth of the shells against me. I liked to look at the light through my eyelids – the red glow and the pulse of my blood. Mama explained it to us once. I played the shells through my fingers. Everything was silky. Then came the shushing sound of the shells moving and Charles's voice close to my head – 'Ah' – which startled me and made me turn to see.

He was lying with his hands folded across his stomach. His eyes were already closed and his face was quite smooth. 'It is comfortable.'

'I told you,' I said.

'You did. I'll believe you next time.'

'But you still need to do it. It's not enough to believe me.'

'I will do as you say, of course I will.' His voice was just a murmur. 'Hester.'

There was the touch of his hand against mine. I thought it was a mistake and pulled away, but his hand followed mine and curled about it and held it. It was as warm, warmer than the shells. I don't know why I didn't move it. His thumb stroked up and down, idle almost, but it was all that I could feel. The sounds of seagulls and waves and the hum of distant wind fell away. And he lifted my hand to his mouth and held it there and put it to his cheek, which prickled after the softness of his mouth. 'I missed you.' He opened his eyes and turned to his side and gave one of his slow smiles. 'I've been thinking of you.'

'I didn't know.'

'Now you do.'

'Yes.'

Our faces drew closer by small movements of our bodies and we reached together – his face was large close to, his eyes very blue before they closed – and our mouths touched and pressed closer. Suddenly the world began to come clearer to me. Addie too. How would you resist this?

15

THE COORONG
OCTOBER 1860

I thought I would laugh when I first saw Stanton. He swung the dining room door back and stood against the light. He was wearing a tartan suit and a silk waistcoat, which could not have appeared more ridiculous in those surrounds.

Everything and everyone was unsettled then. Papa and Tull were still away at Point McLeay, and Charles had left for Melbourne. Hugh and Stanton were full of tales of high adventure and brawls and gold strikes and the size and entertainments of Melbourne. They had made a little money, but not their fortunes, and by the sound of it spent more than they saved. The house could barely contain them. They would try and order us around with Papa not there. They had prospects according to Hugh, and planned to leave again soon, but wished to 'ruralise' a little first. By their second day home they had already pronounced farm life dull.

The baby kangaroo died two nights after they arrived, I don't know why. Perhaps it was only that it was too young to be without its mother, or it was the noise and strangeness of new people.

Stanton watched Fred at work one evening: 'Still doing your scribbles, I see.'

Fred didn't answer, but after Stanton left the room, said, 'I wish Charles hadn't gone.' They had often talked of art.

All I could think about was Charles. It made me short-tempered and drear. I could not forget what I'd said to him. *He* would never forget it; I was sure of that. It did not really matter; I would never see him again.

*

When Charles and I first kissed on the peninsula there was nothing in it but hesitant wonderment. It was a kind of perfection to lie on our bed of shells under cover of sun. How quickly it was not enough. We returned a second and then a third day, for Charles to draw again, we said, and so he could teach me how to use the musket. He did not like to think of us unprotected while Papa was away.

We were bolder each time, as if chaste life – cooking and drawing and playing the piano and seeing to the cows and pretence – had fuelled its opposite. Without a word we hurried the paths and lay on the shells. It was cloudy on the last day, cooler, and Charles pulled the front of his coat across me and we lay in that dark cocoon. His shirt had pulled loose and my hand was on his back – soft, but also hard with muscle, unlike a baby's or child's – and his fingers rimmed my bodice and his fingertip edged beneath. We kissed deeper and lay closer. Then he rolled and was on me, his face above mine, his hands holding me still. He gave me such a look: not perfectly in control of himself, but intent. I had never seen such an expression before. It frightened me.

'No,' I said, blood boiling up in my cheeks. I shoved at his chest with my palms. 'Charles.'

He came to himself and fell away. 'I'm sorry.' His face was twisted with shock but still lovely to me; it was hard to see danger in it.

'I can't.' I shook my head. I was shaking all over. Part of me wanted to see that look on his face again. I had frightened myself. I could see how it happened now, how without meaning to give anything up, I might, to get something else.

'I'm sorry,' he said again.

'I believe you. We should go now.'

He reached for my hand. I pushed it free and shoved it when he tried again. 'No, don't,' I said.

'I can't touch you?' he said.

'No.'

'Or be with you.'

219

'It's not safe. I can't—' If I said more, he would know how much every part of me but my rational self longed for his touch.

'You don't hate me?'

'No, of course not.'

'Do you think I might … because I would not.'

I shook my head and got to my feet.

'I don't understand,' he said.

I looked down at him. 'I can't forget my mother. I swore I would not become like her. And now I can see how it happens.'

'I won't again,' he said.

'It doesn't matter. We can't come back here.'

We just looked at each other. I didn't smile or soften in any way. I would not yield at all and stood as tall as I was able, and he said, finally, 'If that's what you want.'

'Want? It has nothing to do with that. It is what must be. Think ahead.' I was shaking and held my hands tight together to still them. 'We should go now. I must see to supper.' I did not look at him in the boat, but rowed steadily, thinking only of scooping the water cleanly, and feeling my strength put to this familiar work.

When we had almost reached the home shore, Charles said, 'I'd best be leaving for Melbourne.'

'I suppose so,' I said.

The day after that he rode out. At the veranda steps he kissed me lightly on the cheek. 'I hope I will see you again on my return.'

'Yes,' I said. 'That would be nice. If you journey this way another time, do stop and see us.'

I was sure I would never see him again. I thought that was the kindest thing – for us both. There would always be someone else for a person such as Charles; I wanted there to be no one for me. I did not presume the worst of him. But men did rule over women and tell them what to do, as if it were their nature to. No one said they should do otherwise; not the world or anyone. It was not Charles that I did not care for. It was the thought of giving my life away, what I might allow myself to do, and the future that would then unfold. I would not risk it. And the only way to escape such a fate that I could see was to become independent, to keep myself from temptation and never to marry.

By the third day of their homecoming Hugh and Stanton were restless for excitement. Perhaps it was the weather: the first warm day of September. Somehow, while out working that morning, they had persuaded Fred to visit the Travellers Rest with them later that day.

Fred did not look comfortable when the subject came up in my presence. His glance flickered from Hugh and Stanton to me. He seemed trepidatious, which I could not understand.

'What is the purpose of the expedition?' I said.

'A visit to the Travellers Rest is all. The joys of life,' Hugh said. 'Not that you need to know.'

'And I say that Fred may not go,' I said.

Relief flashed across Fred's face.

'Oh dear,' Stanton said in his jeering way. 'Freddie has to stay home with Hester.'

Of course Fred's temper flared up. 'You be quiet, Stanton. I will go. You can't stop me, Hester.'

'You may not,' I said. 'Papa left me in charge.'

'He did not know at the time he left that we would be here,' Hugh said. 'In fact it is I, and not you, Hester, who has guardianship over Fred at this moment, since I am the eldest here, and a man.'

Stanton gave one of his insolent grins.

'Fred is seventeen, which I should not have to remind you,' I said.

Hugh leaned in the doorway and folded his arms. 'I think I know my duty,' he said.

'So I would have supposed.'

Hugh's eyes narrowed at that.

'Only perhaps Papa would prefer us not to leave Hester and Addie here alone,' Fred said.

The rage was a hot red weight in my chest, but I would never show Hugh and Stanton that. 'No, you go along, Fred. I know how to use the musket quite well. We will be quite safe.'

'You can fire a musket?' Stanton said.

'Charles taught me. I am quite a good shot.' I took a chair from the table to the doorway so that Hugh and Stanton were obliged to move, and climbed up and lifted the musket from its pegs and fetched the cartridge box from its hook and began attending to it. It was like an equation. I had only to remember the sequence and the result was assured. I loaded the musket and rammed the ball, doing it without haste to make sure I had done it right, swinging the muzzle past them – they flinched – before setting it on the table. The boys continued to watch. It was as if they were waiting for me to release them.

Finally, Hugh took hold of the door handle. Fred looked at me.

I said, 'Be careful, Fred,' very calm. 'Take Birdie. She's sensible. I'll leave the lamp burning.'

He said, 'If you like.'

Addie came from the parlour to watch them depart, Fred trailing behind, and we went for a walk around the curve of our point late in the afternoon. Birdsong increased as the sun reached towards the peninsula, swooping and ricocheting all around, from the lagoon too, and finally the shapes of the birds turned to shadow rather than substance: trailing parabolas of flight above us.

We strolled home. I lit the fire in the dining room to make it cosy, the wind having turned south, and we spent a pleasant enough evening: Addie sewing, and I reading. Addie sighed over her stitches. 'Do you suppose Papa and Tull will be much longer?' she said.

'Not much longer.'

We played a game of chess and a game of draughts and when Addie went to bed, I hung a lamp on the veranda and put another in the parlour window. I took a quilt and settled myself in Papa's big chair before the dining room stove with Skipper at my feet.

It was the middle of the night when Fred came crashing through the door. I had never seen him in such a state, poor boy. He fell back against the door and shut his eyes for a moment. Skipper rushed to him, whining at his feet and sniffing at him.

'Fred. Are you all right?' I threw the quilt off and hurried over, and felt his arms and inspected his face for bruising or injury, for anything. He was dishevelled and stinking of ale and having been sick, and of something else, but that was all that I could see. 'Come over here, close to the fire.' I sat him in the chair and wrapped the quilt about his shoulders. Once I had brought the lamp in and turned it up I began to see him more clearly. He was pale and trembling, with distress as well as cold, I thought. 'What's happened? Where did they take you?'

Fred shook his head. 'Could I have some water please?'

He drank two glasses of water, retching once or twice between mouthfuls, but shuddered each time I questioned him. 'I'm so tired, Hett. Just let me sleep. Please.' His eyelids were drooping. There was no point in asking further and he groaned when I tried to make him stand and go to bed. By the time I turned the lamp down his eyes were quite closed. Skipper curled up on the rug at his feet and I left them there.

He was still asleep next morning when I went to milk the cows. I set the milk in the larder for the cream to rise and went inside. Fred blinked and looked around, his gaze resting on the table, the window, the stove, me, until comprehension began. His look was of such naked pleading that I did not have the heart to ask him about the events of the night. I put some wood on the fire and went out to the kitchen and stoked that fire too and put the kettle on and began a bread dough. Presently, Fred came through the door, looking a little better. He had washed himself and changed his clothes. He sat in a chair, quiet, watching as I kneaded the dough on the table. I made him a cup of tea and he clasped the mug and shivered and drank a little of the hot tea. His wet hair had begun to spring into curls around his face before he talked.

'I hate them. I wish I had not gone. I wish it.' He shuddered and was quiet for several more minutes. 'We went to the Travellers Rest. It was nearly dark when we got there. Mrs Martin was there and I met Mr Martin. I didn't like him very much. He's like a wolf. Mrs Martin had a bruise on her face. She's nice. You know the way she talks: "Come inside, my ducks. You'll be after refreshment and a bite of my pie, am I right?"'

His Irish accent was quite good; I would have laughed at a different time. 'I like her,' I said.

'Hugh bought me some ale and said I should drink it, so I did. I didn't like being there. It's not very clean now. The tables were sticky. I thought we would go home after that, but Hugh and Stanton bought some more ale and liquor to take with us and said the night had just started. An adventure, they called it. We just rode into the bush. I wanted to turn around, except I didn't know where we were. I didn't feel very well. I am not accustomed to drink.'

He stopped talking again. I put the dough in a bowl and a cloth over the top and set it to rise at the side of the stove. Fred cut a slice of bread and opened the fire door on the stove and held the bread over the coals with a toasting fork. He scraped some butter over it and ate it slowly, then had another cup of sweet tea.

As if he'd never stopped talking, he said, 'I kept thinking of a drawing I'm working on, of some little fruits – *muntharies*, Tull calls them. It's hard to get the blush on them right'. He stopped and rubbed his cheek before gathering himself. 'We went to a native camp. I heard the dogs first. Hugh and Stanton weren't worried about them. It was horrible. There were a lot of sick people. I thought an old woman lying by a fire had died. She stared so fixed. The shelters were falling apart. Their weapons were lying about. Hugh and Stanton got down. I thought I would stay mounted until we left. A man came out of a wurly and they made me bring the drink over, so I had to get down. The native was quiet until he saw the drink. He wasn't well, coughing and so on. He called two girls out of the wurly. They were only young, a little younger than me perhaps. They went into the bushes with Hugh and Stanton.'

'Don't tell me,' I said.

'I couldn't do it. Stanton came out after a while. He said it was my turn.'

'Stop.'

It was as if he didn't hear me. 'She had scars across her front. I remember that.' He inscribed three lines across his chest with a light stroke of his fingers. 'I would not have expected them to feel like that, hard and smooth. She smelled strange.' His breath came rather short. 'I was sick. I couldn't help it. It was the drink. Hugh and Stanton laughed. That's when I ran away. I found Birdie and sprang up before they could stop me. I didn't care where we went, but she found the way home. Thank you for putting the lamps out.'

'That's all right.'

'I'm sorry, Hett.'

'I suppose you are.'

Hugh and Stanton arrived home in the middle of the morning, sauntering in as if there could be no doubt about Fred's safety. (Perhaps they had been concerned. Before they came inside they would have seen Fred's horse, unsaddled, and known he had come to no harm. I will allow that that might have been true.) There would be no work that day – Sunday – or worship service with Papa not there. A working day would have been easier – a distraction. Addie hung about like Skipper when in need of reassurance. When she asked me what the matter was with the boys, I told her it was nothing.

Fred sat on the veranda. Hugh and Stanton clattered about the kitchen, banging pans to the stove and cooking eggs and thick slices of salt pork and sawing hunks of bread as if they were a conquering army in need of victualling. I left them and went inside to the dining room. Hugh and Stanton clattered up the stairs to sit near him. I could hear them quite well through the window.

'You're a man now, I hope, for your troubles,' Stanton said.

'What was it, Fred?' Hugh asked, mopping his egg with bread. 'Not what you imagined?'

'A spree,' Fred said. 'That is a spree?'

'What did you think?' Hugh asked.

'Something different. What should I have thought? How would anyone think such a thing?'

'Oh, I think there are many who would,' Hugh said. He sounded quite mild, considering the matter with distant interest.

'It turned my stomach,' Fred said.

I peeped through the window then, since he seemed rather

desperate. I should have gone out to stop them. I was shocked, and I confess I was curious.

'The ale?' Hugh asked.

'The smell.'

Stanton leaned towards him. 'Of her? Because of that? Her flesh, her titties, her sweet girlish—'

'Shut up,' Fred roared and there was a thump and scuffle.

'Oh brother dear, dear Fred. I begin to know you.'

'What do you mean?'

'Can it be that you do not know? I may not be your equal in intellect or in learning, as people do not tire of reminding me, but I do know what is right. It is right to want that, even with one such as her.'

'And I begin to know you. It was the stink of Hugh on her. I should tell Papa.'

They both laughed. 'Speak to Papa, eh, Hugh. Oh no,' Stanton said, as if Fred had said the drollest thing. His laugh stopped as sudden as musket shot. 'Who do you suppose first took us?'

Papa returned and was happy to see Hugh and Stanton. He did not mention them running away. They were able to give him a little money, which softened him somewhat towards them. It was as if he had given his blessing to their departure the year Mama died, and in this way could take some credit for their modest success. A big strike would have been more difficult; it would have shown him to have been wrong. I hardly knew how to look at him after the conversation I had overheard. I thought of those girls and wondered if they ever ran from their lives, and where.

Worst of all was that Papa had left Tull behind at the Point McLeay mission. He was to study with Reverend Taplin at the mission school for native children, which any sensible person would know was an absurd idea even if Papa did not, but at least it meant I would not have to talk to him of the connection growing between Tull and Addie.

'To do such a thing without telling us, without telling Tull,' Fred burst out. 'What are you thinking? He knows how to read and figure and more besides. They won't know anything.' He spoke with such passion. I had not seen him so before.

I glanced up again from my sewing at Fred all flushed and Papa fiddling with his watch chain and not looking at Fred, and not remonstrating either, and I said, 'But it could be an opportunity for him. We shouldn't stand in his way.'

'I thought you liked Tull,' Fred said.

'I do.'

'He doesn't need school. He'd learn more here with us than at some school for—'

'Blacks?' Stanton said. 'Tull *is* black, Fred. He needs to be reminded.'

'You don't know him. You're the one who needs reminding,' Addie said. 'Not Tull. Tull never forgets a thing. Only say something once and he remembers it forever.'

'Of his colour and his place, I mean.' Stanton imagined himself a man of the world now. Hugh always had, so the change was less marked in him.

'I think it's an excellent notion,' Hugh said.

'As if we cared what you think,' Fred said.

'Now, now, Fred,' Stanton said softly. His mouth curled up a little as if he were toying with him.

Fred made a furious growling sound in his throat. 'What do you do each morning, Stanton? Throw a dice to decide what you'll be that day: adventurer, libertine, oaf?'

'Boys,' Papa said.

Stanton turned his hands into fists. Hugh held his arm. 'Very droll, Fred,' he said.

There had been a strange dance of feeling between the boys since their expedition. Contempt and loathing and rage and other things besides. Addie could not understand, and I would not tell her; I did not perfectly understand it myself, despite what Fred had told me. 'Not a matter for young ladies,' Stanton told Addie. Really, I could not wait for them to leave.

'Tull wanted to stay,' Papa said. 'And he might be of assistance to Reverend Taplin in his work. It was because of my high regard for him, which I spoke of to Taplin, that he thought to ask whether Tull might be willing.'

'How did you persuade him?' Fred said. 'What did you say?'

Papa drew himself upright in his narrow black clothes and set his narrow face. 'I do not have to answer to you and neither does Tull. Think of the good he might do, the service he will be to his people. I wish only good for him. Believe that.'

'He belongs here, with us,' Addie said, almost sobbing with rage.

'Addie's right. They're not his people there. Why would they listen to him?' Fred said. 'If Tull stayed of his own will it's for his own reasons, not yours.'

'He is there, and there he is staying for the time being and let that be the end of it. I consider Taplin's work to be truly Christian and I will do what I can to support it.'

After supper, Papa sat on the veranda writing in his journal and I pulled a chair to the veranda edge where the light was still good for sewing, and presently Hugh came out and sat with him. Neither of them said anything for a while and it seemed quite companionable. Papa had never mentioned missing Hugh and Stanton; perhaps he had though, or missed talking things over with them. He and Mama had enjoyed their conversations.

Papa said, 'Tull made a proposal while we were travelling.'

'Did he now?' Hugh said. 'And what was it?'

'That we share the land with the natives.'

'We do that already.'

'He had in mind a more formal arrangement, I believe. They would help manage it, or we could give them some land and cattle.'

Hugh fell back in his chair. 'Ridiculous.' He leaned towards Papa. 'The blacks have no right to anything. They didn't improve the land or work it. They did nothing. They don't own it. And they know nothing about farming. Why should they benefit? Send them away, I say.'

'They have known nothing else, but they might learn. Tull could teach them. We are right; we have the right over it. But we have done them no good. Not only us, I know that, but the fact of it cannot be denied. Only a native who also knows our world could be of any use working with them. Tull is such a person. The scheme might work with him.'

'You operate within the law, above it I would say,' Hugh said. He stood.

'Yet I cannot feel easy. What my own father would— It may be the law, but as to justice.'

'Papa,' Hugh said. 'You are no worse than anyone; in fact you are a great deal better. The familiarity you encourage. Look at Tull, a native in your own home. It's madness to think of sharing it with them. Sell it, rather, and move back to town if it troubles your conscience.'

'There's no selling to be done. I borrowed from Stubbs against Salt Creek. It's all I can do to pay him the interest and there's the lease too. If I don't pay Stubbs, the lease is his. What else could I do, as hard as things are?'

'I did not realise.'

But Papa shook his head, and his hair, which had grown untidy, fell across his face. 'No, there is nothing for us but this. I cannot risk working with the blacks, but they do need their own land. Tull has made me see that. I must think.' Hugh left to find Stanton, who was trying his hand at fishing again. Papa remained behind, tapping his pipe stem on the arm of his chair. He was still there when I went to bed.

The next morning he had become purposeful. At breakfast he ate with appetite. We all noted it, even Addie, who looked to him when she burst through the door. Sometimes it seemed as if every door, every window had to be opened to allow the house to encompass her energies. He was neat, his shirt buttoned at wrist and chin.

Passing behind his chair, she slowed, glancing at him curiously as did we all, sideways or from across the table, as if some clue might be gleaned from his hearty sawing at his food.

None of us spoke. Papa appeared oblivious to the unusual silence. 'Bread of heaven, bread of heaven', he sang under his breath, and drained his cup and held it out: 'A little more tea, Hester, if there is some.'

'What is it, Papa?' Addie said. 'You are cheerful today.' Her cheeks flushed so that I saw that her boldness was sometimes an effort for her, and that she was not always certain how Papa might respond.

He put down his knife and fork and cleared his throat. 'It was the condition of the blacks at the lakes that has been on my mind. So many are ill. It will come here too, I don't doubt. I could not be easy in my conscience if I did not try to do something on their behalf. If it were not for Reverend Taplin's work with them I think they might die out entirely. Their suffering—'

'From what, Papa?' I said. 'What ails them?'

'Consumption, pneumonia—' He broke off, discomfited by some memory. 'Other contagious conditions. Skin disorders. They are the most miserable of wretches. There is to be an enquiry into their condition. Mr Baker has asked me to make a submission.'

'The Mr Baker Albert works for?' I said.

'Yes. He is opposed to the mission, which I am not. But I am … constrained in what I can say.'

'They are well enough around here,' Fred said, 'but up behind the Travellers Rest—'

'For now, but they have no resistance; they are weak.'

'Charles Darwin says—'

'We'll have no talk of Mr Darwin, if you please, Fred,' Papa said.

'Yet your spirits have improved,' I said.

'Tell us, Papa,' Addie said.

'I have thought of a solution that would suit us all: natives and settlers. They could be gathered and sent to Kangaroo Island.'

'Kangaroo Island? Do you know what the blacks call it?' Fred said.

'I know of the sealers, but they could be induced to leave, or would be less trouble if they were outnumbered. The land is suitable.'

Addie said: 'What are you saying? Send them all away? And Tull? Is Point McLeay not far enough? What can you be thinking?'

'I have been there.' He turned his whole self slowly and stared her down. She subsided. 'I know it to have game aplenty.'

'It is the Island of Death to them, where spirits go after they have departed,' Fred said. 'They are in mortal dread of it.'

'Indeed? How have you discovered this?'

'Only by conversing with Tull, Papa. How else? As you wished us to do, to civilize him, and now that he is civilized you have sent him away.'

'Superstition, which we cannot indulge. I had thought we had cured Tull of such beliefs. They would soon find that was not the case. They won't all die of terror.' He wafted a hand through the air. 'Natives such as Tull might stay. In any case, they are useful. It is like enough to here. It would do very well.'

'What do you know of their lives?' Addie asked.

'That they are superstitious in the main, and that they are in great need and that sharing the land has not worked.'

'Do you know what birds live there, what rushes grow?'

Papa said nothing.

'Because not all are suitable for their purposes.'

'Be careful, Adelaide.'

But her voice kept coming: 'There are some for baskets, and some for bags and some for fish traps. Is there somewhere they can build fish traps? The water needs to be shallow and not too fast flowing. But I'm sure you knew that.'

'Enough,' Papa said, louder. 'I do not wish to remove them because they are a nuisance.'

'But they are a nuisance, stealing the stock, burning fences, God knows what else,' Stanton said.

'Thou shalt not take the Lord's name in vain,' Papa said. 'I suggest Kangaroo Island for their safety.' He made a coughing sound in his throat as if that would release the next words. 'To preserve them.' They sounded false to my ears, as if he had repeated them several times already in the quiet of his mind. 'This will be my recommendation to the enquiry. That will be unexceptionable.'

*

231

In November, Papa and Hugh and Stanton went to the inland run and mustered and sheared the sheep and returned and did the same on the Coorong. Many of the older sheep had succumbed to the wet weather and dingoes. There were some lambs, though, and the fleeces were a little better than previously. In time, a long time, the flock would build, but Papa was not a patient man. He began reckoning spidery columns of figures again and even if he would not say it, I could read well enough that what small profits there were would keep us in food for the year to come, but not give hope that we would one day have enough to leave.

Hugh and Stanton blamed the blacks for some missing stock and Hugh advised shooting one or two, if not to kill at least to wound and thereby warn them off. 'Everyone does it, Papa,' Stanton said.

'There will be no harm done to them by us,' he said. 'Do not contemplate it. I will not have it. My Kangaroo Island solution might come to something. We will wait. Let us have faith, and hope.'

Papa took supplies from the missionary society to a native encampment he knew. It seemed to relieve him in some way, for a while at least. He began to take a bible with him wherever he went as if it were a talisman or a charm that might protect him against whatever came his way. I saw him slip it into his saddlebag one day. He fastened the leather strap and rested his hand on it, his head bowed.

'Do you speak to the natives of what is contained within?' I asked.

He threw his head up. 'Sometimes. I should more often. It is the comfort of it. The reminder to do what is right, that the Lord is with me always. It is for me.'

Yet he did not look comforted.

Sometimes I could persuade myself that it was not all his fault, what happened, that he was just a person luck didn't run smooth for, that it snagged on things, like wool on wire, and caught and tore and became useless.

He began to drink again in the evening, sitting outside at night. His conversation was not as it had been, being reminiscent in nature, but his tone was pleasant, which is to say that it was a welcome change from what it had been of late. He dwelt more often on the far distant past. Perhaps all of us who have children will do the same one day. I speak of the Coorong to Joss. I had thought we had heard all the stories of his adventurous youth, but two of them were new to me and they have often been in my mind since. I make a note of them now in case they are of interest. Of course, to recall some things is to consign others to obscurity. My brothers and sister might tell their children other stories and it will seem that they come from different families. It is only that these two stay in my mind.

The Whale Calf
'Did I ever tell you of the time we caught a whale,' Papa said one night. 'This was before I met your Mama, when I was young and ran away to sea. Oh, she fought the barb.' He drank. 'We drew her in by degrees, her calf at her side. It would not leave her but stayed close, touching her all the while, and her crying out her alarm and thrashing, but fearful of hurting the calf and protecting it with every bit of her that remained. An argument broke out in the boat. Some wanted to kill the calf; others wanted to drive it away. We did what had to be done to the mother and she did not go easy and pulled her on board and the work began. I went to the rails more than once to watch the calf, which swam all around looking for her, very desperate and agitated. It disappeared beneath the ship and surfaced and plunged down again – more than once it did this, mind – and a seaman came up with his eyes as wild as if he'd seen into the pits of hell. "The ship's haunted, so it is," he said. "There's a crying and a moaning down there."

'"It's nothing but a whale calf," I told him, and he went back down relieved but was up again directly saying that it was more than a man could bear to hear. "Kill it," he said. I went below thinking to scoff and put him at his ease, but it was as he had said a most piteous sound coming through the wood and water. It went through us all.' He closed his eyes and put his hand to his waistcoat front, over his heart. 'I returned to the railing and the calf appeared once more sobbing. It rolled on its side and looked up at us hanging over the railings – only a fish, mind you – and I could not do it, nor the captain order us to, and we had to go below later to sleep, which we could not do because of its cries.'

Papa poured a little more liquor into his glass.

'And the calf, Papa?' Addie said. 'What of it?'

'Oh, it stopped crying after some hours, towards dawn. The horizon was beginning to show, you know how it is: as if someone has drawn the line there. The watch had just changed.'

'What about the calf?'

'It was dark around the ship. I could not see. But where there is whaling there are sharks. By the time the sun came up it was done.'

'No, Papa,' Addie wailed.

'It is just the way of things. There was no saving it. I did not feel right about it. None of us did. We have dominion, and it is not always a comfortable thing. I am too soft I think. Your dear Mama thought so.' The idea seemed to give him some satisfaction. The gaunt lines of his face eased.

In bed I thought of the whale calf in the black sea, searching and finding nothing but unyielding wood, and when the wind moaned across the peninsula and through the reeds I could imagine a whale calf to be searching the lagoon.

Papa's drinking became more frequent and steady and he dipped deeper and travelled more often to the Travellers Rest to renew his supplies. After supper he took a bottle outside instead of pouring a little into his glass and after a while he did not bother to replace the cork in the bottle.

Hearing his voice on the veranda one cool evening when the rest of us preferred to be indoors, and thinking there might be a native come to speak to him on some matter – more often now they arrived asking whether there were jobs to be done about the run, which they would do for a little packet of sugar or flour, or even a twist of tobacco – I went to the door to see. There was only Papa and he a black shape hunched into the chair. He could have been a bundle of rags or an old coat, sacking, but for his high cheeks showing pale in that light above his beard. He seemed to be speaking to someone I could not see, the words coming out in a sort of song.

'I said I would show thee and so I shall. Thou shalt see what I be made of. Remember what thou sayest. I remember; I cannot forget. I will bring coin and gold and pour it upon thee until thou art covered and cannot move for it or speak or breathe. Then we shall see who is the black sheep, the prodigal. It is not I, never was and never shall be.'

I went out to him. His eyes were open and looking towards the thin moon and its reflection on the water and the darkness which by some illusion seemed always to be drawing inwards but never reaching us.

'Papa,' I said.

He jerked and closed his eyes and rubbed them in pretence of waking from a dream, which he was not; he had been as awake as I. 'Hello, dear. Hester. What is it?'

'Nothing. Just you. I wondered who you were speaking to.'

'Why, no one. A dream.'

'Of whom?'

'No one of importance.'

'Come inside, Papa. You will catch a chill.'

'Worse things happen at sea.'

'Not only at sea.'

He looked at me sternly then, and reached for his pipe and banged it against his chair and the ashes went spinning away. He came inside. The evening was grown late and we should be going to bed, but a reluctance at the prospect of solitude had fallen across us all and we sat on in quiet waiting and Papa drank some more and presently he spoke again, recounting the second of the stories.

The Hanging

'You know I came this way many years ago,' he said, 'during the whaling station days. For a matter that had to be attended to. A sort of matter that was not within my control. *The Maria*. You remember.'

235

Hugh said, 'The massacre? Everyone knows. You were there? You never said so before.'

'Afterwards,' Papa said. 'Major O'Halloran would not be denied. He was following orders. He wanted some men from the whaling station to accompany him and his troopers to investigate. There had been reports of untoward events. He asked that I accompany him, and I could not refuse. It was my duty as I saw it. So we rode out.' He stopped, as if each part of the story could be dealt with in no more than discrete fragments. He went on. 'Whalers are rough men. They wanted to go. We took two or three days to get there – I forget precisely – but presently arrived nearby the place and found some blacks who were willing, with some persuasion, to show us where the passengers had met their unfortunate ending. It was a piteous sight: women, children, the men, half-buried, in wombat holes, clothes missing, and items strewn around. You do not need to know more.

'I regret those actions I helped to set in train. Dogs that are unleashed are not easy to control. But I let the men go and went with them. The blacks should not have killed the survivors, yet I cannot say that there was not some provocation. When I asked one of my men what might have happened when the blacks were always previously so helpful – indeed they saved many other shipwreck survivors – he said that perhaps the men had been too forward in their attentions to the women. He said the blacks don't like that – most protective they are. I have remembered that. There is that which I should do and that which I will do. I do not intend to fail but the failing is sown at the beginning. It is certain.' His eyelids fluttered here and he nodded as if agreeing with himself. 'But that is not part of this story. Do not attend to it.

'It was right; it must have been right to act. Something had to be done. They were wearing the clothes of the poor murdered souls. Blood on the clothes, but dried, you know.' He drew in a big gulp and his throat moved. 'They saw what our muskets meant. One or two were wounded. And another was less fortunate. There was no trouble holding them. We were a large party. We had our orders, which were to choose and execute the guilty parties, up to three, and we must follow them. So two of the roughest, most villainous of them all were chosen. They did not make any objection, which I could not understand. We built the gallows and we hanged them. It was a piteous sight. They were fine built – fine for any men. And I will not speak against their courage. They did not flinch. Their toes touched the ground. They got it wrong you see. They could hold themselves to life. We had to stop and fetch different rope and hang them again, and dig a hole beneath them so they swung free.' He pulled his whiskers, curling an end into the corner of his mouth. A nervous habit of his; his moustache had a raggedy edge. 'The one I think of was a tall fellow, very well made. I felt his severe countenance on me – grave, you know. He stared into my eyes and I tell you I could not look away try as I might. Oh, I wanted to, but he would not let me. I do not suppose even God would strike such a feeling into me on Judgement Day. Call that blasphemy as you will. No doubt you are right. He was a man, same as you or I. I don't know what else he meant by looking at me like that. We had our orders.' He drank and did not speak much more and did not look at the boys, but at me. I felt he was saying or asking or showing me something and I was not sure what.

Later still when everyone had gone to bed and I was tidying the dining room thinking of Tull talking of Papa and of his hat, Papa spoke once more. 'He saw to the marrow of me – do you see that, Hester? When I pray to my maker for forgiveness in the hereafter I see that man's face. Could I have stopped it? Could I have counselled different? I was young, but I had the captain's ear and his respect I think. But there were orders to be carried out and we did this up to the very least and not beyond. Sometimes we must do things that we prefer not to. Do you see?'

'I am not sure I do.'

'One day you will, I daresay.'

16

THE COORONG
FEBRUARY 1861

That summer burned itself into me, and if I have thought of it with longing during cold winters since, it was otherwise then. The air vibrated and the sky was elemental blue and had the unyielding perfection of a proof. It eyed us all, ants beneath. We became narrow eyed and slow and walked barefoot until the ground burned, and the heat filled my skirts until they felt like a kite that might lift me right up into that sky. The trees and shrubs and smaller plants drew back what moisture they could from their leaves until everything appeared shrunken, as skin draws close to bone with age. The smaller sucks dwindled to staring salt-rimmed eyes of luminous pink and finally there was nothing for it but to open the fenced sucks to save the sheep. Papa had to go to the expense of having a deep well dug for our use. It filled quickly with sweet water.

Billy and George (whose true names Papa could never remember and which I never heard), the two natives from long ago, approached Papa one day and he went with them. 'Very agitated, they were,' he said. 'It was the loss of their sucks. But what could I do? I tried to explain. I showed them the sheep. There is nothing else to be done and so I told them. They wanted Tull. I told them he was in Point McLeay, but they didn't understand.'

'Because they call it Raukkan,' Addie said.

We all stared at Addie, that she knew something that no one else did.

'Tull told me once,' she said.

*

I watered the vegetable garden each day, not from habit or even hope, but as something that measured the day – beginning and end – and altered the slight events between by their difference. Between one pail and another Rimmilli appeared and converged with me, cautiously and obliquely, as if she had started with another purpose and direction and happened upon me by chance. But she was a deliberate person, she had never been this close to the house before, and I had not seen her for a long time. She wore a sort of tunic made of something nubbly and dark, perhaps seaweed, but was otherwise unchanged: straight-backed and with her chin up so that she seemed to be regarding me from a height, though we were much the same as I recall, and spitting out her mouthfuls of words as if she hated herself for uttering them and hated me that I was their target. Being near her left me scorched. Her eyes were glittering black and fierce and I could never understand why – except for the time with the reeds, which I had never done again, and I did not think it was so bad a thing to have done. Anger was the essence of her, deeper than bone, from the profoundness of her self. I do not believe I have ever wanted a person's respect more. I think I never had it. I cannot blame her for it.

'Where is Tully?' she said.

'Hello,' I said.

She stared. 'Where's Tully?'

'Point McLeay. Raukkan? Is that right?'

'Why?'

'To go to school there.'

I thought she might strike me then. She was fearful too, I think, and opened her mouth to speak and stopped. I couldn't help stepping back.

'He's been gone for a while,' I said, but she said nothing more to any of that. 'Were you in need of something else?'

'Water.'

'We have water. The well. Come and see.' I put my hand to her arm. She threw me off with a little grunt of disgust before she could help it and stilled all of herself, even her eyes. By some loosening of the muscle of her face I understood her to be regretful. But I had nothing, no words, to verify that.

Keeping space between us now I took her to the well and showed her how it worked, how to remove the lid and winch the pail up, making sure I did not touch her. The skin of my hands and arms was freckled as eggshell and browner than the hidden parts of me. Her hands and arms so close beside were sleek with muscle and marked with accidental scars of different lengths and sizes and unlike the even, neat cicatrices of her chest. She flicked the long sharpened nail of her thumb against the next finger as a man might shift a dagger in a scabbard, alert and from unease.

'See, it's quite simple,' I said.

She was stern and not at all impressed, testing the movement of the handle herself and winding with ease, though the pail was heavy. She would not need to be told again. When it was up, I pulled the pail across to the well edge and set it there and she took a big shell from her bag and dipped it into the water and drank and filled it again and drank. 'Have as much as you like,' I said. She looked at me very direct and filled the shell and drank, more slowly this time. Her gaze tracked down the slope to the shore, stopping at the privy, the old suck, the stable, the dairy, the washroom, the kitchen, the house, back to me. She didn't thank me, just returned the shell to her bag and flowed away past and between the buildings and over the fences as if the gates and every other thing Papa had created did not exist, even in my imagination.

Late in the afternoon Fred burst into the kitchen. 'Have you seen what's happening?'

I went out, and around the well were several natives and Rimmilli showing them how to get the water.

'Papa won't mind, will he?' Fred asked.

'I suppose not. I don't know.'

They were gone before Papa came home and we did not have to say anything. But there was no pretending that they were not there the next Sunday. Papa saw them from the veranda when he was preparing for the service. His face fairly blazed at the sight. 'Faith is its own reward, of course, but sometimes there are others.'

'It's the well, Papa. They're waiting their turn, that's all,' I said.

'The well?'

'They are short of clean water. I showed Rimmilli. I thought you wouldn't mind.'

'When?'

'Only this week. Truly. We didn't know how to stop them. I meant it for Rimmilli.'

'Just water then? From whence cometh refreshment of their spirits?' He clapped his hat upon his head and strode towards them, beckoning, but they scattered, disappearing into a stand of scrubby trees.

Inside, he gave an incoherent sermon on the verse: 'And the light shineth in darkness; and the darkness comprehended it not.' I took him to mean that we were light and perhaps Tull also, but everything else on this glittering blue and white day was darkness.

After lunch he brooded on the veranda and fondled his pipe, edging his shoulder against one corner of the chair. A man came riding down the slope on a tall bay horse.

'Stubbs,' Papa said, sitting forward. 'Well, well. Quickly go inside and put things to rights, Hester, if they are not already. Find Addie and make sure that you are both neat. Now. And scones I think.'

When I came out again having delivered my instructions Papa and Mr Stubbs were sitting on the veranda together.

'See who has come to visit, Hester,' he said. 'Mr Stubbs, passing by on business.'

I was unused to new faces and his face was so different from any familiar to me that he might have been another race. He was a florid sort of man of thirty or thereabouts, sun roasted and pale haired and pebble eyed. His hands were damp to touch and he had the nervous habit of licking his lips, his pink tongue darting out like a lizard's as if to sample the air. But he was pleasant enough. He stood and bowed and I gave a half-curtsey, which I judged to be sufficient for him. He sat again, tugging his waistcoat down to ease the strain on the buttons.

'Passing by?' I said. 'Have you moved near here? I thought you lived at the lakes.'

'Two days ride only – a pleasant journey. Visiting a little run of mine east of here,' Mr Stubbs said. 'Thought I'd stop in and see Mr Finch here, and meet his family, about whom I have heard so much.' He seemed pleased with this neat compliment and regarded me expectantly.

I did not know what to say to that, and looked to Papa, but his attention remained fixed on Mr Stubbs.

Mr Stubbs relaxed against the settee, an arm along its back, his stubby fingers stroking it. 'A very fine view,' he said. But his gaze did not linger on the islands breaching the water or the birds scudding its surface, settling instead on the veranda roof of rough hewn boards and the spider webs spun at every angle across posts and rails and the way the stable listed and the stockyard fence wavered. Addie came to the door and he looked at her and smiled.

'Ah, there you are, my dear,' Papa said. 'My daughter, Adelaide. And this is Mr Stubbs.'

'Really, I'm Addie,' she said. 'Only Adelaide when I have forgotten to do something very important – such as feed the chickens.'

Mr Stubbs laughed. 'Well, chickens are a serious matter.'

'You may call me Addie. Mayn't he, Papa?'

'If you say, my dear,' Papa said, inclining his head as if he were conferring a blessing.

'Would you like a cup of tea, Mr Stubbs?' I said.

'Yes, that would be splendid. Thank you,' Mr Stubbs said. 'Miss Adelaide – Addie – will entertain us quite well. We must not be greedy and keep both of you here.' He winked at her, which I could not like.

I went down to the kitchen. Addie could not see what Mr Stubbs might be to Papa or what Papa might hope. It was too late to warn her. In the habit of pleasing Papa and everyone else, she was the coquette once more. Perhaps she would like him and Tull would be forgotten. That might be the best thing.

'Not too hot I hope?' Mr Stubbs was saying when I returned.

'It's the coolest place we have,' Addie said. 'So it would be bad luck if I were too hot. But I am quite comfortable, thank you.'

His accent was not that of a well born or educated man – I am sure Mama could have told in an instant where he came from and what his family might be like. He curled his little finger when holding his tea-cup. He trumpeted his nose into a crisp white kerchief and wiped it until it was red before thrusting the scrap of cloth into his pocket. Despite these failings I made sure to be polite since Papa had business dealings with him. Also, Mama said one should always put one's social inferiors at their ease.

Some blacks approached the well, a small family I would say. I hoped the men would not notice, but Addie's shifted gaze alerted them. Papa looked with a sort of sad confusion.

Mr Stubbs stared from them to Papa. 'Are you not going to do something about them? What are they here for?'

'Water, from the well,' Papa said. 'Their sucks have dried.'

'They should move on then. I'll send them on their way for you if you like. It doesn't do, Finch, to have them about your place so. They're just looking for the chance, the opportunity, and then—' He clapped his hands together, loud enough that we all jumped.

'No need,' Papa said, moving slowly towards the stairs. At the sight of him the blacks edged back and were gone.

'They'll likely need a reminder they're not welcome.'

'They are welcome,' I said.

'Indeed?' And he turned to Papa.

'Hitherto,' Papa said with reluctance, 'we have tried to be generous.'

'Generous. That's all very well. It's a fine thing, but the wisdom of it. There's the rub, eh, Finch? Keep a musket about you and don't be afraid to use it is my advice. And now, look at that sun. I must be on my way.'

He stood to leave. 'I hope I will see you again, Addie. Miss Adelaide.' He chuckled as if this were a witticism, then, remembering himself, 'And you of course, Miss—' He struggled for a moment, the slow machinations of social awareness working, and his eyelids fluttered.

'Finch,' I said. 'Miss Finch.'

'Indeed yes,' he said with relief. 'I hope I will see you too, of course.'

I smiled.

'Poor man,' Addie said when he had left us and we were watching him ride away. Halfway up the slope he turned in his saddle and raised his hat with a gay flourish and kicked his bay into a sluggish canter.

'Poor man? Why is he poor? I wonder that Papa was so civil to him. Shooting the blacks. He and Hugh would get on famously.'

'You frightened him.'

'I did not. I was everything that Mama could wish. Was he amusing you?'

'I like company, Hett.'

'But such company. And his terrible horse. Did you ever see such a thing? Cow hocked.'

'It distracts me.'

Papa's recommendations about Kangaroo Island came to naught. The committee instead recommended the appointment of a protector and the removal of children from their parents, the better to provide moral and religious instruction, which Papa did not agree with: 'For say what you will about them, they do love their children.' He spoke as if from a distance, as if it were a report from another country. Having made this final effort to save the natives he was done with it. Society, civilization, had made its decision.

'We'll have to move them on then. I think that's the best thing: to encourage them to leave. We need to give some inducement. Or stop giving them inducements to remain. We cannot afford the loss of any more stock.'

'Papa,' I said. I didn't know what to say next; all my thoughts would not sit smooth. What I wanted to know was how something – caring for the natives, civilizing them – could be important, and then not. It made humanity seem such a simple thing, that it could be separated from the rest of a person's actions in such a way. Had he been persuading himself of this new course in small increments, while waiting to hear from the committee, and now it was done? What else could be excised if that were so? What if I were made up of fragments and the things I held to be important could be peeled away, quite delicately even, almost without what remained noticing. I couldn't say why that frightened me so. If it could happen to Papa, if he could act against his sworn self, perhaps it could also happen to me.

It might have meant more to me, but it was forgotten so quickly in the events that followed. I found Tull on the veranda the next week, shivering despite the summer warmth, and grey and slick with sweat, gripping the handle of the back door. His four months away had changed him.

'Tull,' I said.

His clothes were new: a wool jacket and a shirt with a thin grey stripe, a good belt of leather, trousers that were the correct length. He looked as if he had been dressed to become visible. His mass of hair had been cut short and his head exposed, and something else about him was exposed too – I couldn't say what.

His eyes moved to me but with no great certainty. It was as if he'd become untethered and there was no knowing what he might do next, as if he did not know what he should do. He had become a stranger to himself even. (The truth of it was that he, dear Tull, frightened me.) He was trembling, fearful of and missing the thing he'd lost whatever it was, and beyond that terribly ill.

'They cut my hair.'

'I see that. Who would do such a thing?'

'Reverend Taplin's wife, Mrs Taplin, she did it, her hands on my head.' He trembled afresh at these words.

'It's just a haircut,' I said.

'He said I could still be a man.'

'You can. You are.'

Then with a flicker of bravado he said, 'I don't need them. They can't tell me what I should do.'

'Who?'

'My *lakalinyeri*, my family.' He shivered again. 'I will die now.'

'You won't. I won't let you.'

'I cannot be *narambe*. It is true, what they said, what's happening,' he said. He shivered again, violently, and coughed.

'Who?'

'My family. They came to get me, but too late.' His hand skittered across the outlines of his head.

'Never mind that now. Some inflammation of the lungs is all. Come inside and warm yourself.'

He sat by the fire and I put more wood on, opening the flue to make it burn fast. Then Addie was there, rushing at him. 'You're back. I knew you would come. Oh, your hair.' Her hand almost reached it, but she stopped herself.

I left the room to fetch a quilt and when I came back Addie snatched it and wrapped it close about his shoulders. Not knowing what else I should do I made some good sweet tea, which Tull drank, his teeth rattling against the cup. Addie drew a chair close to his side, on the brink of touching. After a few minutes she bestirred herself to make him breakfast, fussing about him, but he could not eat it, so I collected that and the other scraps remaining from breakfast.

'Come help me feed the chickens, Addie.'

She glared, but I said nothing and she had to give way.

'Addie,' I said, once we had quit the house.

'Don't. Don't say anything, Hester. I will not listen. I am glad he's back. Do not tell me to be otherwise.'

'You will have him sent away again.'

'Did you tell Papa before?'

'No. Of course not. I thought of it.'

She became wheedling. 'It's nothing, Hett, truly. Just that he's ill. I was worried to see it. You know how they succumb.'

When we got back Tull went to his room. Addie heated a brick in the oven and wrapped it in flannel and went and put it under his covers – I watched from the door, her shadowy movements in the dimness – drawing them back very gently and covering him with the same gentleness. Addie pressed the tips of her fingers against her mouth. She watched the shape of him change as he curled himself around it.

'Addie,' I said, and 'Addie,' again.

'Coming.'

But I had to go in and take her by the arm and lead her out.

Papa's face fell when he came home and heard the news. It was another failure, but a different one. 'I had hoped. Well, he will be useful about the run. It's good to have him back, yes. And he has been spared initiation at least, for that we must be grateful. Poor wretch. Let us count our blessings.'

'Is it wise to take him back?' Hugh said. 'We might all catch it, whatever it is that he has. Put him outside at least.'

'Where is your charity, Hugh? For shame. Have you listened to nothing all these years?' Papa said.

'You know, Papa, I sometimes think you care more for him than for any of us.'

'Now you are being ridiculous,' Papa said.

Addie and Fred took Tull broths and books and put him in the sun and he recovered from his illness – his body did at least; the lingering contagion of his spirit remained. He could not lift our spirits now with his games and distractions and company. I missed that.

The level of water in the well began to drop and Papa was obliged to put a lock on the lid to prevent the blacks taking any more. He would not re-fence the soaks. The sheep could not do without them. 'I do not like to do it, Hester,' he said when I looked at him holding the well key. 'I must harden myself, we all must. There are the Chinamen's wells, north and south. There is no money to drill another here.'

From the parlour window one morning I saw George and Billy. Tull was with them, all of them talking at once, loud enough so that some of the sound drifted down to me. Their voices were harsh, shouting over Tull, and striking the well lid. I don't know what Tull said, but whatever it was did not give the natives any hope. When I spoke to Papa, although he looked pained, he said, 'They will have to move; we cannot.' He could not allow himself to be more lenient.

Tull came inside and talked with Papa. So many of the natives had become ill, he said, since they went to rescue him from Point McLeay, and could neither move themselves nor be moved by others. His voice was soft and deep. He knew the right way to be with Papa, as the boys did not. And of his sincerity there could be no doubt.

Papa gripped the arms of his chair. 'You do not understand, Tull. I will not go so far as some, but I will not have them eating my stock and so you may tell them. And we do not have enough water to share. Tell them that too. It's the truth. Explain to them if you please the importance of the farm, how I depend on it. My family depends on it. They are my first consideration. If they must go, they must. I have done all that I can and that is a great deal more than others and so you may remind them.'

At that, Tull appeared wild and stricken. 'Sir— Mr Finch.'

'Yes?' Papa said, with less patience than he was wont to show towards Tull. He stood and drained the last of his tea from his cup.

'My mother.'

'What of her?'

The strangest thing: I had become so used to seeing Tull as ours that I had forgot about the family that he must have. He came and went, it was true, but I had never wondered overmuch at that. 'Your mother?' I said.

'Yes,' Tull said. 'She made the basket you have. You gave her sugar.'

'Rimmilli is your mother?' The feeling was vertiginous almost, as if everything around me that I had thought clear was not. I did not know. I could not, and how could I ever learn? I had never thought to ask. I wondered if Fred had on their explorations.

Tull looked from one of us to the other. Finally, he said, 'My mother is sick.'

'Ah,' Papa said. 'How sick?'

Tull moved his shoulders, and I saw how he was just a boy, and confused and did not know and was even scared. I supposed he had other family who might look after him, and of course he had us, so perhaps he did not fear what the future held as I did.

'Well,' Papa said, 'You may take her some water.' He rocked on his heels, pulling at his moustaches before he spoke once more: 'And bring her back and she may stay here until her health is improved. Yes. The others must make their own way. We all have to cut our coats, do we not? We do. Off you go now to fetch your mother.' He opened the door and Tull was gone and it was my turn. 'If you would make up a bed in the dairy shed,' he said.

While Fred was gone with Tull, Addie and I took the old cheese moulds from the dairy and stacked them in the sun and swept the room out. A sour smell lingered. We propped the door open, and raised the window and scrubbed it, walls and floor, sluicing them down as best we could.

'That's better,' I said.

Addie sniffed and wrinkled her nose and left, returning not long after with some of the young eucalyptus leaves that had sprouted from the old felled tree, which she strewed on the floor, and our feet moving across them with Albert's old bed, and while making it up, crushed them and released their scent and the room began to be more pleasant. Addie put a jar of flowers on a wooden crate. There was nothing to do but wait after that. They did not return for some hours. I did not observe Rimmilli's arrival and only learned of it when Fred came to ask for more blankets since she was cold despite the summer heat. Evidently, there had been some trouble taking her from the camp, and with moving her here. I heaved two winter quilts out to the dairy. The door was ajar and Tull moved around in the darkness stoking the stove we had used in the cheese-making days.

'Tull,' I said and when he came to the door handed him the quilts, one of which he laid over Rimmilli. I left to fetch water and when I went back – Addie with me this time (she wished to help, she said) – he opened the door wide to let us in. Addie halted just inside the door, perhaps from fear of contagion. Whatever sickness Rimmilli had we could not help being exposed to now, since Fred and Tull had all but carried her here. I would not make Addie come further in; that was for her. I took the water to Rimmilli and poured some from the pitcher into the tin mug and set it at her side. She gave me her old look and lay back.

'If you have need of anything more, Tull, you have only to say,' I said, and left. Addie stayed; I don't know why since she still hadn't left the doorway when I departed, and did not return to the house until luncheon, of stew and bread and hot tea, which she took back with her. This became her habit over the next few days. I was glad to see her thinking of someone other than herself.

For the first two days Rimmilli continued to sicken. Addie came to me very agitated asking what she might do to bring her fever down, but there was nothing I could offer but cool water, so Addie took a bowl and old cloths and for that afternoon and into the evening from the veranda I watched her and Tull coming and going, replenishing the water from the well. I went to visit them the next morning. The door was ajar and Addie was there. If she had come to bed, I had not noticed it. I watched Tull curved over Rimmilli, touching the wet cloth to her forehead and arms; on a chair at her side Addie looked on.

'Do you need some help?' I said, pushing the door.

They both started. Addie spared me an oblique glance. 'We're managing quite well, thank you.'

I should have seen what was happening, I suppose, from the strange feeling I had, as if I should first have knocked. It was a private world that they had built at the dairy and I told myself that it was from busyness that I did not return for some days.

A week later Rimmilli had recovered sufficiently that I saw her sitting in the sun one morning, weak and swaddled in blankets, but upright. She continued to improve over the next few days. As for the contagion, we none of us caught more than some slight congestion of the lungs, which we did not suffer from overmuch. Tull and Fred and Papa left to return her to the native camp. Addie watched them dwindle up the slope, her eyes fixed on Tull. I wondered how she saw him: was it his slender back and neat head, his long legs, his easy seat on a horse?

'You must stop this, Addie, the way you are with him. You must,' I said, 'else where will it end? What is it about him? Why do you like him?'

'Everything. I like everything. He sees me. Me, if you can imagine it.'

'And we cannot?'

'No. You see what you have always seen: silly Addie, spoilt Addie, frivolous Addie. Tull sees me different.'

'In what way?'

'Why, that we are both pretenders, appearing to be something that we are not.'

'He's black. He's no one you should be thinking of the way that you do.'

Addie's face flushed scarlet, but she remained calm when once she might have succumbed to a fit of passion. 'Don't say that, Hett. You don't know him. You are supposed to be the clever one.' Her eyes were bright with sudden tears.

I took her by the shoulders as Papa had done to me when we arrived in this place, and pressed them in, narrowing her and shaking her with each phrase. 'You cannot, I tell you. Nothing can come of it. Nothing can ever come of it. You know it.'

'We could live here.'

'Who?'

'Tull and me.'

'What do you mean?'

'Why, as husband and wife. Here at Salt Creek, and help Papa manage it.'

'Husband and wife?' It was worse than I had thought, then. Things had progressed to this point. 'You are mad. You cannot. You would bring shame on us all, not only on yourself. You will fall beyond recovery. Your life will be ruined.'

'What do I care of ruin? I seek it. I wish to be beyond redemption because then I may be with him and you need not try to save me any longer.'

'Addie.'

'It's true, Hettie. So nothing you can say will shift my course. I am fixed on him. On *him*.'

'As if that made a difference. You may not.'

'*May*. Oh, rules.'

'Yes, I know your regard for rules.'

'They are nonsensical.'

'To you. They keep you safe. They keep us all safe.'

'Do you believe as Papa does that they are people?'

'Of course.'

'Then they are people as we are and I do not perceive a problem.'

'They are not as we are. They do not live as we do or think as we think. They must be improved. They must want to improve themselves. Then, perhaps—'

But there was no perhaps, as Addie knew. For a moment I saw their hands touching, and imagined their faces touching. Tull all but naked when he was not living with us. Addie and all her clothes and petticoats. What manner of life could they enjoy together? 'Nothing can ever come of it. It's dangerous for him too, don't you see? How do you think you would live?'

'Papa needs the help. Tull knows the run better than anyone.'

'People won't recognise him or you if you are with him. You like company, Addie. You like pretty things.'

'Do you think I don't know? It doesn't stop me feeling.'

'If you cannot prevent the feeling you must control your actions until the feelings pass.'

Addie said: 'I suppose you mean Charles. Have you ever so much as touched him? I don't mean taking his hand in assistance or by accident. I mean did you ever mean to touch him and do so?'

'I—'

'Ah.' She fell back with a pitying look. 'Truly I feel sorry for him for you are a cold thing, Hester, the coldest I know.'

'You know nothing about me, Addie.'

'A person could not know you when you show so little. Love is not something you decide.'

I did not want her pity. 'Not love itself, but what you do – that, you can decide. Charles—'

'Yes?'

The memory of Charles touching the side of my face, sure, tipping it to the light so my eyes caught it, and his face close and unexpected. 'Beautiful eyes,' he'd said. Heat rushed up my chest, my neck, my face, at the thought of our times lying on the shells of the peninsula.

I would tell Addie nothing; I would keep those memories safe. I said, 'I am not free. I may not do as I please. You do nothing but what pleases you and do not think about what I must do as a consequence. You and Stanton: lilies of the field. I suppose Stanton at least helps with the mustering. They have spoilt you that you think as you do.'

'But have you not seen him?' And she swayed in the direction he had departed as if she could sense his presence yet. 'I must be with him.'

'Stop it.'

'It's too late for me. It is all too late.'

'I will have to tell Papa.'

'No, Hester.'

'If you had children.'

Addie's hands flew to her stomach.

'Stupid girl.' I slapped her and she blinked once and my handprint appeared on her cheek so sharp it could have been painted there. She turned and ran, throwing the door wide so it bounced the hanging coats against the wall and back again with a groaning of hinges. I did not follow but watched her through the scullery window as she flew down the path towards the lagoon – a grey afternoon with the tongues and mouths of waves whipping up in spittlish peaks. Her hair was a fat black rope down her back now. It had been short when we first came here.

*

Papa and Fred rode out of the trees in the evening trailing Tull's horse behind. Their faces were gold masks in the last sun and behind them the trees were massive and their outlines sinuous against the darkening sky. The horses were down at head and walked slow and Papa and Fred were not talking to each other and didn't call out to us. I had never seen such an arrival home. Hugh and Stanton went out and met them, taking the horses away to water them and remove their saddles and wipe them down. They drank a long time from the trough. But this was not the thing I was paying attention to, only that which I used to distract myself from what Papa and Fred were telling us.

Sickness had come to the natives of our run. There had been deaths and more would follow, Papa said. 'They were well three weeks ago. Quite well. If you saw them now—' His face was almost blank. 'If only they'd gone when I said.'

Tull had stayed. Rimmilli's husband – Tull's stepfather, who I learned then was the native Papa called George – was one of those who had died. And I had always thought Tull a sort of orphan.

'Who will look after Tull if he sickens again?' Addie said.

Fred shook his head. 'He won't catch it twice.'

'But how could you leave him, Papa?'

Papa said, 'He chose to stay.'

Addie and I wished to take them some rations but Papa would not allow it. He shook his head, and though his tone was gentle, he would not be swayed. 'If we give them food they will stay for longer. We have done wrong in teaching them to expect it, and must harden our hearts now, for their good too. There is no future for them here and once they learn this they can start afresh elsewhere.'

Addie was stony quiet for days, furious with Papa and, for other reasons, with me. At first she left a room if I entered and when that became inconvenient refused to talk to me, paying great attention to the vegetable garden and the chickens as if she were a woman grown and teaching me what should be done.

'Wash your hands before dinner,' she told Fred one evening.

'Wash your hands yourself, Addie,' Fred said. 'Don't tell me what to do.'

'Are you ill?' Papa asked her at supper one evening.

'Not ill, Papa. No.'

Papa took time and some surgical skill in the removal of a piece of gristle from his stew, which I took as a reproof of my cooking skills and as a more general reproof.

'If you would sharpen the knife, as I asked last week,' I said.

He made no sign of having heard me, just laid the gristle on the edge of his plate as if his burdens were too great to be shared. Skipper would eat it and with pleasure.

Addie's mood had a way of spreading through the house so that we all were out of sorts. I found her crying on the bed one morning, her face to the wall, her hands to her breast and her legs curled up as if she were herself a baby, and when I touched her shoulder thinking to comfort she shook herself free and rose stiffly before stalking from the room. I looked for her later for help hanging the clothes but she had disappeared. I went outside. The chickens were at the far side of their run asleep in the midday sun, a few with beaks open, feathers puffed out like dandelion clocks, one or two looking at me with half-shut eyes as I went up the rise to try and spy her from higher ground. There was no one between me and the water; neither could I see her when I walked the house's outskirts or the yard's perimeter. There was just sky and saltbush and paths and lagoon, and all of them empty.

Late in the afternoon the house cows began to low at the stable door and I sent Fred to milk them and to give them some feed. When he returned to the kitchen with the pails of milk, he said, 'Tull's back,' rather short – distracted I would say.

'How is he?'

'Well, I think. Up at the stable. He'll be along in a minute I should think.' He went out again.

I set the milk in the pantry for the cream to rise and went outside under the grape vines to see if Tull had finished in the stable, but it was Addie who was coming down the slope. I called, 'Tull's back, Fred says. Did you know?'

'Yes. I just saw him.' She smudged the curls from her face and could not stop smiling. The edges of her mouth went down, with effort, and flew up again. She was all lit up.

'Addie,' I said.

'No, Hester.' And she went on, the tendrils of grape vine reaching for her in the draught of her passing.

I looked back to the stable, from where Tull was now coming without haste towards the house. He put his jacket on as he came and eased it at the neck, adjusting his collar against it.

'Hester,' he said when he came close.

'Tull. How are your family?'

'They are— Some of them are recovering. Some not.' He looked past me to the veranda, which was empty of people, and along the lagoon. 'Is Fred about?'

'I thought you saw him in the stable.'

'Just outside. I had something I wished to ask him.'

'He went out again – perhaps down to the shore.'

'Ah.' And he disappeared down the path.

It seemed so long since we had last sat on the veranda in the evening, all of us together watching the stars come out: the Southern Cross, the Ship's Sails, the Telescope. Fred claimed to be able to identify them all from his study of Burritt's *Geography of the Heavens*.

'You have a lot of stories,' Fred said to Tull.

'I suppose so,' Tull said.

'Do you have stories about the stars?'

'Yes.'

'Tell us.'

'I couldn't,' Tull said.

'You said you could.'

Tull shrugged. 'I said I know some, but I have nothing to say about them.' He spoke quite plain, and not unfriendly or cold, and looked up at the stars with a sort of reverence, not only interest. I had seen an exchange finish just so in the kitchen, more than once. In the early days Fred would ask again to see if a story could be teased out of him. Now he merely looked at Tull curiously. There was no offense meant and none taken.

There was still some constraint between Tull and Papa on account of Papa refusing to help his family any further. They spoke a little of a repair that was needed to the stable door before Papa turned to his book. Addie rested against the veranda railing across from Tull, who leaned back on the settee, his hands in his pockets. Fred was reading by lamplight at the other end with his cheek rested on his hand, as was his habit. He looked up once or twice and took us all in with a slow sweep of his eyes, or perhaps to follow a thought to its proper end. He had an orderly mind.

After her days of moodiness Addie was calm – calm enough. She leaned over the railing towards a late bunch of grapes and picked it and crossed to the settee. Tull moved up and she sat between him and Fred. There was space between them all. Addie pulled a few off and handed them to Tull. They did not speak or look at each other, but ate their grapes, their hands moving up and down with utmost slowness. Tull finished his. Addie held out her bunch, tightening her hold on the grapes as he tugged a few more free. I could not say what was so mesmerising about them eating grapes. Presently I looked about to see if anyone else was as transfixed. Papa was reading – a glass of drink at hand – and Hugh and Stanton were playing draughts. Fred's eyes had stopped moving across his page. His head turned on his hand and he watched Tull and Addie aslant. His expression was concealed by his eyelashes and his hair so I did not know what he was feeling or what he might suspect about them. But there was nothing wrong in what they were doing, and so Addie knew. She looked at me until I had to drop my gaze.

The tranquillity lasted until the following afternoon when from outside there was bellowing and hollow wet sounds and deep groans and a scream that was as shrill as Albert's old tin whistle. All these half-heard and then heard fully and comprehended. I ran outside.

Hugh and Stanton were beating Tull with their balled fists. They were halfway up the slope to the stable and dragging him as I had seen them do to a beast reluctant to slaughter and cleaving to life. They could lift him well enough despite his height, but containment was something else entirely. He was all muscle and billowing energy twisting in their meaty hands, his legs and arms flailing, his body bucking and his head become a bludgeon. Hugh was grunting with effort. Stanton, flushed and shining with sweat, had blood pouring from his nose and a fixed grin on his face as if this time, this time he would not be denied. Papa was at a distance, watching, with his hat pulled low and his arms folded and feet planted and his lips parted as if words of judgement were still sliding out.

The screaming started again: 'You'll kill him.' It was Addie at the stable and Fred holding her back, his arms wrapped around her body binding her arms tight. 'Let me go. Stop it.' Her face was red and her hair wild about it.

I should ask what had happened, but I knew. I could save no one and comfort no one and have no influence on events, which I could see unfolding as if time and the things that filled it were rolling out before me and past me without stopping, and were unalterable in all of their details. Finally Tull broke free. His face was red with blood and he made for the trees. Hugh and Stanton took a few steps after him but they would never catch him again and so they knew. Their shoulders were heaving from their efforts. Fred released Addie, who fell to the ground.

Papa came down the slope. 'Hester,' he said.

'Papa?'

'Did you know?'

'Did I know what?'

'About Addie and Tull?'

'That they are friendly, yes. We are all friendly with Tull. I don't know what we would do without him.'

'We will have to find out. He is gone now.'

At this, Hugh gazed at his hands, rubbing his knuckles, and Stanton went to a pail of water by the stable and poured a beaker of water over his hands. The water ran pink into the ground.

'Gone?' I said. 'Where?'

'I can't bear it,' Addie said. 'How could you, Hugh! You wanted to kill him.'

'I did not. I wanted to teach him his place. But he's lucky to be alive, I'll tell you that, and you're lucky you're not getting a whipping. Bringing shame on us all.'

'What were you thinking? He's a black,' Stanton burst out.

'He's different.'

'He is not coming back,' Papa said. 'Let that be an end to it.'

'Who told you?' Addie said.

'I said that was enough. I do not want to beat you. I should have before, and perhaps I should now, and I will if you are not quiet. Do you hear me? Go inside now, out of my sight. Hope that I will feel different in the morning.'

17

THE COORONG
APRIL 1861

After Tull's departure Papa worked outside as late as he could and ate sparingly and left the table to sit in the parlour or on the veranda. He spoke little and preferred his own company. Hugh and Stanton's brutality had sickened me towards them, as it had Addie, and Fred also I suspected. If we made them uncomfortable that would be no wonder. They left two weeks after Tull, and Papa was obliged to employ another native to work on the run, but he seldom came to the house. It was very soon after that that Addie first fled the table at breakfast and was ill over the veranda railing. My eyes flew to Papa's and I saw that he thought the same as I. About our discovery of Addie's condition I will say no more, except that when Papa had recovered somewhat from his shock and anger he came to believe that the matter could be concealed. No one spoke of what would happen afterwards.

Some days that autumn Addie would be merry and speak as if she had a future. 'I will go back to town, you see if I don't, Hester. I'll be a lady again one day.' What she was thinking about Tull I had no idea. She cried as often as she laughed. Skipper had two puppies and they were a diversion. One of them, a black scrap with dark eyes, attached herself to me. I called her Sal. Mr Stubbs took the other, a brindle, on one of his visits.

He had become persistent in his attentions to Addie, arriving twice more unannounced, on the slender excuse of the need to visit his inland station. 'I all but pass through here in any case,' he said, when it must be twenty miles out of his way at least. He had a swag on his horse, it was true, but for a station owner visiting his sheep his style was embellished: fine town boots, a sateen waistcoat and a fat gold fob. No one could blame him for his interest in Addie. Her condition became her; it magnified her: the winter cream of her skin became high blooded at her cheeks, her eyes were clear as any summer sky and each of her movements – picking up a tea-cup, arranging flowers in a jar, brushing a curl from an eye – was filled with languorous grace. She knew she was beautiful, and part of that was a conscious queenly sadness, as if she were presiding over her disgrace or mourning what was to come, or both.

The second visit from Mr Stubbs was on a Sunday in June, when he must have known we would all be about. I made scones and used Mama's Wedgwood jasperware for the preserves, cream, milk and sugar, and took the tray into the parlour. Fred was there too – the lure of afternoon tea. Papa began a performance as affectionate father to us all, even Addie, which startled her at first. She fell into her old teasing way with him: reckless behaviour. Fortunately Mr Stubbs was a great deal more interested in his own opinions than in hearing those of others.

'Yes, chickens, a very useful fowl. Ducks, now, I do not agree with. Their eggs are too rich, and spoil too easy, and there's no meat on the birds at all, but a good capon: delicious, or even a hen bird poached correctly is very nourishing. A few small root vegetables to enrich the stock.'

'Papa loves chickens too, do you not, Papa?' Addie said, knowing very well that Papa hated them – their combs, their flat bead eyes, their scaled feet. He was not rational on the subject.

'Yes. A most excellent bird,' Papa choked out.

'Oh Papa,' Addie said. 'You cannot say so. You know you hate them. God will sit in judgement on you one day.' She shook her head sorrowfully.

Papa's face twisted. 'Adelaide,' he said.

'And what breed do you favour, Mr Stubbs?' Fred asked. 'White leghorns, such as we have?'

'Interesting question,' he said. And he really did seem interested and opined at length and would not be diverted even by the blankest of expressions from his audience.

Having diverted Mr Stubbs, Fred smothered one scone after another and ate them absently, his mind drifting through the parlour window I daresay. He was becoming solitary since Tull went, even in his thoughts.

The warmth of the parlour fire contrasted with the iron skies made us cosy. Addie leaned back, which Mama would not have approved, and the folds of her dress fell away to either side of her stomach revealing for the first time a curve. Papa's eyes became wide. 'Adelaide,' he said in such a voice that she sat up straight.

'Yes, Papa?'

'Would you please see to a little more tea?'

'Cannot Hester go?'

'I am asking you, my dear, and Hester can help, if you wouldn't mind?' And now there was a desperate edge in his tone.

'Of course,' I said. 'Come, Addie.'

'Two of us to make one pot of tea,' Addie said, but she stood and her belly was concealed again and we left the parlour.

'Think, Addie,' I hissed when we were further down the hallway. 'It was to spare you. Your stomach. Did you wish Mr Stubbs to see?'

'Oh.' She cupped her small palm against herself, low, and blushed. 'I couldn't help it, Hettie. I didn't know.'

'Never mind now. We will walk until Mr Stubbs has gone, rain or no rain, and hope we don't catch a chill.'

Addie was dismal and silent all along the sandy path. We passed one of the remaining cows, heavy with calf. She regarded us, chewing, before lowering her head to the grass.

'Do you miss Mama?' Addie said.

'Of course. I will always.' And when she said nothing, only kept walking, I asked, 'Do you?'

'More than anything, more than you could.' She touched my arm. 'I do not mean to insult. It's different for me. I need to talk to her about things that you do not – the baby and to ask how it was for her, what I might expect. You only miss Mama because of what

262

she was to you, not what she might have become. She would be someone new to me now and I to her, closer. I would like her to see how changed I am. Papa does not speak to me. No one here knows. I am alone, as alone can be.'

'I am here.' I drew her arm through mine and we moved together, clumsy and warm.

She sniffed and hunted in her pocket for a handkerchief and wiped her nose. 'You don't know any more than I. Less.'

'I know other things – that love did Mama harm, and that it has done you no good. That's what I would ask her: why she married when she need not have. She gave her life to Papa, the whole of it, Addie. Don't tell me I know nothing.'

She would have become argumentative in the past, as I would have. It was such a quiet conversation. 'We can only be what we are. We cannot help ourselves,' she said.

'I think we can. I believe it. It is my only anchor, not Papa, or God or anything. We can resist ourselves. And we can resist others.'

'Oh Hettie, don't you see? You think that because of who you are. Look at us now. Here.'

'You *are* changed.' I would never have expected to converse in this manner with Addie. To know that she had thoughts of her own that were of interest to me was a revelation. For the first time, even though she was much younger than I, I felt her as a comfort and was terrified of losing her. But this was all there was for us. There was nowhere we could go to make her safer.

Papa's fury upon our return was a shock; we had forgotten him in the closeness of our conversation. We had hardly stepped inside the back door before he was berating Addie: 'Shaming us all. We can be thankful at least that your poor mother is not here.'

Addie paled at that. 'I am sorry, Papa. I didn't know.'

'Get out, get away from me now. I cannot bear you in my sight.' He turned from her and stood at the stove, holding its rail, sliding his hands up and down the smooth wood, and gripping it. When Addie had left the room, he said, 'There'll be no more visits from Stubbs until the baby comes. I told him she would be visiting relatives in town, and so you may tell her. When this is done, I will let Stubbs know.'

'Why will you do that?'

Papa turned and folded his arms and leaned against the stove railing, bouncing a little against the flex of it. A small smile played on his face, but there was no warmth about his eyes, no amusement. His gaze would not meet mine, though I watched and waited for that moment. It made him appear sly.

I removed my coat and bonnet and hung them on the door and smoothed them, my hands resting there. The remnants of outside chill drifted from them. Papa's voice came from behind. 'He is a good man and a notable business person.'

'I see,' I said, and without looking back opened the door and went out. I would light the fire in the outside kitchen and cook there, winter or not. I did not want to be in the same room as Papa.

There were no more visits for Addie after that. But it didn't matter; she turned inward. And really, the secret of her shame was easy to keep. She could not go any great distance towards the stock route, but it was safe enough to walk the lagoon path as long as she concealed herself when Mr Kruse's boat came into view.

All through spring she sat in the sun, her hands over her belly, stroking it or holding her arms about it as if it were already a babe in her arms. Once or twice I heard her talking to it in a low voice, pushing her belly with precise fingers: 'No, don't *do* that. What's the matter with you?' and she laughed. 'It won't be still today. Feel, Hester.' She took my hand and held it against her. The strangest feeling: the slide of a limb curving the wall of my sister, animate, someone, through flesh and cloth.

'Addie, have a care. Don't attach yourself so.'

And she turned her head, slow, as if she could not bear to give me her attention. 'Don't attach myself. What can you mean? What is inside you, Hester? What would you know?'

'I don't know, Addie. I'm sorry for it.'

'I suppose I know why you told Papa.'

'I didn't tell him, but I should have.'

'Do you wish me unhappy?'

'No, of course not. Never that. It can come right. Life can come right. No one need know. Don't you think there is more than this?'

'I didn't want more; I don't still. That was you,' Addie said, and in a soft plain sort of way that persuaded more than if she had lunged at hope: 'You could ask Papa. He would listen to you. You are always sensible.'

'I am not sensible,' I said. 'If I were, I would not be here. I would be anywhere else. You know you can't have Tull. Papa will never allow it, not even for you. Especially for you.'

'But what about me? There is nothing else.'

I made myself speak to Papa on the subject one evening after Addie had retired.

'Afterwards, do you mean?' he said, lifting his head from his paper.

'Yes.'

'I have plans, naturally. The baby will go to the mission to be raised there. I suppose that is what Adelaide wishes to know.'

'I'll run away,' Addie said when I whispered her this news in bed, but she was too far along for that and so she knew.

Papa wrote to Reverend Taplin at Point McLeay to procure the services of a wet nurse for Addie's baby if one could be found, though how he explained such a need I do not know. He would not have told the truth; I was certain of that. Some weeks later he went to the mission to fetch a young native woman Mrs Taplin had trained in domestic service. Flora had a child of her own, a fair little boy called Bobby, just walking, who hid about her skirts, clutching them and peeping out when spoken to.

Addie wouldn't be friendly with either of them but her eyes followed Bobby as intently as if she were seeing her own future child. 'Look at him, Hettie,' she said. 'He is not so dark.'

'No, Addie,' I said.

'*She* has kept her child. I am sure she is not married.'

'She is *black*.'

'I wish I were black then.'

'Now you are being absurd.'

How Flora came to be at the mission and what had happened to her own family Papa did not say; perhaps he didn't know. She was quite pretty, and would have presented to greater advantage had she smiled more. She was not as well grown as the native women about our run, quite submerged in her striped dress, petticoat and apron. We were accustomed to blacks whose clothes and cloaks were made of rushes and seaweed and skins, and who were ornamented in shells and feathers and weaponed with wood and stone – things so much part of the land in colour and texture and movement that they might have fallen on the people and which stayed there so lightly that they might fall again. They moved across our land, certain and complete, not sparing us a glance unless there was a pressing need to converse. At least, they used to when there were more of them about. The ones we saw now often wore articles of clothing that Papa had brought from Point McLeay: a shirt, trousers, a jacket, a tunic. Flora was eager to please, which was disconcerting, but she was capable and well trained and I saw no reason not to relinquish cooking duties to her – washing too. It gave me time to sew clothes for the baby, even to smock them, which Mama had taught me to do.

Mama's last hours were always on my mind. What would I do if Addie suffered in the same way? I would go through it myself rather; at least I told myself that. And if she died, how would I forgive myself when I had done nothing to stop her and Tull? I admit that my fear was for me too. We were so different, yet the thought of life without her if something should go wrong, of having nothing but Fred's preoccupation and Papa's distance for company, and the only hope that one day Albert would return to us, was not welcome.

With Papa so cold and distant, Addie looked for affection from me, lying on the sofa with her feet resting on my lap while I sewed, or sidling up to put her head on my shoulder while I cooked or sitting near the vegetable garden while I worked on it, and for the first time I was not wishing for Papa to look at me as he did her. I never liked her as well as I did then, when she was so frightened and in such need, which I cannot help thinking now was a poor reflection on my character. But I am almost become used to that.

We fell into whispered conversations after putting the lamp out. We did not know exactly when to expect the baby. Mama had never spoken to us of such things. But by November we thought from Addie's discomfort that it must be soon.

'I am frightened, Hettie, I cannot help it. You will be with me, won't you?'

'Of course. I won't leave your side. I promise.'

'I don't know what frightens me more,' she whispered. 'Living or dying.'

'Don't, Addie. Please don't say it.'

There came the sound of her moving about and rearranging herself and her covers. 'I cannot get comfortable. Oh, *stop* it.'

'Stop what?'

'It's the baby moving. I don't know what that is, knees or elbows. It is not peaceful. Mama was so calm.' She was quiet for a minute or two, and then: 'How was it for Mama? Was it fast when she went? Papa never said, but you can tell me now. I'm not a child and never will be again. She cannot tell me. I would like to know, to be ready.'

'I don't think you do.'

'Please.' And when I did not speak immediately, she said, 'I do wish to know, as I wish her here.'

Finally I said, 'It was not so bad. She was in some pain but she became quiet at the end and thought herself in England with Grandmama, safe and warm. She remembered their house and farm and the waterlilies that grew in their pond.'

'Did she speak of us?'

'Yes. She did. Of course she did. She did not know how it would end, though, else I think she would have said more on that subject.'

'How could I have been sleeping? I am the most unfeeling thing in the world. I should have known and woken.'

'It was not only you who slept. Mama would have wished it so. What would you have done here? And there was no more room in the boat.'

'Oh, Hester. If I live, I will lose my baby and already I know I will miss it. I know it. I'm not sure I can bear it.' Her voice quavered at that.

'Don't think of it now, Addie,' I said.

The labour went well enough, better than Mama's at any rate. I was glad to have Flora there during the worst parts when Addie was suffering most. She moved around, soft on her bare feet, and held Addie up when she wanted to be raised, and walked about the room with her, her arm circling Addie's waist, as if she were the sister. She knew better than I what might help. The screams and cries did not appear to affect her. I could not stop shaking. There were no complications, thank fortune, and at the end the baby, a slippery wet scrap, a girl, slipped out in an easy rush and was nuzzling at Addie's breast soon after. It was not so different from a cow or a sheep. Addie's face and the baby's as they gazed, falling into each other, were suffused with the purest wonderment, which I remembered in the moment that my own boy was born safe and never to be taken away, so that the pleasure of it was marked with the horror of what I helped Papa do to Addie and the baby.

I did not know that then. It was hard to watch Addie and to know what was coming. What would the baby's life be? Addie named her Grace, which even Papa thought was suitable. In all the time she had her Grace hardly left Addie's side. Even Papa could not help sometimes smiling at the picture they made in the evening when he returned home – Addie was so doting and careful – but he checked his weakness and became grim again and sat in the parlour alone.

Supper was finished, yet Papa continued to sit, his hands resting at either side of his plate, as I might rest my hand on the piano keys before playing or a dog its paws upon a floor while waiting. It was a sultry evening in January, and the night breezes just picking up along the lagoon came pouring through the open window and door. I began to gather the plates. Addie fanned first herself with a folded newspaper, and then Grace, who shut her eyes in startlement at the sudden rush of air.

Without lifting his eyes from his plate Papa said, 'I have found a position for you, Adelaide, at the Travellers Rest. In two weeks I will take you there and Flora will take over caring for the baby.'

Addie groaned. 'No,' and she gathered Grace in so close that she gave a little cry. 'No, Papa. You cannot make me. Not my girl. She's only six weeks old. Please.' She looked at him wildly. 'We can find a story to explain her. Hester?'

She was so earnest and stricken that my mind began to run. I had persuaded myself that Grace being with us would drift on and Papa would weaken and do nothing. I was not prepared. I said, 'We could be caring for an orphaned child, Papa, could we not? There are enough deaths to explain it.' It was true. I had seen a body on a tree platform while out riding the day before. Fred had seen others on his explorations. Some contagion spreading again.

'Hester Finch,' Papa's voice rumbled. 'I beseech you: do not encourage your sister in her foolishness. Do not be a fool yourself. I have been blinded enough by her and spoiled her and see what has happened. Look at the infant' – he nodded but did not shift his gaze towards Grace – 'and tell me who other than Adelaide might be her mother. One word, one whisper and we are ruined. Adelaide, this will give you time to forget, and the money will pay for Flora and—'

'What? More sheep?' she said. 'They will die like all your sheep. Or rot, or be eaten, or run away.' She stopped at the sight of Papa who held the arms of his chair, his face set like a flint.

'You will obey me in this, Adelaide, as you have failed to obey me in all else.'

'A little longer, Papa. Another month. Please,' I said. 'I will do the work in Addie's stead. Send me.'

Fred leaned away from us all into the back of his chair.

'You will not. She will learn of the wages of sin,' Papa said. He faced Addie. 'You will not see her again, Adelaide. The mission will take her by and by as I have arranged with Reverend Taplin and will raise her up to be decent and find a suitable position for her in a

God-fearing home. Her life will be of some use. I hope that they will succeed with her where I failed with you.'

Fred occupied himself with his cutlery and with moving about the remains of his food. Noticing him now, I saw how completely he had separated himself from us all, and Addie especially of late. He must have been lonely with Tull gone and Albert away working. I no longer knew his thoughts, but observed that the work of his book continued in the little time he found at day's end; he was dogged rather than joyous these days.

'Fred, you tell Papa,' I said. 'One more month. What would the harm be?'

He slid a glance at me and at Addie. 'But won't it be harder if you leave it longer?'

'Fred,' Addie wailed and began to sob and leapt up so that Grace woke and began to cry too. Addie buried her face in the baby's neck and they wailed together.

'It's what I think. Don't ask me if you don't wish to hear it.' He took his plate to the washbasin and placed it so it did not clatter. 'A walk, I think, now that it has cooled.' And he went outside.

Addie would not talk of her future to me, or of leaving Grace, but went about for the next two days very quiet and acted as though Papa were not there – her old way of showing him (and Mama once) that he had displeased her. In the past, after bearing her disdain for some hours, Papa would have chucked her under the chin and said he was sorry he'd hurt her feelings and she would be merry again. But this time Papa did not yield to her temper, which frightened me before it began to frighten her. He was resolved to carry through his wishes and what he considered right to the end. It was the oddest thing to watch him behave as Addie did, averting his gaze from her, neither smiling nor speaking at breakfast or supper, but revealing his displeasure by his stiff bearing and hard expression. It made me wonder if he had been to his father or mother what Addie was to him: most beloved of all, the greatest disappointment.

On the third night Addie refused to come to supper, but sat in our room with Grace. After I had cleared away the dishes and set the kitchen to rights I went to see her, lying on her side on the bed, curled around Grace and dangling a bobbin above the baby's head and smiling to see her eyes following it and her hands waving about at it, trying to touch it. Addie moved the bobbin into the path of her hands and when she bumped it, Addie cried, 'Clever girl,' and kissed her and Grace gave one of her gummy smiles. She was the bonniest baby and her skin still so fair, and if her hair was dark and curled, well what of it? No one would have known. Seeing them lying together occupied in the same amusement, I felt so for poor Addie; she was not much more than a child herself.

I sat on the edge of the bed and rested my hand on Addie's back, and stroked it. She stilled, as if she could not decide whether she wished to throw me off and berate me or encourage comfort to continue.

'Come and sit with us, Addie. Please do,' I said. 'Ask Papa's forgiveness.'

'Forgiveness? *I* should ask for forgiveness? I think not, Hester. It is he who has wronged me. To take me from my baby? Who would do such a thing? He's a monster. There is no feeling in him.'

'Addie. Think. He is not a monster. Truly he is not unfeeling. You must apologise else there is no chance at all that he will do different. If you won't do it for yourself, you must do it for Grace. At least make the attempt.'

'He can wait until Judgement Day for me to say I am sorry. It will not come before then.' But her voice at least had dropped, and she turned her head too, tucking her face against the baby. Grace rolled her head as far as she could and her legs began to thrash with the effort of trying to discover where Addie had gone or what new game they might be playing, but her mama's face was hidden and her shoulders heaving and Grace set up a moan like that of a calf when calling for its mother. Addie reached a slow arm about Grace and rolled her into her side and undid her bodice to bare her breast and the baby settled, gulping and snuffling in the pleasure of comfort restored. I had such a strange feeling, watching them, wondering what it would be like to bring forth life and keep it alive from my own self. More than that: I wished for it; I envied Addie the closeness of it. I would not allow it though. I would not have a baby or that would be my life. There would be another and another and nothing left of my self; my life being decided for me.

I left them, hoping that Addie would see the sense in my words, and went back to the dining room to do some sewing – that night finishing the new dress for Grace that I had been working on. Even if I would never see her wearing it, Papa would surely allow it to go with her when she left for the mission.

The hall door opened and Addie rushed in and across the room as if the momentum of her desperation carried her, and flung herself at Papa's feet, burying her face against his knees.

From habit, he placed one of his hands on her head. I can see it so clear in my mind's eye still, after all these years, pale and long-fingered and gentle against her dark curls.

'Oh Papa, Papa. I am sorry, truly I am, only don't do this thing, don't make me please, I beg you.' Her voice came out muffled against the cloth of his trousers. 'I will learn my lesson, I will, Papa, you will see. Let me keep her.'

He pushed her away from him, with the design to create distance rather than to hurt her, so that she had to rock back onto her heels to prevent herself falling. 'Look at me please, Adelaide.' She lifted her face, which was smeared and blotched with tears. 'I see you are penitent and am glad of it. Remember this: that you believed your behaviour to be wrong, and in so many ways. But I will not change my mind. Do not expect it of me; do not hope; naught but disappointment can follow. You will pack a bag and next week we will ride to the Travellers Rest. The baby will be cared for, of that you may be sure. I am not cruel or wicked. It is for you that I follow this course. I would not leave you destitute, though others might. If you do not understand today, you will one day. I do not doubt it.'

There was nothing to hope for now but that Mrs Martin at the Travellers Rest would show the kindness to Addie that she had once shown to me.

*

I should not have been surprised by the events before Addie left. She had been fussing through her clothing for days, putting things aside and discarding them, and not taking as much as I thought she would need. 'I must do it myself, mustn't I? As Papa told me to,' she said, shrill, when I asked if she needed help after supper one night, rolling a petticoat into a ball and rolling some more before stuffing it into a bag.

Papa, passing by, said, 'Leave her be, Hester.'

Now I wonder if he knew what she was doing and did not want her to be disturbed in her plans, but to deal with events once they began to unfold. Perhaps the prospect of dispensing justice felt like an action that was clear and measurable, that it might allow him to think something of himself. (But I might be wrong in this. Memories are just the survivors of complete events and are not easy to interpret; in the recalling they can be used to create a story that is only partially true or not true at all. I have sometimes found it hard enough to know what is real even when events are unfolding around me.) Papa had foreseen what she might do where I had not for all the time I was with her. It didn't seem right. He knew Addie better than I. Why was that?

When I woke the morning before Addie was to leave, she was no longer in bed. I dressed and made my way through the house to the veranda and finally to the kitchen and did not pass her along the way. Fred was coming down the path with two pails of milk, and the cows were ambling away from the stable. There was no sign of Papa. Flora had stoked the fire in the kitchen stove, and was busying herself cutting bread and making tea and stirring porridge. Bobby was at her feet with Skipper and Sal curled against him.

'Tea, Miss?' Flora said.

'Please,' I said and she poured me a cup. I supposed that Addie was visiting the privy, or had gone to visit the shore, as she liked to do.

Fred came in with the milk and set it at the end of the table. 'Did you know?' he said.

'Know what?'

'About Addie of course.' Then, seeing my blankness, 'She's run away. Left before daybreak taking Grace with her.'

'Why aren't you looking then? What are you thinking? Never mind breakfast. I'll go myself.'

'No need,' he said. He pulled out a chair and sat, legs outstretched and hands in pockets. 'Papa was expecting it. Flora has been watching for days.'

My eyes met Flora's; hers were fearful. Deliberately, she dipped a beaker of fresh milk and handed it to Bobby. Sal nosed at it and he pushed her snout away. She ladled some porridge into a bowl and brought it to Fred with a jug of cream.

'Flora,' I said.

'It's not her fault,' Fred said. 'Don't go blaming her. Papa told her to, and what else could she do? She made sure of what Addie was doing and her direction and came back to find Papa. He's gone to fetch her.'

'She might do anything,' I said. 'Why didn't you tell me, or warn Addie?'

'And leave her wandering alone?'

'Did she take a horse?'

'She did, but she can't go fast with Grace. She's not you, Hett. Papa will catch her soon enough. He'll have it in hand. What good would come of it? Addie can't run away and care for a baby on her own. Where would she live? How would she live? She has only herself to blame and yet she is surprised that hardship falls on her.'

'Yes. Tull is gone and now Addie bears this on her own.'

'What would he do? What could you expect of him?'

'He might find employment. Papa could employ him. He is intelligent.'

'Oh, yes,' Fred said.

'And trustworthy.'

'I think one thing we have found is that he is *not*. I know him – at least I thought I knew him – better than any of us. The hours we spent together. And see? I knew nothing of his attachment to Addie, nor saw any sign of hers to him. Did you?'

'No,' I said, which was not true.

'He asked about leasing a run, the cost of it. Perhaps that should have made me wonder.' Fred shrugged. 'As to accepting a marriage, Papa would never agree, so do not encourage Addie to think of it. He believes that crossbreeding creates weakness. Of course he is wrong, as Mr Darwin has shown, but Papa will not hear of it. Social ruin. It would be easier to be an animal. People have considerations that no animal does.' He let his spoon fall and watched it subside into his porridge.

'Eggs, Mister Fred?' Flora asked.

'None, thank you.'

I was on the veranda when they returned: Addie stricken and wet-faced on her horse, trailing Papa. There was a red mark across her cheek and her eyes had become small with weeping. And poor Grace was in her arms. I ran to meet them and took Grace when Addie handed her down. Papa, dismounted, grabbed her by an arm and yanked her down. She landed awkwardly, half-sitting so that she appeared to be mired in the marsh of her skirts. 'Papa!' I said, and crouched at her side. She was like a small hot bird, heaving with sobs. Papa pushed his gaucho's hat to the back of his head, and took Addie's arm in his clenched hand and dragged her from me, heading for the stable. Addie pulled back, huffing out small sobs.

I ran to catch them up, Grace screaming in earnest against me now, and her head battering my chest. 'Papa,' I said. 'Enough. She will go.'

'I will not go,' Addie screamed. 'I will not.'

'You will mind your business, Hester,' Papa said, the words flinging out. 'Had you been more careful of your sister we would not have come to this. Be grateful you are not next.'

I followed at a distance after that, for Grace's sake, but continued to the stable. They had gone inside when I reached it. I peered around the doorway.

'I do not beat you for punishment, or for the joy of it,' Papa was saying to Addie, calm as could be in his smooth preacher's voice. 'I do it because it is right. You *will* do as I say. I will let you go now but do not dare to move, Adelaide. There, see my hands, how steady they are.'

Addie stood before Papa shaking, her stare fixed on him. His outstretched hands were pale against the shadows and his black coat and appeared almost to be floating in the darkness. His right hand trembled. He dashed it down his coat front and held it out once more – still this time.

'There. You will not forget about right and wrong another time. I *will* save you. I will restore you.' He lifted his riding crop from where it had fallen to the ground. I did not want to see this and drew back, but I could not help hearing it. 'You will not disobey me again.' Between the words came the hiss of leather cutting air and the solid sound of it striking her and her cry, which was not only of pain, but also of shock at what Papa was capable of. Five more strokes.

'Enough, Papa!' I said.

Papa stopped to speak in a voice become breathless. 'Be quiet, Hester, I say.'

'Do not, Hester,' Addie said. 'Think of Grace.'

So I held the baby's warm body close and rubbed her hiccupping back and thought of wee Mary those years ago and how often I had held her like this, curled into me when Mama was sad.

When it was done and Papa released her, Addie stumbled from the door and seeing me there took Grace, very gentle and murmuring soft words, and carried her to the house, walking upright but jerky, as if a mechanism had come loose inside her and she could no longer move as a whole. I found her in the bedroom where she fed Grace to stillness, never taking her eyes from her, stroking her dark hair until they both were soothed.

She rose. Her back had become stiff.

'Let me see,' I said. She stood still while I drew her dress from her shoulders. Stays would have saved her from some of the force of Papa's blows, but she had not worn any for almost a year. Her back was flushed red, and striped a deeper colour where the crop had struck.

'Oh, Addie. He should not have,' I said.

'Please, Hester. I will not talk of it again.'

She stayed in our room that day, packing Mama's old travelling bag neat and careful, without haste or speed, hardly looking at what her hands did.

The next morning we waited on the veranda – Addie with Grace, Flora with Bobby, me with the dogs – while Papa saddled the horses and strapped on Addie's small case.

He came and stood at the steps. 'All set?' he said, a trifle too hearty.

We walked down. Addie would not look at him. She held a kiss to Grace's cheek and buried her nose to her neck and breathed her in.

Papa stamped his boot heel into the dirt more than once and glared at me.

I put my hand to Addie's arm. 'Will you let me hold her?' I asked.

'Oh, Hester. I will die of it. I will.' She flung an arm about my neck, Grace in the middle, and when we drew apart I was holding Grace, who shifted and murmured. She was sweet and soft. She was made for this, to be held and loved and soothed, and I could see what the doing of it meant to Addie, how it made her and how it became her.

'Come, Adelaide,' Papa said. 'Do not make a show.' His face was a mask of kindness, an uncomfortable fit with his tone. He took her elbow.

She snatched it from him as if his hand burned. 'Do not make the mistake of ever touching me again, Papa. Else things will end badly.' She walked away up the slope to the horses not looking about at anything. Flora took Grace from me, hitching her weight into her side. I went after them – Flora coming behind more slowly – and steadied Addie's horse while she mounted.

'Goodbye, Hett,' she said. 'I will see you again, I suppose.' She swung her horse around and dug in her heels before Papa could give any signal, and he had to hurry to catch up. It made him appear undignified, as if he were the one being led away in disgrace. I looked around when they had gone to see the small figure of Flora returning to the house, carrying her new burden. Bobby went at her side, as he would have to always from now.

18

THE COORONG
MARCH 1862

Wherever I went I was looking beyond: out to sea or at the mail boat or at the dust that sometimes rose from the stock route. I watched that slow brown smudge and it was as if a wind blew me towards it. I could cut my hair and dress as a boy and put on my riding clothes; I could be a drover or make my fortune on the goldfields. Only I could not be easy leaving Addie at the Travellers Rest and Fred on his own with Papa, who I could never trust again.

Papa had taken Flora and Bobby and Grace to the mission early in February. He said there was no reason for them to stay and there was nothing I could do except weep over the loss of Grace, and not only for Addie's sake. The longing she had set up in me would not pass. Was this where will began to crumble, at this point, with desire for a baby of one's own? It would go. I would wait it out. It was not as if I had a choice.

Papa had persuaded the bank to lend him further funds, on the basis of what he called 'significant improvements to the land'. I could not help thinking it fortunate that we were so far down the lagoon; it was not likely that they would visit and discover our true situation. It was enough to pay for two more native shepherds – cheaper than white men, but needing more direction, Papa said. There was too much to do without them. He was seldom home at midday.

Fred began to stay out overnight after working all day on the run. He was wild eyed and hungry on his return, and had an air of sort of desperate triumph. I asked where he had been after his first night away.

'On the peninsula, seeing if I can survive there without Tull.' He blinked and rubbed his eyes and his hair. When he took off his jacket sand fell from its folds.

'Do you think you can?'

'I can learn to. It's lonely. He said it would be.'

'You must tell me next time,' I said. 'Promise me, Fred.'

Papa was often gone overnight too. I did not ask where, but tended the garden and did the washing and went along the shore, remembering bathing there that hot summer, and walking with Mary and meeting Rimmilli. It was late afternoon – a good time of day in the heat. Once, everyone and everything would have emerged blinking from shade and shelter and done the work of a day in an hour. But there was no one about – I had seen no natives for months – and no pressing tasks, only birds moving about in the trees. A flock of pelicans came in a few yards above. They are enormous in flight and look around with intelligence and they continued at that height, cruising the length of the lagoon (one of the tracks of their world I suppose) until they were gone from sight. I stood at the last to see them for longer.

In the distance Skip barked, which Sal took up and I looked about: Charles covering the ground in big strides and the dogs dancing about him. It was as if he'd left the day before.

'You,' I said.

'I've been watching you since the house. I could tell what you were thinking from there – the same as always. Still fighting your nature.'

'Which is what?'

He stopped, his hat tipped back, and gave the question some attention. 'Why, to leave. To flee and never to look back. You know that.' He had changed. He was older, more defined. His voice rang out but his expression was less certain, assessing me as I was him. Was I glad to see him?

'How would I do such a thing?'

'I think you would if you could.' He came closer.

My face was hot and I turned from him so he would not see. 'All the time you've been gone and that is the first thing you say.'

'The second. And I am the opposite – always trying to come back even while I am travelling away.'

'That makes no sense at all.'

'No. I tell myself the same. It makes no difference.'

'To what?'

'Everything. That's what I was thinking, looking at you.'

'Oh.' I had forgotten him, how dangerous he was to me, and folded my arms to make a wall between us.

He leaned in and kissed my cheek, a prickling touch; he had grown his whiskers. He smelled of sweat and the road and of himself.

'Why did you come back?'

'I said I would.'

'I thought you would not.'

'I thought that too. I told myself I was done.' He lifted his shoulders and let them fall, as if there were no accounting for the behaviour of some people, and looked along the shore and back to the house and stable. 'Where is everyone?'

I told him some half-truths about Addie (that she had been working at the Travellers Rest for the past two months) and explained Fred's current activities.

'A sort of Robinson Crusoe?' Charles said.

'I suppose.'

'Is Mr Finch about?'

'Out working.'

'Tull?'

'Away.' I considered this true, as far as it went.

'So it's only you here.'

'And Skipper and Sal.' They lifted their heads and panted a little and flopped back down on the path. 'Papa will be home later, and perhaps Fred. Would you like something to drink? Tea?'

'Just to be here.'

I returned to my tussock and he sat beside it, his legs outstretched. I pointed out a suitable seat a yard away but he shook his head. 'It's nice here.'

'It's the same over there.'

'In the sun.' He held his face into it and turned slowly until he was looking at me. 'Near you, I mean.' He took a fold of my skirt in his fingers, idly, and felt it.

'Oh.'

He lay back and shut his eyes and the dogs circled him and collapsed at his side, resting their slender heads across his belly so they rose and fell with his breathing.

'Stop it,' he said.

'What?'

'Looking.'

'You've ridden from Melbourne and now you're sleeping in the sun.'

'I've been thinking of this. Being here. You. That's all.'

'This particular moment?'

'I am but a simple man, a poor player, strutting, fretting etcetera.'

'You *say* that.'

He lifted a hand to stroke Skipper's head and fondle her ears.

'I'm sorry for how I was,' I said.

'It's all right.'

'It's not.'

'I did not expect … anything … anything you might have been thinking. I was too forward. I'm sorry for it.'

'So, friends.'

His hand on Skipper stilled and his eyes opened with the startling blue flash of a kingfisher's wing. 'Friends, eh?'

'Yes. I'm going back now. Are you coming?'

'Where you go I must follow. Help me up though.' He lifted a hand and I pulled him up and before I could step away he put his arms around me very tight, like a dare he could not resist, and said, 'I missed your little self, Hester,' and released me. 'Come along then, *friend*,' and we walked up the path with the dogs at our side.

He kept me company through the afternoon, milking the cows while I grubbed up a few potatoes and fossicked for late tomatoes, and sat in the kitchen doorway as he had done in the past with his feet against a post and when I joined him he told me of Melbourne and the gallery school.

Papa rode in late. Charles went to meet him, taking his horse.

Papa came down. On his way past the kitchen he said, 'Did you know of this?'

'No.'

'He might have sent word. Is he staying long?'

'I don't know.'

'Did you tell him about Addie?'

'No.'

'Tull?'

'No.'

'Good.' He went inside.

It was not restful with Papa around. It was difficult for him to pretend that all was well with so much evidence to the contrary. When Fred did not come home we sat down to dinner and after a pipe and a drink on the veranda Papa went early to bed. I took the lamp and made up the bed in Tull's room, which I had not been into since he was sent away. His old shield, curving a little at its edges as it dried, and his weapons were still there, also a shirt on the door and a round white stone on the shelf by his bed, which I picked up. It was about the size of a quail's egg and fitted perfectly into my hand. I remembered the feel of it; the day we came here.

'He won't mind?' Charles asked, leaning in the doorway.

'No,' I said.

From the veranda we watched the stars. The air was thick between us.

Finally Charles said, 'Remember the first time I was here? Fifty-seven it must have been.'

'Yes.'

'There were so many of you, and all of you so lively, talking and laughing, and your ideas. And you were like a wasp buzzing around. That sting of yours.' He smiled. 'Keeping everyone moving. Father told my mother that you – your family that is – were very advanced in your thinking. My mother was very shocked at *Jane Eyre*.'

'A long time ago. I remember it differently.'

'Well, who could ever know what you think, Hester Finch?'

'You would. But what you think: that's a mystery. You *seem* quite open. I don't believe it.'

'Why, at this moment only that I am glad to see you again.'

'See?' I said.

We fell silent.

'I don't expect anything,' he said.

'What could you expect?'

'Nothing. Your company.'

'You can have that.'

At breakfast next morning Papa asked Charles to stay for a few days. He had to visit the inland run, he said. 'It's providential that you're here. I don't like to leave Hester alone.'

'Of course, sir,' he said blandly. He had a way of looking transparent. No one would think him dangerous.

'I am quite sure Charles has better things to do, Papa,' I said. 'He is on his way to town to see his family. I can look after myself. He taught me to shoot.'

'Indeed?' Papa said; his tea-cup halted between the table and his mouth.

'Yes, so I don't need him.'

Charles said, 'A break in the journey would be just the thing.'

Papa left. A wall of cloud was gliding towards the peninsula. It seemed likely to rain – a good time for planting. I went inside to fetch the cabbage seeds from the dresser, passing Charles sitting quiet outside drawing with his old concentration.

I watched him through the window – no harm in that surely, no risk. His hair was shorter now, cut by someone other than himself, but the fringe fell across one eye. He pushed it back and looked over his shoulder at me and I couldn't turn away. For once he didn't smile, but was serious, rather. He stood and passed by the window and came inside.

'You should not have stayed,' I said.

'I thought we were friends.'

'We are.' I could not tell him the truth: that he frightened me, that he made me fear myself. 'The best I ever had. That's the truth, Charles.'

'It's no use, Hett. I do not feel friendly towards you. That's not what I feel at all.'

'I meant what I said.'

'You said you were sorry.'

'For the *way* I said it. Only for that. I will not become like Mama. If you had seen her.'

He came closer and reached, pleading, and took my hand. 'If help had been close it would have been different.'

'It might have, but it isn't always enough. It was not only that. That was just the end of everything. It was bad before then. To lose control of my life …' I pulled my hand away. 'I tell you, I will get it back and when I do I will never give it to another.' And I pushed past him, outside, and leapt from the veranda and ran.

I stayed out all afternoon, first in the garden, and then roaming the shore. High above, birds coiled and twisted with dazzling speed, knitting into expanses and unravelling – a long thread stretching out, trailing the garment behind them. And the sound they made was not so different. A thread to a garment was as a single note to music, or a symbol to an equation. There are patterns and similarities in so many things if one can but learn to see. Six hours of distracting myself with such thoughts when I could have been with him.

When the sun was a few degrees above the horizon and the clouds were closer and pink light was flooding through and beneath, there was no putting off my return. There was a lamp in the kitchen window and darkness outside and through the swaying vines I watched Charles moving about inside, turning salt pork in the frying pan and lifting the lid of a saucepan to poke its contents with a knife.

'I know you're there,' he said. 'It's almost ready.'

'Just back from a walk,' I said, stepping through the door.

'Of course you are.'

'You cook as well?'

'Camp food only. Plates?'

I fetched two and he put the food out – meat, salad greens, buttered potatoes – and picked up the plates and took them into the house. We were quiet while we ate. The sounds of night: frogs in the old suck, the ratchet and shrill of crickets and cicadas, a distant splash. The wind gusted through the house and the back door slammed. Sound died.

'Sometimes it feels as if nothing happens here,' I said. 'But things do all the time. I wouldn't know how to tell you everything.'

'I'd like to hear.'

'One day. There's a war in America, did you know?'

'I had heard.'

'Think how many people you would need to have a war.'

'More than there are here.'

'Fred should have come home,' I said. 'This weather.'

'Too late for that.' He poked a potato and set his fork down and rocked his glass on its base. The water lolled. He looked up from it. 'I don't know what to say to you. I don't know what's right, what will make you understand.'

'It's the same for me.'

'Nothing dishonourable. If you have no feelings for me … That is, I wish to … to know your feelings for me.' The words rushed at the end; he could not hold his gaze steady.

'I like you. I told you.'

'Not what I mean.'

'They don't matter.'

'I cannot help mine.'

'Nor I,' I said. 'But that is not all there is in life. I don't want them. I wish I felt otherwise. Indifferent. With all my heart I wish that. I cannot prevent what I feel, but I need not give way to it. I know what happens then. Mama was contented in England, but left it for Papa. It might have been the same for your mother; I don't know. And then we came here, all through Papa's choices, his risks, because of him. One day I will leave here, and it will not be with another man or because of a man. Men make so free with the lives of others, and judge themselves so little when things go awry. I wonder at the presumption of it. Where does it come from? How could I respect such a person?'

Charles reached across the table and grasped my hands. 'I am not all men, only myself. I presume nothing with you, Hett. It would take a brave man to do that.'

'Charles.' I pulled free. 'Find someone else. A woman who wishes to please.' I put my hands to my mouth – a sob came out – and shoved the chair back and fled the table. He caught me at the door. A sliver of cool air came in. He pushed it shut. I buried my face against the coats. Charles's arms were on either side and he was against my back and there was a touch at my neck, very light and delicate – him smoothing my hair aside – and his warm breath on my neck and his soft mouth, soft, and I could not think.

'I don't wish to be pleased. You think I am free. I am not. How can I be when I know you?' He pulled me against him and turned me around. 'Hettie, I want you so. You.'

I kissed him on his mouth, hard, and wrenched away. 'Let me out now, let me go. You know what I feel.'

He lifted himself away and I flung the door wide and was through. The first drops of rain were falling – heavy, sparse. I sat on the settee. A gust of wind hurtled in and the rain began. After a while the air stilled and the rain settled and made a dripping veil of the veranda. I was cold but not wet up against the house.

A shadow fell across me. Charles slid the window up. 'Are you coming in?'

'No.'

The shadow moved. He came outside with two cups of tea and we sat apart.

After a long time he said, 'Would you … would you think of marrying me?'

'For what purpose?'

'To be with you. For us to be with each other.'

'No. We couldn't do it.' I would not look at him. 'You'll find

287

someone,' I said after a while. I began to shiver, not only with cold.

'I could take you from here.'

'I will find a way myself. I will not be beholden.'

'Come inside, Hettie.'

'I can't.'

He went in and came back a few minutes later with a pile of quilts. 'Lean forward,' he said. He wrapped a quilt about my shoulders and flung one about his own, and it might have been sumptuous possum fur. I was warmer then, but still shaking, my arms wrapped tight about me as if my own will and strength would stop me flying apart. The tears welled and fell. There was no end to them and no reason that I could tell.

'What can I do?' he said. 'Tell me.'

I shook my head.

He moved along the settee.

'Don't.'

'I can't make it any worse.' He pulled me onto his lap and turned me into him and wrapped his quilt about us both. 'I won't do anything.' He pressed his face to my hair and breathed it in. He was my favourite smell and my favourite feeling. His heart pounded next to me; he was a living thing and warm and himself. Night turned. I slept a little I think; between closing and opening my eyes the clouds had broken and stars webbed the black between. Charles's shirt was loose at the throat. I touched the backs of my fingers and then my mouth to his skin, against his pulse. I was thinking only of this moment. I kissed him so lightly, hardly moving; that was all. I would allow myself that and he would never know.

He woke. I knew the moment – his arms tightened and stilled again – but he pretended he had not and I pretended the same and in this way I could go on kissing him softly: across his cheeks, around his mouth. It was very hot. With utmost care I undid three shirt buttons and put my hand on his chest and eased the cloth aside and touched my mouth there and kissed my way up his throat – he lifted his chin a little – towards his mouth. He was quivering by then. It was a game almost to make him admit he was awake even though part of me didn't want him to, and when I reached his mouth I kissed him and didn't stop and he couldn't pretend any more and kissed me back. It was the best feeling of my life up to then. He held me very tight and laughed and groaned, fumbling at my dress and kissing what skin was bare.

'Once,' I said.

'How do I get you out of this?'

We went into his room. It didn't seem so wicked or terrible to help each other undress – all those buttons and our hands trembling – or for his hands and body to touch and move against me and for me to know at last what he felt like. It was everything, not only pleasure, and shocking.

We woke late and did not get up until hunger drove us. Fred came home early in the afternoon when Charles and I were finishing lunch. He said little and did not bring out his work to show Charles. He had in mind dry clothes and going out again.

'I'll be gone for two more nights,' he said.

Charles gave me a questioning glance.

'He misses Tull,' I said after he had gone.

Once, I had said. There could be no harm in that, no risk, or not much. I could live with the odds whatever they were, but surely they weren't so bad. I had no conception of what might come after. The things you feel and experience are not shut away so easy. They will have their way with you and live with you. Two more days and two nights – that was all.

Later, I told myself that I was tired, I was upset, I was not in control. It was not true. I was never more aware. It was a recalibration rather of my mind and body and the ways they worked together. In those moments my rational mind cared more for touch, for the exact now, than for any future.

19

THE COORONG
APRIL 1862

There are years that pass in which nothing at all seems to happen but the change in seasons, and even those can't be called events considering the way in which they dissolve into each other. And there are days in which entire lives turn on their axes, grinding against each other like mechanisms, crushing the things that fall between. Afterwards there are only pieces remaining and people must make of them what they will and what they can.

Dusky afternoon was draining away when I went to shut the chickens in and feed the horses. Around all things – trees and house and fences and cows – darkness gathered and began to spread, and out of the obscurity of trees a shape moved soft and sure towards me.

'Skipper, Sal,' I called and they bounded from their explorations at the other end of the yard. Before they reached me Skipper's name sounded again and for an instant I thought it the faint echo of my own voice, as sometimes happened when a sea mist came up the lagoon or rolled across the hills of sand from the open water, muffling vision while it amplified sound. But it was clear that evening.

Skipper and Sal began to bark and at a low whistle leapt towards the shape, which now resolved into a person, and wriggled with delight when they reached it.

'Skip, down,' a familiar voice hissed. 'And you,' speaking to Sal.

'Tull.' For it was he, looming clearer, desperate and stricken.

'You shouldn't be here. What is it? Is something wrong?'

'Addie.'

'What? What of her? You know where she is?'

He gave me one of his old patient, pitying looks. 'I've been there all this time.'

'Of course you have,' I said. 'What is it then?'

'Mr Martin, at the inn. He means ill by her, I am sure of it. Mrs Martin has gone to see family in Goolwa – left last week. I'm afraid of what happened to the other maid. She's missing. She went before Addie went there. A letter arrived from her family asking about her. Addie took it and opened it. Mr Martin didn't see.'

'Jane? What's happened?'

'Mr Martin told Addie she went back home, that she did not like a place so wild and desolate, but the stable hand never heard her say such a thing. He said she was glad of the work. She needed the money to send to her family.'

'Could she be working elsewhere?'

'No.' Tull shook his head. 'Her family are looking. There's been no news from her since December. I've seen him like this.'

'Like what?' I grasped his arm.

'Angry.'

'That's all?' I let go of him. 'We are all angry sometimes, I think.'

'The temper he has. I believe he has killed before.'

'Killed? No one knows who killed Mr Robinson. There was no proof of anything.'

'Proof is only part of the truth. You heard of the black who drowned?'

'A story. The police said so. No one found him. I do not believe he existed.'

'No white man found him. He was killed and he was found, sunk in a waterhole – the big one behind the Travellers Rest – by the blackfellas down that way.'

'It was true?'

'He sold fish to Mr Martin. Like … others. Mr Martin owed him money but would not pay. No proof that it was Mr Martin, true enough. But everyone knows. Three months Addie is owed now. It's her money and she will not leave. He did not pay Jane either and now she is gone. No one to watch for her. I didn't like to leave her there on her own, Mrs Martin being away. Mr Martin says later, next week, but never this week. I cannot make Addie leave. She doesn't believe me. She won't listen.'

'She has always been stubborn.'

'Would Mr Finch fetch her?'

'He's not here. You must make her come, Tull, on your own. She'll listen to you. I know she will.'

Tull said, 'I tried, I tell you.'

'He wouldn't hurt Addie, surely.'

'Because she is white? That makes her safe?' He regarded me in silence for a few seconds, as if he saw something in me that filled him with melancholy. 'You don't think you are better than black people. You *know* it, don't you? It is inside you, this belief, like your heart.' He thumped his chest. 'Birds don't think: I will fly. They *are* flight. It is what they do and what they are. In what you do, what you are, you know that you are better, but not to me, not to blacks, to yourselves only. You have forgotten that Jane is white. It did not protect her.'

I could hardly take in his meaning – and whether my recollection is correct I don't know. 'What I think doesn't matter. And what is right doesn't matter. The only thing now is keeping Addie safe. Hasn't she been ruined enough? You would not ruin her further.'

Tull shuddered and collected himself. 'I want her safe and you think I'm the one she must be saved from. You don't know Mr Martin. In a rage he does anything. Mrs Martin—' He broke off and looked at me. 'Well. When his temper is up it's better to be quiet. Addie should not be around him. I told him Mr Finch would know of it, that I would make sure he knew. He said he would make sure Mr Finch learned that I had seen Addie. It would be strange if I did not when I have known her so long and wish her safe.'

'But seeing Addie? Oh, Tull. You cannot. Papa will— I don't know what he might do. He is determined. He will never allow you and Addie to be together.'

'Where is he?'

'At Tinlinyara.'

'Mr Martin showed me his musket.'

292

'Did he threaten you?'

'No. He shot a magpie from a tree. It fell at our feet, its wing broken, and he put his boot-foot on it and pressed it down slow. The bird looked at me. No need for him to say anything.' His gaze was unwavering.

'It's too late to go now. The horses will go lame. You can leave in the morning with Fred. The two of you can make her come.'

He spoke louder then, very desperate. 'You should come too. You must. She will listen to you.'

He was right. Of course he was. Three of us might persuade her. It was only that I felt rather ill. It was a month since Charles left, and even though I believed I had done right in remaining at Salt Creek, I had been listless since and could take no pleasure or interest in anything. Charles was constantly in my mind. By the end of his stay at Salt Creek, but for Addie and Fred, who I would not leave to manage Papa on their own, I would have gone with him, I think. 'Yes,' I said. 'I will. Of course I will. Come in now. Use your room.'

'The baby, Grace? Can I see her? Addie will want to know.'

'Oh, Tull, she's gone. I'm sorry for it. Papa took her and Flora and Bobby back to the mission. He said there was no reason for them to remain here. It would only make things more difficult.'

'Ah,' he said on a breath, as if he'd been struck. 'How will I tell her? How can we be together again? What can I do?'

'Addie. First we must get her.'

'Yes,' he said. But his face was despairing.

We rode off a little after daybreak, the dogs loping along behind and disappearing into the bush and reappearing further on. There was no ease between Fred and Tull. Fred's face, which had lit up at first sight of him, by some deliberate means dulled again and he didn't meet Tull's gaze. I hadn't known he had taken Addie's plight to heart so, or that he felt so bitterly towards Tull.

It was before the worst of the autumn rain started. When I travel the Coorong in my mind, as I do often, it is like that day at the turning to cooler weather, almost the last day I ever spent there with Tull and Fred together and the last that I travelled in that direction. The sky and the lagoon were sapphire, and the peninsula was that strip of white and green, and the sucks were pink rimmed and the last birds that left for winter were wheeling the sky and dipping to earth and sea to gather up more of their number before rising again, higher – clouds of them separating and cohering like shoals of fish. The noise of it. I wish I could remember it exactly; I dream it sometimes. It was never more beautiful and now I wonder if some part of me knew that it was close to the end of everything.

We rode three abreast where the track permitted, Tull a step ahead between us, making haste, but we did not speak for a long time. I could not understand it when Fred and Tull had always talked so much.

All the way down that broken road, which was still dusty and soon to turn to mud, the weather biding on the horizon for the moment, at every corner, every outcrop, every island, Tull said a few words, not in English when he always spoke English.

'What are you saying?' Fred said.

'Names.'

'Of what?'

'This.' He cast his eyes slow, a line floating out and gathering the world within its arc. 'All of it,' he said.

'It's lovely,' Fred said.

'Other places?'

'Not as beautiful.'

'Ah.' He clicked his tongue and resumed his low intermittent recitation.

'What do the names mean?' I said.

And Tull began to say them, first in his own language and then in English: Eel Lagoon, Place to Trap Mullet, Pelican Island and many others which I do not remember, and some that he did not know the words for in English. It seemed as if every part of the lagoon had a name and a story and a meaning. The stories were all around us wherever we went. There was scarcely a place without one and it felt as if we were nothing but one more story inside this world and the stories were without number. No one would have time to write them all down. But that day it was as if he were reciting a litany – as if there were a chance that he might not remember everything that we were passing. I wish that I had paid closer attention.

And then Tull said, as if this were the true direction of his thoughts, 'I thought she had been married to Mr Martin.'

'Addie? Why would you think such a thing?' Fred said.

'Because I watched Mr Finch take her and all her things to live with Mr Martin and his old wife. I thought Addie was his new wife.'

'To work, that's all. He may only have one wife.'

'Addie said this too. I didn't know if she spoke the truth or was saying what she wished to be true. So we are not stealing her from him?'

Fred shook his head. 'No.'

'If she leaves will Mr Martin follow to get her back?'

'No.' I did not like to say the next part but I thought he should know that nothing was changed whatever happened this day. 'Papa will want her to be away from you still. But she's not, is she?'

Tull shook his head. 'Am I so bad?' he asked.

I hardly knew what to say. There was no badness in him that I had ever seen, but I knew that I had not seen all of him. 'Bad? Of course not,' I said. 'You should have stayed away from Addie, though, Tull. You must know that. And she should have stayed away from you.'

'Hettie's right,' Fred said.

'Mr Finch said to me, "'We are all men, all equal, in the eyes of the Lord".'

'You've seen for yourself you can't trust to everything he says,' Fred said.

'I believed him,' Tull said.

'He would say that we are not all equal in the eyes of men. It is other people who make things difficult. He loves Addie the best of us,' Fred said.

'Does he think I do not?' Tull asked. 'Is it because we have nothing to give for her?'

'No. Not that,' Fred said. 'We do not buy and sell our women. They can marry who they please.'

'But she may not marry me even though she wishes to.'

'She's only seventeen, too young to decide.'

'Is seventeen young?'

We rode past a treed headland and for a few minutes the lagoon was hidden from view. 'You must see, Tull, the way people think, what sort of life she would have with you. And for Papa and his work, for Hester, all of us, what it would mean for that.'

'We could get a lease and run our own farm,' Tull said. 'Take Grace back. Or move somewhere.'

Stupidly, I said, 'Perhaps you could.' But he was not a child who could be told a nightmare was not true and believe it. There would be white people wherever he went. He knew it too.

'How would I hide who I am?' He slapped his hands to his chest and his arms. 'I have read in Charles Darwin the things that white men do to people like me. I read all of it, including the parts that you did not read me, Fred. I knew it would be like this, but thought it could be different, that I could make it different because I knew. Knowing is not enough.'

'No. Believing something is not enough either.' Somehow I had held onto the idea of our family as enlightened. Yet I did not altogether think Papa wrong and I also thought that Tull was a better person than Stanton or Hugh. I could not make the thoughts run clear. 'He likes you, a great deal. Not for Addie though. The money that Addie is waiting for, is it for a lease?'

He didn't speak.

Fred said, 'Papa is expecting that money. It's not for you. In any case, it's not enough for a lease. What other money do you have?'

'From selling fish to Mr Martin. My family and I shared the money. We built another fish trap where Stanton could not find it.'

'Where?'

He shrugged.

Fred dropped his head at that and when he lifted it he said, 'It doesn't matter, Tull,' he said. 'They will never sell you or Addie a

296

lease. And what of your family? Addie will not live like that. She is not born to that life. You shouldn't expect it. It's wrong.'

I wished then as now that Fred had not said those things. But it was the truth. What life would there have been for Addie cut off from all company but Tull's? I wonder now that I never considered what a life with her might be like for him. It is not easy to turn your back on your family and deny them, if that was what he planned. 'And if you did get a lease, would people do business with you?'

'Will they always hate me?'

'I don't know. Perhaps not hate. They don't see you.' But it was that they would not stop seeing him.

Tull fell back into silence.

The Travellers Rest came into view before mid-morning. We slowed at the sight and called the dogs close. It had been almost picturesque when I visited with Mama and Addie those years ago; now the yard was untidy, the wagon gate swinging loose so that anything might stray in or out, the flowering plants about the doorway straggling out thin arms, and there were sacks of grain leaning against a stable wall, two with mouths agape – an invitation to spoil. I could not feel easy.

We tethered the horses to the outside of the railing, none of us mentioning that flight might be necessary, and brought the dogs within and shut the gate behind us, leaving the musket strapped to Fred's horse. When no one came out we went into the inn, pushing the door and stepping down into the vestibule. Some leaves had blown under the door and crunched underfoot. The paint at the doors had chipped. We first looked in the dining hall, a gloomy space. Its wooden walls were weeping sap and the rough tables were marked and scarred from careless use. No one was there. We returned to the vestibule.

'The parlour's this way,' I said, and began down the hallway to the left. There was no runner to soften our footfall. Our boots sounded against the rough boards.

'What will he do if surprised?' I whispered.

Fred shook his head. 'Mr Martin?' he called. His voice cracked, but he cleared his throat and it came out firmer. 'Mr Martin?'

'What?' The voice that came from further within was deep, rough, a trifle slurred.

We stopped.

'Come on, come on now,' came the voice again from the end of the hall on the other side of a door. 'Don't be shy, you'll find me if you just keep walking. Not open for business quite yet, but open for conversation right enough.'

We went on and pushed the door open and Fred stepped into the room, with me a pace behind him. Tull remained in the hallway, though there was space for him to enter, if he wished. The room had changed so since last I was there. It had been neat and pretty. The chairs had faded now, and the dresser was shoved awkwardly into a corner. The rug at its feet had been moved there not so long ago, by my estimation, since the large area of pale wood in the room's centre where the sun had not touched it corresponded exactly with the dimensions of the rug. The room had recently been whitewashed; the smell of it lingered. But all these things were by way of framing Mr Martin who now heaved himself from his easy chair in front of the dresser. At its side stood a little table with a single glass and a bottle of rum. Mr Martin looked at it, and looked away. He had the air of one who was guarding something, though I could not see what that might be.

He was not tall, but was deep chested and wide shouldered and his moustaches were like horns, being massive and curved, sweeping across his wide cheeks to join his side whiskers. He was like a bear in a dollhouse. He lowered himself with a grunt and poured a glass of rum.

'I know you, boy, do I not?' Mr Martin said.

'Frederick Finch.'

'And who would that make you?' he said to me.

'Hester Finch, sir.'

'Another Finch, eh?' At that, he rubbed his hands together, which were white and hairy knuckled and hairy backed, and their fingers long for a person of his bullish build. He rubbed them together as if there were something inside he wished to squash. His small dark wet eyes watched unwavering and made me wonder if the thing that he was grinding in his hands was the thought of a creature or person and the thought pleased him. 'Come to see that sister of yours? You do not favour her overmuch.'

'Is she about?'

'About, about. She should be, what I pay her, but if you've not seen her yet she's run off again into the bushes to see that black bastard of hers, I'll wager. And there'll be trouble when she returns, I tell you that, and pay will be docked. Said she'd be a willing worker, your father. Mr Finch.'

'We'll step out to see if we can find her,' I said. 'We have to take her home. Our grandmother is visiting and wishes to see her.'

'A fucking good riddance to the little miss then.'

Fred said, 'If you would get the money that is owed her, we—' He turned his head a little, glancing over his shoulder. I wished that we had brought the musket inside with us.

'Who else is there?' Mr Martin said. He peered around me, leaning from the side of his chair. 'The black bastard himself. You should leave now. Get out. I'll have no blacks in here. Thieving scum. She'll have your hands on her, will she, and turn down decent white folk? So high and mighty is she. I'll be glad to see her gone. But as to money, I don't believe I can see my way clear to that. Board and lodging, time taken off to see your good self' – he sneered at Tull – 'leaves, let me see. Nothing. I should kill you now. It would not take but a minute.'

At this, Tull stepped into the room, casual, standing next to me. His face was still and his gaze almost lazy. He could have been thinking anything. He bent over, reaching for his boot with the utmost calm so that we all watched with nothing more than idle curiosity. I would have said his trousers had caught at the back of his boot or something of the sort. When he straightened, there was a knife in his hand: bone-handled and with a sharp blade. He swung it there between thumb and finger, in a very particular way, and we were all transfixed.

299

I backed up to the door and Fred moved to one side. Mr Martin blinked several times in rapid succession and half-closed his eyes and a grin twisted his mouth as if the scene provided an unexpected amusement. He put a hand to his glass and with a single finger began to rub its side up and down, steady, so it was hard to look away.

'Well, well,' he said. 'That puts a different complexion on things. What are you proposing exactly? To stab into my heart or slice across me neck?' He lifted his chin to expose his black-whiskered throat and drew one long finger from behind his ear to the bulge in his throat. 'You must mean it, don't be shy about it, and get the place right, here' – his finger found the hollow point beneath his chin – 'do not miss it and you will succeed. And then a small matter: I am not easy to move. Fifteen stone I would say. Would you be thinking a horse? Over the saddle? The two of you – maybe you could do it. And as to disposal, a good deep suck and the body weighted down, the bottom of a sand hill dug in, wombat holes, the entire peninsula if you could row me across unseen. Quite a choice I would say.' He lifted the glass and sipped and his marked Adam's apple bulged and receded, and with scarcely a change in the tension of his body or a shift in his position the glass flew from his hand at Tull. I cried out, but Tull swayed out of its path as easy as if it had been a ball of feathers, as if he had seen it coming minutes before, and the glass smashed the wall directly behind his head. Mr Martin lunged from his chair at Tull, but before he reached him Tull lifted his blade. Mr Martin stopped, panting.

'We won't kill you,' Tull said, 'or harm you, if you will give us Adelaide's money and tell us where she is.'

'Money first,' I said. I felt a little better seeing how cool Tull was. 'Three months' wages.'

Mr Martin drew himself up, almost calm, as if Tull's knife had punctured his rage, and regarded me: 'You Finches – I include the black Finch here, listen to him speak as if he's a lord or an admiral – you think yourselves so fine, so superior, but you're the same as people the world over. All of you with your eye on the main chance. Mark what I say, for I am a judge of character.' He swayed, the weight of him shifting from one foot to the other, as if trying to decide what to do next. And then he moved forward in small steps of resignation. 'Men, women, blacks, I hate them all, what is one less?' He clomped between us through the doorway, his words become indistinct. We followed him to the dining room where he knelt behind the counter and taking a long iron key from his pocket unlocked a trapdoor concealed beneath a foot mat and pulled out a calico bag which by the weight and sound of it must contain coins.

'Now, what will we say she was worth, eh? Give you too much and I shall have to accuse you of theft and what would happen to a black accused of such a thing? So, not too much for the sake of your own good selves.'

'What is fair,' Tull said.

'Fair is nothing. Has she ever worked a day in her life? The hands on her, smooth and dainty as you please, and the complaining.'

'What was agreed, then,' I said. 'If you could not make her work to your satisfaction, that is your fault I think.'

'Oh, you think that do you, Miss Finch? Right enough then, I'll let you be the boss, shall I?' He shoved some coins towards me. 'Take that and that will be the end of it and do not ask for a penny more.'

I scraped them into my hand and felt the weight of them and handed them to Tull who dropped them into his pocket.

'Where is Adelaide?' Tull said.

'Stupid girl took fright. She's out there somewhere, I daresay.' He waved a hand towards the grimy windows, and the yard and trees beyond. 'Told her a little story was all.'

'We'll collect her things then and go looking,' Fred said.

'You will keep us company, I hope, Mr Martin, until we are gone,' I said.

Tull inspected the blade of the knife.

Mr Martin swore very freely then and after that took us – the dogs at our sides – to the room that had been Addie's and the other maid's before her. It was small and dark and unpainted and contained nothing but two narrow iron beds and a rough plank wardrobe and a plain washbasin and jug. 'Everything here is the fine young lady's.

Take it. Take it all.' He sat on one of the beds and watched while we gathered Addie's clothes. I looked about and found Mama's little case shoved under the bed. I pulled it out and threw Addie's clothes into it.

Mr Martin came out to the horses then, with not overmuch encouragement I would say, though some grumbling, and leaned up against a fence post, one leg crossed over the other with the greatest nonchalance while we strapped Addie's case to one of the horses. Fred held the musket to Mr Martin, which he snorted at the sight of. Tull took the dogs and walked into the trees.

'Nice bit of horseflesh,' Mr Martin said. 'Happen you want to sell it, I might know a buyer.'

'We don't wish to sell it,' I said. 'It's mine.'

'Oh yes? I've heard of you, you know. The tall one, proud, disdainful.'

'How would you have? Your wife, I suppose.' It stung, if that were true. I had liked Mrs Robinson.

'Nellie likes you well enough. No, it was not she. Word has a way of spreading, Miss Finch, about all sorts of things up and down here.' His smile stretched his face.

Every word that came from his mouth seemed to insinuate something other than what the words said, but I could not guess at all his meanings. He was an uncomfortable, uneasy sort of person to converse with: friendly almost, and not altogether unpleasant.

When Tull did not immediately return Mr Martin directed Fred inside to collect some chairs and some bread and cheese. It seemed safer outside, and Tull would know immediately that all was well with us on his return. Fred handed me the musket. 'She knows how to use it, Mr Martin,' he said.

When Fred had gone into the house Mr Martin uncrossed his legs and by degrees straightened a little.

'I would not disdain to shoot you, Mr Martin. I think you would not be mourned,' I said.

He smiled at that. 'I believe you. You would keep a man on his toes – or in his bed, I daresay. I'd not get rid of you hasty.'

302

I aimed the musket at his chest.

'Bitch,' he said, in a mild way.

By degrees Fred brought the things out. It was almost pleasant sitting in the April warmth. I ate some bread, but declined the cheese since I still felt a trifle ill. Mr Martin put his feet on the fence railings and tipped his hat lower at the front. He chewed heartily. Presently he held his bread and cheese aloft. 'It's a good cheese your father makes. I'll say that for him. He's paid for many a bottle of grog with one of them. I've not seen him of late, though. Is he well then?'

'Quite well, Mr Martin,' I said.

'Ale, young Mr Finch?' he said.

'I thank you, no,' Fred said.

'I remember. Water it is then.'

A lake of parrots flew overhead, all calling to each other. There were distinct notes to their conversation: a sort of music, though I would not know how to write it. They were desirous of company and careful to stay together. Finally, late in the afternoon, Skip and Sal wriggled beneath the fence and came tearing down the slope to us, and Tull emerged from the bush beyond the fence with Addie. I had thought she might be hysterical, but she was quite sensible and walked contained and her face did not show much of what she might be feeling – neither frightened nor relieved. I ran to them and embraced her. Her hair was tangled and her face smudged with dirt. 'Where were you?'

'Gone to look for Tull, of course, only I could not find him and it was cold out last night,' she said. 'But I am well enough now. Hungry though.' We walked back towards Fred and Mr Martin. Addie did not approach close, but stopped for a moment to consider Mr Martin. 'I think you will be dead soon.'

'The fine young folk here have assured me not,' he said.

'Because of Jane.'

'Gone home to see her family. Pining. Took a ride with a bullocky passing through.'

'Murderer,' she said.

'Adelaide,' I said.

'Yes, Adelaide,' Mr Martin said. 'Fly away, Finches – all of you be gone. Leave me be here.'

Fred strapped the musket to his horse, and we mounted. Tull threw Addie up onto his horse and leapt up behind and she settled into the curve of him, his arms loose about her on either side and her curls in his face, which he rubbed his cheeks against, and we rode away from Mr Martin. I turned once to see if he were fetching a musket or anything of that sort. He remained at the fence and did nothing but watch, and watch, as if now he was waiting for something else. When I looked from the top of the hill, all had changed. He must have gone inside. In that light with the winking lights in its windows just beginning to show, like eyes, the low building put me in mind of an animal readying itself to spring. The creek at its feet licked out and the bulrushes lining its course were as bright as burning wicks in the orange light. I shivered to look at it and made haste to catch up with the others.

Fred rode in front and was silent and I was hungry and wishing to be home. The wind had turned cold and the heavy clouds had surged closer in a long line above the peninsula.

'Fred,' Tull called after we had gone a mile or two, and sparse drops of rain had begun to spatter down. 'We'll stop here, else the storm will get us.'

'It'll pass us by,' Fred said.

'If Tull says it's coming, it is, and we should do as he says.' Addie spoke as if it were a matter of fact, not a point of discussion.

'Too dark for riding,' I said, 'rain or no.'

'And shelter where?' Fred said. The trees were no cover, and in the breaks between them, looking inland, there were only a few rocky outcrops and saltpans and distant flats, which by morning would be turning to bog. 'Better to keep going.'

But without acknowledging Addie's words or Fred's dissent Tull wheeled his horse around and hardly thinking what I was doing I followed him and Addie from the track onto unbroken ground, the loose stone rolling beneath the horses' hooves. What could Fred do but follow? We dismounted to save the horses and stumbled more than once. Bushes and a small species of gum tree grew about the base of a low boulder-strewn hill that we circled a little inland, thicker at the back, and we pushed past them and came to a limestone overhang. It was lower than head height – no one but Addie could stand there – and invisible from two or three yards away for the scrubby plants around it, yet Tull went directly to it as you might go to a barn or a wood heap or anything else in plain sight. He knew it was there; it was nothing to him to have found it with such ease.

We tethered the horses near some grass and removed their saddles. Addie collected what sticks and branches lay strewn about; it was a novelty to see her become industrious and to know what we needed. She and Tull had done this before. The rain began and the ground steamed and such a smell of wet bark and wet leaves and damp soil rose around us. Tull struck up a fire with his flint. We had nothing but oat biscuits to eat so we sat about the fire in the deepening dark, eating around their edges and slowly inwards to make them last longer, and watching the flames and the wood turning to frail coals. Skipper and Sal crept close. I fed them half a biscuit each and they licked at the crumbs and that was all there was. They sighed and put their noses on their paws.

'You called him murderer,' I said to Addie.

'He is. I'm sure of it.'

'Then why did you stay when Tull tried to make you leave?'

'I thought it was just stories. I thought I could manage him. I managed Papa well enough – until Grace came, at least – and those troopers and Mr Stubbs. Men don't frighten me. It *was* all right until Mrs Martin left. I managed him; I had him on a string. And I wanted my money.'

'Papa's money,' Fred said.

'He will never see it,' Addie said.

Fred would have spoken again. To distract them from one of their old bickering exchanges I said, 'But you changed your mind.'

'Something he said. It doesn't matter now.'

Tull said, 'What?'

'A stupid thing. He said, "Women are so soft. Plump little pigeons.

Their necks are so small." And he did this.' She stroked her throat with the tips of her fingers and thumb, and shuddered.

'Poor Jane,' I said.

Tull stood and went, half-crouching, to the edge of the overhang and remained there hunched, looking out into the darkness. 'I should catch something.'

'Don't,' Addie said. 'Stay. You'll get lost; you'll go missing; I'll never see you again.'

'How would I get lost?' Tull said over his shoulder to her, puzzled. 'I could never get lost here.'

Addie went to him and rested her cheek against his back and slid her arms around him. I saw her gentleness and how she had done this before; also from her grave face that she wasn't a child any longer. 'Just stay then, for me. I'm not hungry.'

'Addie,' I said, but she paid me no attention. Tull turned and put his arms around her and pulled her deep into the shelter.

Fred said nothing. He took a saddle and one of the horse blankets and withdrew to the far end of the overhang. He pulled his collar up about his ears and his hat over his head and rolled himself in the blanket behind the wall of his saddle. I was beyond caring, and could see no way for anything to come good, not for a single one of us, and put some more wood on the fire and curled up with the dogs, a blanket around us, on the other side of the fire from Addie and Tull. I could hear nothing but the hiss and snap of burning wood and threw myself into sleep to be done with this day and my life if only for a few short hours.

Tull had the fire going when I woke next morning and the billy was on its way to boiling. Addie sat beside it, her skirts wrapped tight about her ankles to keep them from the flames, and poked at the coals and twigs with a long stick. Her face had become hectic in the heat, and smudged, and in other circumstances this could have been some childhood adventure to the peninsula to see if whales or ships might be seen. But Addie was not in an adventure; she was in the midst of some grim reckoning by the look of her.

'Papa is away?' she said, her eyes unwavering on the flames.

'At Tinlinyara.'

'Expected back?'

'I don't know. Soon, I suppose. The rain will slow him.'

'We won't risk stopping then, Tull and I. There's no gain in it.'

'Where will you go?' I said. I did not even think to try to forbid her. How would I? I could not restrain her or save her, or send Tull away. I would not hold a musket to her. She had set her course, and I would not try to change it again.

'To Raukkan, of course, to get Grace back.'

'And then?' Fred asked.

'People make their way, Fred.'

'They do, but you need not, not today anyway. He will be at least two more days I think, three with the rain; he's always longer than he reckons on. He might think differently when he sees what Tull did for you.'

Addie looked up from the fire then and her eyes moved across his face in some judgement. Did he believe what he was saying? Something like that. She knew as well as any of us, especially now, that Papa was not a mutable person. Still, some fear made her clutch at the hope of him changing his mind. Her expression became earnest. 'Do you think so, Fred, really?'

For a moment, Fred's sincerity almost persuaded me that he was right. It was his hope too. Then, as if they shared the same memory at the exact same time, their faces became suffused with doubt. I felt it too. Papa beating Addie: that's what I thought of.

'No,' she said. 'We will not risk it. We will ride on through. We have my money, and will collect Tull's and be on our way.'

Tull came back with a possum he had beaten from a tree and singed the fur off it all over – which smell I loathe – and flung the bald creature on the fire and buried it in coals. Once, Addie would have sighed over what a sweet thing the possum was and how cruel boys were, but she said nothing in this vein to Tull, only leaned forward and sniffed at the roasting smell wafting from the fire, and smiled at him. In everything that they did there was

307

awareness of the other; their movements together were a slow dance of fine adjustments. Addie placed a stick just so and Tull passed her another; she handed him a beaker of steaming tea, which they shared as they sat leaning against each other and staring into the flames. Addie put her hand on Tull's leg and he put his hand over hers. How could I stop them? Fred glanced at them from the other side of the fire, then pushed two wet leaves into the fire and watched them steam and smoke and finally burst into flame. They burned fast.

When the rain had quite stopped we packed our things and after we had finished, our shelter seemed more an empty room than a rock formation. How quickly it had become home. We knew what might happen there and now everything was uncertain.

Between the rise we were on and the distant track the ground had become a mosaic of standing water and drowned succulents and marsh. We began to pick our way across it, keeping to what high ground there was, following Tull, who moved more surely than the rest of us. There was no keeping our feet dry, and if mine were miserably cold I was sure it was the same for us all. The only sound was of feet and hooves splashing and the wind buffeting past and very high overhead and faint the sound of birds fading north. Addie and I held our skirts, but they got in our way and we couldn't see our feet. More than once I tripped on a submerged rock or uneven ground. My skirts became muddied and heavy, and the wind chilled my wet hands. It was no wonder when Addie, walking ahead of me, fell hard with a quick scream. Her eyes were wide and stricken, and try as she might she could not regain her feet and cried out again when she tried to put her foot to the ground. She sank back and clutched her ankle and her face was so grey and bloodless looking about at us all that I became truly alarmed and hurried forward.

She moaned. 'Not broken. Please let it be all right.'

Tull pulled his horse about and plunged towards her ungainly as a drunk in his haste; we reached her side together. Fred stumbled up and took our reins. Tull sank to Addie's level and felt about her ankle, which was plainly swelling. I crouched then and unlaced her boot and took it off. She sobbed and put her hands to her ankle. 'No. No. We will keep going anyway. I don't care if it's broken,' she said.

I did not know if it was broken or not. It looked straight enough. 'Just a sprain, I think. But you can't walk,' I said.

'On the horse now,' Tull said. He helped her stand on her one good foot and lifted her up and her wet stockinged foot hung against the horse's flank. She couldn't put it in the stirrup.

And so we kept going and regained the stock route; at least we were off the ground then. But mud flopped from the horses' hooves and flicked up and they slid about and Addie could not help crying out once or twice, though I think it was a little better with Tull behind, holding her. She was terribly white still. 'I'm so cold,' she said once, and I could see her shivering.

Tull caught my eye.

'One or two days' rest before you go on, Addie,' I said. 'You can't travel like this.'

'No,' she said, but it came out on a moan. Tull rubbed his cheek against hers and murmured something. She shook her head. 'I'm frightened to go there.' But the horse lost its footing and Addie cried out again. 'One night then,' she said.

Clouds scudded the sky, plunging us in and out of shade, and all around were the sounds of water dripping from trees and the flashing movements and raucous calls of birds. I am not sure we would have heard anyone approaching even had we been alert. Skipper and Sal lifted their heads, though, and darted ahead; I should have taken note of that.

Tull said, 'Addie!' and lunged for the side of the path.

It was too late. Papa came riding at a canter around a sharp turn in the track and was upon us.

20

THE COORONG
APRIL 1862

'Thank God, you are here,' Papa said, 'all well and unharmed. I thought I would ride up the track in the hope that you were coming. And Tull too. Good day to you.' He came close. His face was like some weathered escarpment. Grey dirt had settled deep into the crevices and lines that fell at the sides of his mouth and down his cheeks, and the rain had splattered him too. It gave him a deathly sort of appearance.

Dismay made us mute. Addie stared at Papa with horror. Tull's gaze, frantic, darted past Papa and off the side of the track.

'No need to run, Tull. Come back home now and you can all tell me what has happened.'

'But how did you know we'd be coming this way?' I said.

'Did you not see the police? The maid from the Travellers is missing.' Papa shook his head. 'Of course you must know that. They've come from Wellington to make enquiries. I got back late yesterday, and found the house cold, and was worried at you all being gone, and Adelaide at the Travellers Rest. The troopers came to see if we knew anything and stayed overnight. They have suspicions about Mr Martin.'

'We were off the track last night,' Fred said. 'They must have passed before we started this morning.'

'That will be it,' Papa said. 'Well, come along now. We can have tea when you get home. I suppose you will be hungry too.' He swung his horse about and, without deciding to, we were riding together. 'He did not harm you, Adelaide?'

'Thanks to Tull. And Hester and Fred. They came to keep me safe.'

Evidently Papa heard the reproof in her voice. 'We had no reason before to think you unsafe. Mr Martin deceived us all. I would not have thought it of him. However, be that as it may, thank you, Frederick and Hester, and Tull.' His voice was calm reason and he bent his head courteously towards each of us in turn. Everything about him was designed to smother an outburst. (I did not see that then, only that I was glad that our voices were low.) Papa rode alongside Tull and Addie, perhaps a half-head in front and rather close, which made it appear that he was leading them. His leg bumped Addie's and she cried out and Tull pulled his horse a little further away. Papa moved to stay with them. 'You have hurt yourself, Adelaide?' he said pleasantly.

'Only a little,' she said. She did not look at Papa. She would not.

'We think it's a sprain,' I said.

'But we'll keep going,' Addie said. 'To get Grace.'

'Indeed?' Papa said.

'You will not stop us,' Addie said. 'Not this time.'

Tull held Addie tighter and glared at Papa. 'We are leaving the Coorong,' he said. 'No one will know. We will collect Grace and be on our way.'

'You surprise me, Tull. Addie can't travel, and you will wish to see your family,' Papa said.

'Why?'

'You have not heard about your mother?'

'No,' Tull said.

'She has just died, as I discovered last night. I am sorry for it, if you didn't know.' He turned to see the effect of this on Tull and a secretive look slid across his face. 'It was fortunate I found you.'

'Do you lie?' Tull said in a harsh voice. His face blazed and for a moment it seemed he would lunge across the gap between them and attack Papa.

Papa pulled his horse sharply away. 'No,' he said. 'I swear it, on the holy bible.' He leaned and touched his saddlebag and Tull appeared suddenly so desperate that I thought he might plunge from the path right there. Addie gasped at another misstep and Tull held himself in check. 'Come then. We can travel together for now.'

We rode on, Fred and I behind, beneath the iron sky. Tull and Addie, their heads together, spoke so low that I could not hear them. Papa was quiet, but he turned often to watch them, close as they were. Then Addie's voice lifted. 'No, Tull. Take me with you. Please. It will end badly if I go to the point. I am sure of it.'

'You can't come, not for this. I can't take you. But I will come back. Wait for me here. You'll be safe.' He turned to me. 'Hester? Will you care for her?'

'Of course,' I said, though I could not help wondering what Papa might do.

'See?' Tull said.

We arrived at the turnoff to the point and stopped. The horses shifted their feet and their heads, mouthing their bits, eager to be home.

'Take the horse,' Addie said. 'You'll be faster.'

Papa's hands rested easy on his pommel. 'I think not. That is my horse. Tull would not want to take something that is not his, would you, Tull?'

Addie said, 'How can I stay here without you?'

'You must. You can't walk,' Tull said. 'And I can't carry you so far.'

Addie had been calm, but she cried out again, 'Please, dear Tull,' and clutched his arm and began to cry.

Tull, desperate, said, 'I don't want to leave,' stroking her wild hair back and wiping the tears away as much as he could, as he had wiped flour from her cheeks once. 'I must first do this and then come back for you. I will. Believe me. It won't be long.'

She took his arm and shook it. 'How long? Tell me quick now. I can't bear it.'

'I'm not sure. Two weeks?'

'Ride me down then. Stay with me a little longer.'

'He can take his leave here, now,' Papa said. 'I'm sure you can ride that distance on your own, Adelaide. Hester can lead you if you cannot manage.'

'One minute,' Tull said, cutting him off, and looked so fierce that Papa fell silent. Tull drew their horse a little further away, his back to us, as if he had closed a door. His hand rose and from the way it moved, delicate and slow, I thought he must be stroking Addie's hair. Then his arms were very tight about her, and a high wail broke free of her. Fred rolled his eyes and picked at a thumbnail and adjusted his hat. He stared down the path. Tears pricked my eyes. I put my hand against my mouth to hold sound in. Birdie, restless, circled, and when I had pulled her round again Tull was on foot and Addie was looking down at him as if already she were seeing him from a distance: across a valley, the breadth of the lagoon.

Tull briefly turned his attention to Papa. 'Do not harm her, Mr Finch. She will tell me.'

'And do not threaten me, sir, over my own daughter,' Papa said.

'We are all equal, are we not, in the eyes of God?'

Papa flushed at that.

Tull turned and walked away. His legs were so long and his pace so rapid that he was quickly among the trees. Addie watched until he was gone from view.

'Come along now,' Papa said.

We followed him down the sodden path. The lagoon came into view once more: gouts of water lifting and falling away on its surface, and rivulets of mud bleeding into it from the banks. I drew alongside Addie and took her hand and squeezed it. 'Not long, Addie. He won't be long.'

At the house, I helped her from her horse and up the stairs to the veranda; Fred and Papa removed the saddles and loosed the horses and came down the path to the veranda stairs. There was nothing overt of threat in Papa's manner, but his stillness and quiet and calm as he stood below us frightened me. 'We'd best see to the fires, eh, Fred?' he said.

I sat Addie down before the dining room stove and pulled off her stocking. 'It feels a little better I think,' she said, pressing her fingers to her ankle, and then, wincing, 'No worse at any rate. Is it broken do you think?'

'I don't know.' It was swollen and bruised violet at the joint, and tender to the touch. Would a break do that?

'A week or two only, I hope. That will surely be enough,' Addie said. 'If only Papa had not come back early, or we had left our camp later. I wish Tull had not gone, that we were riding now. He will be hungry. And Rimmilli. Poor Tull.'

'Did you ever talk to her?' I asked.

'Sometimes,' she said. 'She tolerated me, no more. The other women were quite friendly.'

'It was the same with me.'

Fred passed through the room with wood for the parlour, and then with more for the dining room. I made a cold compress and strapped it to Addie's ankle and put a stool before her to rest her foot on and she was more comfortable. Her shivering abated and her cheeks flushed pink as the fire warmed the room and I began to think of lunch – a hot broth for this cold day. There is comfort in the ordinary, not only for people. I fed the dogs and soon they came to sit at the stove side with us and I rubbed Skip's belly with my foot and she sighed and stretched out.

Fred and Papa rode out in the afternoon and were home in time for milking. In the evening Papa was at pains to be pleasant, as if he were trying to persuade us all, even himself, of his decency. He expressed proper dismay that Addie had slept alone in the bush overnight, and the story of our rock shelter set him reminiscing about his adventures in Patagonia. It was normal, or what might have been thought normal once but was no longer. Addie was with us again, and it seemed a month at least since our departure for the Travellers Rest only the morning before. It was hard to know which felt more unreal: the events that had passed or this pretence of tranquillity and amity. I could not be easy. Mr Martin had troubled me less; he did not hide his badness, even from himself. It was the opposite with Papa. There was no predicting what his politeness concealed. I watched him warily, and saw Fred and

Addie doing the same. We were early to bed.

The following day passed quietly. Papa and Fred were occupied at the stable and about the sheds. Addie rested in bed in the morning, and in the afternoon began a new dress for Grace from remnants of dresses too worn to repair. I found her in the dining room over faded scraps of material, touching them with her fingertips and moving them as aimless as if they were seaweed in water.

'What is it?' I said.

'How much will she have grown? My own baby a stranger. Will she know me?'

'Make it a little bigger and she can grow into it,' I said.

She sniffed and wiped her nose. 'Yes.' And so the time passed, with Addie moving from one distraction to another. I could not see how the next few days would unfold. Addie would not be able to walk freely for a week at least – longer, even – and I could not imagine what Papa might do if she tried to leave with Tull.

The next afternoon, Papa sat on the veranda humming and 'catching up on his book-keeping', he said, and cleaning the musket. When I asked him why, he said only that it might have got some mud or water in it on our journey to the Travellers Rest, but when the task was done he kept the musket at his side.

Addie hobbled about on a stout stick, coming to sew by the stove in the kitchen while I cooked, and talking, her words and tone following her moods, which were swooping and inconstant. I shaped bread dough into tins and set them to rise and churned fresh butter, stopping for a few moments only to run outside to be sick. Addie didn't notice. She resumed talking as soon as I came back.

'We plan to go to the hills, to see what positions we might find there.' She paused in her sewing to address me directly, as if I had disagreed. 'They must always be in need of good workers, and I can cook and sew besides. We don't need a great deal, and we have our money. If we keep saving we should do well enough. And we will have Grace. Tull will finally meet her. I hope they have cared for her as they should, that she has not forgot her own mama. Oh, I cannot wait, Hettie. If only you could be as happy.'

'I am not sure about happiness. Charles was here while you were gone.'

'Charles,' she said, in a wondering voice, and she scrutinized my face, which I kept very still, paying attention to the carrots I was peeling and chopping. I did not want to talk further of it; I could not without revealing too much. 'Not for very long. A few days only.'

'And what? What, Hettie? What happened?'

'We spoke a little, and I don't know the rest. There is nothing more.'

'But you like him.'

'I do like him,' I said.

'I hope he knows.'

'He does. I told him so.' I bit my lip to stop smiling at the thought of him. Love was clear to Addie and confusion for me. She would never bite her lip at the thought of Tull.

At supper Addie poked at her food. She said, 'I wonder how Tull is. When he will come.'

'Two weeks at least,' I said.

'He might come sooner. You don't know.'

Papa chewed his mouthful and swallowed. 'As it happened I wished to talk of the future.'

'My future is no business of yours,' Addie said.

'You will not stir me to anger, Adelaide, try as you might,' Papa said.

'I am not trying; I simply do not care,' she said. All her words and her manner were reckless.

'Nevertheless, I have some news, which I think it is safe to say now.' He returned to fussing the food about his plate, chivvying a hillock of potato across to a scrap of chicken. 'It is certain now that Tull's mother is dead; otherwise Tull would be back.'

'She was dead before. You said so. If she was not, then you lied to us,' Addie said. 'You swore it on the bible. Why would you do such a thing?'

'The bible was not in the saddlebag.'

'In your words you swore it,' I said. '"On the holy bible", you said.'

'A small untruth only,' Papa said, looking sidelong at me. 'To ease their parting. That was all. For a greater good. I was sure that she would die.'

'To ease our parting? What can you mean?' Addie spoke slowly and my thoughts ran slowly, both of us trying to understand his meaning.

'I was waiting for the best moment to tell you what has been arranged. Naturally I did not wish to hurt Tull's feelings. However, all is in train.'

'It was to make him go, wasn't it? To get him out of the way.' Addie said, 'We will be together again.' Her mouth twisted. 'It doesn't matter what you do or say. You cannot compel me to stay. You can't tie me here until I'm twenty-one. Tull and I will walk if we must. Disown me if you like. We will fetch Grace and keep walking. We will live somewhere else – no need to worry about the disgrace. You cannot stop us.'

Papa lifted his gaze and looked about at us all. There was a moment of quiet, a gathering up of attention. The lamp hanging from the ceiling moved in the breaths of the house. It cast its subdued light over us, the dishes of food, the surface gleam of our glasses of water, and felt its way towards the dark corners of the room. Our eyes were wide with attention, and the shadows on the deep lines of Papa's face gave him the appearance of some immutable ancient, a Pantocrator. 'In fact I believe I can,' he said. 'I have news for you, Adelaide. The best news. Better than you could ever have hoped for. Mr Stubbs has made an offer of marriage.'

'Papa,' Fred burst out.

Addie shuddered and dropped her knife and fork. 'Even to entertain such a thought. Now I know you are mad.' She leapt to her feet. 'My answer is no and so you may tell him. I will never marry him.'

Papa rested his hands on the arms of his chair. 'You *will* marry Mr Stubbs, Adelaide, and enjoy a finer life than you deserve.'

She began to shout. 'There is no one for me but Tull. You can't make me. I'd sooner live like a savage.'

'I have advised Mr Stubbs that you have returned to us, and we have made arrangements,' Papa said. 'I was going to collect you from the Travellers Rest myself to tell you of his most advantageous offer. I was not aware of your disobedience in continuing to see Tull, but that matter is resolved. We need not expect Tull here for some time. And, happily, Hester and Fred spared me the journey.'

'I said I would look after her. I will not be her guard,' I said. 'I will help her if I can.'

'I would not have thought it of you, Hester. Such disloyalty.'

'I wish I were surprised at you, Papa, but I find that I am not.'

Papa eyed me coldly, and returned his attention to Addie. 'Sit down, Adelaide. If you do not accept Mr Stubbs, I will notify the police – whatever their names were' (he stopped and fluttered his fingers irritably) '– that Tull was involved in the disappearance of Mr Martin's maid.'

'You would not,' Addie said.

'You know Tull would never do such a thing,' Fred said. 'Mr Martin threatened to kill him. We were there. He saved Addie and this is how you reward him?'

'I am grateful to him if, as you say, Mr Martin is a violent man. But my gratitude does not extend to the ruination of my family's name and reputation. I will not harm Tull – though he has sought to harm me and has repaid our charity in the worst possible way – as long as Adelaide relinquishes him and he her.'

'And I marry Mr Stubbs?' Addie said.

'That too.'

I thought that Addie would faint, so white and horror struck was she. She reached out a hand. I pulled a chair towards her and pushed her down. She swayed beneath my hand and began to sob – a piteous sound.

When I looked up again Papa was regarding her as unyielding as ever I saw him.

Fred stared at him, as if he were a stranger almost. 'I told Tull we didn't sell our women, that they have a choice, and now I see that we are worse than savages; we are hypocrites. Let me guess: you owe Stubbs money. I do not say that she should marry Tull, but to compel her to marry someone she does not care for—'

Papa eyed him coldly. 'I hope I know my duty to my children, and what is best for my daughter even if she does not know it herself.'

'Oh Papa,' I said. 'You cannot believe that. It's cruel in you.'

His gaze flickered at that but he did not speak.

Addie raged – all night, it seemed – her voice a sort of growl at my side. I was unaccustomed now to sharing a bed and had forgotten how she tossed and pulled at the covers when upset.

'How could he think of it? To threaten me, to threaten Tull. I will ride away. He would not stop me.' She smacked her hands against the covers. She breathed loudly and knocked my arm with the back of her hand. 'Do you think he would, Hett?'

I lay flat and straight, my fingers laced at my chest and looked into the moth darkness above and the faint moonlight falling on the room's dark shapes. 'I do,' I said. 'I think he will do anything.'

'I will try anyway. Could you help me? I cannot get onto a horse on my own.' She turned her head and the whites of her eyes gleamed.

'I don't know. I would not see Tull imprisoned. I do not wish him dead.'

She began to cry.

Sergeant Wells and Trooper O'Grady rode in the next morning and were relieved to see Addie alive since they did not believe everything that Mr Martin had told them. 'Very unreliable I would say,' Sergeant Wells said. They did not have proof of his guilt, and had not yet found any sign of Jane. They questioned Addie about her time at the Travellers Rest, also Fred and me about anything that we might have seen. Papa sat with us, quiet and intent. We spoke only a little of Tull, mentioning that he had been with us to help collect Addie. Addie's pallor and the dark rings beneath her eyes could as easily be ascribed to her fear of Mr Martin, her night out in the cold and our flight, as to her sleepless night and the crying fits that overcame her.

From the end of the veranda we watched the two men depart for the lakes, where they planned to fetch a black tracker known to them. Papa and Fred were gone soon after. I wondered at Papa leaving Addie free until I saw that the horses were missing from the home paddock. I went up the rise to the stable, which was also empty, and returned to the house, to Addie.

'What is it?' she said.

'The horses are gone.'

We knew without asking that Papa had moved them. I would not give him the satisfaction of asking why or where, but Addie was not too proud to ask Fred when he came into the kitchen before dinner.

'Everything must have you at its centre, mustn't it?' he said, looking at her over his cup of tea. 'I will not tell you. I do not treat Tull as lightly as you. He will die, you will have killed him, if you follow this course. If Papa will not waver, you must, for Tull's sake. Think of him.'

'It isn't me. It's Papa. I cannot live without Tull.'

'You can.' His voice, turned soft, was still insistent. He was not unfeeling; it was that he saw things so clear; he understood consequence. 'You don't want to. But either way you will not have him. Better to have him alive in the world; better not to cause his death.'

'What if we told the police?' Addie said.

Fred shook his head slowly. 'You know what Papa would say. He would tell of his wilful daughter, grown reckless without a mother's guiding hand, her infatuation with a black outgrown his station, who has taken advantage of her youth and ruined her innocence. Think,' he said, angry now, and took her shoulders and shook her.

She threw him off and slapped his hands and pummelled his chest. 'Let me be. What would you know?'

'It does no good, Fred,' I said and he flung his hands up and stepped back. 'Addie. Addie.' Finally she gave me her attention. 'Perhaps the police will find evidence of Mr Martin's guilt. There is still a chance.'

She stopped then, her breaths heaving. 'Do you think so? They might, I suppose.' She bent her head and lifted a skirt to wipe her face.

'Mr Stubbs will be here in ten more days, Papa says,' Fred said.

Addie lifted her head. 'Ten days. I will run before then, with or without Tull.'

'Don't, Addie,' Fred said.

She did not speak to Papa during that time, but kept watch on the path, running to the parlour window or the veranda end at any noise, looking both for Tull – who I do not think she could have resisted running with if he came, whatever Fred said – and for the troopers. Once, in the second week after our return, I spied her limping up the hill away from the house, leaning on her stick, and ran after her.

'What are you doing?'

She kept on in her halting way. 'Only going to the stock route to see if anyone might be passing by. Anyone with news, that is.'

'You might stay there for a week and not see a soul. And if you go along the track you might miss Tull, and if you go searching for him inland you might miss the troopers.'

'I can't wait. I don't have a week. Leave me, Hettie. Let me be. I must try else I shall go mad. If only I knew where he was.'

'Addie, dear Addie.' I took her by the arm. She jerked free and in doing it stumbled and cried out and sank to the damp path. I crouched at her side and put my arms about her and rocked her. She burrowed her head against my front. 'I want Mama,' she said. 'I want her. She would stop him. I know she would. You said you would not guard me.'

'There's no need for a guard. There is nothing we can do. Your ankle is not ready. You'll only make it worse and then if the troopers come with good news you will not be fit to walk. Come now, Addie.' I took her arm and we went back to the house, which I hated to do. Even if we rowed away I could not do it on my own for the length of the lagoon. And that would not help Tull, who despite the great expanse of land and water that was his home was as trapped as us, even if he did not know it. Only Addie's marriage could set him free.

I could not help counting those ten days; I was sure Addie did too. We did not talk of it. Two days before Mr Stubbs was expected at Salt Creek, after breakfast, Papa went to his room and returned with a slithering armful of material. 'Your Mama's wedding dress, for Adelaide, to make her suitable.' He put it on a chair and stepped away from it, clearing his throat as if there would be a further announcement, and when I did not reply took his hat and coat from the door and went out.

After he had gone, I shook out the rustling folds of cream silk. Heavy wings of skirt and underskirt fell away from a whalebone bodice; it was trimmed in lace and satin ribbon and had mother-of-pearl buttons up its long wrists and up its back. It seemed to gather all the light of the dining room into it and send out some light of its own. It was an uneasy sort of garment, made from things of land and sea. Addie limped in, bleary from sleep, and stopped. 'It is real then,' she said. She sat at the other end of the table. 'It will happen, I think.'

I did not mention trying it or fitting it, but after she had picked at some food, she dragged it away to our room and a while later called for me. She was a forlorn sight with the dress unfastened, not draping as it should. She could not do up the buttons, and neither could I.

'It's no use, Addie. You'll have to wear stays.'

She shut her eyes. 'In the drawer,' she said.

I found her old corset rolled at the back and pulled it out and held it above her head. Obediently, she lifted her arms and I lowered it over her and began to tighten the laces. Twice we pulled the dress up to see if her waist was small enough, and twice had to tighten further. My fingers were red and sore from the cord.

'It's because of Grace. Mama had not had a baby when she wore it,' Addie said.

'You're as small as her. It's because you've gone free for so long.

Heavens, what would Grandmama say?' Addie brushed her face with her palms and I saw her tears. 'It's all right. It will fit. I will make it.'

Addie said nothing; she rocked on her feet as I tugged, bracing herself against a chair, and her breaths became shallower. 'Stop, stop,' she said once in sudden panic. 'I can't bear it.' Her hands beat at her ribs. 'I can't breathe.' She drew in quick, shallow breaths. 'No.' She shut her eyes. Her hands stopped their fluttering and settled against her chest, pressing hard. Her light panting sobs died away finally, and her face settled, deliberately. She mastered herself. When she opened her eyes again, I said, 'Ready?' and when she nodded, I drew the dress up her body and pulled the sleeves up her arms and forced each button through its tight corresponding loop, all the way up the dress's back and its high, slender neck, throwing her plait over her shoulder to her front. She was obliged to hold her chin high. Lace foamed at her throat.

'Your hair,' I said.

She had hardly bothered with it for days, just plaited it and left it. Now she touched it and felt about and shrugged. I led her outside and sat her in a patch of sun on the veranda and brushed it out. The forgotten past flew up at me as if startled, like the ground parrots that grazed hereabouts. How often I had done this for Mama. Addie's tangled hair smoothed and I drew the mass of it back until it was sleek, plaiting the sides in as intricately as I could and coiling it into a bun. We forgot ourselves for a while. Finally it was done and she stood and turned for me to see.

'Well, you are beautiful,' I said, which was nothing more than the truth. She did not belong at Salt Creek. She was a lady in this dress, and every part of our house was dull brown as a sparrow. The longer I looked the more that impression of civilization seemed an illusion. The greater thing that it did was to frame something in Addie, not only her looks, but also something barely containable: her rage.

'That's done then,' she said.

The dogs set up a barking on the tenth day and for a mad moment the world changed. It would be the troopers and Addie would be spared, and Tull too. It would end well. How quickly we rushed at hope. Addie was at the veranda in seconds and I was fast behind. A lone rider, that was all. A man in a tall hat on a terrible horse. Mr Stubbs. We watched him all the way down the path – Addie as if she had set eyes on her executioner.

'Mr Stubbs,' she said in a faint voice when he approached.

He removed his hat and held it in front of him. 'Miss Adelaide,' he said, with an uncertain smile. 'I am a little early. I could not wait.' His cheeks flushed very bright; almost, he seemed shy. Then, noticing me, 'Miss Finch.'

'Won't you come inside, Mr Stubbs. Papa is out at present, but I hope you would like some tea.'

'Yes, please,' he said. He came up the stairs and approached Addie and put his hands to her upper arms, and though she reared back in surprise, his head followed and he touched his mouth to her cheek. 'A little signal of affection for my future bride,' he said and laughed, 'Huh, huh,' like that, as if relieved that some test had passed.

Addie looked at me.

'Into the parlour,' I said, and opened the door so that Mr Stubbs would enter.

Addie followed, wiping his touch from her cheek as she went. Afternoon tea could hardly have been more awkward. Poor Mr Stubbs could not understand, Addie always before having been so lively. She sat opposite him, her gaze travelling from his smart boots up his thick legs and snug waistcoat to his florid cheeks and flat eyes. I thought of Tull's dark elegance, as I am sure she did.

'Won't you take me for a walk, Mr Stubbs?' she said after a time, which startled me. From the way she did not look at me for approval or sympathy or anything else I could see that her thinking had moved beyond mine. She was as alone as could be now. Nothing I did could make any difference. It was fantastical to imagine otherwise.

'Why, certainly. Only your ankle— Can you walk?'

'If I may take your arm, I believe we will manage,' she said.

I watched them walk away, very slow, Mr Stubbs bending his head to her. He supported her quite tenderly. I did not think him a cruel man, at least not to people he regarded as his equals, but he was inferior in every respect but wealth and social standing to Tull, and watching him I felt some of Addie's anger. She deserved better.

It was my melancholy task late the following morning to row out to fetch Reverend Taplin, who was to perform the wedding ceremony, from the mail boat. The great surprise was that Albert was standing on the deck at his side, as tall and strong as Stanton, though with Mama's soft brown hair – the hair Mary would have had. He was burned by the sun and had the beginning of a soft moustache: he was sixteen now, and somewhat watchful. There was little of the boy in him, and a distance between us.

'Hester,' he said, holding out his hand to take mine when he had lowered himself down.

'Albert.' I pulled the oars in and leaned forward to embrace him.

He patted my back awkwardly. 'It took Addie getting married for Papa to summon me. I suppose I should not be surprised.'

'It's because of the money.'

'Nothing's changed then.'

I turned my attention to Reverend Taplin once Albert had helped him down. The boat rocked; he quickly sat, flicking his coat back fussily so he didn't sit on it. He was dressed in black and had a beard that I considered ridiculous, circling the bottom of his face only and leaving his upper lip quite bare. He had a flat face and an unsmiling countenance, whether from disposition or disapproval, I was not certain. Remembering Tull's distress on his return from the mission, I found it difficult to be pleasant.

We walked up the slope to the house. Fred spied us from the veranda and ran down the stairs to see Albert, and after some awkwardness they began to laugh and talk. Soon they wandered off – to explore old haunts I supposed. I did not see Albert meeting Papa, but later saw them speak politely enough. Papa took Reverend Taplin on a tour of the house and its immediate surrounds and I observed Mr Stubbs wandering the short path from house to stable and back in his bobbing gait, his hands folded behind him and bent forward a little from the waist.

There was only Addie now and I found her easily enough. She was sitting in the bedroom with tears sliding down her cheeks. 'Oh, Tull, Tull. I want him, Hettie.' She mopped them with one of Mama's handkerchiefs.

'I know you do.' I could only help her once more into the dress and do her hair and by the time we were finished her tears had stopped. 'I'm so sorry for it all, Addie,' I said.

'Papa will regret what he's done. He might have an agreement with Mr Stubbs, but I have too, and so Papa shall discover.'

'What have you done?'

'Talked to my future husband.' She would tell me nothing more, and if she looked grim and stricken when she left the room to be married, she was still beautiful enough to light up Mr Stubbs's dull countenance. She would not have noticed that. She was looking past him, through the parlour window to the slope – and seeing it still empty, the wind drifting over the silvered grasses of summer and the brilliant green shoots of approaching winter, her eyes dulled.

Papa's demeanour during the wedding ceremony ill became him. He rocked on the balls of his feet and smiled at the words 'I do' and 'obey', and paid no attention to Addie's monotone. From his manner, I deduced that Mr Stubbs had waived some, perhaps all, of his debts in celebration. But observing how Mr Stubbs did not meet Papa's eye or return the heartiness of his tone after the ceremony was concluded I began to suspect the agreement that Addie had reached. Mr Stubbs was not as jovial as I had seen him at other times. He could not fail to be aware of Addie's sadness; he was not unfeeling I would say, but he was determined.

We had afternoon tea of Mrs Martin's layer cake. She had taught it to Addie while she was at the Travellers Rest. At sight of the rich cream I fled around the side of the house and was sick. I could no longer pretend or even hope that what had happened to Addie was not happening to me. My choices were so few and my feelings on the matter so desperate. But I had to shut them away for just a little longer, until Addie was gone.

At the last, when Papa approached her in farewell, Addie turned to him, as a boat turns in water, cumbersome and reluctant seeming, against its own nature, and held him off with an outstretched hand. 'Do you remember what the bible says, Papa?' she said. 'Amos, five: twenty-four I believe; you may check it to be sure. "But let justice roll down the waters, and righteousness like an ever-flowing stream." Think of that, as I will. It will roll for you one day and I will do nothing to stop it.'

This discomfited him, as might be imagined, yet he rallied. 'When you are more yourself I am sure you will understand, my dear.'

Addie ignored that and drew me aside, holding me tight. She spoke soft into my ear. 'Listen to me, Hettie. You must get word to Tull for me. Tell him I will get Grace, I will make her mine.'

'But how?' I said.

She shook her head. 'Doesn't matter. I will. Stubbs wishes to make me happy, I believe. Imagine.' She released me and took my hand. 'Tell Tull, oh, everything: my feelings, what Papa did, that I am sorry. My whole life I will be sorry for it. Then you must leave.'

'Come, my dear,' Mr Stubbs called. Mr Stubbs and Addie rode away on their horses, with Addie's meagre possessions strapped to a third. Her back was very straight. She did not look back.

Albert, standing between Fred and me, said, 'She doesn't seem very happy.'

'She loves Tull,' Fred said. 'Tull loves her.'

'Tull. Good God. So that's why he left. Papa sent him away?'

Fred nodded.

'Don't tell anyone,' I said.

'As if I would. A black in the family. They'd kill him up at the lakes. They'd kill him for less. I'd not shed a tear.'

'Why ever not?' I said.

Albert shrugged. His face twisted. 'I was the one sent away; he stayed.'

'How could Papa send him away to work? He wasn't family,' I said.

'Yes he was.'

The mail boat's horn sounded its return from the south and Papa and Reverend Taplin strolled to the shore. Fred and I followed with Albert.

Before stepping into the boat, Albert said, 'I might not see you for some time. I am to oversee Mr Baker's new station in the Flinders Ranges. Leaving quite soon.'

'Well,' Papa said. 'He thinks highly of you then.'

Albert regarded him coolly. 'I believe he does.'

'It's so far,' I said.

Poor Fred was stricken – from his old shame with Albert perhaps. He clasped Albert's hands in his own and pressed them. 'We missed you; we did.'

Papa rowed them out and on his return we stood together watching the boat ride through the choppy waves. Papa said, musingly, 'Perhaps Addie might send you some new clothes, Hester, if you ask her nicely, and we will see what sort of husband we might find you.' He had an air of gaiety, as if he were offering an unexpected treat.

'Do not think of marriage for me. You will not compel me.'

He looked startled. 'Yes, well, perhaps in time.' He rocked on his heels and stared towards the departing boat. 'She will come around, my Adelaide. Her sweetness will out,' he said.

I thought it would not, that it was gone, that the steel of her would out, but did not say so. She was like Papa. She did not forgive and she did not forget. These things were not in her nature.

My dread was that Tull would return that very afternoon, that he might even see the boat making its way up the lagoon without knowing who it took away. We were spared that, at least. Papa and Fred left early the next day to begin rounding up the sheep. While they were gone I took the musket down and hid it in the stable. Later, as exhausted as he was from his hard day, Papa did not notice its absence from the wall. Fred hardly spoke. He washed when he came in and ate and worked on his drawing and writing until bedtime.

*

It was the third day that he came – the third day after the wedding, that is. The dogs leapt from their place by the stove and threw themselves, whining, at the door. I crossed to them and put my hands on the door, and stopped there. There was nothing good on the other side, only more distress. The dogs fell away, waving their tails and panting and looking up at me. It would be Tull. That was his footfall bounding down the stairs, slowing as he looked around. I opened the door. He was so joyous in that moment crossing the walkway beneath the bare vines, the basketwork of their shadows falling on him and about him, and his face alight, smiling at the thought of Addie who must surely be behind me. Seeing my face, he changed in an instant, before I said a word. The dogs leapt at him and he patted them absently, and pushed past them, past me, into the kitchen.

'Where is she?' he said, looking around.

'Tull, it could not be worse. I'm so sorry. Come inside now.'

'Quickly, tell me where she is. What has happened?' He turned grey almost. 'Is she dead?'

'No, not dead. Not that. She is married to Mr Stubbs and gone to the lakes.'

He stilled. 'She would not do that. I don't believe it. It is another lie.'

'It's true. *I* say it's true.'

He roared at that, and smote the door, which flung back with a squeal of its hinges, and clutched his hair. 'No.' Tears streamed down his face. He let them. 'Why did she? I said I would come. She could not wait? I'll get her back. I will.'

I took his arm and drew him into the room. 'Listen. Let me tell you. Please, Tull. Addie asked me to, so you would understand. It was for you.' I told him everything that Addie had asked, and more, and when I had finished speaking his tears had slowed. He seemed dazed. The dogs lifted their heads and went to the door. Papa and Fred would be home. Tull stood, his face become still. 'Tull,' I said, but he rounded me, making for the stairs, which I could not immediately

329

understand, since when I went outside Papa and Fred were in plain sight coming down the track. Tull was up the stairs in three bounds and moving along the veranda and I began to comprehend his intention. He went into his room and in seconds came out again, carrying three of his spears, which he held horizontal, feeling the weight of one, bouncing it in his hand, reacquainting himself.

'Tull, Tull,' I said. 'Don't.' But he was past me again. Then I screamed as loud as I could, 'Fred.'

In the distance, Fred's head reared up. He turned to Papa and set his horse to a gallop down the slope towards us. Tull drew a spear back in a smooth arc. It was as if he circumscribed the space around him, cut it clean and made it his own: something profound and alien.

'Not Fred,' I said.

Tull waited with the same fixed expression of rage and determination. Fred reached the gate and threw himself off the horse. 'Don't, Tull, he's not worth it,' he said. He faltered at sight of Tull's ferocity.

Papa began to come down on foot. 'Get the musket,' he bellowed. 'Get it now.'

'I will not,' I said.

Fred ran inside, and came out again. 'Where is it?'

'Hidden,' I said. 'You would use it?'

'To stop Papa. To stop them both.' He leapt down the stairs.

'You cannot stop me. I don't care,' Tull said.

'I will finish you,' Papa shouted and kept on. Madness when Tull was poised ready to throw.

'Why?' Tull screamed. 'She was promised to me. Her own promise.' He pulled the spear a little further back at his shoulder.

Fred shouted at him. 'Stop. She did it for you. To save you. Because of you, because she loves you.'

'I'll kill him. I'll kill him,' Tull sobbed. 'They can kill me. I don't care. How could you let him? You should have cared for her better.'

'We tried,' I said. 'We, all of us, Addie too, wanted you safe.'

'This is how you do it? Sell your sister?'

'Not for money; that was Papa. For your life,' I said. 'Papa is not worth it.'

'Give it to me,' Fred said. 'Give me the spear. Don't do this to Addie. Think of Grace. Grace, Tull.' He was shouting in his ear at the last.

Tull threw it to the ground.

'Hah,' Papa said, reaching us. 'That's the way. The musket.'

'Hidden,' I said. 'I will not tell you where.'

'Foolish girl. Hold him for me, Fred.'

'I will not.'

Tull lunged at Papa and grabbed him by the collar and squeezed it tight at his throat until the flesh of his chin wrinkled up and his cheeks turned a choked pink. His arms flailed. Fred took hold of Tull at the shoulder, from behind, and heaved. It was enough to break his grip. Papa pulled at his collar and coughed.

They stood there, three points of a triangle, all panting.

'Get off my land,' Papa said.

Tull thrust out a long arm and punched him in the chest with the heel of his palm and strode past his sprawling shape in the dirt across the slope.

And that was the last I ever saw of him. He sank back into his life for all I knew, as soft as a whale into the depths, and disappeared and was never more seen by me before I left.

Two letters arrived the following week: one from Mr Stubbs for Papa, which threw Papa into such a state that I thought it best to leave the house, and one for me from Addie, which I read on my old seat by the lagoon, where Charles had found me not so many months ago. I felt closest to him there.

Remember how I once dreamed of pretty things, money to spend, a household to run and a kind gentleman for a husband? Though they are pleasant enough, I would give them up in a minute for Tull.

You must leave, Hester. Papa will never change. There will only be this and he will bend you to his will or you will die resisting. This money is for the journey: a little pocket money that Stubbs gave me, but enough to get you to town. I have no better use for it than this. Only get out. I hope you will see Tull and can tell him what happened. Perhaps he has been to see you already.

Remember what I said. It was for him that I did it. Tell him I will get Grace.

When I judged that enough time had passed I went back to the house. Papa, against the veranda railing, was speaking again before I reached the top of the stairs.

'He agreed to release me from the debt and now he says he will not. Unforeseen circumstances.'

'Did he sign anything?'

'Word of a gentleman.' He paced up and down and wheeled around. 'The rain falls on the just and the unjust alike, Hester, as you know. But it does fall and sometimes the just do get it. I try to remember that.'

'It does not fall on us. You should not have treated Addie so.' My voice was so hard that it surprised me. 'It was wicked.'

Papa stared. 'I was looking after her.' He fumbled along his fob chain. 'I thought that good would come to me because I believed and acted with faith in all that I did. But what if there is no pattern or principle in the world? Have you thought of that, Hester?'

'People prefer to ignore those things when it suits them,' I said. I looked at his hand, a thin dried up brown thing. I did not see how it could wield anything, much less power. 'You're cold. Come inside where it's warmer.' He followed me in and watched as I made a pot of tea.

'There is nothing now,' he said. 'I do not see the way out.' He glanced at me from the corner of his eye as if I might approve this remark. I did not give him the look that he wanted: warmth about the eyes, understanding, complicity. I could do it no longer. And then he faced me straight and unguarded, the glimmer in his mind sudden and visible, and was like the child Fred presenting Mama with a special shell: *See, Mama, see what I found.* He touched the cuff of my faded muslin. 'There *is* one more thing. Where is Frederick? Fetch him to me please.'

I called up the hallway, and Fred came down, stopping in the doorway to take in Papa's mood and unroll his sleeves and button his cuffs. Papa settled into his chair.

He said, 'There is no avoiding it this time, Fred. It is your turn to leave and to work.'

With equal calm, Fred said, 'No, Papa. I will not.'

'Let me explain. We do not live on air, Fred. Our property is mortgaged. If we do not pay the interest on the mortgage we lose Salt Creek. We must hold on until the values increase. It is not difficult to understand.'

'No, I tell you. I am almost done and will leave then. I will even send you money. But a station or a farm? No, that will not be my life. What interest do I have in sheep or cows? Sell the horses. Sell the boat. My work on the peninsula is finished.'

'We cannot sell the horses.'

'Why not?'

Papa raised a hand to silence him. 'Never mind that; we cannot. No one wishes to buy the boat. It is a shame that this is not the country for gentlemen scholars.'

'I work on the run, I always have. It's never enough for you.'

'Show me your work now, Frederick. Your books. Let me see what you have done.'

Fred looked from Papa to me and when I did nothing but return his gaze and perhaps also his confusion he turned and went slowly to his room and came back carrying his three thick sketch books, which he relinquished into Papa's hand. Papa held the books very gentle and turned the pages, each of them, giving them their own attention and pausing at some. 'Well,' he said, 'they are something. Some fine work here and your work has progressed, of that there is no doubt.'

'Thank you, Papa.'

He bent his head with deliberation, as I have seen an axe fall at a troublesome knot of wood. 'I think you can write another book one day when you are done here. Now we will walk the fences. We will go, Fred, we two, men, and remind ourselves of all that we have created and we will contemplate our futures. Let us do that now, eh? What say you, my son?'

I do not know how a voice can be at once ringing and quiet, but so it was. He stood and moved almost leisurely. There were just his strange words and the horror on Fred's face and the sound of wood crackling and snapping in the fire – the good hard wood that Tull said was forbidden. No matter. Soon it would all be gone and that would be one less rule that we were breaking. A small mercy. Papa pulled the stove lid aside and put the kettle on and opened the fire door, and as if they were no more than twigs and without rush dropped Fred's drawing books in and shut the door.

Fred lunged forward.

I leapt up. 'No, no, no. Stop it.'

Papa stood against the stove door. He said, '"When I was a child, I spake as a child, I understood as a child, I thought as a child: but when I became a man, I put away childish things." Sometimes we need help to put away childish things.'

I began to cry. 'What would Mama say?'

'But she is not here to say it, is she?' Papa said. 'There is no choice now, not this time. It makes it easier, do you see?'

'I do see,' Fred said. 'I can see what you have become, very well.' His skin never took the sun, but it became deathly pale now and his chest heaved as if he could not draw breath. His gaze fixed on the musket over the door. He seemed almost dazed. He shook his head as if to clear it, as I have seen a beast do after a blow to its skull. 'Who are you? Who would do such a thing – to his child? I see that you were trying to save Addie, but this— You did this to destroy me. And yet you demand obedience.' His eyes were wet. He smudged a hand across them and turned away, almost stumbling from the room.

'One day he will understand the difficult situation we are in. Fred's money will tide us over and Hugh and Stanton will be back and then we need only hang on. You know there's talk of an inland canal system to transport, oh, everything. Stock and crops, anything you could want. And land values …'

'No,' I said. 'I did not know that.'

'It will be like England. If your Mama could have seen it.'

'She hated it here.'

'Hester, dear,' he said plaintively, as if it were we who had failed to understand him.

I went to get one of Mama's handkerchiefs. I kept one, ironed and starched by her hand, in one of my drawers and held and stroked it sometimes for the comfort of it; the others were soft and worn these days. Folding them smooth was the most I did for them. I chose one and tucked it into my bodice and went into Fred's room. He was stuffing his possessions into his old duffle bag.

'You're leaving,' I said.

Fred rubbed the heel of his palm over one cheek and the other. 'Why would I stay?' He could not make his voice run smooth. 'He wished to bind me, but he has cut me loose. Will you come with me?'

'Walking?'

'How else?'

I took a moment to consider. 'I will write to Charles first. He will come for me. No need for you to wait. I'll only slow you down.' I had been so tired of late, as Mama had been when she was with child. I felt that secret deep inside me, and how it was changing me already, and although I did not know what would become of me as a consequence, I would do anything to keep it safe.

'Ah yes. I suppose so.' He wrapped two books – Darwin – and put them into the bag. 'I thought of Tull, seeing if he might like to come with me, if things are quite done with his mother.'

'You know where he is?'

'I can find him.'

I folded a shirt and handed it to him. 'You can ask at any rate.'

'Where will you go?'

'Grandmama and Grandpapa first. And then, do you know what

Darwin says? I have held it in mind for so many years: "Nothing can be more improving to a young naturalist than a journey in distant countries". I am ready to discover whether he is right.'

'You're leaving Australia.'

'You know I always planned to.'

And now I was the one crying. 'When will I see you again? Nine children. What has become of us, Fred?'

He put his arms around me. 'Life,' he said.

I could not think of what else to say. Nothing could make any difference to Fred's circumstances or feelings. He had been pulling away from us since Tull went. This was merely the end of it. I left him to his task and drifted through the house.

Papa was on the veranda putting his boots on. There might have been no difference between this and any other day.

'Papa,' I said. 'Look.' Coming down the path were the two troopers, Sergeant Wells and Trooper O'Grady, also a shabby native in a rough old policeman's jacket, its frayed collar forming a tawdry sort of lace, and a fourth person slumped in his saddle at the rear. His hands were tied behind his back and his hat was drawn low, but I could not mistake that moustache. It was Mr Martin.

'Well, well,' Papa said, and went to meet them. I followed.

Sergeant Wells removed his hat. 'We thought you would wish to know, Mr Finch, that the maid, Jane Macmanamin, has been found in a wombat hole by Mickey here. He saw crows in a tree above. Most ingenious. It is quite certain that it is she. And we have arrested Mr Martin here' – he nodded in Mr Martin's direction – 'on a charge of murder.'

Mr Martin scowled at that and catching my eye, said 'Miss Finch.' Although he was reduced by his situation, something in him – unseen but felt – could not be contained. It seethed against rules, and feeling those things myself often enough, even though he revolted me I could not help feeling for him a little, which I judged in myself. He was a murderer.

'Mr Martin,' I said. He smirked in a familiar manner, as if he knew quite well how discomfited I was feeling.

Sergeant Wells looked surprised at that. 'Your other daughter, Mr Finch. Is she about? Would she be willing to make a written statement?'

'That she saw nothing? I would suppose so. She is lately married to Mr Stubbs of Lake Albert,' Papa said, drawing himself up.

'I see. We best see her again then. Make a note, O'Grady.'

Trooper O'Grady pulled a shabby notebook from his pocket and licked his thumb and flipped it over to a new page and licked the end of his pencil and slowly wrote, breathing loudly through his nose.

When he had finished, Sergeant Wells said, 'We'll be on our way. Quite a ride before the day is done.'

Mr Martin spat in the dirt. They reined their horses around and Mr Martin's horse had to follow. It was too late to make a difference to Addie and Tull.

21

CHICHESTER
OCTOBER 1874

Two letters came on the day before the trunk: one from Addie, one from Hugh. Addie's scrawl said that Mr Stubbs had died in a horseback riding accident – an event that did not seem to trouble her more than was proper. There was news also of her several children. Her herds and enterprises were prospering and I believe her to be a businesswoman of note. She asked at the end, almost in passing, whether Fred or I had ever heard word from Tull. She would be glad to hear from him, she said, and that was all. So she had not forgotten him. I had never heard from him, and if Fred had, he had not mentioned it to me.

There was no mistaking Hugh's flourishing lettering. He ever held himself in high regard: strange how such a thing can be evident in a person's hand. His news reached out and twisted my heart in a curious combination of anger and grief.

Melbourne
The 5th of May, 1874

Dear Hester,

I write with the news that our father died this April, after a gradual weakening and decline. I last saw him in January, when the heat, indeed everything, was troubling him.

The past preyed upon him. He wrote to me of mistakes he had made. It was not of his financial misjudgements that he spoke, though I think we are agreed that he was in error in the risks that he took, with so little prospect of success. Of recent years he was often in need of funds. I gave what I could, despite my family and the position I must maintain. Adelaide has never forgiven him for the events of '62, though he saved her from ruin and arranged a most advantageous marriage. I have not seen her since '64, I suppose. I had thought becoming a mother might have softened her. Her son Harry was a fine little fellow, but it was a girl she found at the Point McLeay mission who she doted on. She and Mr Stubbs took her into their home as an act of charity, and she quite stole their hearts. Such familiarity never ends well, as she should know, and so I reminded her (Stubbs must have been quite nutty on her to have permitted it). At that point she requested my immediate departure, and I had no choice but to comply.

But to matters at hand: It is my hope that you will see fit to make a contribution towards moneys I have outlaid on the family's behalf since our father's death. There are obligations to consider, regarding which I have provided a separate balance sheet. Stanton, I am afraid to say, has Papa's head for business. Adelaide and Frederick have neither spoken nor written to him since leaving Salt Creek. I have not heard from Albert for many years. Perhaps, if you know his location, you could forward it to me.

You will, I am sure, be surprised, in view of your scant communication with Papa, that he left the bulk of his estate to you. The portion of the will that pertains to you is as follows, which you may make of what you will:

To my daughter, Hester, I bequeath my land, house, and all its effects to use as she deems fit. I make one stipulation only: that Flora and Bobby, natives, and any other natives who are currently dwelling at Salt Creek are permitted continuing use of the land, and may move across it without restriction for their own purposes.

You should see from this that in fact he has left you nothing. There is not a person who will wish to purchase an estate so encumbered. But no matter: the land is worth nothing, and likewise the house. I would not call it a bequest – rather, a millstone, and do not envy you the duty of discharging the terms of the will. The good furniture was long since sold to cover some portion at least of the debts. The pianoforte is all that remains. Papa would not sell it when he might have, and now it is all but ruined by salt and damp. I cannot imagine that you have any need of it. If, however, you do wish for it, send me word to that effect in addition to funds to cover the costs of shipping. I am sending also a trunk containing miscellany, as Papa requested me to in January. This does not appear in the will, but as in all else I try to do my duty.

There was a little more about Flora and Bobby and how they had been living in the house with Papa, 'quite as if they owned it' – but no other information about when they had returned to live there – and how Papa sat each day on the veranda.

That, I could imagine: him in his driftwood chair staring the length of the lagoon as if he were the captain of a sinking ship unable to abandon the hope of rescue, and from pride would watch the disappearing view to the end. I had repaid the mortgage and paid the lease on Salt Creek each year and sent him money besides, and Hugh never knew. How like Papa. There were only five more years to run on the lease and the land would be owned outright. He concluded with remarks about his many fine children, his excellent wife and good address and his future political hopes. He remained my affectionate brother, etc.

Then the trunk arrived. It being a school day, I was before a classroom of girls and could only watch as it was carried up the stairs. I hurried to the drawing room at luncheon and at the sight of it square on the rug could not help trembling. It was at once familiar and strange. Ruby hovered as I lifted the lid.

One of Mama's thick blanket quilts was folded at the top. I picked

340

it up – it was heavier than I remembered; I must have been stronger then – and was overcome with a strange sensation, as if the world itself had listed. For a moment I was at Salt Creek, running from house to dairy shed with this quilt bundled in my arms, to warm Rimmilli, to save her. There was the smell and crunch of eucalyptus leaves too beneath my boots, and Addie and Tull. I held the quilt close and breathed it in. I am sure Ruby thought me quite deranged. I put it aside, and looked in the trunk again. There was Tull's old bark shield, its muted red and white, nested against another quilt. It was bowed, but had travelled safe, and was marked and chipped in places – doubtless from where Stanton had landed his blunt spear. With it was a short note in Papa's hand: 'To do with as you think best'.

And so began my strange week plunged into the past. I could not look further then, but that evening I found Papa's old leatherbound journal. It was held together with a cord wrapped around and circling a metal disc on its front. When unwound it sprang into stiff curls, like unravelled wool.

On the first page Papa had written:

It is not easy, always, to shoulder the burden of this family's direction. I must pray to our Heavenly Father for guidance and trust that all will become clear.

Truly this is a land of riches, which it is our duty to make use of for the betterment of society and ourselves, and to bring enlightenment to the poor wretches living thereon, who possess so little and want for so much. I do truly believe that all men are created equal in their potential and that if circumstances where deficient are improved then civilization and enlightenment will follow. As surely as I rejoiced in the abolition of slavery do I rejoice in the prospect of fulfilment of this goal.

Papa had used to keep his accounts and records in it, which I read now for the first time, seeing more clearly the ways his various enterprises intersected, the purchase of one thing always relying on the value of another, so that if the new venture failed the former one must be sold. And if it did succeed, he would borrow against it to speculate further, always gambling what he had on the chance of a better future. He had borrowed against the value of town properties to buy the Encounter Bay whaling station; the shipload of sheep that drowned had been purchased against our dairy farm. It seemed that the house in Adelaide had paid for the cattle from the dairy farm and the lease of runs in the Coorong and further inland ... two more than I knew of. There was more about stock losses and appointment of native shepherds for Tinlinyara and Salt Creek. He had borrowed against each of the leases, but paid only interest on the loans. When the sheep did poorly, this was what we lived on. A shopping list fell to the floor: tea leaves, mustard seed, raisins, flour, sugar and so on.

Here and there were sparse passages of his thoughts or descriptions of things he had witnessed. There was the time when he and the boys had come across the winter encampment of some natives, and found them suffering from chills and fevers and something he called 'the French disease', and were in a 'most miserable condition'.

They are hungry, the stock now being driven from Mt Gambier to Adelaide all through their old winter grounds, scaring away their game and consuming the vegetation. One of them showed us their suck, which is spoiled, and with clean sucks and land become so rare, and prey as they are to illness, their situation is desperate indeed.

I remembered Papa's return from that trip, how he obliged Addie and me to gather some items together to give to the blacks who lived on our land. We took the things down to the shore: flour, dripping, some meat, and a little sugar too. They wanted more, but with sugar so dear, we could not give it. I did not like to disappoint, especially Rimmilli. She took our charity but was not grateful. We used to say that we didn't know how they lived without us and Papa didn't correct us. Our house had been built on their old summer camp, Tull told me one day; their good deep suck had been spoiled; our cattle and sheep had trampled their grounds. And Papa's charity, what lay behind it …

There were records of loans from Mr Baker and Mr Stubbs, but nothing from the few months after Mama died. Only this:

> *This evening Hester asked why we did not return to Adelaide and I did not give her the reply that I should have. I meant only to reassure, and the truth could not do that. The truth is that I cannot live there any longer. All around are men and I see myself in their faces, and in all their failings. I cannot be with them and know myself to be one of them. I thought I could make amends, but in all that I do its opposite comes about. Naught came of it but death upon death. This land is cursed. I fear I am forsaken.*

I found his notes to the parliamentary enquiry and further below, hastily written and scored through, but still legible:

> *I said I took my bible for comfort. It was not true. It was to remind me to be a protector. I find my comfort elsewhere. The fault is not so great, I hope. But I should not. I do not mean harm. It is not my intention, but a curse. I do not believe in curses.*

A page on which he had written, 'Tull sorely missed', as if he had nothing to do with his departure.

There were so many figures in it and many notes, but the meaning drained out of the words. The journal spelled only failure, the gradual drying up of hope, but I had known that. The last thing he wrote was about Addie's marriage. There was nothing about Fred or me leaving. It was as if we had ceased to be.

22

CHICHESTER
1874

There are two pictures of me on the Coorong – two in my possession, that is; Charles sketched several, as I recall. One was a watercolour from Charles and Mr Bagshott's first visit. Joss found it in the back of a book when he was a small boy and liked it, so I had a frame made for it and put it on the wall in an out of the way corner of the landing. I do not pass it in the normal way of things, but sometimes go and look at it, at myself, almost despite my conscious inclinations. Mama's old brocade chair holds me within its arms and behind me is the window, a curtain lifting, a smudge of yellow grass and blue sky, and within the room the hulking shapes of the barley twist bureau (gone now, I daresay, bartered in exchange for debt) and the piano. Did I ever look like this? I appear, if this is possible, watchful and also about to jump up or speak although my hands are clasped as ladylike as anyone, even Mama, could wish for. Charles very kindly left out my freckles. I appear young. I was young, with full cheeks, and hair that no one had time to quell. The dress I wore was a favourite: blue with the lace trim afforded by prosperous times in Adelaide. It was faded by then, although this is not apparent in the picture. I appear well bred and contented – or not discontented at any rate. It is as much a lie as Mr Angas's drawings. Clattering around the kitchen or dealing with the chickens or the garden or the children's lessons or walking the pathways of the lagoon or galloping the tracks would have shown a truer likeness. But I did not look at the picture to see myself. As long as I looked at it seldom – no more than once or twice a year – I could surprise from my memory the sight of Charles sitting opposite, concentrating and irritable, his jacket off and shirt-sleeves roughly turned, his hair falling on his face so that he had to push it from his eyes when he looked up, his mouth working as he tried to render what he saw and telling me to be quiet and stop moving.

The other picture I have only now found, tucked in a paper packet in the side compartment of the trunk among a bundle of letters tied with the finest native-made twine. The faded writing on the front of one of these was in Papa's hand: 'To be paid for in full with interest when the boat comes in!' It had the hopeful sound – almost jaunty – of his voice when we first moved to the run. Within, was a list of things – the piano, three horses, the barley twist bureau and Mama's chaise longue – and a signed note from Grandpapa that the items were a loan to us for the duration of our time on the Coorong. It appeared that he had bought them from us in 1854, the year before we moved to Salt Creek, and lent them back so that we had at least some requisites of civilization; also to prevent Papa selling them again. I suppose Papa would permit the arrangement only if an account was kept. I wished I had known and could thank them. There were also letters to Papa from Mr Stubbs and Mr Baker and the bank, reminding him of payments due. And one more.

The direction on the front of the envelope said: Miss Hester Finch, Salt Creek, Coorong. I could not tell whether the contents had been looked at, the dampness having buckled the envelope and lifted the seal. It had not been cut open at any rate. It contained two slips of paper, one of them a letter dated the 21st of May 1862, which began 'Dearest Hester'. The hand was untidy – exuberant even. I turned the page over. The final words, smaller, as if they were whispered into my ear, said: 'I remain yours always, always Charles'. Then, below: 'P.S. I await your reply, Hester. I cannot stop thinking of you.'

At that, I felt faint and shut my eyes, seeing the words before me still, untouched since Charles wrote them. I opened the other piece of paper, which was a drawing of me lying in the valley of shells on the peninsula. I appear to be sleeping. The wind has blown a strand of hair across my face, my bonnet is in my hand and I am peaceful.

'Hester, Coorong, 1862', it said beneath. It was a private drawing and it seemed an intrusion to regard it, but it was only of me and would have been drawn from Charles's memory unless I had been asleep for a short while on the last day, when the peninsula was the one place we could be alone and he had drawn it before waking me.

I returned to the letter, which told of his father's explorations for Adelaide's city council further inland, a journey Charles had accompanied him on during the months of April and May, also of his family: mother, sisters and brother. It put me in mind of my own family as it had been before we moved to Salt Creek. He wrote of his wish to return to the Coorong as soon as may be to see me and to talk of 'various matters and about the future, which I beg you to consider'. But first he had to go on another short trip, no more than a week or two, with his father. And there was his final paragraph:

> *If you have need of ought in the meantime, I hope that you will let me know. If I have not returned to Adelaide yet, my mother will help you, I am sure, as I have told her what you mean to me and of my future hopes. The direction on the back of the envelope will reach me and you may be sure that any word from you will be welcome. Or you. Nothing could be more welcome than that.*

Close to the bottom of the trunk there was a creeping dampness, and a silvering of salt where seawater had wet and dried the lining and crept into bundles of documents. Papers clung to each other and some could be separated only with care: a slender wooden knife inserted between them before they dried completely worked best. Mould had begun its stealthy growth across them; still I persevered. I might have been digging for bones or shards of pottery or arrowheads or fossils, as people did hereabouts, for their amusement only. It was otherwise with me, I was between urgency and reluctance.

An image emerged from amidst a few items, pale as a body dragged from the deep. A picture of Tull sitting in the chair he favoured by the kitchen fire. He was oblivious to the artist, reading intently – *A*

Naturalist's Voyage Round the World, I had no doubt. The thickness of the book was right, as was its dark cover and the rough rendering of a lengthy title. He preferred it to the bible, which was the other book he studied. He was intent, as if there were a mystery there that he might unravel if he could find the end of it. I must have seen him sitting so one hundred times or more. The lamplight threw his face into relief against the shadowy corner and cast a glow across his cheek and the sweep of eyelash and the fullness of lip. It was a tender portrait – more than that. I did not think it was Charles who had done it. I would have observed that and it was not in his style. No one but Fred could have done it. Still, something in it put me in mind of Charles's drawing of me.

I wrote Fred a letter that very night, to his home in Regent's Park. In it I told him news of Joss and Beecham and the school, mentioning at the end that I had discovered a sketch of his in the trunk, and Papa's journal.

> *I hoped I would find more. Your drawings were very fine, which I did not know then, when you were working at the big table. They gave you so much trouble – remember? This one at least has survived. There are a few other things of Tull's that you might like to have, since he was a particular friend of yours.*

Fred's reply arrived at the end of the week – last week:

> *As to any drawing of mine that you find, you can keep it or burn it as you wish, dear sister. I have no need of it, or to be reminded of Papa and what he did. There is just one picture I would be pleased to see again. I doubt it will have survived. It is of Tull in the kitchen, a drawing, which came out better than I expected. Happier times. No matter if you cannot find it. I have it well enough in my mind. As for the others that were burned, they were false. They showed nothing of the entirety of that world. I did not see anything there. Understand it, rather. I could not. It*

347

was not knowable; nothing is on short acquaintance. I confess
that I am curious to see what remains of Tull. Come and see me,
Hester. I should be glad of it.

I am seldom in London, but have occasionally visited by railway, combining it with my efforts to avail myself of the joys of civilization. I had only previously seen Fred in Chichester; he had been travelling each time I visited London. The hansom cab let me down before a tall, white fine-featured terrace, like a well-bred horse with all its points correct. I could not imagine Fred living here without falling into boredom. There was a restlessness in him that could not be sated. Letters from him might be postmarked Madagascar or Newfoundland or the Azores or Argentina. He wheeled around the world in the way that I had dreamed of once.

I climbed the stairs and rapped the knocker on the gleaming black door, twice, and peered through the window. It was as if I were standing at the lip of the past, unsure of what I might discover. A maid opened the door. I had hardly spoken a word before she was standing aside to let me in, for I was expected, she said.

'Mr Finch is out for a few minutes, but will be back directly. Mr Alexander is here though.'

'Mr Alexander?'

'Yes. A particular friend of Mr Finch's down from Cambridge, doing some work in Mr Finch's collections. Shall I fetch him? And some refreshments. Mr Finch was very particular about that.' She was gone up the carved staircase.

I removed my pelisse and placed it and my reticule and the shield – this wrapped in brown paper – on a chair in the entrance hallway and looked about the walls at paintings and drawings of places I had never seen and never would and at strangely carved masks and engraved metal discs whose purpose I could not guess. A great brass lamp hung overhead, light sieving from it as if sunlight were filtering through leaves. Through a nearby door I glimpsed a wall of books and a chair and table heaped with papers and more books. Curiosity overcame me and with the tip of a forefinger I pushed the door wider and stood at the brink of the room. I had time to gain one more impression, of a painting above a marble fireplace – an orange butterfly with lustrous wings – when the sound of racing footfall came down the stairs and I turned to see a young man jump the last few and land light as a cat. His abundant hair was dark and curly and his eyes bright and his manner merry. Perhaps he improved Fred's spirits when he became low.

'You are Hester? Miss Finch? Mrs—?' he said, plunging towards me with his hand outstretched.

I couldn't help laughing. 'Yes. Hester will do very well. Fred's sister.'

'I shouldn't be so familiar. But I have heard so much of you. Ralph,' he said and shook my hand. 'Fred will be back in a minute.'

'Yes, the maid said.'

'I am staying here just now, cataloguing and so on. His collections are very fine.'

'I think they always were. Of course we didn't know it then. Fred's rather—' I could not find the word. Secretive, private, wounded, concealed, brilliant?

'Yes,' Ralph said after a pause. 'He is, isn't he?' And gave a smile of gentleness, also sympathy, I think. 'Come, let's have tea and you can tell me of your childhoods running wild with the blacks. I don't like to ask Fred too much. It makes him sad.'

'Yes,' I said, wondering that he called him Fred and not Mr Finch. They were close friends, then.

The maid brought tea and little oat biscuits. 'Rather rustic, but Fred insists on them and now I have developed a taste too,' Ralph said.

With the constant noise of horses and cabs passing by I did not hear Fred's return. Suddenly he burst through the door. He had changed so little. He was tall and still narrowly built, and rather careless in his dress. His neck tie was loose, as was his collar, and his jacket was crumpled. When he took it off and threw it on a sofa I began to perceive the cause. 'Hett,' he said, and kissed my cheek. 'You've met Ralph then.'

'I have. You've become terribly respectable, Fred.'

'Yes. It's not so bad. I have the zoo on my doorstep. The British Museum is not far, and the collections in South Kensington.'

'Stop. You have convinced me. This is the centre of the world.'

'There you would be wrong. And you, Hester, what a lady you are become.' He turned to Ralph. 'If you had seen us.'

Ralph smiled and poured Fred a cup of tea. I could not help noticing how fondly his gaze rested on Fred. When he had finished his own, he left us. 'For it's clear that you have a great deal to talk about,' he said.

'Tell me, Hett, I can see you are bursting with it, what did you find in that trunk?' Fred said.

'Wait here.' I went into the hallway and collected my things and came back. 'First this.' I handed Fred the parcel, which he took without a word and undid the string and folded the paper back. His face, which had been animated, stilled. His fine fingers felt delicately along its edges and at the cracks opening down its length. He might have been a blind person. And watching it I felt it again myself, how it was not as smooth as polished wood, but was alive with the texture and muscle of the tree it had come from and caught at fingers as if its entirety was an invitation to be held. He took it onto his lap and stroked its convex face and rested his palms against it. 'Oh' on an inward breath; he shut his eyes. His head moved, slightly. He drew it against his chest, fitting it to him, and put his arms around it. His thumb stroked it.

'I'm so sorry, Fred.'

He shook his head again, and sat back on the sofa, the shield resting against him, and pressed his hands to his face. A stricken sound came from him. I went to his side and sat and touched his arm, which quivered and stilled, and left it there. Presently he opened his eyes. He cleared his throat. He looked at me and like that, in a single blink of time, it was as if a pond had stilled and I could see beneath its surface. I never before understood Fred, and never knew it. Perhaps I did not understand him then, not completely. How could I? I did see the pain that was in him, I am sure of that, and knew I could not take it away or ease it. It was his and part of him. Were all people so burdened by the past, I wondered, or did some sleep as easy as a fox after slaughter? Fred pulled a handkerchief from his pocket and wiped his cheeks. 'All right now.' He laid the shield against a cushion at his side, his hand lying on it.

I took an envelope from my reticule. 'Now this.' I handed it to him and he pulled out the drawing of Tull.

'This is the one I meant,' Fred said. 'Do you remember how he read that book?'

'Yes.'

'As if it held every mystery in the world.' His gaze moved across the picture, lingering on Tull's face. 'He never did me wrong and see how I repaid him.'

'What do you mean?'

'I discovered him and Addie to Papa. You didn't know?'

'I thought Stanton must have seen them.'

'So I'm worse than Stanton.' The thought seemed to sicken him.

'I thought it was right to do it. I should have.'

'You knew?'

'For a while. I saw it start.'

'There is a day I think of. You asked Tull how long he could live on the peninsula and he said forever, but he would like some company, and Addie said she would keep him company. And he smiled. Do you remember that?' He frowned a little in a wondering way, as if he were witnessing it again and wondering afresh. 'At the beginning of that day I thought life was one thing, and at the end of it, it had changed entirely. It was not the *Origin of Species* that changed the direction of my thinking. It was Tull's smile for Addie. I saw it and began to understand. But I didn't know enough then. Even if I had, I don't know if I could have changed anything.'

'I warned her, but Addie was so determined.'

'She was.' He smiled at that. 'I would like to return his shield to him one day. I hope I will be able to.'

'I thought you might know where he is by now.'

'I've not seen him since Cape Town. He missed the ship, by accident or on purpose. I don't know which. When I left Salt Creek and found him I asked him if he would like to come with me. He was sitting by the fire, not doing anything. He just stood up and put on his cloak and bag and we walked away. He would not talk of it. I would not have blamed him for killing Papa. I thought of it myself. There was nothing left for Tull. No reason to hope. His family didn't care. I asked him why and he said he had failed them, that he could not do what they wanted or make them understand.'

'Poor Tull.'

'Only at the end. He wanted Papa to agree to working with the natives on the station, did you know? He was like one of their ancestor stories. There should be a story about him. He was in a terrible state on the walk to Adelaide. No one would blame him for that. He talked about Genesis.'

'The Fall,' I said. 'Yes. To me too.'

'Taplin told him that blacks were sinful, and Papa told him that the serpent was knowledge, which was the root of sin. Do you know what he said about that?'

I shook my head.

He closed his eyes in concentration. 'Something like this: "It is the white man who is the serpent, who destroys, who whispers in our ears. The curse of the serpent is upon you already: *dust shalt thou eat all the days of thy life, cursed is the ground for thy sake; in sorrow shalt thou eat of it all the days of thy life.*"' His voice was like a song sung on only one or two notes and with even beats. I could have listened to it forever. 'I have often thought of it. Darwin saw it. He called it progress rather than sin. It was a long walk. The country did look cursed. The stock had chewed all the grasses. We hardly saw a kangaroo or an emu. It was grey weather. And there were just the two of us walking through this wasteland.'

'How was it when you reached Grandmama and Grandpapa?'

'To them?'

I nodded.

'I think it was as if I'd risen from the dead.'

'Yes. More for you, I suppose. They were waiting for me, since you had been and gone already.'

'Grandmama would not stop feeding us.'

'She had so many things made for me. "Nothing but rags and tatters", she kept saying.'

Fred smiled. 'I dream about Tull sometimes. That I find him and know what to say. He understands. He forgives everything. He's out there somewhere. I've met people who know him. He's quiet, they say, a pleasant fellow. Good with his hands. He still likes to read. I ask for him at every port and leave a letter with the harbour master. Sometimes I tell myself that nothing has really changed. I used to walk through the trees looking for him, and now it's masts all around. Wooden docks instead of dirt tracks; the water is still at my feet. I'll be leaving again soon. Perhaps this time.'

'Remember to mention what Addie said in your next letters, about Mr Stubbs and that she would be pleased to hear from him.'

'I will. That might bring him to the surface. I would like to make amends, if that's possible. He was closer to me than any brother. I cannot help wondering what would have happened if I had not spoken.'

'She was with child. They would have been discovered.'

'Or they would have run.'

'Or that. But what then?'

Fred took another biscuit and began to eat around its edges.

I said, 'Do you remember that night? Oat biscuits, and possum for breakfast. Malachi Martin the murderer. Life is dull here.'

Fred leapt to his feet. 'Come on. Let's go for a walk.'

I put on my pelisse and bonnet and Fred his coat and hat and we strolled along the road. The trees were almost bare – just a few leaves still falling. People brushed past, carriages and hansoms came towards us and receded; there was no end to them. 'Look at us, Fred. No one would know that we ran wild in Australia. No one. I thought I would feel free here.'

'It's why I go voyaging. Not so many rules.'

We walked to the park and climbed to the top of Primrose Hill.

There were few people about, it being rather late in the afternoon by then, and cold. Our breath huffed out in clouds. The sun was like an old penny sliding above the horizon. The clutter of London spread into the distance. Below, along the road, the lamps were being lit and the light that glowed from each of them seemed to gather the dark closer. 'I miss it, but it makes me sad to think of it,' I said. 'Not only because of Tull.'

'You never told me what happened with Charles.'

'If you don't ask me about Charles, I won't ask you about Ralph.'

Fred was startled at that, but said, very quiet, after some consideration, 'I cannot change my drives, even knowing their wrongness. Perhaps that is what it means to be human. I do hate myself for it. I will not say more than that, and that only to you, Hett.'

'No.' I tucked my hand through his arm. 'We can't help our natures. Addie believed that.'

'I saw you and Charles. I came back early that day and went to Tull's room and you were both there, lying so peaceful. I could not think it wrong, only wished that I had someone too.'

'Well,' I said.

'Yes.'

'Why did you tell Papa, Fred?'

His gaze slid away from me and he moved his body and face very slightly, helplessly. Finally, he said, 'I would think you would know why.'

A breeze picked up, and I tucked my hands into my pockets, and pulled one out again. 'I meant you to have this.' I handed him the small white stone.

His fingers curled around it. 'Oh, Tull,' he said.

23

THE COORONG
JUNE 1862

Fred did not trouble to conceal his departure the morning after Papa burned his books. I made him a batch of oat biscuits and wrapped them in a paper packet and we went onto the veranda.

'Perhaps I will see you at Grandmama's,' he said.

'Be careful.'

The wind was gusting cool as he left: a tall, slender figure hefting a bag upon his shoulder walking away from me in plain view up the path to the stock route, not bothering to see if Papa were about.

I never felt more alone than I did at the moment he turned the corner and was gone from view. I knew no one but a few natives and the wife of a murderer. The time for waiting had passed and I must do something, else be forced to discover myself to Papa and that I would never do. There was no reason to stay. Jane Eyre ran away across the moors and made her own way; I lacked her courage, and she had not been with child. There was nothing for me between Salt Creek and Adelaide; there was nowhere further to fall. I went inside and lit the fire in the parlour. The familiarity of the task and the flames crackling up and the warmth touching my face were a kind of comfort.

All I had left was pride, and there was no room for that. I did not doubt my feelings for Charles, only mistrusted where they led. I wished it were otherwise. And now there was so little of choice left to me. All I could do was keep the baby safe, give it a name, come what may.

I fetched paper and pen and ink. What might Charles expect

from a union? Surely not obedience. I would not stay; I would leave him rather when I could. I would find a way. We had never spoken of it, only soft words at the end. I thought of the day he rode away from Salt Creek.

He had been mounted, his horse restless to be gone. 'You remember what I said: to leave, to flee—'

'And never to look back.'

'That's it.'

'I do.' I had put my hand on his knee.

He bent until his head was close. 'I would go with you, anywhere. You know that I hope. Only say. Or come to me.'

It was the hardest thing to let him go, and to stay. All I had were those words.

I began to write: a letter to Charles, asking him to come for me, and to Grandmama and Grandpapa, asking if I might stay with them. I did not mention my condition to them. They would surely disown me if they knew. There was nothing for it but to conceal it until Charles and I married.

Once the letters were sent, there was nothing to do but wait. It was almost winter. The house was quiet and my chores were done quickly. There was one cow to be milked – I let the other two go dry – a little washing, small meals. It was all I could do to disguise my wretched sickness. Papa hardly spoke. I played the piano softly. It was out of tune and the pedals stuck sometimes, but I had grown to like the wayward sound. The piano's old sparkling grandness would have fitted ill with my mood and circumstances. When the mail boat next made its ponderous journey down the lagoon I rowed out to meet it. There was no news from Charles, only a letter from my grandparents. Mr Kruse hung over the railing, scratching his beard idly, waiting while I read it. The boat bobbed in the swell. I paused to be ill over the side. They would be delighted to see me whenever I should arrive, they said.

'Would you please stop on your return this afternoon?' I asked Mr Kruse. 'I will be travelling to Adelaide.'

'Certainly, Miss,' he said.

356

'You don't seem surprised, Mr Kruse.'

'Mrs Stubbs mentioned the possibility. She said to keep watch for you.'

'You've seen her? Is she well?'

'Well enough. A nice little thing, en't she?'

'She is. I'll be bringing two dogs,' I said.

'Anything up to and including sheep,' he said. 'It'll cost you, mind.'

I packed a case, at the last minute collecting one or two of Tull's things: tools and a weapon and a stone. I did not like to leave Tull's shield behind, but it would not fit. I put the money that Addie had sent me in my pocket and sat on the edge of our bed. There was nothing to do but wait.

Papa returned at lunch.

'Are you hungry?' I said.

He ducked his eyes. 'I'll get some bread and cheese and take it with me. No need to trouble yourself.' He opened a drawer on the dresser and pulled out a roll of twine and went out into the cold.

'Goodbye, Papa', I called from the door. He raised a hand but did not look back, just went across to the kitchen. It was as if he had been wounded and I was nothing but salt. I tidied the dining room and straightened the dresser and left a letter there for him to find and went down to the shore and sat watching the lagoon for Mr Kruse's boat, which emerged from the mist and slid across the silver water – so still now that the boat by some illusion appeared to glide above it – and drew closer. I had tethered our boat to the shore by the longest piece of rope we had (when Papa found my letter, he could pull the boat back to shore), and now I put my case in the boat, and persuaded the dogs in too. I rowed out to the mail boat. Mr Kruse sent a harness over for the dogs and heaved them and then me aboard. The rowing boat drifted away from us to the end of its line and with the dogs on either side of me I watched it and my home and everything I knew slide away and grow smaller, the water flowing so smooth, so quiet beneath the boat and up its sides, until all of that world disappeared.

*

'Oh, I'm glad to see you, my dear,' Grandmama said when I arrived at her door. Her face was thinner and her hair quite grey. She held me within her arms and patted my back, and patted it, as if she were comforting herself as well. 'I've been waiting and hoping for this moment since Freddie was here, and for so long before that. While there was a chance, we could not leave, and now I think we never will. But come in, my darling, and tell me your news.'

My memories of that time are all fragments: the snowy folds of unmended sheets, the strangeness of people, noise, Grandpapa's humour and the softness of his hands. I could not let go my old habits of thinking. Before I could stop myself I had calculated that at least two dresses could be made from the curtains in the drawing room, and that the roast beef served one night could have been stretched to three meals had it been stewed and served with dumplings. The plenty left me uneasy, and sad at the thought of Papa, and fearful at the thought of him too. I started at each knock on the door, and shook, until Grandmama made a sound with her tongue behind her teeth and looked at me as if I were a flighty horse. She sent me out riding, 'to give you something sensible to think about, my girl', she said. I found Charles's house and spoke to his mother, a sombrely dressed woman with faded brown hair and Charles's startling eyes, and she looked at me as implacable in her own way as Papa – I, a girl who would appear at a door without introduction, and perhaps looking as desperate as I felt.

She knew who I was and took the letter I left with her for Charles. 'He and Mr Bagshott are not expected back for some time, perhaps months, but I will give it to him then, you may be sure.'

I was not gambler enough to wait that long. Papa had taught me the dangers of hope and expectation. Grandmama agreed. It had been quite bad telling her. Exclamations of shock punctuated our conversations.

'Beyond the reaches of civilization,' she said. 'What did he expect? Nothing to temper you. Running wild. I blame myself. I blame your father for taking you there.' She quivered with rage and her eyes snapped; a moment later it gave way to regret: 'We should have come and taken you away. And your Mama – poor, dear Bridget.'

'Papa would never have allowed it.'

'Perhaps not. He's a proud man. Proud and improvident. But we should have tried. It's England for you, my dear, and we can keep things quiet. Only you will have to go alone. Francis, your Grandpapa, will not withstand the voyage, I fear. He is not at all well. Oh, what were you thinking though?'

'I was not thinking.'

'No, I daresay you were not.'

Before my ship left there was news of the impending trial of Malachi Martin. He was like a creature from mythology that had lurked at the Travellers Rest, at the mouth of the creek, waiting. I thought of Addie at the other end of the Coorong now, beside a lake, caught in the trap of Papa's devising.

It did not seem fair that I should be the one to break loose. It is hard to discern design or justice in life. I was healthy and thanks to my grandparents without need. Because of them I had the means to provide for my boy. I could not help seeing that it was losing control, having a child, that had led to my escape and thereby set me free, as I had dreamed of for so long. Would I have had that if I had received Charles's letter and stayed on the Coorong in the hope of his arrival, if I had waited in Adelaide in growing disgrace? No knowing when he would return: I had to keep reminding myself of that. Still, I hoped for him until the day that Grandmama settled me in my cabin, and looked for him as the ship sailed from Port Adelaide, until all the white faces watching from the shore were as blank as polished shells.

I survived without him, but I did not feel quite human.

Chichester, 1874

We are all fettered by the past no matter how we struggle to free ourselves. Papa carried all of England with him it sometimes seemed: its grandness and vision and civilizing power. And I feel always that

I carry Australia with me. I am thrifty when I need not be; I have a longing for space and heat, the scent of eucalyptus, and still, after all these years, for Charles, so that there is no true comfort for me. The search for it in my memories is futile and leads only to despair, but I cannot prevent my thoughts from travelling.

I often wonder what Mrs Bagshott would have thought of me had she met me in Chichester. It is as watery in its own way as the Coorong, with marshes and birds aplenty; it is the safest, most respectable place in the world. We are civilized here, you see. We have keys as big as your hand and walls of stone that are a foot thick and houses so bristling with flint that they would cut you to ribbons if you brushed against them. The stresses on the walls are such that bands of iron skewer the walls to hold them, as coarse stitches do cloth. In South Australia we lived in the bones and skins of drowned ships. A spear could pass through a wall with ease, but none ever did, and we lived among savages, people say.

I attended the cathedral service this morning. I move to different parts of the building from week to week. It allows me to vary the reading material: tombs, burial stones, epitaphs. My favourite seat is between two such markers in the north transept. One is a white marble column for Edmund Woods, husband, father, J.P. (1751–1833), and his two wives and three of his daughters, all of whom predeceased him. I think of Papa when I read the epitaph, which speaks of Mr Woods's 'conscientious discharge of all the duties of life in the advancement of true religion and in constant acts of benevolence and charity'. Papa would have liked this said of him, he would like to have been 'esteemed and regretted'. I prefer the other marker. It is a simple one of mottled grey stone set into the floor, damaged by the look of it when the cathedral spire fell; the carved letters and numerals are chipped and some ambiguous. It looks like something that has endured.

John Barnard
Deccaled 5 March
1715 Aged 32

Nic Son of his Died
February 1711 AGED 3 YEARS
Also Mary His Wife who died
1733 Aged 47 years

I felt for her in her sadness. At least I had my son.

24

CHICHESTER
1874

I have read that some species of finch become distressed and grieve and cannot settle when separated from their true mate but once returned to each other are restored to life. As to whether this is true I do not know, never having observed such birds.

The events of this afternoon and the evening will not cohere, yet I am strangely peaceful at the end of the day. It is as if yesterday and even most of today was the end point of a journey across a salt plain that had seemed without limit until the final step. I will say, though, that there is an austere satisfaction to traversing such a plain, to stepping forward each day. I took some pride in it. These things I recall clearly: Charles meeting my gaze through the window; that I ran past Ruby and flung the door open; Charles leaping the stairs; Ruby's shocked face; Charles holding me in my private sitting room.

'You are very forward these days. How do you know I'm not married?' he said.

'Are you married?' I put my hand to his chest and felt his heartbeat against me. I had been thinking of it for so long.

'No I am not. I could not find anyone. But you did, Mrs Crane. Is your husband about? Should you be here on my lap? Should you be doing that?' He laughed as if he did not care and tightened his arms about me and rested his cheek against my hair.

'There is no Mr Crane.'

'You are widowed?'

'And never was.'

He stroked the backs of his fingers down my cheek. 'You've become so pale.'

'Yes.'

'Why are you Mrs Crane then? So your father would not find you? Why did you leave?'

I told him about Joss.

We pieced the past together, what we could: his parents had not given him my letter or direction, and my father from bitterness had not forwarded his letter to me, and when Charles went to the Coorong Papa would tell him nothing; he sent him away. We have Hugh to thank. It was through a chance meeting with him on Collins Street in Melbourne that Charles discovered where I now live.

Whether we will ever make something complete I cannot know. It is a fractured thing, life; it is in its nature. These things are true: a fallen cathedral can be rebuilt, a wall held up with a clover leaf of metal, a house brought back to life, and broken people can survive and find each other and become whole. And the people of Salt Creek: some of them have persisted despite all, if Hugh's letter is to be believed. Charles and I cannot be what we were, but we might become something other. I am not reconciled, not to any loss of freedom, which is part of my dearest self, nor yet to life without Charles. But I will live the life I have. I will take the chance.

This is our plan: we will go walking tomorrow and look for fossils or Roman artefacts, or we will ride to Bosham or Chichester Harbour to see the boats and breathe the salt wind, and we might discover what may be made of the future, the three of us: Charles and Joss and me. Perhaps we will go to sea.

AUTHOR'S NOTE

Salt Creek is a blend of fact and fiction. Although there are parallels between my family's story and this fiction, my forebear and his family (about whose characters little is known) were not models for the fictional character Stanton Finch or his family, and my family's property was not in the location of the fictional Salt Creek property.

Malachi Martin, Catherine (Nellie) Robinson/Martin, the missionary George Taplin, and Jane Macmanamin are historical figures, as are the murders and suspected murders depicted. The events of the wreck of *The Maria*, with the exception of the presence of the fictional figure Stanton Finch, are based on the historical record. The Bagshotts are modelled on Herschel Babbage and his son Charles, who had the connections with Charles Darwin and the Brontës that appear in this fiction.

There is not the scope in a book of this size and type, and it is not for me to depict in any depth the subtle and sophisticated culture of the Ngarrindjeri. It would be inaccurate for them not to have a presence though. In my thinking and writing about the Ngarrindjeri and the Victorian era I have been particularly influenced by the following books: Diane Bell's *Ngarrindjeri Wurruwarrin: a world that is, was, and will be* (1998); Bill Gammage's *The Biggest Estate on Earth* (2012), Charles Darwin's *A Naturalist's Voyage Round the World,* better known as *The Voyage of the Beagle* (first pub. 1839) and *On the Origin of Species* (first pub. 1859); Philip Jones's *Ochre and Dust* (2007); Norman Tindale; Christobel Mattingley and Ken Hampton's *Survival in Our Own Land* (1992); Iola Hack Mathews' (with Chris Durrant) *Chequered Lives* (2014); Graham Jenkin's *Conquest of the Ngarrindjeri* (1985); George Taplin's *The Narrinyeri*

(1874), the archaeological work of Roger Luebbers on Chinamans Wells and Hacks Station, Charlotte Brontë's *Jane Eyre*, and the King James Bible.

There was no Salt Creek Station. The Travellers Rest, which exists today as a service station and restaurant, lies in the small town of Salt Creek, at the mouth of the creek itself. I have been assured that they serve a very good meal of Coorong mullet, which has probably been on the menu for the past 160 years.

ACKNOWLEDGEMENTS

The Coorong is strange and secluded and grand enough to humble, though the sensation of remoteness experienced when visiting it is these days a trick of geography and landscape rather than distance. The Ngarrindjeri inhabited this region with great sensitivity for millennia; many live there still, working towards its restoration. I have been grateful for the opportunity to visit it.

Thank you to Jane Aitken, Emily Boyce, Jimena Gorraez-Connolly and everyone at Aardvark Bureau for the wonderful job that they do and for being such a pleasure to work with. Thank you to Pan Macmillan Australia: Alex Craig, Cate Paterson, Geordie Williamson, Samantha Sainsbury, Tracey Cheetham, and Rebecca Thorne. Thanks also to Robyn Molyneaux for her beautiful artwork, and to my agents Gaby Naher and Rachel Calder.

The writing of *Salt Creek* was supported by Creative Victoria and the City of Melbourne. Thank you to both.

Thank you to dear friends Jenny Green, Kate Richards, Trish Bolton, Clare Strahan and Dana Miltins. I am indebted to Iola Mathews, Chris Durrant, Annie Keeley, Drusilla Modjeska, Fiona Wood, and Margie Long-Alleyn for their support and insight at various stages.

I'm grateful to my parents, Aileen and Ted Treloar; my aunts Patricia Kelly and Nancy McWaters; my grandmother, Alice Kelly; and to Andrew Treloar, Sophie Treloar, and Tash Chiew.

Particular gratitude to my children, James Howes, Catherine Treloar, William Howes, and Jack Howes, who explored the Coorong with me and were the best and funniest of company; and to David Howes, who made the work possible.

READING GROUP GUIDE

What do you make of Papa's attitude to and treatment of the Indigenous people? Were his beliefs and behaviour consistent or contradictory? Self-serving or altruistic? Genuine or applicable only when convenient? And how much was a result of unresolved guilt?

What kind of life do you think Addie and Tull would have had if they had managed to escape and be together?

What did 'love' mean in the Finch family in the mid 1800s? Which characters demonstrate what kind of love, and is one more valuable or worthy than another? Why?

In the mid-nineteenth century, industrialisation and empire-building were seen to make western European countries progressive and powerful as well as being of great benefit to the 'savages' they encountered, but the beginnings of the dark legacy colonisation would leave are already evident in the Finches' world. What are the signs of it?

Pioneer pastoralists are often lauded as heroes in Australia for their courage in creating a new land where 'no one' had been before, and for doing it on their own. The reality was far more complex, though, as Fred indicates when he sets out to stay on the peninsula alone to see 'if I can survive there without Tull'. How might life have panned out for these 'pioneers' without the cooperation and assistance of Indigenous people?

Threading through the whole story is the notion that some peoples and practices are 'civilized' while others are barbarous. What makes a person 'civilized' or 'uncivilized'? Is civilization always a good thing and barbarity always bad?

Hester feels a strong sense of obligation to her family. But is the unquestioning performance of one's duty and sacrificing oneself to others always the 'right' thing to do? Does it always benefit others, or can it do just as much harm as good?

Although there was a flowering of education of women in Victorian England (and its colonies), women remained subordinate to men. What were the possibilities for women in the Finch family?

How does the author's evocation of the landscape echo what is happening in the story itself? What was your emotional reaction to the landscape evoked, and how did each of the Finch family members respond to it?

What does the movement back and forth between time periods add to the drama and suspense of the way the events of the story are revealed? Would it work as well if the narrative moved in a straight line from 1855 to 1875?

How does the author's adoption of a nineteenth-century prose style help us to understand the characters and their actions? Does it make the story more authentic?